Mrs. Richard Linton   august 23, 1971

LIGHT FROM THE DUST

LIGHT
FROM
THE
DUST

A HISTORICAL NOVEL

By Winifred M. Milner

Copyright © 1971

HERALD PUBLISHING HOUSE, INDEPENDENCE, MISSOURI

Library of Congress Catalog Card No. 72-147023

ISBN 0-8309-0040-3

Printed in the United States of America

Prologue

This is the story of how the Book of Mormon came to be. The Book of Mormon is acknowledged as scripture, along with the Bible, by many religious scholars, and it is the hope of these believers that thousands who are skeptics now and thousands still unborn will come to revere the truths contained in it.

A story must begin somewhere. I have chosen to start this one when Joseph Smith, Jr., the translator, was eight years old.

In order that the reader may glimpse the boy with wider vision I shall tell the little I have been able to glean about his predecessors.

Robert Smith, the first of his line of whom I find record, came with his wife Mary from England and settled in the bay area of Massachusetts in 1632. To them a son was born on January 26, 1666. They named him Samuel. Samuel was married to Rebecca Curtis on January 15, 1707, and to them nine children were born, one of whom was Samuel II, Joseph's great-grandfather. He grew up in Topfield, Essex County, Massachusetts, before it became a state. He was a man of integrity, industry, and learning, and was known as the Right Honorable Samuel Smith. He provided various services to his city and country and was a delegate to the first and second Provincial Congress. In Topfield a monument was erected in acknowledgment of his work. Five children were born to Samuel Smith and his wife Rebecca. The youngest son, Aesael, was Joseph's grandfather.

Aesael was born in March 1744 and grew up in the midst of strife and war. Like his father, he grew up to speak his mind. On February 12, 1761, he married Mary Duty; eleven children were born to them. Mary was a brave woman, as were other pioneer wives. She stood with one baby in her arms and four clinging to her skirts while she watched Aesael shoulder his gun and walk away to fight with Washington and his men. One of the Smiths' sons, Joseph, grew to manhood and married Lucy Mack on January 24, 1796. They were the parents of Joseph, Jr.

Lucy's great-grandfather was John Mack. He came from England to America in 1699. Her grandfather was Ebeneizer Mack who at one time was a man of considerable property. He commanded all the attention and respect shown to those who live in fine surroundings and observe habits of strict propriety. Her father was Solomon Mack, born in Lyme, New London County, Connecticut, September 26, 1734. At the age of twenty-two he fought in the Revolutionary War under the command of Captain Henry and was later annexed to the regiment commanded by Colonel Whiting. In 1759 he was with Major Spencer. He fought at Ticonderoga with Majors Butnam and Rogers, and in the spring of that year received his discharge. Perhaps his greatest victory came at Crownpoint where he met a schoolteacher, Lydia Gates, daughter of Nathan Gates, a man of wealth who lived in East Haddam, Connecticut.

Soon after Solomon and Lydia were married he made an investment in real estate, contracting for the whole town of Granville, New York. The stipulation called for building a number of houses, and he went to work to fulfill the contract. He had the misfortune to cut his leg and was unable to do any manual labor for several months. He paid a man to continue the building, but the man absconded with the money without doing the work. Solomon lost the land but, undaunted, set about to rebuild his lost fortune.

Lydia and Solomon had eight children. Lucy was born in the town of Gilsum, Cheshire County, New Hampshire, on July 8, 1776. While helping to care for older sisters Lovisa and Lovina before their death of consumption, she contracted the disease and went to live with her brother Stephen. At his home she was miraculously healed and promised God that she would find a church and give Him special service in any way that he might choose. It was at Stephen's also that she met Joseph Smith. Following their marriage they established a merchandising business in Randolph.

Lucy tells this story:

Soon after we opened business in Randolph, Joseph learned that crystallized ginseng root sold very high in China. It was used as a remedy for the plague which was raging there.

Taking what money he could scrape together he began crystallizing the root, and when he had enough to export he took it to a merchant by the name of Stevens, of Royalton, who offered him three thousand dollars for it, which was about two-thirds of its value.

"I'll take it to New York and ship it myself before I'll let you have it at such a low price." said my husband.

In New York a vessel bound for China was in port, and Joseph made arrangements with the captain to take the ginseng. Everything would have worked out fine except for the trickery of Mr. Stevens, who planned to swindle him. He sent his son to follow Joseph to New York, found the ship, and made arrangements with the captain to take full charge of our ginseng along with his own. The voyage was made and the ginseng sold, but all we ever got out of it was one small chest of tea, for he made us believe the trip had been a complete failure.

A short time afterward though, he [Stevens] hired a business house of my brother Stephen and employed six to eight hands in the work of crystallizing ginseng.

One day Stephen found him intoxicated at his place of business and said: "Well, Mr. Stevens, you are doing fine here, you will soon have enough ginseng for another trip to China." Then he added in an off-hand way, "Just how much did my brother-in-law's venture bring you?"

Stevens led the Major to a chest, and opening it showed a large amount of silver and gold. "There, sir, are the proceeds of Mr. Smith's ginseng."

Stephen left at once, riding a swift horse to bring us the news, but the trip took several hours. Together he and Joseph returned, only to learn that young Stevens had dismissed his hands, called a carriage, and fled with our money to Canada.

Joseph and the Major tried every way they knew to find him, but he had hidden his trail too well, and at last we resigned ourselves to our great loss, a loss that left us badly in debt.

At the time Joseph sent his ginseng to China we owed eighteen hundred dollars in Boston for store goods, an account we planned to settle with gensing money. Now the debt had to be paid, and the only way to do it was to sell the farm in Turnbridge. There wasn't time to make a good sale, and we sold at great sacrifice, a heart breaking experience.

This was the beginning of a series of debts, school teaching, moves, and children. One child, little Ephriam, born March 13, 1810 died before he had hardly lived. By 1813 five moves were made to various cities and states, and the children had increased to seven, but it was a happy family, dwelling in love, and a richness that money cannot buy.*

---

*Adapted from *Joseph Smith and His Progenitors.*

Part 1

Spring came early to Lebanon, New Hampshire, in 1813. Earth, warmed by the sun, awakened sleeping seeds, and young shoots sprang from the ground to grow and flower. Birds held riotous choruses in the woodland, and wild geese made early morning and late evening flights undisturbed by hunters' guns. This was not the usual thing in Lebanon, for geese were common food in every kitchen.

People, with grim faces walked woodenly. When they met one another they exchanged hurried words and hastened to perform whatever their errands might be, anxious to return to their houses, yet fearful of what they might find there. Fresh new graves appeared in the churchyard daily. Never before had such a siege of typhus fever come to Lebanon. It raged in almost every home. Night after night candles burned like small, incandescent stars, as if by their constant light they might discourage the entrance of death.

At the Smith home, Mother Lucy, bone-weary from many nights of constant vigil, lay in bed beside her sleeping husband. Both were fully clothed although the hour was past midnight and she knew she ought to be sleeping. Two of the neighbors had come to keep watch over the children so that she and Joseph could get some needed rest. Was it habit that kept her staring at the shadowed ceiling and listening to every sound?

A gentle wind stirred the window curtain. She felt the coolness of the night. The burning candle on the table beside the bed flickered, and she moved it out of the draft so it wouldn't go out. How boyish Joseph looked in sleep. How dear he was. His body was as tired as hers, but he placed all his worries on God and slept like a child. She placed hers, then snatched them up again, fearful lest her Maker should fail to see their importance.

When would the fever leave this house? Ninety-five days it had raged here; ninety-five days she and Joseph had fought and prayed, despaired and hoped. First it had been Hyrum, sent home from the academy in Hanover. Then Alvin had been sent home from the same school. The disease was everywhere, like wolves pouncing on the innocent. The ravaged bodies of her seven children were living witnesses of the scourge, but they were alive, and the crisis was over for all of them. All? What about Sophronia? Eighty-nine days she had been under the doctor's careful watch. Lucy sat bolt upright in bed. What am I doing resting here? Why am I leaving her to the care of the neighbors? Were they seeing to it that she took her medicines—each dosage at the right time? She climbed out of bed, careful not to disturb her sleeping husband. Then from the next room she heard one of the boys moaning in his sleep. She walked into the room where her sons lay, and the moan came again. It was little Joseph, and she went to him. "Are you all right, child?"

There was no answer. She pulled the quilt over his small, thin body.

The wall candle was burning low, but it would last until morning. By its light she could see all her sons. Hyrum, asleep beside Joseph, looked older than his thirteen years.

She moved to the bed by the north wall where Alvin and Samuel were sleeping. Alvin moved at her touch, opened his eyes, and smiled at her. She brushed a lock of hair from

10

his forehead. This oldest child was one she could always depend on. "Aren't you sleeping?"

"Sure, Mamma, we're all sleeping."

She covered Samuel's foot, then knelt beside William's trundle bed. He was breathing peacefully. Two seemed so young to have suffered so much. But they were a blessed family; although the fever had gone through Lebanon like the devil's destroyer, ravaging the bodies of her children, their lives had been spared. "Let there be an end to sickness and trouble," she breathed as she opened the door of her daughters' room and went in. The candle burned brighter here.

Catherine, the baby, lay in her cradle like a beautiful doll. But Lucy's glance had barely fallen on the sleeping infant when a gasp came from one of the neighbors who was attending Sophronia. Then her cry came sharp and clear. "Mrs. Smith, all night long there has been no change in your child, and now . . . Bring Mr. Smith!"

The other neighbor went racing to awaken him, and Lucy hurried to Sophronia's bed. The girl lay altogether motionless with her eyes wide open. Dark hair tumbled upon the flat little pillow. The very air about her seemed charged with death.

Lucy said, "We must have cold water—lots of it. Tell Joseph to bring it from the well." She was moving with precision now. Towels, basins—they must bring the fever down. She brought a tarpaulin. Then she lifted the nine-year-old to the arms of her neighbor as if she were no heavier than the infant Catherine, and began remaking the bed. She placed the tarpaulin under the sheet and smoothed out the wrinkles. This would keep the bed dry.

Gently she placed Sophronia in bed, removing her nightgown. The little body was so hot it almost burned her

11

hands. These things she did with experience, for she had done them many times before in the past ninety-five days.

Joseph came with the water, and they worked like a team, wringing out towels, wrapping the child, wringing . . . wrapping.

Alvin went for the doctor and came back alone. So many fever patients needed a physician's care. He would come when he was free. In the meantime . . .

Minutes grew into an hour, then two. Alvin went again to find a doctor. Suddenly, without warning Sophronia flexed her muscles, her eyes rolled back, her body alternately relaxed and contracted; she was having a spasm. Lucy watched helplessly while Joseph worked with her. When it was over, with hope all but gone, she and Joseph clasped hands and fell to their knees by Sophronia's bedside, pouring out their grief and despair.

Lucy was trembling. She had never felt so frightened or helpless or alone. Then as Joseph prayed aloud, a strange feeling of God's nearness seemed to fill the whole room. They were his children, bringing him their great need. She knew they must relinquish their hold on Sophronia and place her entirely in his hands. For almost ten years she had been their child, but she wasn't really theirs; she had only been loaned to them. And she had been like an angel from heaven. It was at this very moment when she was fighting hardest to say thy will be done that an unexplainable feeling of assurance came to her. It was such a positive feeling that she knew Sophronia would get well.

But when they arose from prayer, Sophronia had ceased to breathe.

Without pausing to think, Lucy snatched up a blanket, threw it around the thin body, and with the child in her arms began pacing the floor.

12

The neighbors, who had been keeping the other children out of the room, came running in.

One said, as she tried to take the child, "Mrs. Smith, it is of no use."

The other stopped Lucy's pacing long enough to examine Sophronia, and her tone was like a sob. "Your girl is dead."

Joseph's eyes were brimming, but he didn't try to stop her pacing, and when they tried to take Sophronia from her he said, "Let her be."

Then . . . Lucy would remember forever what happened next. Sophronia gave a little sob, then a gasp, as if she were finding her breath. Her eyes opened, and her breathing started again as if it had never stopped.

Lucy's eyes met Joseph's. They were brimming with grateful tears. Her voice was a prayer. "She lives. Thank you, God. Thank you for letting us keep her, and help us to remember our blessings."

Sophronia slept. By dawn she was awake and asking for food. Lucy fixed a soft-boiled egg and milk toast. The child ate it and slept again. After several hours she awakened and asked for her clothes.

The children were waking up. At the sound Lucy stirred and stretched her aching body. Had she slept at all? She wasn't sure, but it was morning and the children would be needing her.

Father Joseph opened his eyes. "What time is it?"

"About six."

"Why don't you stay in bed awhile, Lucy? I'll dress the baby and William and help with the other children."

She was wide awake now and sitting up in bed. "I'm fine," she said. "Anyway, who can sleep? It's a soul-stirring sound."

Two weeks had passed since the night Sophronia had

almost died, and with each passing day the children had grown stronger. Now the house was alive with commotion and laughter, a sound Lucy had missed during their long illness.

Joseph had himself and William scrubbed and dressed before she had hardly begun to get baby Catherine into dry clothes and nurse her. Now she could hear him in the boys' room, a welcome addition to their jolly banter.

With Catherine fed and content, she carried her to the kitchen, put her in her play box, and gave her a gourd to rattle while she made porridge. It was a cheap, nourishing breakfast, for they had to be frugal. Bills for the doctor and medicine had mounted during the past three months, and the school where Joseph taught had been closed since the beginning of the epidemic, leaving him without a teacher's salary.

The children began crowding into the kitchen, but she wanted them there. Sophronia, moving like a wraith, began setting the table and pouring milk into mugs. Before the fever Sophronia had been excellent help, but now Lucy watched, fearful that she might misjudge her strength and overtax herself. Alvin and Hyrum pushed the stools into place, and William and Samuel climbed into their places at the table.

When everyone was seated and quietly awaiting grace, Lucy caught Father Joseph looking at her. "You look haggard," he said.

She tossed him a smile. "That's a nice early morning compliment."

"Now that the children are well again we'll both learn how to sleep." He gave her a quick, tender glance and bent his head to ask the blessing. Lucy's eyes moved swiftly around the table before she bent her head. She had made a silent roll call—Alvin, Hyrum, Sophronia, Samuel, William, Catherine. Young Joseph was missing!

14

When the prayer ended she arose quickly and went to find him. He was sitting on Sophronia's bed, a too thin figure for his eight years. He sat clutching his shirt with tight fingers. His face was drawn in pain, and his eyes were filled with tears which he dashed away quickly at sight of her.

"What is the matter, Joseph?"

"I—I—thought Sophronia was here . . . and I . . . came in to see if she could see . . . anything wrong . . . with my shoulder. Her touch is . . . very gentle you know."

Lucy touched his shoulder and he cried out in pain, although her touch too was very gentle.

"Child, show me the exact spot where it hurts."

"I . . . don't know just where. It's my shoulder."

She examined the shoulder carefully but could see nothing wrong. "I'll get your father."

At her call the whole family came trooping in. Joseph examined his son with grave eyes. "Did you hurt it?"

"No, Father."

Big Joseph looked grave. "We'd better have the doctor see him. Alvin, saddle up your horse and go for him at once."

Alvin left the room quickly. Lucy's face grew a shade whiter and a shade more weary. Where would the money come from for all these bills? Long ago Father Joseph had refused to accept help from her people. She was glad that he was a proud man, in the sense that he wanted to provide for his family. But there was the jewelry, most of it gifts her brother Stephen had given her from time to time. Joseph refused to let her sell even a brooch, yet the fine pieces seemed foolish luxury when money was needed so badly for everything. Stephen would not care if she sold it, although he might insist upon replacing it—a kindness she would never allow, for with each material setback they had, Joseph always found a way to remind her that her brothers were men of considerable property, as if it were important to her. He

15

couldn't seem to understand, even after all these years, that she preferred him and whatever came in life with him to all the substance that had once been a part of her existence.

Then there was her painting. She loved to paint on oilcloth when time permitted, and it was something women would buy, but Joseph refused to let her sell it. Why did men feel it was a disgrace for wives to help with finances?

The doctor came, and with all the family gathered around the bed he made his examination. His fingers moved over Joseph, pressing here, pressing there, lifting the arm, moving the shoulder. From time to time Joseph would cry out, although he kept his teeth clamped together in an effort to keep still.

"It's a bruise," he said at last. "I'll leave some bone liniment."

"But, sir, I didn't bruise it," Joseph told him politely.

"We'll treat it for a bruise anyway," the doctor said with a smile. "I'm sure it will be better in a few days."

But it was not better. For two weeks Joseph suffered excruciating pain. Lucy tried all the home remedies she knew, but it grew steadily worse.

"We must bring the doctor back," Big Joseph said.

When the doctor came the family gathered around as before. This time he found that a large fever sore had gathered between Joseph's breast and shoulder.

"If you'll remove all the children from the room I'll lance it," the doctor said.

Lucy sent Alvin and Hyrum away with the children.

Joseph's eyes met his father's. "Will it hurt much?"

"I'll hold you, son." He took a chair to a spot by the window, and Joseph climbed on his lap.

The lancing was soon over. Lucy clenched her hands together and watched white faced as the sore discharged over a quart of foul-smelling matter. As soon as it had drained the

16

pain left young Joseph's shoulder and shot like lightning down his side into the marrow of the bone in his leg. Joseph was sobbing now and clinging to his father. "The pain—the pain—how can I bear it?"

"Is this a natural thing, Doctor?" Concern was in Father Joseph's face.

"We must wait and see." The doctor put the instruments he had used into his carryall.

Lucy placed herself in front of the door. "Tell us what is happening."

"Mrs. Smith," his grave eyes met hers, "we must wait and see. You want the truth, and the truth is I don't know yet what is happening." He looked worried as he left the house and walked to his waiting buggy. Father Joseph went with him as far as the porch.

Day followed day, and each was filled with such suffering for young Joseph that the family could have cried for him. He could bear no weight on his leg, and he had to be carried from place to place. Most of the carrying was done by Lucy.

With school closed because of the epidemic, Father Joseph felt he should spend all his free time working the land. Alvin and Hyrum were going to the fields too, giving what time they could. They loved to be outdoors, and the sun seemed to be giving them new strength. Seeds must be planted for, with the closing of school, the land was the only source of food for the family. Lucy knew that her husband would leave Lebanon and seek a better living in another place if the crops were not abundant. Although he had not said so in words, she knew his heart yearned for New York State and the large wheat crops he had heard could be raised there. Sometime soon they would be making up their minds whether to go or to stay.

With Joseph and her older sons busy in the fields Lucy overtaxed herself caring for the family and trying to interest young Joseph in things that would help him to forget his pain.

One morning she awakened to find herself too limp to get out of bed. She was surprised to discover that the hour was late. Her husband and sons were already in the field . . . she could see them through the window. "I must get up," she told herself fiercely. She sat up, but the room began spinning crazily, so she lay down again. "Lord," she whispered, "I'm so tired that daytime sleep would seem like a gift from heaven. But if you plan to treat me to such luxury at this inopportune time, then please take over the house, the children, and young Joseph. There is a hungry calf in the barn to feed, bread to bake, washing to do, and ironing left over. . . ."

When she awakened, Alvin was sitting on the edge of her bed. "Everything is in order. We're all helping," he said. "The children are dressed and fed. Sophronia has made the beds, straightened the house, and fed the calf. About the bread, you'll have to tell us how to do that. Sophie wants to try the mixing, and I'll do the kneading."

Her face wore a puzzled expression. "How did you know about all these things?"

"The work you do isn't exactly hidden," Alvin told her with a grin. "We know pretty well what goes on around here."

"Where is Hyrum? Isn't he helping you?"

"Father excused us from field work. He told us to keep you in bed, and to help Joseph. Hyrum has found a way to really help. He's holding the sore part of the leg and pressing it between his hands. I don't know how long he can hold out, but it's stopping some of the pain. We put Joseph on William's bed to make Hyrum's job easier. Hyrum says he will sit there all day if necessary, and I guess he will for the swelling is like an elephant's leg."

For two days Lucy remained in bed. On the third day she made her way to the kitchen and was amazed at how well her husband and the children had managed without her. It was now three weeks since the doctor had lanced young Joseph's sore. "I have sent for the doctor. He and Alvin will be coming soon." The concern in Joseph's voice sent her hurrying to see young Joseph.

This time the doctor's face was grave. "I'll have to make an incision." Then to Lucy, "Please take the children a long way from here. Keep them away from the house. This is going to hurt. I want Mr. Smith to remain to hold the boy, but this house will be no place for a woman."

"I'm staying," Lucy said. "I'll send Alvin with the children."

The doctor shook his head. "I will not touch your boy while you are here."

Lucy's eyes met her husband's. His were imploring her to go.

She knelt beside William's low bed where young Joseph lay. He looked so small and worried and pale. "Brave darling, tell them you want me to stay."

"No, Mamma. I want you to go. I want only Father. Now please go."

"Then God be with you." She kissed him, fighting back the tears that brimmed her eyes.

"Don't cry, Mamma."

Through tears she gave him an encouraging smile, then she arose and walked out of the room to where the children were waiting. She didn't trust herself to look back.

On any other day Lucy would have welcomed being with the children out of doors, for she loved the land, a part of which was plowed and planted, the rest virgin timber.

19

They walked to a grove of trees some distance from the house, and she sat down on a little knoll with baby Catherine on her lap. Alvin, Hyrum, and Sophronia sat near her. Samuel and William ran a short way off to play among the trees. Nobody seemed in the mood for talking. It was so still that a little squirrel stopped beside Alvin, looking at him with bright, inquisitive eyes. Alvin could have reached out and touched it.

Lucy bent her head, and Hyrum said in a voice hushed and full of meaning, "You are praying for Joseph."

Lucy nodded, and he said: "I've been praying too."

"That's good." She was remembering Joseph the way he had been before the fever, always running, always climbing, always in a hurry, even when walking. He needed that leg! She asked for faith as she prayed, but the fear would not leave her.

Sophronia's voice broke into her meditation. "Mamma, why must Joseph bear so much pain?"

"We don't know why," Lucy told her gently. And then, as if she were also reassuring herself, "We must trust God to make things right for him."

The waiting seemed endless. When at last Father Joseph came out of the house to beckon them, baby Catherine had fallen asleep in Lucy's arms.

Lucy went to Joseph's room quietly. He looked haggard and pale, lying in bed between clean white sheets. Every sign of the bloody ordeal had been removed. He gave her a wan smile as he showed his bandaged leg. The doctor had made an incision of eight inches on the front side of the leg between the knee and the ankle.

During the next few days Lucy did her work with a light heart. The pain in Joseph's leg was gone, and there was laughter in the house again. Then the wound began to heal and the pain became as violent as before.

20

Again the doctor was called, and again Lucy took the children and left the house. "Oh, God, why?" she cried in anguish. But there was no answer.

This time the doctor enlarged the wound, cutting the leg to the bone. Surely, Lucy thought, there would be an end to it now. But as soon as the leg commenced healing the swelling began again, and Hyrum resumed his vigil, holding the leg and pressing gently, careful not to hurt the wound.

This time a council of surgeons examined the leg and held a private consultation in the living room. Lucy sat tense and silent in a chair beside Joseph's bed awaiting their verdict.

"Mamma," Joseph asked, white-lipped, "are they going to hurt me again?"

"I don't know, son." She bent and kissed his brow.

Minutes ticked by leadenly. At last Father Joseph stood in the doorway. He tried to make his voice matter-of-fact when he spoke, but Lucy knew by his stricken face that the verdict was not good. "Lucy," he said, "the doctors want you to talk with us downstairs. I'll send Alvin and Hyrum to stay with Joseph."

"What is it, Father?" Joseph's voice came out too shrill.

Big Joseph reached for his son's hand and pressed it to his cheek, "Whatever it is, lad, we'll face it like men together."

"Will it be worse than other times?"

"I won't lie to you, son." He turned his face away to keep young Joseph from seeing the tears that filled his eyes suddenly. "Come, Lucy, the doctors are waiting." He pressed Joseph's hand to his lips, forcing a smile. "What are we all so long faced about? We're going to get you well, and I'll butcher a young steer to fatten you up."

The doctors sat in the living room with grave faces.

Lucy looked from them to her husband. "What is it?"

The principal surgeon got out of his chair. "Sit here, Mrs. Smith."

Lucy sat down.

The doctor paced back and forth and Lucy said, "Please, I must know the truth about my son."

The surgeon spoke as if he were measuring each word. "We don't know how to soften the blow, Mrs. Smith. We find that amputation is absolutely necessary to save his life."

For a moment Lucy could say nothing at all. She was seeing Joseph, who loved to run in the wind, stumbling through life as a cripple. Oh, no, she simply could not have that for Joseph. When she spoke her voice had finality. "You must not take off his leg until you try once more. Cut around the bone and take out the diseased part. If the wound doesn't heal properly, perhaps then I will resign myself and permit this terrible thing."

"Would you have your son suffer more and then lose his leg?"

"I would have him suffer to save his leg." Lucy's eyes were swimming, but her voice was determined. "I will not consent to let you enter his room until you promise to try once more."

"Get plenty of water boiling on the stove then," the principal doctor said. "It is my idea to do it now and not wait."

Lucy prayed as she filled the water vessels, and she knew big Joseph was praying as he pumped the water and carried it into the house. "Our boy will be fine," she told herself fiercely. "God knows he needs two legs. Please don't let him down, God, because I think he would rather die than lose his leg." Then she took herself in hand. "Lucy Smith, you've got to trust that the boy will be all right."

When the time came they went up the stairs. It was their

own doctor who approached the bed. "My poor boy, we have come again."

"Yes," the young patient said. "But you haven't come to take my leg off, have you, Sir?"

"No." The doctor glanced at Lucy. "Your mother insists we make one more effort to save it and that is what we have come to do."

"You mean . . . you are going . . . to do it now?"

The principal surgeon came and took his hand. "Waiting won't help." He ordered cords to be brought to bind Joseph to the bed.

"I won't be bound, Sir."

"You must be bound. It's unthinkable to operate without tying you, lad."

"No, Doctor," young Joseph said as if the whole thing were definitely decided. "I will not be bound, for I can bear the operation only if I am free."

"Then," said the doctor, "you will drink some brandy."

"No, Sir, I will not."

"You must take something or you can never stand the pain. We are going to take out all the diseased bone in your leg." He turned to Father Smith. "Reason with him, Sir."

"Please." Young Joseph's eyes went from one doctor to the other. "Let me tell you how this must be done. I will have my father sit on the bed and hold me, then I will let you do what you need to do to fix my leg."

Father Joseph said, "The other times were very bad, and we did it this way."

Young Joseph looked at Lucy. "Go, Mamma, take the children . . . and go a long way from the house . . . so you won't hear me scream." His eyes were swimming as he looked into her face. "Father can stand it, but it is not for you. Please go!"

"Oh, Joseph!" Lucy was crying and holding him the

way she used to hold and rock him when he was very small.

"Please go, Mamma."

She brought a number of clean, folded sheets and put them under his leg.

His arms went around her, and she clung to him.

"Mamma, please don't cry. I'll . . . be . . . fine."

Hyrum was waiting in the hall. He walked with her down the stairs and out of the house.

She saw that Alvin had hitched their best driving horse to the wagon, and the children were in.

He called to her. "Come, Mamma, your place is in the seat beside me. Father says I am to take us a long way from here."

"You go, Hyrum," Lucy said. "Help Alvin with the children."

"But you must come too. I'm sure Father . . ."

She went with Hyrum to the wagon. "I think it is fine that you are taking the children, Alvin. Drive very carefully, and don't take chances with the horse."

He looked troubled. "Father said . . ."

"I know. You children must go without me. Do you have food and everything you need?"

Alvin nodded. "You ought not to stay here."

"You've brought everything for the baby?"

Again he nodded.

Her eyes moved over them tenderly. "I'm sure you all understand. I want to be where I can tell how things are going with Joseph."

She watched them drive off. The younger ones were waving and the older ones looked worried. Baby Catherine seemed quite content on Hyrum's lap.

Lucy walked briskly away from the house and sat down in a wooded spot with her back against a tree trunk. The blue sky was filled with feathery clouds, and she felt a kinship with the universe and God as she sat crying for help for Joseph. Her lips moved as she watched the clouds. "Oh, God, strengthen him. Be with him. Ease his pain, and heal him if it is thy will."

She closed her eyes to blot out the images she was seeing in her mind's eye, but the sight did not go away. The doctors would be boring into the bone, first on one side, then on the other. With a pair of forceps they would be chipping, taking out pieces of diseased bone. How could he stand it? Why must it be? Sweat began pouring from her, and she stood up, clenching her hands.

Suddenly the air was filled with piercing screams. Without realizing what she was doing she began running toward the sound. Then she remembered that the way was barred to her. She began walking away from the sound, crying and praying.

Time stood still. Minutes seemed like hours. Then the screams became so wild that nothing could keep her away from the house. She ran toward the sound and stumbled up the porch steps. Pushing open the door she raced madly up the stairs to Joseph's room. Now she was beholding the horror of her child's suffering. The wound lay open, blood gushing from it. Young Joseph was pale as a corpse. Large drops of sweat were rolling down his face. Mingled with his panting and screaming he was crying, "Oh, Mamma, go back . . . go back!"

She tried to run to him but was forced back by a doctor who pushed her from the room.

Lucy went into the adjoining room and closed the door. She was trembling and sobbing. Then she was on her knees "Oh, God . . . please help!" The screams became wilder, then softened to moans. Lucy felt each one as if it were her own bone that was being chipped away. Why was there not something to still the pain? In the city hospitals doctors were trying anesthesia. Some persons thought it was good; some said it was a killer. Surely it would be better than this butchering with nothing but mind and will to endure the pain.

At last the room became quiet. The silence hung in the air like a breath. Then she could hear the voices of the doctors mingled with her husband's voice. She got up from her kneeling position and went to the door of Joseph's room, but it wouldn't open.

"You'll have to wait." It was the voice of their family doctor. "Your boy came through fine."

"Thank God, oh, thank God," she said softly.

When at last she was permitted to enter the room every appearance of blood had been removed; even the instruments that had been used in the operation were not in sight. Father Joseph had made many trips up and down the stairs.

Young Joseph lay between clean sheets. He was completely spent, but he gave her a fleeting smile, then his eyes closed. He would sleep now.

Big Joseph reached for her hand. He looked haggard and pale, but looked proudly on his son.

The operation was a success. Very soon Joseph was on his way to becoming well again. Only one thing was different—he walked with a limp. It would be a long time before he would stop favoring his lame leg, but his determination was strong. That the leg would function adequately for him nobody in his family doubted. They knew Joseph.

The Smiths had few books. For this reason the Bible they owned became worn from use. Memorizing favorite passages became a pastime for all the family. Even little

William could quote short scriptures, and he enjoyed joining the family in repeating the Lord's Prayer or a psalm.

As soon as the children could read, each had his own favorite stories. Some of these they wrote into plays to be acted out. Often they did these so well that they learned to quote verses and sometimes whole chapters for their dramatizations.

Other times the family, or just the children, would read or quote verses or chapter, while the others guessed where the quotations could be found. In this way the scriptures sank deeply into their minds so that they were never alone; God was their friend. Often they would discuss the meaning of their readings, until they began to build a pattern of what Christ's church on earth should be like, and a desire grew in them to belong to such a church.

They looked at the earth and sky, and God was there. He was in the sun, stars, clouds, trees, grass—all living things. They were convinced that some of their dreams had spiritual meanings. All these things opened up new vistas of thought. It was not unusual to hear them talking to Him as they went about their daily tasks. Lucy would say, "That William! There isn't any fear in him at all. I caught him climbing the corral fence with the intention of riding the cow. Now, it was you, Lord, who put that fearlessness in him, so protect him, please, until he is old enough to get some sense." Or "God, help us to understand young Joseph. He asks questions we can't answer. He reads less than the other children, but he goes deeper into your mysteries than we can comprehend. He will read and then sit and think as though he would drain extra truth from every sentence. He is an unusual boy. I have never heard him pray aloud, yet I feel he does talk with you about everything that you have made. I don't know what you have in mind for him, but please stay close to him, and help him grow according to your will."

And so it went. She continually prayed for the welfare of each member of her family as she would talk to a friend.

Big Joseph's faith was humble and direct. He brought his children together at bedtime for prayers, where they learned reverence. When he picked up the Bible to read aloud, they sensed his regard and respect for the words written there, even as they were enchanted by the way he read; he could make stories come alive, and cause words to sparkle with meaning.

Six times big Joseph had had strange dreams of a spiritual nature, and Lucy had had one. They wrote these down and read them to one another. In a way these writings were a substitute for the books they were too poor to buy. Lucy announced her dream one evening when the family had gathered for worship. Sitting down at a little table, she pulled the candle closer and began to read what she had written:

"I stood in a large and beautiful meadow where everything around me wore an aspect of peculiar pleasantness. Running through the meadow was a pure, clear stream of water. As I traced the stream I discovered two trees standing upon its margin, both on the same side of the stream. The trees were beautiful and well proportioned, towering to great height. Their branches commenced near the top, and spread themselves in luxurious grandeur. As I gazed with admiration, I saw that one of them was surrounded by a bright belt that shone like burnished gold, but more brilliantly. Presently a gentle breeze passed by the tree encircled by this golden zone, and the tree bent gracefully before the wind, waving its beautiful branches in the light air. As the wind increased, the tree assumed the most lively and animated appearance and seemed to express in its motions the utmost joy and happiness. Even the stream that rolled beneath it seemed to share every sensation felt by the tree, for as the branches danced over the water it would swell gently, then recede with a motion as soft as a baby's breath, but as lively as a sunbeam. The belt of light also moved in unison with the motion of the stream and tree until it became exceedingly glorious.

"I looked at the other tree. It was surrounded by no belt of light. It stood erect and as fixed as a pillar of marble. No matter how strong the wind blew over it not a leaf stirred, not a bough bent. It stood obstinate and stiff, scorning the gentle breeze and the strong wind."

Lucy stopped reading and looked at big Joseph. "I asked the Lord the meaning of this strange dream, and this is the interpretation that came to me. The stubborn and unyielding tree is your brother Jesse."

Big Joseph looked surprised, though he knew that Lucy had never particularly cared for Jesse Smith.

"The flexible, pliant tree is you, Joseph. And the breath of heaven passing over the trees is the pure and undefiled gospel of the Son of God. This gospel Jesse will always resist, but you, Joseph, when you are more advanced in years will hear and receive it with your whole heart, and it will bring you intelligence, happiness, and everlasting life." As she finished speaking, her eyes were starry and her face had a kind of glow. Joseph listened and made no comment. Another time he might have teased her a little about disliking Jesse.

Joseph's dreams all seemed to have the same meaning. One night after he had been contemplating the different religions, he fell asleep and dreamed he was traveling in an open, barren field. He looked in all directions and could see only fallen timber. There was no sign of life, and a deathlike stillness pervaded the air. No sound could be heard in all the field, yet he knew he was not alone, for an attendant spirit walked with him and seemed almost to be a part of him.

29

"What is the meaning of what I am seeing, and why am I in this dismal place?" Joseph asked.

"This field is the world, inanimate and dead, awaiting the awakening of a true religion," the spirit said. "But travel on, and by the wayside you will find a certain box, the contents of which, if you eat of it, will give you wisdom and understanding."

Joseph proceeded a short distance and came upon the box. Immediately he raised the lid and began eating of its contents, finding it delicious above anything he had tasted before. As soon as he commenced eating, ugly beasts appeared. They began roaring, tearing the earth, tossing their horns, and bellowing. They came so close that he was compelled to drop the box and flee for his life. Yet in the midst of all this he was perfectly happy, although he awakened trembling.

The sixth dream came soon after young Joseph's surgery. Early one morning big Joseph came into the kitchen where Lucy was preparing breakfast. In a tone half serious, half teasing, he said, "I've had another dream, Lucy. What would you say if I told you that we were to have two more children?" She tossed her head. "Who needs more? We already have seven."

"Do you have time to hear my dream?"

"If it isn't contagious I'll listen."

He pushed a stool against the wall out of her way and sat down. "I thought I was traveling in a desolate, barren field, with my guide beside me. As I walked I thought I had better reflect upon what I was doing before going farther, so I asked, 'What place is this, and what motive can I have for traveling here?' "

Lucy moved from stove to table, listening. She liked these intimate times with Joseph without the children, and

30

his strange dreams fascinated her more than she was willing to admit.

His voice followed her. "My guide said, 'This is the desolate world, but travel on.' I wanted to turn back, for the place was not to my liking, but after a time I came to a narrow path, and after walking in it a short way I saw a stream that ran from east to west. I couldn't see its source or its end, but as far as I could see a rope ran along its bank about as high as a man can reach, and beyond me was a low and very pleasant valley. In the valley was a tree different from all the trees I have seen. It was such a handsome tree that it caught my admiration. Its branches were beautiful, and it bore a white fruit shaped like a chestnut bur. I gazed at it with considerable interest, and as I looked the burs began to open, shedding particles of a white fruit. The fruit was dazzling, like snowflakes in the sun. I tasted it and found it delicious beyond description. As I was eating I said to myself, 'I must bring my family to enjoy this with me.' Then I brought you and the children and we commenced eating. While we ate we were thankful and prayerful.

"Then I noticed a spacious building opposite the valley we were in. It was so tall that it seemed to reach beyond the sky, and it was filled with doors and windows where proud, richly dressed people had gathered to watch us in the valley under the tree. They pointed scornful fingers and treated us with contempt, but we completely disregarded them. I asked our guide the meaning of the delicious fruit, and he said it was the pure love of God shed abroad in the hearts of all those who love him and keep his commandments."

Joseph paused, and a slow twinkle filled his eyes. "Then the guide told me to go and bring the rest of my family. I raised my eyes and saw two small children standing some distance off. These I brought to the tree, and they commenced eating with the rest of us."

Lucy showed her dimples, but he was suddenly serious again. "The more of that fruit we ate, the more we wanted. Finally we were scooping it up by the handful. After a little while I asked the guide the meaning of the spacious building. He said, 'It is Babylon, and it must fall. The people in the doors and windows are the wicked ones who despise those who love and serve God.' "

The fever in Lebanon ran on into summer and schools remained closed. Money was scarce everywhere, and the Smiths felt the pinch keenly, for they had grown to rely on Joseph's teaching salary.

The summer was a scorcher. Worried farmers scanned the sky for rain that did not come, and the draught took precedence over the war as the topic of conversation. All growing things were withering in the heat. Water holes were drying up. In some places the stench of dead fish in ponds was almost too foul to breathe, and water became so polluted that animals would not drink it.

Joseph had scanned the heavens so often that now the children were doing it too. Even baby Catherine would stretch her small arms toward the sky and Samuel or William would say, "Tell God to make it rain, Cathy."

"We'll be leaving Lebanon very soon now," Lucy said aloud to the chickens as she gathered the eggs. Wonderful how chickens went right on laying eggs as long as they were fed, without knowing or caring about crop failures, but if the drought continued they would probably sicken and die too. It was evening, and the heat was still so thick she seemed to be walking through it.

The thirsty cows in the corral stood by the dry watering trough with heads lowered. Joseph was hauling water for the livestock from their one good pond now. He should be coming soon with just enough rationed to sustain livestock and family. It was necessary to measure the water, for without rain this pond too would soon be gone.

She looked back toward the house. She would miss Lebanon. Their life here had started with such promise—a house almost adequate for their large family, fertile land, schools for the children, a teaching position for Joseph, and Alvin and Hyrum attending military school in Hanover. Why at one time she and Joseph were laying aside a savings account for later years when they would be too old to work. They had even talked about higher learning for the children.

She moved toward the house slowly, pulling her eyes away from the dry land that at one time had been green with promise. She did not know whether it would be wise for them to leave Lebanon. When she was sure about a thing she could hold as firm as a rock until Joseph came around to her way of thinking, but now she did not know what was best for them. She only knew that Joseph had been spending much of his time alone thinking, and that he was restless at night. Now he had come to a decision. Something in his posture, the lift of his shoulders, and the way he had walked toward the wagon an hour ago told her that very soon he would be speaking his mind.

It was not until after the children were in bed and the house had become silent that he said, "Lucy, would you consider moving to Norwitch, Vermont? Esquire Moredock says I can manage a farm of his for a small salary and a share of his crops. There is a house, though probably not like this one. In fact," a twinkle replaced his solemn look, "we are likely to all be comfortably pressed together."

Lucy felt a lump gathering in her throat, but she knew there was one in his too so she waited for him to continue.

Her eyes took in each familiar object in the living room that had somehow this minute become very precious.

His voice was not altogether steady. "If we sell almost everything good that we own, Lucy, we can leave here with every debt paid and—" a corner of his mouth turned up a little, "we'll have a little manna left to feed the hungry nine of us until Norwitch gives us a full cupboard."

She searched his face. "Are you sure you want to do this?"

"If you can endure the arrangement I think it would be a wise move."

"How soon will you . . . want us to go?"

"Very soon, Lucy. We can't get water from our neighbors, for they have none to spare, and our last water hole is drying up fast."

She sat very still. Tomorrow perhaps when he was out of the house she would cry, but not tonight. His heart was heavy too. She reached and touched his hand. "It's late," she said, "and time we were in bed."

At the top of the stairs he spoke again. "Lucy . . ."

"Yes, Joseph . . ."

"I can't help feeling glad our troubles are only material. So many people have lost loved ones as well as crops this year. We are a blessed family."

Lucy reached for his hand. They both knew what death was like. It had come to them a year before William was born. Little Ephraim . . . what a rosebud of a baby he had been! Small dainty hands, features like Joseph's, soft, dark hair—she would carry his image in her heart as a part of herself forever. Eleven days—what a short lifetime! The marker on his grave told the story: Ephraim Smith—born March 13, 1810, died March 24, 1810.

"We had better look in on the children," she said. "They are probably smothering in this heat. And you are right, my dear." They were together, and life seemed suddenly abundant.

The move to Norwitch was a mistake from the beginning. What they did not know was that the drought had spread throughout New England. It was in Norwitch as well as Lebanon.

The house was better than Lucy had expected it to be. The stables were well built, and the barn was filled with fragrant hay.

In good weather Alvin, Hyrum, young Joseph, and Samuel would sleep in the haymow. Sometimes long after time for the boys to be asleep Lucy and Joseph would hear them singing together. There was a blend to their voices that was rich and melodious.

"It's a talent," Father Joseph would say. Then to tease Lucy he would add, "They get it from my side of the house."

In spite of these things that were good, Lucy knew that Joseph had begun to worry almost from the moment their feet touched the land.

It did no good to work from dawn until dusk, for crops parched and withered, curled and dried. Nothing much grew except the fruit, and it was scrubbier than it ought to be. But poor as it was, they managed to sell enough to keep bread on the table. Their bills began mounting again, and Father Joseph began talking about New York, the way he had talked in Lebanon.

Winter came and went. Strangely enough on a diet of whatever Lucy could scrape together, the children stayed healthy.

Again Joseph plowed and planted, but the year was the same as before—a total failure. This time they survived only because Mrs. Mack, Lucy's aged mother, came from Royalton to stay with them. One evening after Grandmother Mack and the children were in bed, Joseph and Lucy were alone in the cook house taking stock of their scanty provisions. Lucy said, "Remember the dream you had in Lebanon when you saw our family increasing by two?" There was a twinkle in her eyes.

"Are you . . .?"

"Yes."

He kissed her, and some of the worry left her face. "You aren't sorry when times are so hard?"

"Times aren't hard." He smiled down at her and caught her face between his hands gently. "Our crops aren't all bad. We raise mighty fine children."

That fall an untimely frost destroyed the crops. Now Joseph and Lucy both knew they must leave Norwitch, and they must go before cold weather set in.

"Will we go to New York State this time?" Lucy asked.

"If that is God's will. We've both had strong impressions to go there."

Lucy was not surprised when a few days later Joseph came to her and said, "There is a Mr. Howard, a dependable man, leaving for Palmyra, New York, very soon. I can go with him as one of his drivers."

"Then we must go, Joseph."

"It isn't that simple, Lucy. He wants me to drive for him without you and the children."

She stood silently thinking. If he went ahead, how would she ever manage seven children and a team of horses all the way to New York State. True, Alvin was strong and almost as big as a man, but sixteen was young, and he was no more used to following a map than she was. She dismissed the thought of the baby on the way. She could cope with that and drive. Well, she would make a copy of Joseph's map before he left, and she would memorize every landmark on it. They simply could not survive another winter in Norwitch.

Joseph broke into her thoughts. "Our debts must be paid before we leave, and God only knows where the money will come from to pay them."

Lucy's mother had been listening. Now she said, "You and Joseph should move to Royalton, Lucy, where Daniel can give you everything you need until after you have your baby."

The room became too quiet suddenly. Lucy resented the unspoken implication that Joseph was to blame for the heat that had withered crops and the cold that had frozen them. And certainly Joseph wanted no help from Daniel or any of Lucy's brothers.

That night Lucy lay beside Joseph in the comfortable stillness of their bedroom, thinking of the prayer Joseph had prayed with her and the children. "We thank you for the beauties of earth, the warm colors of fruit and flowers, the peaceful sight of cattle grazing in a field, the joy of knowing that all living things are in your hands. We do not ask the easy way. Brave men are made by facing hardships and wisely solving problems. But we do ask you to walk with us, show us your will, and give us courage to meet bravely whatever the future holds for us. Let us be calm in adversity, humble in prosperity. . . ."

She reached and touched Joseph tenderly, careful not to awaken him. Here was a man who could be thankful in spite of trouble or worry, a man who loved beauty so much that he could mention colors of fruit and flowers when his own were frozen and useless. She moved closer to him, proud that he was her husband. He was honest and good. If he had a

37

fault it was in trusting others and expecting them to measure up to his standards. This Mr. Howard, what was he like?

Next morning Joseph said, "Lucy, if we sell the livestock, wagons, and most of the furniture that we have been able to scrape together it should bring enough to pay for everything, with a little left over to get you and the family to New York." Lucy felt her heart wrench, but she gave no outward sign. "How can we go without a wagon and horses?"

"I'll come back after you, or send someone to get you. I'll never let you drive those strange roads alone. We'll keep goods enough to make one full wagonload. What do you say?"

She nodded. "It sounds like a workable plan."

"Mr. Moredock has promised to buy one wagon and team and two cows from us with the understanding that you will use them as your own for as long as you remain in Norwitch."

His words gave her added assurance. "With those we can manage," she said.

Joseph had only a few days in which to settle his accounts, so he set a special day for his creditors to come to the house and bring their books so that everything could be properly settled and the payments receipted. Each creditor came, but two neglected to bring their account books. Without the books no "paid in full" entries could be made, but Joseph supposed witnesses would be enough to prove the payments, and settlements were made accordingly. Again Joseph and Lucy had the satisfaction of knowing they were entirely free from debt.

It was a busy time at the Smiths after Joseph left for Palmyra, but packing to go away was exciting, and to the children New York seemed a faraway magic place. Lucy caught their enthusiasm, and she too began to feel that the

38

move to New York would be a turning point for good in their lives. The map she had insisted upon having was becoming soiled and crumpled from use. The older children studied it as much as she did.

At last the packing was done, and everything was ready for loading except for last-minute necessities that would be attended to after the wagon and team came for them.

Lucy knew that this transportation would have to be hired at expense, and that Joseph would expect them to leave immediately, so as to keep the transportation bill at a minimum. Lucy's mother would ride with them as far as Royalton, where she would again live with Lucy's brother Daniel. They would spend one night there, after which they would begin the long trip to Palmyra. Lucy dreaded it, but mentioned her fears to no one. If Joseph were here he would be teasing her about morning sickness that lasted all day.

At last the wagon pulled by two teams of horses arrived. The excitement of the children was electric. The driver was a man past thirty, a relative of the Mr. Howard Joseph had accompanied to New York. His name was also Mr. Howard. His manner was stiff and distant, and Lucy sensed at once that he wouldn't warm up to the children. She was one to make quick judgments about people. She either liked them at once or she didn't, and she seldom changed her mind about the way she sized them up. She didn't like this man. He made her uneasy. Her mother spoke her thoughts when they were in the house alone. "That young man has cold eyes. Watch him Lucy. He may be cruel."

When Lucy went outside again she asked Mr. Howard for the papers so that she could see what sort of contract Joseph had made with him. She read them carefully, handed him his copy, and kept the second copy for herself. The papers pledged a safe delivery of family and goods to

Palmyra, and Joseph had paid two thirds of the fee. It was probably all the money he had been able to raise.

Lucy superintended the loading of the goods into the wagon and this displeased Mr. Howard, but at last all the belongings were in, with space enough for the children to sit down, and a place in the wagon seat beside the driver for herself and Mrs. Mack.

Lucy went through the house a second time to be sure nothing belonging to them had been left. She also examined her leather pouch, concealed in a secret pocket she had made in her petticoat. In it was her money and her jewelry.

They were almost ready to leave when two buggies appeared in the road that led to the house. These were of the finest make, and the horses were high-spirited thoroughbreds, elegant and graceful. Lucy's heart sank, for as she recognized the men a feeling of foreboding came over her. These were the two who had withheld their books at the time of settlement, and the books had not been receipted.

The men pulled their horses to a halt, and the fear in Lucy grew. The schemes of these men had come to her ears before. Even good, trusting Joseph had doubted their honesty. They pulled their horses to a halt, and commanding Lucy's sons to tether them, they climbed down from their high seats.

Lucy didn't ask them in. Instead she came out on the porch to talk to them. After the usual salutations she waited for them to state their business. The smaller children gathered around, and she asked Mother Mack to herd them back into the house.

As soon as they were alone, the manner of the men became bold. "Mrs. Smith," one of them said, "you are not planning to leave without paying us what you owe, are you?"

Lucy faced them with defiant calmness. "You both know my husband paid you before he went to New York

State. The payments were made before witnesses."

The men smiled amiably. "Here are the books, Ma'am. If the payments had been made they would be entered and receipted, and they are not."

"You failed to bring your books the day my husband paid you," Lucy told them stubbornly. "But they were witnessed by a Mr. Flogg who lives in Hanover and . . . and . . ." It occurred to her suddenly that she didn't know the name of the other witness, nor did she know where the papers were that Joseph had had the witnesses sign that day along with the signatures of these two men. "Mother," she called, "will you come out here a minute?"

Mrs. Mack came out on the porch. Lucy was going to ask her about the papers when the other man said, "Mrs. Smith, unless you can produce the witnesses or the papers, your debt is one hundred fifty dollars."

"Oh, dear," Mrs. Mack said. "That is more money than Mrs. Smith and I have together."

"Mother, Mr. Flogg from Hanover witnessed Joseph's payments to these men that day. Who was the other witness?"

"I don't know, child. I spent most of the day at the Moredocks so I would be out of the way."

And the children wouldn't know, Lucy thought frantically. Alvin had kept them away from the house all day.

Alvin and Hyrum had finished tethering the horses, and now sensing that something was wrong they joined the gathering on the porch.

"What's it all about, Mother?" Alvin asked, trying to assume the role of a man.

"These men are asking for money we don't owe." Her eyes left Alvin's face, and she addressed Mother Mack again. "We'll have to unpack the wagon, and go through trunks and dresser drawers until we find those papers."

41

"Joseph took the papers with him, Lucy. The suit he wore to New York was the one he had on the day he was making settlement with everyone. I know. I pressed the coat and trousers, and saw the papers in his coat pocket. I put them back after I pressed the coat."

"You put them back—oh, Mother!"

"I'm sorry, Lucy—I'm real sorry."

Lucy could have shook her for blurting her confession in front of the men, but she kept her composure and asked the men to leave.

All this time Mr. Howard had been standing impatiently by the loaded wagon. Now the two men walked high-handedly down the steps, stopped by Mr. Howard to show him their books, and made Mrs. Smith a mocking bow. "If you try to leave town without paying us, Mrs. Smith," one of them told her, "we'll attach your goods." Then they were gone.

"What will we do, Mother?" Alvin asked as they drove away. His face was lined with worry.

"Let's get our last-minute things done, and the children in the wagon. We have to go through town on our way. We'll stop there, and I know just the man to talk this over with."

In Norwitch Lucy went at once to see an attorney, a friend of Joseph's, and laid the unjust claims before him. He listened in grave concern. "You must stay here a few days until we can contact Mr. Flogg in Hanover, Lucy. Now, go over all you have told me again, and try to remember the name of the other witness."

But it was no use. In her mind the last men to leave the house that day and the last men Joseph had paid were Mr. Flogg who had his books and these two men without their books. All the other creditors had gone home.

"These things can't be settled in a minute," her friend said. "You must stay and prove your claim."

"But we can't," Lucy said. "We gave our house back to

Mr. Moredock, and his new tenants are moving in this afternoon. Do you realize what it would cost for three adults and seven children to put up at the inn for several days? There would be food and lodging plus extra wages for the driver and feed for two teams. These rogues say they will attach my goods. It isn't that what we own is so valuable, but we can't get along without it."

He walked to the window where he could see the well-loaded wagon, and behind it now were two waiting black buggies. "Those are clever men," he said, thinking aloud. "They must have learned from some source that you couldn't produce the papers Joseph took with him to New York, or the witnesses, otherwise they wouldn't have tried this bold maneuver. They're counting on the fact that time is important to you, and that you are a woman. It's something they must have planned from the beginning. That is why I wish you would stay and see this thing through."

"We should be on our way this very minute."

He turned to look at her. "We'll have a case once we contact Mr. Flogg."

"Mr. Flogg may be dead. Maybe there wasn't another witness since I can't remember one. Joseph trusts everyone. All I know is we paid them, and I can't prove it. And they must be very sure that I can't."

She joined him at the window. There was steel in her walk and determination in her proud, pointed chin. "If I pay them will you try to recover the money on a percentage basis? I don't know of any other way to honestly promise you a fee." She gave him a smile that was half defiant, half wistful. "To tell you the truth we have barely enough money to get us to New York."

"Then let me advance you some."

Her face became warm and lovely all at once. "You have always been a good friend to us, and Joseph will bless you for offering, but we can't take money from you. We might never be able to pay it back."

"Give me a couple of hours," he said, "and I'll raise the money you need by subscription from the townspeople."

The thought seemed so absurd that she laughed in spite of the seriousness of her situation. "That would be a clever get-rich scheme," she said. "I'd be in the same class with our two friends out there." Then suddenly her face became serious. "Do what you can for us, and thank you for listening. I'll sign whatever you'll need to give you power to act for us, then I'll be off to try to raise what money I need."

"How will you do that?"

"I have some jewelry. Most of it is quite valuable." She was smiling through tears.

"Don't do it, Lucy. Don't pay those scoundrels. Give me time to act for you."

A dimple appeared in each cheek. "You have all the time there is. Just get the money back for us." There was a proud lift to her shoulders as she left the office.

Lucy paid the unprincipled men and left them. Her head was held high and red flamed her cheeks. She did not mind that her anger showed. It hurt being imposed upon to pay for the settlement a second time; but it hurt even more that her jewelry had been sacrificed on account of their scheming. It was, as their friend had said, a loss she could never recover. The luxuries she had known as a girl were gone. Not that she would exchange her life with Joseph and the children for any other, but sometimes it was nice to remember that once there had been music and beautiful clothes, balls and socials, warm nights under the stars, laughter mingled with the sound of tinkling crystal, fine food, delicate china, gleaming silver, and New England's carefree hospitality with leisure to enjoy it. These things perhaps would never come again, but they were

44

bred into her being so that nothing could ever erase them. From the Mack jewels she had managed to keep her watch, which she needed, and one plain brooch. She also had her wedding band from Joseph.

She sat silent and prim on the wagon seat beside her mother, hardly aware that they were moving away from Norwitch and everything that had been a part of her life there. She hardly knew when they left the town behind them.

As the day wore on Mr. Howard began to show the manner of man he was. The children were behaving well, but he was gruff and silenced even their singing. Sometimes when he reproved them Lucy found it impossible to hold her tongue, and this added to the tension, making a situation that was almost intolerable, but since they must travel together she did her best to control her irritations. Nothing seemed to please the man, not even the pleasant weather, with the sun so warm that coats were not necessary. The children even removed their shoes, putting them with the new ones Lucy had bought for "fit and proper dress" or to be ready for an emergency.

They came at last to Daniel's lane. Mr. Howard drew in his breath sharply and straightened himself on the wagon seat. His face registered surprise. Lucy knew he hadn't expected to see the broad acres of fertile land and timber or the fine buildings that were Daniel's.

Before they could enter the lane Mr. Howard had to pull the horses to a stop and wait, for Daniel's milk cows filled the lane. They were slowly wending their way to the barn to be milked and were being herded along by a hired boy of perhaps fifteen and his shepherd dog. Actually the boy and dog had nothing more to do than to walk behind, for the cows knew their way and followed the lead cow contentedly, as if the whole thing had been rehearsed. The boy whistled a lively tune that filled the evening air with soul-lifting sound. It was a pretty sight—the sleek, fat cows, the road lined with maple trees, the sky alive with every color of the rainbow blended in the sunset. Half a mile away a white church nestled in the tree-covered hills, and all the earth seemed filled with the peace and quiet of New England. Then they too were moving up the lane.

Vermont had always been dear to Lucy, and now as they rode along she drank in the beauty of the Green Mountain state where all her children except Catherine had been born. She would miss the rugged beauty of mountains and streams, and the proud, independent people who lived here. She would miss the wind, heat, and snow. Vermont was the only state in all New England without a seacoast, but its beauty was indisputable.

"*Ver-mont*," she said aloud to no one in particular. "Green Mountain!" The words lingered on her tongue lovingly.

Her eyes moved over Daniel's land. Royalton was mostly a community of small farms, and Daniel's place was like those surrounding it, except that his maple groves were a little bigger, his cows a little fatter, and his cheeses and butter somehow seemed a little richer than his neighbors.

There was granite and marble on his land, some of which had been used to enhance the beauty of his house. They were nearing the house now, and off in the distance they could see wooded trails, perfect for riding or hiking.

Nothing seemed changed. Daniel's home was Colonial in style, and the white pillars of the porch stood like welcoming sentinels. They drew up in front of it, and the next thing she knew she was in Daniel's arms. Then they were all being welcomed inside and placed in the care of his competent housekeeper. At once Lucy's mother assumed her role of being Mrs. Mack, head of whatever needed managing within the confines of the house. If Daniel noticed he gave no sign. Later, Lucy knew he would have to mediate whatever trouble came between the housekeeper and their mother.

It was good to wash up and rest, to be pampered by a jovial and loving relative, to eat from his bountiful table. Even Mr. Howard warmed to these comforts. He drank claret fresh from Bordeaux, France, passing the small crystal wine glass time and again for a refill. Daniel was a gracious host, and Lucy, watching, appraised him almost as if she were seeing him for the first time.

A villager had once called him the tall, handsome, beloved Mr. Mack. But Daniel wasn't tall; he merely carried himself with an unassuming dignity. He wasn't handsome, but he was clean of mind and body, and his attitude was one of interest. The villagers loved him, for he gave love and received it in return. He was quick to see another's need, and he had the knack of helping in such way that the benefactor never felt obligated or put down. Children gathered around him, and he had time for them. He shared himself with anyone who had a need—the old, the lonely, the sick, all came under his watch and care. He had his faults—a quick temper, an impatience with indifference and slothfulness—but he was a strength in Royalton, and Lucy knew his influence went deep. It was good to have such a brother, even though he was showing Mr. Howard far more kindness than the man deserved. Perhaps it was just as well that Daniel didn't know what manner of man Mr. Howard was.

That night when the children were in bed, and Mr. Howard was at a tavern owned by Daniel's friend Willard Pierce, she and her brother sat beside a friendly fire in the parlor and talked about old times and new plans, catching up on things that had happened since the last time they were together. Eventually the conversation drifted to religion.

"Did you ever join a church, Lucy? I remember the promise you made years ago—that you would find a church and give your full devotion to it."

"No," she said slowly. "I haven't kept my promise." In thought she was a girl of seventeen again. She was feeling what it had been like to fight consumption, to struggle for every breath in order to live. She was feeling the pain of incessant coughing. And then—she was entirely free of it—well and strong without a trace of it left in her body. That was when she had promised God a life of service. She had been earnest and determined when she had made the vow. "I've meant to keep my promise, Daniel. But the children require so much time—and Joseph and I don't agree on churches."

His face was gentle. "Don't be distressed. I asked because I was sure you had found what you have been seeking. I heard the children's devotions tonight. They were quoting scriptures from memory—remarkable!"

"What about you, Daniel?"

"The little church among the trees—you must have noticed it as you drove up here."

"Yes."

"I feel very close to God there."

She didn't tell him that she felt close to God wherever she was. Perhaps somewhere there was a church so close to Christ's pattern that its very walls would seem to lift her. It was for this she was waiting. The night was all but spent when Daniel and Lucy went to bed.

Next morning Daniel paid for Mr. Howard's lodging and breakfast at the tavern. Later he was to discover that Mr. Howard had charged several bottles of liquor in his name, pretending to be one of Daniel's very special friends.

It was time now to say good-bye, and the parting seemed different from all other times, for Lucy felt that she was looking upon the face of her mother for the last time, and that it might be months, even years, before she and Daniel would meet again.

She was crying softly as Daniel helped her climb into the wagon seat, and they argued a little when he forced money into her hand which he convinced her she should keep. Then he helped the children into the wagon, saying it was good that they were getting an early start. She was crying as they rode up the lane to the main road. But the bracing morning air and the demands of the children made her forget for a time the way her mother had clung to her and sobbed, and the tears in Daniel's eyes when he had lifted the smaller children into the wagon bed.

Mr. Howard had watched Daniel give Lucy money, and they had not gone many miles before he demanded his full fee. She allowed him to persuade her against her better judgment, making him sign an acknowledgment for payment in full. He no sooner got the money than she found her problems and troubles multiplied. His manner became very independent, and he began drinking heavily in front of the children.

Then they came to a part of the road that was mountainous and sparsely traveled. They seemed to be set apart in a world alone when he began crowding her on the wagon seat, and she read into his looks and the way his eyes covered her enough to make her apprehensive. When his leg touched hers she said in a low voice, "Mr. Howard, since I must ride in front with you, I would appreciate it if you would stay on your half of the seat and let me stay on mine. My only interest in you is that you get us safely to Palmyra." Her tone was cool and she was careful not to let him see that she was afraid. She was even more careful not to let Alvin or any of the other children know what was going on, for this man would be brutal, and Alvin was no match for him. At sixteen he was gangly and slightly built, although he would be a fine looking young man once he got some meat on his bones. She dare not let him even guess the insult, for fear Alvin would try to take him on. Now she moved as far away from Mr. Howard as she could. There was a duel of eyes, and hers didn't waver.

Because he was angry he began to abuse the children. When this brought no retort from her he stopped the wagon, saying that the load was too heavy for the horses to pull, and ordered them all to walk.

The children jumped down from the wagon. Lucy, angry and thoroughly alarmed, climbed down to walk with the children.

"Go ahead—walk!" Mr. Howard said. Then he took the whip and struck the horses harder than was necessary.

The ascent was steep, and the load was heavy for the horses to pull, this Lucy could see once she was on the ground. But she knew he had ordered the children out to strike at her, and she felt helpless, not knowing how to assume control of a situation that was entirely out of hand.

"Do you think he will make us walk far?" Alvin asked, as he boosted Catherine to carry her piggyback.

Lucy's eyes touched his gently. She couldn't answer because she didn't know. They climbed, digging their feet into the uneven soil. The horses moved slowly, and it wasn't too difficult to keep up. But the climbing was especially hard on young Joseph. His leg, even after all this time, was sensitive. The scars were ugly, long and deep, and the loss of bone had left him with the limp. Sometimes it was slight, but now, watching him climb through ruts in the uneven ground, Lucy became concerned at his white, strained face. He had

50

pride and determination; she knew he would keep going until he had no strength left. Half running, so as to be even with Mr. Howard on the wagon seat she let her rage burst forth. "Mr. Howard, I demand that you let Joseph and the younger children ride."

"Lady," there was quiet mockery in his tone, "I'll wager we are the only folks for miles around. Now you start something and you and the children may find yourselves walking all the way to Palmyra. There is nothing in our contract says I have to keep you in the wagon."

And so they moved through the rough terrain. She was having difficulty now restraining Alvin and Hyrum, for both boys were determined to fight him together, but even together they would be like a puff of wind for this brutal man. They must get to Palmyra without bruises or major trouble. Alvin and Hyrum willingly carried William and Catherine piggyback, but a few times when the children were crying or cross she had carried one or the other of them even though, in her condition, she knew it was not the thing to do. Then, when Howard's whim had spent itself, he let them back into the wagon. As the miles lengthened there were other times when he ordered them out to walk. Once when Alvin challenged him he got a crack across the mouth that sent him reeling; then Hyrum rushed in, butting and clawing, only to find himself on the ground beside Alvin. This was a cruel man, and Lucy was afraid of him. But Alvin and Hyrum were not afraid. When they got up from the ground, she knew that they held their fists only because she wanted it so much.

Mr. Howard was also a foul-mouthed man, and she despised his cursing, but the small children were fascinated by the strange new words and promptly tried out his vocabulary. These things Lucy endured because she didn't know how to stop it. Only one thing was in his favor; he

51

knew the way. Three days and nights were spent before they came to Oneida County, and each nightfall he knew where they could get lodging. The first night was at Comstock, then at Corinth, then at Johnstown. Now they were in beautiful land where there was hardly a farm without streams and brooks.

Cotton and woolen manufacturing was more extensive here than in any other county in the state, and as they drove into Utica Village Lucy's heart swelled at the sight of it. The village was a part of Whitestown, with a population close to eight thousand. On the south side was the Mohawk River covered with a gigantic growth of forest trees. Because Utica Village was the central point for roads and canals to various parts of the state, it was regarded as the great central point of the whole region, and it had the air of an energetic little city.

Buggies hitched to fine horses and wagons and drays loaded with merchandise all seemed to be moving in great haste. Shining surries passed them, carrying elegantly dressed women, and Lucy became suddenly conscious of the condition of her shoes and dress, and the grime on herself and the children. More than anything she wanted good lodging with comfortable beds—but who would take them in such a state? They had managed before, but those were smaller places where innkeepers had sympathetic concern for weary travelers.

On the three preceding evenings they had taken lodging near their wagon. Most of the time Alvin, Hyrum, Joseph, and Samuel had slept in the stables where they could keep watch on their goods. It was a custom often followed by travelers with large families. This way Lucy had managed with one room and two double beds, plus a charge for the horses and wagon. Mr. Howard paid for his own lodging, which had been included in his driver's fee.

Lucy remembered the Oneiyuta Inn in Utica Village.

She had been a guest there with her brother, Major Mack, before she and Joseph were married. She had gone with her hair piled high on top of her head to make her look older, and she had worn a blue silk beaded gown. The thought she had now was ridiculous, she knew, but if there was a modest room—would she dare to take the children? They needed to experience the nicer things, if they could do so without being made to feel inferior. Not giving herself a chance to change her mind she said, "Mr. Howard, if accommodations are available we will be stopping tonight at Oneiyuta."

She had expected him to protest and tell her she had lost her reason, as perhaps she had. But he didn't, and after a while they were driving through an archway into Oneiyuta grounds, and a liveryman was directing them to the stables. He was a courteous and gracious man. If he thought they looked bedraggled, he gave no sign.

Lucy gave Alvin money and sent him scouting for a room or rooms if the sum was sufficient. This had been Alvin's duty each time they had lodged, as Lucy would not trust Mr. Howard to handle any money of hers. Sending Alvin was almost as good as going herself, for he was proud of her trust and took the responsibility seriously.

The family remained in the wagon. Mr. Howard, having turned the horses over to the liveryman, was now gone. Her one hope was that she would see him no more until morning. She could drive the team if they had to seek a different inn.

Presently Alvin came back with good news. "There is a back entrance where you and the children can go to the rooms and clean up." His manner was as mature as he could make it. "Sir," he said to the liveryman, "my brothers and I can stable the horses. Joseph, you stay with the team while I show Mother the room. Hyrum and Sophie will carry our clean clothes, and Mother, we'd better wear our best if you know where to find them, and take our new shoes. The ladies and gentlemen in the lobby all look grand. For an extra fee there is a public bath. We're all so dirty that I ordered it."

"A real bathtub?" Sophronia's eyes widened. "This will be even better than at Uncle Daniel's."

If Lucy had misgivings about her extravagance, they vanished as she witnessed the children's awed excitement. Bathing in the porcelain tub was an experience they would always remember. Each of the two rooms had double beds, and they were impressed by the duck-down mattresses that lifted the beds high, the pillows with their starched bolsters, the sheets so white that Samuel said they resembled snow, and the blankets that must have taken the wool of a dozen sheep. The draperies would make dresses for a queen. The carpets were as thick as Uncle Daniel's, and they covered the whole floor. They examined the porcelain washbowls and pitchers on the commodes, and the small china chamber pots with their tight-fitting lids. Sophronia was sure no princess in a castle could have more elegant quarters than these.

There were other things the children had not seen. Lucy took her clean and shining brood for a look at the main street. Night was falling. At home, if a citizen went abroad at night he carried his lantern with him. Now, for the first time, the children watched the lamplighter light the lamps along the street. He would put his little ladder against a lamppost and run up the steps to light each lamp with his torch. It was an awesome sight—all those bright lights!

"What makes them come on?" William asked in a tone of wonder.

"They are gas lamps," Alvin told him. "The gas comes from pipes underneath the ground. Gas is made from soft coal in some mysterious way."

"It is like a miracle," Joseph said, with his eyes fastened on the golden lights along the street. "It is God showing us

54

another of his many secrets. Don't you agree, Mamma?"

She drew the boy to her. "Yes, dear, each time God reveals one of his secrets it is a miracle. This is a fine time to be alive, when all the world seems to be in a state of change."

They ate in the inn dining room, and here the children were delighted by the soft, gleaming gas lamps. Nothing seemed exactly real; the diners, the food, even the familiar faces of each other seemed unfamiliar in this soft, strange light.

After dinner they strolled on the boardwalks and watched the carts and vehicles that filled the busy, cobbled streets. They watched the people, most of whom seemed to be hurrying somewhere. They saw a policeman break up a brawl; they gave coins to two beggars; they listened for a few minutes to a street preacher; they watched an organ grinder put his monkey through some clever performances; they passed a theater, and Lucy wished that she could take them, but the children were experiencing the drama of real life. To them all this activity was more fascinating than any theater. Just before they returned to the inn they saw a slave owner whipping a colored girl. It was an ugly sight, for the man was brutally lashing her with his whip.

"Why is he doing it? Why doesn't somebody stop him?" Joseph cried in alarm.

"He owns her," Alvin said. "He thinks he has a right to do whatever he pleases with her."

Joseph started running toward the man and Alvin snatched him back. "You can't do anything."

"Somebody has to help her."

"Nobody will. She's a slave, and slaves have no rights."

"Do you believe that?" Joseph asked him.

"No."

"Someday devils like that will be stopped," Hyrum said.

55

They walked back to the inn with thoughtful faces.

Next morning Alvin came to Lucy in great haste with word that Mr. Howard was at the stables drunk, and that he was about to unload their goods and make off with the team.

"This I will not put up with." Leaving the older children to mind the younger ones, Lucy followed Alvin. Her swift, determined feet made a crunching sound on the graveled roadway. The air was brisk and cool but no more so than her voice was when she saw that Mr. Howard had indeed commenced to unload the wagon.

"Don't you dare lay a finger on our goods. I command you to put those things back."

Without paying the slightest heed to her command, Mr. Howard told her thickly, "This is the end of the line. Last night I spent all the money you gave me. We can't go anywhere now."

A crowd was beginning to gather, and the innkeeper, wanting no trouble that might injure his business, demanded an explanation for the quarrel that was brewing.

Lucy, without losing her wits or her dignity, sent Alvin back to their room to fetch the children and their belongings. When they came, she paid her room fee and showed her papers. "He has no right to touch my goods," she explained patiently. "He has been paid for their safe delivery to Palmyra." Then she looked Mr. Howard squarely in the face. "Nothing in our contract says you have to drive. What we have paid for are your horses and wagon. I shall take my goods and my children and drive myself to Palmyra."

Mr. Howard's face had an odd expression. "You'll never make it. You can't find your way alone even with a map."

"I have a map with all the landmarks on it. Alvin and I—yes, and all the children—have studied it. We'll make it."

"I'll be happy to check your map to see that all

important markings are on it," the innkeeper told her. "But I don't think you should try it. I'm sure you can find a responsible man to drive you."

She shook her head. "I have no money to pay another driver. I can manage food and lodging only for us *if I drive*." Then she gave him a warm smile. "We would appreciate your help with the map."

Lucy spent careful time going over each marking on the map with the innkeeper. She could feel her concern mounting, and her hand trembled a little as her fingers touched each landmark while she tried to force her mind to imprint it in memory. But outwardly she gave no sign of her misgivings. Could she really find her way to Palmyra, or was she being foolhardy? With Mr. Howard she had had nothing but problems, yet he understood traveling and could easily follow a trail. Could she? Time would tell. It was true, she had no money to pay another driver, nor would there be any when she reached her destination. Knowing Joseph and their circumstances, she was sure he had overspent himself when he had hired Mr. Howard.

Several bystanders had helped reload the wagon, and now there was a determined tilt to her stubborn chin as she took a quick survey of the wagon and team. Quickly then the children were loaded in—Alvin and Catherine in the wagon seat with her, the rest of the clan in the wagon bed with room to sit down. Everything seemed in order. She took the reins. Could she manage such a load up uncertain mountain roads and across windswept trails? There could be no turning back once they were on their way. With a cluck to the horses and a slap of the reins they were off, waving good-bye to the strangers who had befriended them. The long drive ahead had commenced. She would do her best to bring them safely to Palmyra.

The children were happy and content without Mr. Howard's constant bossing and complaining, and they behaved themselves. The only times Lucy had them walk were in places where the horses really needed their load lightened. At these times the children helped each other over rough and rocky ground or up the steep terrain.

There were times when the road was mountainous and so narrow that Lucy worried about meeting vehicles traveling in the opposite direction, wondering how they would manage to pass one another without disaster. Then she hit upon the idea of having the children sing. Their voices were strong and could be heard a long way off and would warn travelers that their wagon was approaching. In this way drivers stopped and waited where the road was wide enough for two vehicles to pass. Sometimes it was Lucy who would hold her wagon in a wider place when the way was obscure and narrow and she heard a *he-ll-ooo* echoing through the mountainside.

Nights were a problem. With the heavy load and the bad mountain roads the horses traveled at the slow pace of two or three miles an hour. Her plan was to go from Utica Village to the town of Oneida and stop at a halfway house the innkeeper had told her about the first night. In Oneida a good dinner could be had for twelve cents, but for her family this would be ninety-six cents, more than a full day's wage for a man. They would do better to build a fire along the roadside and cook their own meals. The fourth night, if all went well, they could spend in Syracuse, and by nightfall of the sixth day they should be with Father Joseph in Palmyra. Each night stop was carefully planned for and everything seemed to be going well—then on a straight, level road between the curving mountains they went across what looked like just a pleasant stream and broke an axle.

Lucy climbed down from the wagon seat. She was exhausted from the strain of driving on the dangerous mountain roads where curves were never marked and the descent was often so fast that even the brake was not sufficient to keep the wagon from going too fast. Then the voluntary bracing of the horses was all that kept them from plunging into some ravine below.

Now as she climbed down to look at the damage Samuel and William began to quarrel, and Catherine for no apparent reason began a wail that all but strained her lungs. The older children gathered around the wagon inspecting the damage. The axle had snapped on the left side and the wheel lay on the ground—a useless thing.

"What shall we do, Mamma?" Alvin asked.

"I don't know." She put a weary hand to her forehead and pressed some disheveled hair from her brow, a thoughtless act. "We must be at least three miles from Syracuse. The wind is blowing from the north. It will be a cold night."

"We can't fix it ourselves—that we know," Hyrum said.

By this time the three smaller children were out of the wagon.

"Find your coats, all of you. Sophronia, help Catherine. Samuel—William, stop quarreling this instant!"

"William ate my candy," Samuel said angrily. "I've been saving it all day."

William looked triumphant, and Lucy was just too tired to reprove him. Anyway she was as exasperated with Samuel as with William. He should have eaten his treat when the others did, instead of saving it to tantalize the younger children. With the candy in William's stomach Catherine's crying ceased, and she ran after him. He had discovered the stream and a twig and was dabbling.

Lucy's weary mind began to function. We'll build a fire and cook supper. With everyone tired, hungry, and cross the best way to settle was with food. Alvin and Hyrum could unhitch, feed, and water the horses. Farther upstream the water looked clear. They could sit on dry ground there, around a fire, and eat. It would be fairly comfortable. After they had eaten she would decide how to solve the problem of the broken axle.

She sent Samuel, Joseph, and William to gather firewood.

Sophronia brought the iron skillet, eggs, smoked meat, and cornmeal from the wagon. "I'll cook supper," she said. "Alvin can superintend the fire. You rest, Mamma."

Lucy's eyes took on a grateful shine. At this moment she knew why children deserved to be loved.

Night came quickly. It was very dark when they finished their supper of corn cakes, eggs, and meat. Only around the fire was there light enough to see.

"Will you be afraid to ride the horses into Syracuse to see if you can find someone who will mend our axle?" she asked Alvin and Hyrum.

"No, Mamma."

Her eyes strained through the darkness as they rode off. It was wooded country. Would they be safe riding alone in the dark, uncertain of the way? And what about the rest of them? Already the younger ones were nodding. Would they be safer by the fire or in the cold wagon bed?

From where they sat she could see the gaslights of Syracuse, lights her boys would follow while they trusted the horses to find the way and keep to the road. Would wild animals dare venture this near to a city? She put more wood on the fire. The blaze warmed her, and she felt safer with her family close beside her. This then was where they would stay. But if the firewood gave out before her boys returned, what then? What wild animals were in the woods—wolves, bears? Lucy was seldom afraid, but the night was so dark and so cold. Her unborn child began to move and kick, and she asked herself what she would do if the strain of the last few days were to hasten the delivery. "Help me, God," she said. "We are so alone."

Minutes moved woodenly, but the children slept unafraid because she was there. An owl in a nearby tree began its weird night cry, and Lucy shivered. Then she heard something, a stealthy sound. She put more wood on the fire, and the sound ceased. Then it came again . . . a twig snapping . . . the sound came closer. "Oh please, God, take care of us," she prayed.

And then it came into full view of the fire—a fawn of such beauty that she wished the children were awake to see. For a moment the soft brown eyes watched her curiously, then it trotted off, lost in the darkness. Lucy laughed her fright away. "When I pray," she told herself, "I must believe."

She must have slept then. She had meant to stay awake, but she was so tired. It was Alvin's voice she heard.

"This, sir, is our trouble."

Then Hyrum's. "Can you fix it, sir?"

The fire had burned low, and Lucy put more wood on before she joined the men.

"Mamma," Alvin said, "I was told this is the best wagon man in Syracuse."

"I'm Mrs. Smith." Lucy gave him a quick smile and bent to watch his deft fingers move over the wooden axle.

"I can splice it together well enough to get you into Syracuse, but you'll need a new axle to go farther." He stood up, and the wind moved through his dark hair. "I brought my wagon. We'll load the young ones and you in it."

"He knows where we can get good lodging at reasonable rates," Hyrum said.

"And I'll give you a guaranteed axle that should end all your troubles."

That night Lucy, snuggled in a feather bed, bathed in the luxury of being warm. I'll never doubt again, she told herself. But even as she thought it she knew she would.

Next morning she counted her funds. After paying for a new axle and having it put on, and for a night's lodging, and losing half a day while the wagon was being fixed, with the most careful planning and managing she thought they might make it into Palmyra. With the north wind blowing up a gale there would be only blankets enough for Alvin, Hyrum, and Joseph to sleep in the wagon. This meant she would have to pay for a double room an extra night. "You're doubting again," she told herself. Her fingers closed over the money she had left. . . . It would be enough.

On the seventh day she drove into Palmyra with her funds almost gone, but the family and household goods were in fine shape.

It was a humble little rented house that Joseph had waiting to receive his family, but the land was beautiful, the soil fertile, and it was home. Joseph had made a deal with the owners to work the farm on shares.

"Someday," Joseph told Lucy, as they walked together, "we'll own our own home and farm somewhere in this goodly land. And the house will be big enough for the whole Smith brood."

They were walking hand in hand, and Lucy lifted his hand and kissed it. "I'm sure that we'll do all that you say, Joseph. But right now I'm feeling very grateful for what we have—enough to eat, a fireplace in every room, we're together, and the children are well. We're a blessed family."

"Very soon now," he said, "we'll have to make room for one more."

"Babies are small," she told him. "They don't take much room for a long time."

The twenty-first day of March a little boy was born. They named him Don Carlos.

Lucy had the baby at home with the aid of a midwife. After ten full days of lying flat in bed—the customary time for a woman's bones to properly place themselves—Lucy was up, wobbly and weak, looking at a house that was badly in need of a woman's hand, for when the children were not studying lessons, they were out clearing tree stumps so that the land could be made ready for more planting.

It was this afternoon, much to Lucy's dismay, that Martin Harris and his wife came to honor the new baby.

Mr. Harris was perhaps the richest farmer around Palmyra. Nobody knew the extent of his farmland and holdings, but his wealth was considerable. Lucy wasn't sure how Joseph and he had become friends, but they were well enough acquainted now to address one another by first names, and Martin often dropped over to discuss crops, the price of wheat, the best ways to winnow, markets and millers, small and large talk on state and government problems, and anything else he felt worth talking about. He was a shy person with a warmness about him that put everyone at ease. Lucy had never met Mrs. Harris, but Joseph had said "She is not a woman one addresses by her first name."

Now Lucy saw the shining black surrey pull up beside the barn. As she caught a glimpse of the brown bonnet with elegant plumes her heart sank. If only she could throw a quilt over the whole house, or pick up her brood and race for hiding, but there was only time to straighten her hair, and order Hyrum to take the children upstairs and keep them there. With a quick smoothing of the covers in the little homemade cradle where the baby lay, and a glance that assured her he was beautiful, she went to greet Mr. Harris and his lady.

Thoughts have a way of racing quickly, and hers were dark as she walked toward the door. These people were inconsiderate. Why would anyone dare call on her first day up? Her eyes covered the untidy room, then with a forced smile she opened the door and they came in. Their arms were filled. Mr. Harris apologized as he introduced his wife. "I told her this was no day to call, but she said, 'Pshaw, this is the day our call can do her some good.' Where would you like us to put these things?"

"It's your supper," Mrs. Harris explained.

Something about Mrs. Harris made Lucy feel like a child as she took two fragrant loaves of bread and a glass of jelly from her and got her seated in a parlor chair. She was probably only a little older than Lucy, but she seemed entirely in command of herself and each person in the room. She wasn't pretty, but she was perfectly groomed and laced in to hide her plumpness. Now from the chair she said, "Everything is cooked. There is a hot rock under the roast and vegetables that should keep everything warm. You won't have to do much to anything except serve it."

As Lucy led Mr. Harris to the dining area where he could put the food down she was both exasperated and grateful. To have a delicious supper brought in was a gift to rejoice over, but to be caught in such an untidy state was humiliating. She ought not to care, but her heart was lead, and unshed tears stung her eyes. Mrs. Harris would have hired help. Probably in all her life she had never had a house as untidy as this one. She was elegant from her high buttoned shoes to the rich brown of her satin gown, and this too angered Lucy. A thoughtful person would have worn homespun or a simple cotton when making a call on someone so recently out of bed. Even Martin seemed smaller with her in the room.

He apologized again as he set the food down. "I hope you don't mind our dropping in this way unannounced."

"My family will enjoy the supper," she said trying hard to keep her irritation from showing, for she didn't blame him. Lucy had a feeling that Martin always did what Mrs. Harris wanted or suffered the consequences.

"The pastries are in the surrey," he said. "I'll get them."

They went back then to Mrs. Harris. She was bending over the cradle. "You have a beautiful baby."

Lucy's heart warmed toward her a little. "He sleeps most of the time."

Mr. Harris bent to look. "He's a fine young Smith."

Mrs. Harris loosened the covers around Don Carlos, a small gesture.

"Don't you think you have him covered too warmly, Mrs. Smith? These little ones have a lot of natural heat, you know."

Mr. Harris said, "You women get acquainted. I'll get the pastries."

Mrs. Harris reached for his hand, detaining him. "Men are so restless. They can't stay in one place a minute. We were hoping we would get to see the children, weren't we, Martin?"

She wants to see whether they are as untidy as the house, Lucy thought. Aloud she said, "They're busy. They help their father, go to school, study, and soon it will be plowing and seeding time, then the schools will close. They are making the most of learning while they can."

She wanted to add, "In spite of the way things look, my

65

children are good help," but she held her tongue. Had she been talking to Mr. Harris alone, she would have told how Joseph and the children had taken care of her and waited on her while she was in bed, and how they had seen to one another's needs and managed famously, but a woman like Mrs. Harris just wouldn't understand.

He said again, "I'll bring the pastries."

When he had gone Lucy had the lost feeling of not knowing what to say. It was a feeling that was to last through the years. Lucy didn't know it then, but their paths would cross many times. They would be friends of a sort, but always there would be a small, inexplainable wall between them like a veil that neither would penetrate.

That evening supper was special. Lucy had never watched her family enjoy a meal more.

She had begun a recital of her embarrassment when Father Joseph put his fork down. His eyes held the twinkle she had known for so many years. "This roast, potatoes, and vegetables taste real neighborly. And I'd say Mrs. Harris ought not to mind looking at untidiness we couldn't find the time to remedy. You say the Harrises were here about half an hour and saw what we've had to put up with for several days. Well, she'll go home and appreciate her house, and we've got you back at the helm of things. This just shows how much we've missed our lady while she was laid up."

The approving eyes of her family were upon her, and the resentment melted away.

Joseph continued gently, "Sophronia's cooking will be this good someday. She tried hard and did real fine by us."

Sophronia's eyes took on a shine and Lucy thought, There is nothing like a family to make one see things in perspective. Her heart was at peace as her mind caressed them. How good it was to have a family to belong to!

66

Alvin was as good as a man in helping Father Joseph with the farming, and Hyrum, Joseph, and Samuel were eager learners. All the children who were old enough had their special work to do.

Young Joseph and Alvin were alike in that both were extra gentle with the livestock, and for this reason the animals seemed to have a sixth sense in understanding what was expected of them.

Father Joseph called Alvin his veterinarian and credited him with saving the life of a very valuable horse. This led Alvin to read books on animal husbandry, and neighbors began calling on him to doctor their sick livestock. In almost every instance the animals got well, although Lucy declared it was not knowledge but love that cured them. Father Joseph gave Alvin credit for putting into practice what he read. Since there was no veterinary with a degree in Palmyra neighbors were grateful for Alvin, and didn't ask whether his knowledge came from books or experience.

As for growing things, there wasn't a Smith child who didn't love the sight of grain, vegetables, trees, and flowers. Although when it came to weeding perhaps William was the only one who took it to heart. He liked flaying the hoe. The rest helped because they had to.

Lucy and Joseph prayed over their family and their crops, and Lucy prayed especially for William who caused her to petition heaven daily in his behalf. He was a cherub to look at and an elf to keep track of. Usually he had Catherine in tow, climbing trees to inspect birds' eggs, wading ditches much too deep for them, sliding down forbidden haystacks scattering the hay, and any other fancy that his six years could dream up. Catherine, a year younger, found him an enchanting teacher.

The first year in Palmyra was a real success. Wheat—their most important crop—yielded an abundant harvest and was now being winnowed and readied for marketing.

What Father Joseph needed was a reliable and honest miller, someone to grind his wheat into flour. His good friend Martin Harris knew of such a man, a Joseph Knight in the town of Colesville.

The day the Smiths and Knights met began mildly enough. Father Smith and the older boys were in the granary winnowing the wheat. This was done with a large fanlike device that turned with a crank, causing a wind to blow the chaff from the wheat. Hyrum, young Joseph, and Samuel took turns at the crank while Alvin and Father Smith filled sacks with the winnowed wheat.

Young William and Catherine looked in now and then, but Father Joseph's "Tut-tut, you're scattering the wheat," kept them at a distance.

Inside the house Lucy and Sophronia had finished the morning chores, and Lucy had her paints out on the dining room table and was finishing the last design on an oilcloth she was painting for that same table. It was an elegant oil to be used for company dinners.

Suddenly there was a loud clap of thunder, a flash of lightning, and a darkening of the sky. Then the rain came—not in big slow drops but a downpour that sent the Smith boys racing for the house. Father Joseph waited to close and lock the granary door; then he too sped for the house.

Sophronia heard them coming and held the door open, mop in hand, to swish up the mud and water that came in with them.

"I ought to flail you," she said, half laughing, half scolding, as her eyes followed the muddy tracks on the floor she had scrubbed that morning.

Lucy said without looking up, "Wipe the rain off and get into dry clothes, all of you." Then to Sophronia, who was trying to repair the damage with the mop, "Please call William and Catherine, dear. I'm sure they think this rain was made for their special sloshing."

They came reluctantly after being called twice. Water oozed from their shoes, wet clothes stuck to their small bodies, rain dripped from their hair and rolled down their cherub faces. Droplets clung to their eyelashes, but there was radiance shining from their eyes.

"God is giving everything a drink," William said with a kind of awe. "An angel must have busted a hole in heaven to let all that water out."

"Change your clothes," Lucy said.

Sophronia wiped their faces with a towel and took a hand of each. "I'll help you. How did you manage to get so wet?"

"We're only a little wet," Catherine corrected, fascinated by the sloshing sound her shoes made as she climbed the stairs. "You can hear the water when it freckles the roses."

It was at that moment that a knock came on the door.

Lucy half ran to open it, wondering who could be arriving in such a rain.

A man of medium height, about Father Joseph's age, stood at the door, and beside him a merry-eyed lady stood holding a drenched hat to her dark hair. The hat had been a thing of beauty and fashion—green velvet with pink flowers and a black satin bow—but it clung to her head now like a sail adrift from its moorings. As their eyes met, Lucy knew she was looking at persons exactly like herself—folks who could see humor in a rainstorm and even in a ruined hat.

"Come." She held the door open and they laughingly came.

It ran through Lucy's mind that she couldn't take them into the parlor because her "men" were dressing there. Most folks had parlors just for company, but there were so many Smiths that they lived in every available space.

"We're a big family." Lucy's dimples were showing as she led the way to the dining room where she had been painting.

As they walked with her the man said, "I'm Joseph Knight, and this web-footed creature is my wife. We're friends of Mr. and Mrs. Harris. Martin told us to come and see you."

Lucy struck a match to the fireplace that they always kept banked for lighting. "Martin Harris and my husband are good friends. His farm is the finest one in Palmyra." Then to Mr. Knight, "If we put two chairs near the fire, it will soon be warm enough to commence drying you out."

She walked with him to the table for the chairs, and that was when Mrs. Knight noticed the oilcloth.

"How beautiful!" she said, bending to look at it more closely. "I've never seen prettier work. Would you sell it? Something like this would be just perfect for our table, wouldn't it, Joe?"

He was bending over the oilcloth now too, and Lucy could tell they were genuinely interested. If they would buy the cloth . . . She was doing some mental gymnastics now. Father Joseph had never let her sell any of her work, but with her growing brood there was never enough money to spread around. This time she wouldn't ask him.

"How much would a cloth like this be worth to you?"

"You mean you would really sell it?" Mrs. Knight's voice was wistful. "It would be exactly right for us."

The Knights exchanged some quiet words, he nodded consent and she named a price that staggered Lucy. It had never occurred to her that hand painting would be worth so much.

"I'll finish it while you are drying out," Lucy said, and her eyes were like stars. "When it's dry, it will be yours."

The Knights sat close to the fire watching Lucy work. "My friends will want them too. I know they will," Mrs. Knight said. "I mean—they will if you are willing to paint them and sell them."

Lucy didn't know it then, but she was in business. This was a very special day.

Mr. Knight was the miller that Martin Harris had talked with Joseph about. The men made satisfactory arrangements for milling the wheat, and a friendship was begun that was to last through the years. The Knights had children too, and soon the families were visiting back and forth, sharing good times and bad times, play times and work times, and they blessed the rain that had marked the beginning of their friendship.

Three things became special to the Smith children when they visited the Knights. The first was the mill with its sets of rollers that ground the grain into flour. The Knights lived in a large Colonial house surrounded by rolling land, much of which had been cleared of timber, for they were close to the town of Colesville.

Not far from the house the mill was built at the head of a swiftly moving stream. Mr. Knight had made a sluice or gate in the stream, which caused water to collect around the great wheel which had traps around it. Water continually caught and released by the gate would rush over the wheel and into the traps, making the great wheel spin. The turning of the wheel set the grinding stones in the flour room in motion. The children had never watched anything more fascinating than the grinding of the grain into flour.

There were several sets of rollers. The first set broke the

kernels, and each set that followed was placed a little closer than the set before, so that when the grain had gone through all the rollers it came out powder fine. Then some of the flour was sifted through a silk cloth called a bolting cloth which removed all the husks. This flour made delicious pies and cakes. Not all the flour was sifted through the silk. Some customers preferred the coarser, darker whole wheat flour for making bread.

Everyone entering the roller room had to be scrubbed clean from head to toe. The Smith children thought it was a great privilege to help in the mill, and their help was welcomed, for each customer's flour had to be weighed and put into wooden kegs. The tops had to be nailed on, and the kegs labeled with the buyers' names, price, grade of flour ordered, and whether the flour was to be paid for with money, livestock, or merchandise. The Knight children *had* to help, but the Smith children worked because they thought it was fun. Mr. Knight paid the older boys wages during the busy season; Alvin, Hyrum, Joseph, and Samuel would stay for days, bunking with the Knight boys, breakfasting at dawn, and working until dark. Then, after a good supper, they still found time and energy for games.

A second thing all the Smiths enjoyed was Mrs. Knight's tender loaves of bread and delicious pastries. Lucy was a good cook, but the first time she tasted Mrs. Knight's baking, her private remark to Father Joseph was, "Mrs. Knight must run her flour through the bolting cloth several times to turn out such loaves and pastries."

"Maybe she has a better oven," Joseph answered with a twinkle.

"She's . . . just a better cook," Lucy replied.

His smile grew large. "I haven't noticed any runts among the Smiths from your cooking, Lucy."

The third thing was one Father Joseph approved of and

Lucy didn't. Joseph Knight had taught his boys to shoot with rifle and pistol, and now Newel Knight was teaching the Smith boys. Since almost every man in the country carried a gun and knew how to use it, Lucy didn't object to that too much, but he was also teaching them the scientific way to wrestle and how to handle a whip. This Lucy didn't approve of, even though she knew flogging was a common form of punishment in all the states. Persons were flogged for debt evasion, for small misdemeanors, or the breaking of any law too minor for imprisonment. Newel, about Alvin's age, had practiced with the bullwhip and was very good at sending it exactly where he wanted it to go. But what the Smith boys found even more interesting, he was exceedingly good at dodging the whip, so that unless one were very skilled in swinging he couldn't hit him. Now Newel was teaching this skill to the Smith boys, and they were taking to it with great enthusiasm, especially young Joseph, who carried his welts with pride.

And then there was the wrestling. All the bumps the boys got from this rough game they wore like heroes home from battle. This skill was not small under Newel's tutoring for he was a careful teacher, though he made it great fun. Lucy watched, trying to find a reason for stopping the whole thing, and discovered merit which she admitted grudgingly. Her "men" were learning stance and form—learning to move, walk, halt, and keep an upright position; learning foot and leg control and the art of motion; mastering ways to follow through in a certain action; how to meet opposition and resistance; what to do with shoulders and arms; and ways to strengthen muscles.

Newel would bark at them like a professional trainer, "You'll be downed if you do that!" And he kept them working until he could approve their lithe movements.

Was it right? She didn't know. When they first began she

had hoped it would be a passing fancy. It wasn't. After a year of it the boys were as interested as when they began, only now their coordination was beautiful to see, and she was torn between pride in their development and fear of what the skill might lead to.

Father Joseph said that any skill was an asset, and that he wished he knew more about wrestling and whips himself. He bought the best of bullwhips so the boys could practice.

One day Lucy heard the sound of a whirring whip not far from the window where she sat painting. She looked and stopped to watch. Hyrum was throwing the whip with a practiced hand, but it was young Joseph who held her attention. He was dodging with such skill that the whip seemed a useless thing in Hyrum's hand. And he knew exactly what he was about, for his movements inched him toward Hyrum in such a way that with no detected effort he reached swiftly and suddenly, and the whip changed from Hyrum's hand to his. She waited then to see how he would handle it. His hand was deft and sure and Hyrum shouted, "Wait, don't swing at me. Get yourself some other target."

The whip dropped then. Joseph had not intended inflicting pain.

Lucy turned from the window. Perhaps it would never be used for anything more than a sport. Many a man wore a gun who did no harm with it, and this could be the same. With a sigh she went back to her painting.

That same hour she watched Hyrum and Joseph wrestling. Now it was Alvin guiding them while the rest of the children shouted their approval. All this exercise was doing wonders for Joseph. He no longer favored his lame leg. There would always be a limp, but he was in control of his handicap now, and she found her eyes riveted on his every movement. He'd never stood for any babying. He'd mastered these skills in the same dogged way he did everything his heart was set on. He would never be a weakling. The black eyes, the bruises, and the skinned knuckles all her young men bore with enthusiasm, but Joseph had probably profited more than the others. Yet even as Lucy acknowledged this good she could also see the danger, if someday all this should be used to wrong ends.

With James Monroe as President and Daniel D. Tompkins as Vice-President, the country began a great advance toward material prosperity called the "era of good feeling." And this year—1818—Father Joseph, tired of sharecropping, was able to get a farm from a man named Eversten, a tract of fertile land paralleling the Canandaigua Highway in Manchester, which was just across the river from Palmyra. Had it not been for the river these two towns would have joined. However, barges and a ferry made it easy for their citizens to trade and fraternize with one another.

Many of the forest trees on this land had been cleared away, but there was plenty of forest still untouched, which lent enchantment to the farm and quickened the hearts of all members of the family, especially Lucy, Alvin, and young Joseph, for nature's beauties, and the solitude to be found among the trees.

The log farmhouse was located on a pleasant elevation a short distance from the road. Sugar maples spread shade across the lawn. When Lucy first saw the house with the splendid maples her eyes quickened in appreciation. The family walked through the parlor, approving the fireplace with its hearth of bricks showing depressions made by many footprints. They went up the steep stairs to the room above, admiring the quaint balustrade and newel-post. Here were sleeping rooms, if not quite adequate for the family at least exceeding anything Lucy had expected, and she accepted them gratefully.

There was one little attic room with windows and a low

ceiling. Lucy found young Joseph alone there after the family had finished touring the house. He was looking through a window toward a certain grove of trees.

"It's a beautiful view."

She looked with him across the pebbly stream to a rise of tree-covered ground, silver tipped by the sun.

"Is it not lovely?" he asked.

She caught the wistfulness in his voice. "Would you like this room for your own, Joseph?"

"Very much."

"It will be hot in summer."

"But I'd be alone here. I've never had a room alone in all my life."

"You may have it, son." Her eyes twinkled suddenly. "I'm sure there will be no dispute from anyone. Only the two of us, or maybe Alvin, would have this room."

Schools in Palmyra were held in summer only during months when weather was very hot, and in winter when it was very cold. In summer the school day commenced at seven in the morning and continued until five in the afternoon. In winter the day began at eight and ended at four. Small children attended a "dame school" run by a "marm" in her own home.

One day in early January a gentleman from the Manchester council came to the Smiths asking for Father Joseph.

Lucy knew without being told that Joseph was going to be asked to teach. It was a school that had been run by the minister of the Belltower church. She had heard that he had resigned of his own accord, and that Monday would be his last day of teaching.

A little pucker gathered on her brow as she led the caller into the parlor and gave him the most comfortable chair in the house. At the same time she sent William to the carriage house to advise his father.

"My husband is mending harness," she said by way of opening conversation, but her mind was racing ahead of her tongue.

Joseph would hardly do for this particular school, because this master had acted as clerk and sexton of the church, rung the church bell, dug the graves, led the singing in the church, preached the sermons, and taught the school. The only thing Joseph would find in its favor was that the school was interdenominational. He would have nothing to do with furthering church services, and he would not be in favor of following after ways the minister had run his school.

I know it isn't customary for a woman to remain in a room where two men are transacting business, her thinking continued, but I'll find a little mending and sit in an inconspicuous place where I can listen without seeming to. She had heard some ugly rumors regarding the school and now she wanted to find out, if she could, how much of what she had heard was true.

The councilman commented on the freezing weather outside, and they agreed that the temperature was below zero. He inquired about the health of her children, and Lucy said they were fine without going into detail. Then Father Joseph came in looking freshly scrubbed and combed. The men shook hands, and Lucy went for her mending. She came back quietly to take a chair in a bright corner by a window.

The men were discussing schools in general, and her mind raced ahead of their conversation as it had before.

She had heard that the resigning master didn't believe in heating the church either for school or church services. Too much comfort was supposed to be an invitation for the

77

devil's entrance. Instead of a fire, each person was supposed to supply himself a foot warmer and a heat bucket. All these together would make the room halfway tolerable. She had sent hot bricks to school with Joseph, Sophronia, and Samuel all during this cold spell, and they had come home each night shivering, in spite of the warm clothing they wore.

It was said that this man baptized babies in the cold meetinghouse and christened them when ice had to be broken in the christening bowl. And from the pulpit he told parents that as soon as children were two or three years old, their feet should be dipped in ice water daily to make them tough, and children should wear shoes thin enough that when they walked outside ice water could ooze through. "The death rate among children is too great," he preached. "We must make our children strong, that they may survive." Lucy sniffed audibly at the very thought of it.

She had gone with a committee two times to complain about the lack of heat in his building. Both times his appearance had been that of a distinguished gentleman. He was near Joseph's age. He had been immaculate in a tabby velvet coat, the tails of which had seemed to stand straight out. Inside this he wore a waistcoat of tremendous length through which one could see conspicuously the nicely starched ruffles of his white shirt. Around his neck was wound once and a half a stiffly ironed linen which helped to keep his head stiff and straight as became a teacher-minister. And he was stubborn. When he voiced an opinion, it was law.

The councilman was saying, "Our books are few and tiresome; paper is scarce, and lead plummets are costly. Some of the planters' children write on birchbark. The students who can afford it sew foolscap paper into a book and rule it by hand. School opens with prayer each morning and closes the same way each evening. On Wednesdays and Saturdays each student learns to recite his catechism and prayers from a prayer book."

"I won't teach in an unheated building with the temperature touching zero," Father Joseph said.

"We'll see what we can do about a stove and fuel, but too much comfort is bad for learning. There will be complaints if the school is more comfortable than the homes, and you know yourself that most persons heat only a room or two at a time in a home. I dare say your bedrooms are cold."

"Our fireplaces burn at night; our children are warm in featherbeds, and we use bed warmers," Father Joseph replied with his usual twinkle. "It is not the same as trying to study with wind blowing icy gusts through an unheated building."

"Agreed. And I hope you will teach our children. Big families being the rule—ten, fifteen children to a family—reading, writing, and arithmetic is about all the education most of them will get. Many of the parents can't read, you know."

"Get us a potbellied stove, coal, and firewood; then if you want me, I'll give it a try."

Monday morning Father Joseph and Lucy were up before dawn. The new teaching job would require these early rising hours from now on, for work on the farm continued throughout the winter. Livestock and chickens had to be cared for and the usual chores done.

Alvin and Hyrum were attending an academy in Manchester, so there was little help from them. Father Joseph's days would indeed be full now as he shouldered old burdens and prepared each day's assignments for school. Lucy, always hungry for knowledge, had been studying with the children. Now she would study with Father Joseph and assist him wherever she could.

By three quarters past six the family had been fed,

79

lunches made, and the children bundled into warm clothing. For several weeks now William and Catherine had been attending a dame school in town. It was Lucy's intention to leave Don Carlos at this school with the madame this morning; then next week she would spend a day there and assist with teaching to make up for whatever trouble he might cause. He was no longer a baby. In two months he would be three years old. Madame thought an occasional "visit" was good for the little ones, and Lucy had permitted him a day there once before. "School" had been in his talk and his play for days afterward, for he liked nothing better than to copy William and Catherine in all their doings. And, strange as it seemed, they liked having him with them.

Lucy had made up her mind to accompany Father Joseph. There would be ways she could help him get ready for his first day of teaching. It would be a simple matter to drop the children at the dame school on their way to the Belltower church.

They trooped out of the house, each child carrying his lunch and a hot brick. The bricks would help to warm them on the ride into town. In good weather the children walked to school. Now, whether walking or riding, they would enjoy the company of their father.

The madame accepted Don Carlos with her usual graciousness, and a short while later the Smiths were driving up to the Belltower church. The building was painted a drab brown, but the vacant land surrounding it made a fine playground for the children.

As soon as they arrived Sophronia, young Joseph, and Samuel begged for the key and went racing off to unlock the church. They were in a hurry to see the new stove.

While Father Joseph unhitched the horses on ground back of the church and tethered them to the wagon, Lucy looked around.

80

The air was sharp, and the wind whipped her skirts as she walked. There were two latrines behind the church about seventy-five yards apart. One was marked "His," the other "Hers." Each had four holes, and they were clean.

There was a back door to the church, and directly opposite the door was a whipping post. The footmarks around it showed that it had been used often. Lucy shuddered at the thought of a child being strapped there and whipped. It seemed cruel, almost barbaric. One thing she was sure of: with Joseph whippings would be few if any. A child would have to be practically uncontrollable before he would lay a hand on him, and then only after he had exhausted every gentle means he knew to get at the root of whatever was making the pupil unruly.

He came to stand beside her now. "Not a pleasant sight, is it? Children are like horses. They give us just about what we expect of them."

Hand in hand they went inside the church. The room was big and cold and as drab and colorless as the outside, but the potbellied stove was there. The most shining thing in the room was the new black chimney. The children had set the kindling and the coal and were waiting for a match, which Father Joseph supplied. Soon there was a roaring fire, and everyone was enjoying the tingling warmth of the heat.

Lucy asked, "Joseph, what will you do if some of the parents object to the stove?"

The familiar twinkle touched his eyes. "You mean they may agree with the Reverend-Master that too much comfort makes children puny and devilish?" He turned down the damper on the stove and his tone became serious. "I'm going to ask for a month's trial. Even children who hold knowledge like a cup can't keep their minds on lessons when they're cold. Once parents find out their children are learning more and behaving better, they'll cooperate. There aren't many who believe the old Cotton Mather superstitions anyway."

He walked toward the storeroom and turned back, a smile crinkling his lips. "We may find some of the parents enrolling to learn reading, writing, and arithmetic once they discover they can be just as comfortable here as they are at home. They may want to join us to get their money's worth. I'm going to ask them for an armload of wood and a scuttle of coal every day until we build up a supply, then they may not have to furnish quite so much." He went into the storeroom.

The assembly room was warming up nicely now, and Lucy walked around examining everything. Seats were rough, backless, hard benches. Her quick eyes told her at a glance that in this church for adult services the men sat on the right side of the room and the women on the left, instead of being seated together. She knew, because the men's side had cuspidors placed at convenient intervals. Since church lasted the biggest part of a Sunday this was a convenience for men, but for children who were always on the lookout for new experiences it was a shouting invitation to "chew." Lucy felt that they had no place in a schoolroom.

She looked around for a spot to get them out of sight. Across the front of the assembly room was a rostrum with a pulpit and four chairs. To the right of the rostrum was a pump organ that stood out a little from the wall. I'll put them behind the organ, she thought. Then with a grimace she gingerly lifted two of the smelly copper pots with their shining exteriors. "They are like handsome men with foul minds," she told herself as she deposited them in their hiding place.

The children saw her and came to help.

"Lift them from the bottoms; don't touch the rims or insides," she told them.

"Why not put them behind the stove?" Samuel asked.

"They would get hot and smell worse than they do now."

"I thought tobacco just smelled like tobacco," Sophronia said.

And young Joseph added, "Some of the boys in the class chew. They'll be looking for a place to spit."

"Let them swallow," Lucy said.

The job finished, Lucy joined Big Joseph in the storeroom. It was to the north of the assembly room, and she found him putting in pegs to hang coats on. Always before, the children had worn their coats to keep warm. Now it would be a place to put wraps and lunch buckets. It held school supplies and discipline equipment.

"Not much here to study out of," Joseph said.

There were various maps, a blackboard, and a few books. She thumbed through some of the books. They were inadequate and meager. She examined the other equipment. Birch rods—a tap was a reminder that things could get worse. Pink and black ribbon bows, these she understood. If a child wore a pink one home, pinned to a shoulder, it meant he had done all his lessons with excellence. A black bow meant he had failed, and it often meant a whipping administered by a disappointed parent.

There were thong boards. As Lucy picked one up, her face revealed her disapproval. The boards had holes for fingers to fit in, and straps to be placed around the hand and wrist. A child wearing one had no use of his hand, and worse, fingers pushed through the holes would swell. making the removal of the board painful, sometimes tearing tender flesh.

"You won't use these, will you, Joseph?"

"No."

She remembered Hyrum coming home with one of these boards. The strap had been fastened so tight that his hand had swollen to a terrible sight . . . all because he had hit a boy who had stolen his speller. Father Joseph had cut the board around each finger to release the hand, then he had spent half a night making another board for Hyrum to take to school so that he wouldn't be punished again for destroying church property.

Father Joseph finished putting in the pegs and turned to examine the maps. He chose one and carried it out to hang up. That was when Lucy's eyes fell on the stocks.

"Joseph!" she called. At her tone the children too came running.

She stood pointing. "What possible place do stocks have in a schoolroom?"

"You ought to see how often they are used," Samuel said. "You'd be surprised."

They were looking at two contrivances of punishment, each consisting of a framework with holes for ankles and wrists. These were instruments of derision for grown-ups who evaded debts or other obligations. Men were placed in them on the public square where they were made fun of. But here . . . for children!

Father Joseph stood quietly looking at the contraptions. Then in a whisper for Lucy's ear alone he said, "It would be nice to see the Reverend-Master in one." He carried out the blackboard and went to finish hanging the map.

There was one more form of punishment, a dunce stool. This was usually placed in a corner. When a child failed in his schoolwork a clown-like dunce cap was placed on his head and he was made to sit on the stool with his face in the corner. A cruel teacher could keep a child sitting in the same tiring position for hours.

Young Joseph and Samuel carried the stocks out of the storeroom and placed them in their usual spot which was up front facing the students. Sophronia put the dunce stool in the corner.

Lucy, disapproving, went to Father Joseph. "Are you going to keep those things around?"

"We'll keep them in sight, along with the birch rods and ribbon bows. They are church properties. We can't burn them or throw them away, and young folks need to be reminded until they learn self-discipline. I hope soon they will earn the right to do away with them themselves. It will be a profitable experience."

"But you won't use them."

A smile touched his lips. "No. But they won't know that."

The children had filled the drinking buckets and washed the wash basins and dippers. Everything was in order now for the new teacher's first day at school. Father Joseph brought out the few books and scanned them with more care than Lucy had done.

By half past seven children and teen-agers began arriving, some with parents and some without. The students were excited over the warmness of the schoolroom and the new stove. Some knew the Smiths; others met them with casual interest. Each stayed long enough to look, feel the warmth, and say a greeting. But the outside beckoned, and they were gone to fill the vacant school ground with vigorous games.

Not so with the parents. After the students were out of the way, they surrounded Joseph—five men with their wives. Almost at once the women made a sitting row on one of the benches, silently waiting and watching their husbands. Should Lucy join them? No, she would hold her ground, standing beside Joseph, for it was obvious they were not there to be friendly. That the men had something to say to

Joseph was evident, for they eyed one another, silently seeking out one to be spokesman.

These were farm folks, used to grinding out a living from the soil by hard work. Many such farmers could neither read nor write. Could these? Not that this made them less manly, but it would make it more difficult for them to understand Joseph's point of view.

The men stood looking awkward, fumbling, uncertain. Joseph offered them benches, trying to put them at ease, but they chose to stand. At last one of them elected himself spokesman, and while he talked the others acquiesced with approving nods.

"We've come to speak our minds," he said. "It's not right, kids havin' it better at school than at home. We're for 'em comin' to school. We want 'em to get learnin', but if they're cold they'll learn fast so's to get home. Heat 'em and they'll stay in a warm place. We've come to tell you that stove's gotta' go. If it warn't so hot we'd throw it out now. That's what we come aimin' to do."

There were agreeing nods from the women now. These were wives who stood by their husbands.

Joseph, unruffled, said, "Let's sit a spell." He sank onto one of the benches, and Lucy took her place with the women, but not a man sat down.

"If you'll hear us through, Mr. Smith," the spokesman went on, "we're simply tellin' you we've put up with a cold church on Sundays, same as our elders did, and we want no changes, Sunday or any day. The parson says we need sufferin' if we're aimin' for a place in heaven." They waited then.

The pause continued several seconds. Joseph's eyes seemed to be studying the floor, but when he raised them they were friendly, kind, and quiet, covering each man. "Would you be willing to try an experiment?"

86

"To do what?"

"You all must have some idea of the progress your children made in school during the coldest months last year under the previous professor. What I'm asking you to do is to leave the stove in for one month; help supply coal and firewood to keep it running. At the end of a month if your children have progressed at a more rapid rate than usual, if they are healthier and happier, the stove stays. If not—well— I'll give my place to a better man, and you can do what you like with the stove."

Lucy wanted to protest, to say it wasn't fair, but she held her tongue. After deliberation, even though it was against what they had been taught to believe, the men agreed to send firewood for the stove, but no coal, and they left the school grounds feeling they had won a victory. Out of twenty families these were the only objectors.

At eight o'clock Joseph rang the school bell and the students came trooping in . . . a pretty sight. When wraps were hung a few of the girls were in store-bought clothes, but most were wearing linsey-woolseys, a stiff homespun material that was half wool and half linen. The dresses were made with bodices or basques and full skirts. The younger girls' skirts touched the calves of the legs, the older girls wore theirs ankle length. Some had white blouses under sleeveless bodices; others had white collars and cuffs that were crocheted or knitted. Some had pretty kerchiefs around their throats. Each had a little apron to protect her dress.

The boys wore knee breeches, long waistcoats or vests, and coats with wide pockets and wide turnover cuffs. Some wore ruffles of fancy white linen at their necks and wrists; others had collars and broad ties. The first day with a new teacher was dress-up day, and each student was wearing his Sunday best. Lucy's own children were wearing clothes like the rest now. They had brought them to wear when their chores were finished, and they had put them on in the latrines.

Before Father Joseph asked for roll call he had everyone stand for prayer.

During roll call Lucy's quick eyes made some revealing observations. Young Joseph was noticing the girls—two of them—Nancy and Henrietta Stoal. He was quietly showing off for them and would probably earn a reprimand from his father.

Jerusha Braden, a lovely young lady of perhaps fifteen, would probably become Father Joseph's assistant. There was something very mature about her. She had a way of standing and sitting that made her more woman than girl. And then Lucy made a big discovery.

It was when Father Joseph called the name Calvin Stoddard, and a tall, good-natured boy stood up to respond by saying "present" that Lucy caught the quick exchange of eyes between Calvin and Sophronia, and the sudden blush of pleasure that made Sophronia's face a little more beautiful. Why, Lucy thought, my daughter is in love.

First love was something to cherish, for whether it grew or faded, in the heart of a girl it would always be a shining, never-to-be-forgotten part of her. She looked closely at the boy. His face was open and honest, his smile quick and sincere, and Lucy's mind was suddenly at ease. It was good to be here, to observe, to learn firsthand what her children might not tell her. They grew up fast. Encased in their own worlds it wasn't easy for a parent to know them. They could live in the same house, eat the same food, enjoy the same material blessings, yet mingle as strangers. What a tragedy to rear children and have no point of contact. Parents should visit school more often, she thought. It's a good place to make discoveries.

88

A month is swiftly gone. Looking back Father Joseph had no regrets. True, the children had tried his patience as they experimented, measuring how far they could go with him before he took charge of a situation. It was when they found out that he was striving to know them as individuals, that he respected each one as a thinking person capable of self-discipline, that the atmosphere in the school began to change. Some had never been "friends" with a teacher before. The previous master had ruled with commands, punishment, and fear. Father Joseph's love for children begat love. He had the gift of empathy—remembering his own boyhood with vividness—and the children responded. Trouble-making students settled to a new experience, discovering that whetting minds in a classroom and acquiring knowledge was even more of an adventure than plotting mischief. The school was on its way. There were few absences.

On the first day of the new month Lucy was up an hour earlier than usual. She had planned to "visit" school with Father Joseph, until he told her seriously, "If there are dissatisfied parents, I'd best face them alone."

She watched him drive off. Her intention had been to remind him how badly his salary was needed to make ends meet, but his quiet dignity, the way he carried himself with a kind of self-assurance stopped her tongue. Now she worried. "I'm being mercenary," she told herself. But by what right do half a dozen parents run a school and dictate how things shall be?

Back in the house again she tried to talk with God about it, all the time keeping things under her own control, while she gave instructions.

"You know Joseph has teaching ability. Now it's up to

you to put the right words in his mouth so he'll know how to deal with folks who can't tell a road from a gully."

Often during the day her "prayers" ascended to castigate every potential opposer. By Joseph's returning time she was certain that he would never teach in Manchester again and a whole new way of life had been mapped out for the Smiths, ways to stretch income, added chores for herself, until she was irritated, cross, and as tired as if she had fought the enemy with her fists and *lost*.

Father Joseph and the Smith brood came scurrying in just as she was getting the table ready for supper. She tried to read her husband's face, but it was adamant. To the children she said: "Hang your coats where they belong, and stay out of the kitchen."

"Is that my orders too?" His eyes were half-amused, half-indulgent.

"You know better than that."

The room became silent. He hung his coat on a peg and sat down.

"Well?" she waited.

"Well what?"

"Are they against you?"

"The same ones are against heating the school, if that is what you mean."

"I knew it." She sat a plate of bread down so vehemently that some of it bounced off the dish.

"Stop going off like a cannonball, Lucy, and hear me through, Or would you rather wait until hungry stomachs are filled and we can have a quiet talk together?"

"I want to hear it now."

"Folks have a right to their own ideas. They can think their own way without following the majority. You agree to that, don't you?"

"You won't be teaching now, will you?"

90

His eyes held hers so intently that she sat down in a chair.

"Today I saw a man wrestle with beliefs that have been ingrained in his mind by his parents since childhood. He came alone this morning, representing folks who object, as he does, to having heat in the church. There are those who want the stove lit on Sundays now too."

"Fine. Why should folks be cold when they can be warm?"

His eyes brushed hers. "Is it so wrong to believe we can appreciate nothing good until we know its opposite?"

"When does the stove go?"

"Last night a meeting was held without my knowledge. The Stoals, Stoddards, and a number of parents got together to make sure the stove stays."

"Hurrah!" she said. "Let's have supper. Why didn't you say so right away?"

"I want you to see how things really are, Lucy. I want you to see the losers' point too. Mr. Wallace came as spokesman, and he brought five scuttles of coal. These are proud, honest men. At the meeting they were told to take their children out of school, or go along with the rest to furnish coal and wood for the stove. The Wallace children— others too—are not only learning at school, they're teaching their parents to read and write at home. These families know it would be a mistake to take their children out of school, so they are transferring the guilt they feel to my shoulders. Mr. Wallace asked me if I would be willing to take the blame for the sin of heating the church. He seemed relieved when I told him nobody could hold him accountable, that everyone who believed as he did would be absolved from blame, because if there were sin, it was mine."

"And you parted friends."

"Of course we parted friends."

From the time the Smiths had moved to New York they had been approached by ministers of various denominations inviting them to attend church and hoping they would join.

All-day meetings were held at most churches. Some denominations started the Sabbath at sunset on Saturday; all work was stopped then, and the children's play was hushed to prepare their minds for worship. Sunday the attenders got up early; only essential work was done; no hot meals were prepared; and dishes were left unwashed until Monday. Whether the weather was stormy or fair, the entire household set out for the meeting place. Lucy and the children sometimes went. Now that they were in their own home, they enjoyed the two-mile walk through the woods. Long before they reached whichever church they were to attend that day, they could hear the muffled beat of drums through the Sabbath hush. The drums were a call to prayer.

One could join a denomination, change his mind and affiliate with a different church without a ripple or a stir, but when a family belonged to no church at all eyebrows were raised, for this was courting hell. Lucy reminded Father Joseph of this while she was trying to decide which church to join.

Ministers, aware that she was seeking, came to call on Joseph. Each time, he would listen politely to what they had to say, and ask questions about their beliefs; but he had his own interpretations of the scriptures, and since he was unable to find a church that fit his pattern, he refused to attend anywhere. This disappointed Lucy, for the pledge she had made to seek out a church and join it had never been kept, and it bothered her conscience even more, now that her children were growing up without a church. But she didn't want to join one without him. He yielded so readily to most

92

of her desires; why couldn't he see that the children should have the discipline of regular church attendance? They needed to fraternize regularly with other young Christians. Alvin was already a man. In due time he would marry, for girls appealed to him and he to them. She wanted him to have a good Christian wife—someone with more than a pretty face and a well-turned ankle. She wanted a girl who had been brought up to live by godly precepts. What had gotten into Joseph anyway? Surely he could see these needs for his family . . . she had pointed them out to him often enough! Why did he think home teaching alone was enough for the children?

There had been times during their marriage when he had been zealous in church work, even to disappointing his father and brother, since his choice had differed from theirs. He had not complained then of all-day sermons or double work on the second day of the week. Should she join a church or wait for him? And if she joined, which church would it be?

During the month of March, 1820, Manchester and Palmyra became alive with religious zeal. In fact, unusual excitement on the subject of religion seemed to be everywhere in Europe and all the eastern parts of the United States. It began with the Methodists, but soon spread to the other sects. The religious excitement had been prevalent for some time when the people of Manchester and Palmyra began planning for a special revival service. Ministers from several denominations joined to combine their efforts into one great soul-saving endeavor. Leisure time was devoted to clearing out trees and making benches to accommodate the crowds. The skilled and the unskilled worked together. Up in front a mourners' bench was built with a platform behind it for preachers and the choir. Nails were driven into trees for lanterns to hang on. The whole place bordering the clearing was to be one blaze of light. Services were to last a fortnight, and each minister hoped he would make the most converts for his church as well as rekindling whatever waning enthusiasm there might be among present members.

Lucy was excited about the services. She sent Alvin, Hyrum, young Joseph, and Samuel to help build the meeting place, but the revival had been in full swing two days and nights before she attended. She was waiting for Father Joseph, who refused to go with her.

The third night she took all the family but Don Carlos. At least Joseph could mind the baby.

It was a beautiful, cool, crisp night. They were dressed in warm clothing and carried down-filled quilts. Up above golden stars and a bright moon mingled with the lights of many lanterns to give the meeting place a pleasant glow. The air was spiced with the odor of growing trees and fresh lumber.

It was several minutes before evening service would begin, but benches were beginning to fill, although many people were still arriving or milling and mingling just outside the clearing.

Alvin with Lucy led the family down the center aisle where they could see and hear everything that went on.

He folded a quilt lengthwise and placed it on a bench for Lucy, the girls, and William to sit on; then he put another quilt across their knees to make sure they would be warm.

The rest of the family would occupy the bench opposite, and here they put their quilts. Then, leaving Samuel to hold their bench for them, Alvin, Hyrum, and young Joseph left, telling Lucy they would be back in a little while.

Lucy's eyes followed them and saw them separate. Hyrum had found Jerusha Braden. She was a lovely girl, and it was plain to see that Hyrum thought so. They had met soon after Father Joseph's school opened, when she had accompanied Joseph home to help grade some papers. Hyrum had been smitten then, and his admiration had not worn off. Lucy had approved of Jerusha that first day at school, and like Hyrum she still approved and hoped the friendship would continue. Schools were closed now for the revival. It was giving Father Joseph an appreciated breathing spell.

Martin Harris and his wife stopped by Lucy's bench for a moment to exchange greetings.

"Almost every denomination is represented here tonight," Mr. Harris said. "Many sinners will be brought to repentance during this fortnight jubilee."

"I'm sure of it," Lucy said. As they walked away to take a bench somewhere behind her she felt an excitement that seemed to be in the air all around her. She looked again for her boys. After considerable searching she saw young Joseph talking with Isaac Stoal's two daughters. He was teasing them, and they seemed to be enjoying it. Why, Lucy thought, in just no time at all I'll have three young men in the house. Alvin is now, Hyrum thinks he is, and Joseph looks like one for all his fourteen years.

Just then Calvin Stoddard walked up to greet her and the children and to claim the attention of Sophronia. Again, as on that first day of school, Lucy caught the slight blush and the quick smile of pleasure on Sophronia's face. My daughter is a young lady too, she thought, as she watched Calvin and Sophronia walk a little way to stand and talk, as if they alone were the only persons present.

Members of the choir were taking their places, and a hush fell over the congregation. Then the ministers filed onto the platform, and all her young people came back to sit quietly on the benches. Although Lucy's eyes had failed to follow Alvin, she was sure he too had been with the young ladies.

She heard young Joseph whisper to Alvin when he sat down, "How long will the service last do you suppose?"

95

"Three or four hours," came Alvin's low reply.

There were three speakers each night, each one trying to get the most converts. Never in the two towns had there been such eloquence, such long and solemn sermons, such prayers and singing, or such tales of devils, hell, and brimstone. Night shadows lengthened and cast eerie shapes on the trees. Softly blowing wind made lanterns flicker, adding an unnatural gleam to a setting that seemed supernatural and unreal. The congregation became so large that many young persons and adults sat on rugs or quilts on the ground. Lucy's boys had relinquished their seats to the ladies and had spread their quilts on nature's carpet. Walled in by trees and canopied by the sky, Lucy felt as if the worshipers were set apart from the world, a small, glowing spark of living beings surrounded by heaven.

She had made up her mind to join a church, but was this the night? She wanted all her family in the same church if that were possible, and she hadn't talked about their preferences with them enough to come to an understanding. It would be better to wait.

People were coming from every aisle to give their allegiance to Christ. It was an impressive, soul-lifting sight, with each minister standing to accept his own. Baptisms would come later, some by immersion, some by sprinkling, some by the right hand of fellowship.

Days and nights came and went with the same number of Smiths attending services, and still Lucy had not joined a church. She had approached each of her children separately and together. They wanted what she wanted . . . all but Joseph.

During meetings he sat listening intently. Nothing seemed to escape him, but each time she approached him afterward he was unwilling to talk. It wasn't that he was impolite, stubborn, or rebellious; he was simply unapproachable.

"Let him be," Alvin admonished her gently. "Don't you see, this is an individual matter—something each of us has to answer in his own way."

"But what we believe, what we do does matter."

"Of course it matters. What we believe determines what we think, and what we think determines what we are, but Joseph is a good boy, Mamma. Let him be. Let him work things out for himself."

And so it was that on this last night of services, Lucy sat praying with an aching heart. Tonight she must make public the surrendering of her life to Christ. When the call came for converts, her prayer was that all her children would be with her. Alvin was in the choir. If she and the children went to the mourners' bench, would he come too? Would Joseph?

The sermon ended. The choir began singing softly. Above the music came the minister's voice urging the uncommitted to give their lives to God. "This is the way, the truth, and light," he was saying. "This is the road to eternal salvation."

Lucy stood up. Hyrum came to take her arm. What a fine young man he was! Her eyes moved to the choir seeking some sign from Alvin. Would he come? Hyrum was guiding her down the long aisle with the rest of the family following behind them. They reached the place where the ministers were standing to welcome all who came, and Lucy looked back. Joseph had not moved. He sat on the ground where other youths sat. He was looking straight ahead, feet placed firmly in front of him, hands in his pockets, eyes lost in thought. His meditations were so deep he was not even fraternizing with his own age group. Again her eyes sought Alvin's, begging him to come. Ever so slightly he shook his head. But he was ready. Her heart knew it and was still. She had no worries for Alvin. But Joseph . . . !

The minister's hand closed over hers, and she looked up through tears which he took to be repentance. This was her great moment, but without Alvin and her two Josephs something was lacking. This most important step was taking place, and these were not sharing it with her. People at the bench were kneeling, and she knelt with them. Her tears spilled over now, and she fought to control them. "God," she was speaking too softly for human ears to hear, "take care of young Joseph." It didn't occur to her that she had absolved Alvin from blame at the same time that she was condemning Joseph. She could understand Alvin; they were in accord. "Let no wedge separate me from Joseph." She was feeling the ache of her disappointment. "I feel so lost with him lately. We speak together without understanding." She arose when the others ceased their prayers, but her worry remained.

Part 2

Young Joseph's mind had never been so troubled in all his fourteen years. He had sat in the congregation when his mother, sisters, and brothers had given their promise to join a church. He had watched each minister strive for converts, claiming his denomination was right. He had witnessed scenes at the mourners' bench and dedications made in quiet sincerity by certain of the penitent, while others shook and cried that the Holy Spirit had taken possession of their bodies. His father would say that these had been overtaken by their own wild imaginings, that the Spirit of God was a quiet, penetrating, informing Spirit, a part of the divine in everyone. Then why the frenzy? Why would persons of a calm nature indulge in such wildness? He had sat fascinated by women with the shakes whose heads moved with such speed that their hairpins fell to the ground. Others, like those of his family, had approached the bench with such dignity and reverence that the ground where they stood seemed almost holy.

The revival had excited him, moved him, kept him coming meeting after meeting. Ministers from faraway places had joined with lay ministers; nothing like it had ever happened in Palmyra and Manchester before. His mind had been rubbed with as much agitation as soiled clothes on a washboard, but—among other things—he couldn't believe that little children who died without baptism were plunged into the flames of hell to burn in torment forever. He couldn't believe there would be one minute of such torture, let alone an eternity of it. Why even his own father's punishments were just. He expected his children to be accountable for their acts, and if he punished in error his concern was great—so great that once, not long ago, tears had been mixed with his apology. Would God's love be less than this?

And what about deathbed repentance? Could an evil man die with Christ's name on his lips and spend eternity in heaven, while an unbaptized man who had served his fellows all his life wallowed in hell eternally? What *was* hell? Who went there? Was it literal fire and burning? Could a spirit burn? Or was it a place of learning with Christ holding the keys as his father believed? All week he had wrestled with these problems.

He had wanted to join a church with his family, but their choice had not been his. In fact, he really hadn't had a choice. Were all the churches right, or was only one right? If so, which one? Did it really matter which church he joined as long as he served God and loved Christ and his fellows? He did have a preference, but it was not for creed or doctrine—it was for one special minister. Joseph liked him long before the revival services. He was someone to look up to, and he had a way with young people. If the same man were of some other religion, Joseph knew he would want to follow him. But was it right to make a covenant with God because of one man? Most problems he could talk through with his parents, but this time he wasn't sure they had the right answers, even though they thought they did.

Now, walking home, he sensed his mother's silent grieving for him. He had let her down, but he couldn't bring himself to speak with her about his mental turmoil.

As soon as they were home he excused himself from the

family and, carrying a lighted candle up the steep stairway, he went at once to his room. He undressed and went to bed, but sleep was impossible. Everybody who was anybody joined a church. His mother said so; his friends said so; and Calvin Stoddard, Sophronia's boyfriend, had told him he would rot in hell if he didn't join. This he didn't believe, and yet—what if it were so? He wanted a religion that would teach truth and increase his understanding of the divine, but which church?

Several times he got out of bed to sit at the window, to look out at the April night alive with stars. The moon shed a glow on the sugar maples in the yard, and beyond them was the grove of trees that he secretly called his, because of the peace and solitude he always found there.

"God," he silently prayed, "if you have a church, I'll join it. Please let me know which one it is." The Stoal girls, Calvin Stoddard, Jerusha Braden—all of them had joined a church. They knew—or thought they knew—which one was right.

The sun was streaking the heavens with the bright hues of morning, and still he had not slept. When the family stirred he dressed and went downstairs. This was Sunday, the day when each convert would attend his chosen church, and each church would hold an all-day jubilee with baptisms or fellowship.

Lucy studied young Joseph's face as he sat down to join them for breakfast. When he made only a pretense of eating she didn't chide him. But when the horses were hitched to the wagon and he asked to be excused from going, her face clouded with disappointment and disapproval.

"There will never be a day exactly like this one, Joseph. There will be baptisms all up and down the river, as well as the glad hand of fellowship and happy communion. We very much wanted you with us today."

He didn't answer, but he knew he had spoiled her day.

As he stood beside his father and watched them drive off he could feel his father's questioning eyes. He was waiting for him to "talk." Always he had been able to bring any problem to his parents for their wisdom and sound judgment, but this was his soul and its outcome that he was facing. Perhaps someday the time would come when a church and what became of one's soul would be nothing. Without meeting his father's eyes he went to do his morning chores.

His mind was in turmoil as he fed the stock and straightened things inside the house that would help his mother. Which church should he join? He didn't doubt the power of God to give him the answer, but was he making too much of what the rest of the family had seemed to decide without difficulty? There had to be an answer somehow—somewhere.

He finished his work and climbed the stairs to his room. Was it or wasn't it true that every person was of great consequence to God, as Christ in the New Testament had led him to believe?

He closed the door. It was very quiet in his little room. A breeze billowed the curtains, and the air was cool. He made his bed and straightened the untidiness, grateful for the privilege of being alone there.

When the room was to his liking he reached for the Bible as he had done for several days and nights in his searching. Somewhere in those familiar pages there must be an answer. This was God's business, and if he were to know the truth it must come through Him. Prayerfully he opened the Bible at random, as he had done so many times before, and suddenly his eyes fell upon the epistle of James, first chapter, fifth verse: "If any man lack wisdom, let him ask of God, who giveth to all men liberally and upbraideth not, and it shall be given him."

The words seemed to light the page, and his heart seemed on fire as well. Until now he had been telling God what he hoped He would do. Now God was telling him what to do. Without realizing where he was going he laid the Bible on the table and went down the stairs as fast as his feet would carry him. He took a shortcut through the corral where Bess the cow was. She was the favorite animal of the whole Smith family, and Joseph was especially fond of her, but now he went swiftly past her. He was on his way to the grove—the one place he knew that he could be entirely alone.

He made his way through the trees to a familiar spot. Here the forest was cool and fragrant. New life was beginning to spring out of the brown earth that until recently had been frozen. It was a small clearing entirely surrounded by trees. Often when something troubled him he had come to this spot to think things through, and he had come to regard this part of the grove as his sanctuary.

Birds flew out of the thickets that surrounded the small enclosure, startled by his sudden intrusion. Joseph was only vaguely aware of them, for his mind held but one purpose. He was following what he took to be a command from God. Having arrived, he looked around to make sure he was alone, then he sank to his knees and began praying aloud—a different kind of praying than he had ever done before. He was asking in all earnestness for light and waiting for the answer.

Minutes passed, and suddenly he was seized by some unexplainable power that bound his tongue so that he could no longer speak. Darkness gathered around him—a darkness so dense that he felt surely he would die. In agony he cried out to be delivered from this spirit that seemed to be dooming him to destruction. At that moment he saw a pillar of light in the sky above his head. It was more brilliant than the sun, and it descended gradually until he was entirely

103

surrounded. Immediately, as the light fell upon him, he was delivered from the darkness. Then looking up, he saw two Personages above him in the air. Their brightness and glory were beyond description and one of them called him by name, saying, "This is my beloved Son, hear Him."

The vision did not frighten Joseph, nor did it seem strange to him that it was taking place. For days he had been praying to know which of all the churches he should join, and now he asked in all earnestness that he might know which church was right. The light remained, and the answers came from the lips of the two who stood in vision before him.

When Joseph came to himself he was lying on his back looking up at the heavens. Over and over through his mind echoed the words he had heard. After a time he got up and walked dazedly toward the house, still under the spell of what he had both seen and heard.

He entered the corral and was about to pass Bess, the cow, when she nuzzled him gently, expecting some delicacy from his hand or at least a friendly pat. He stopped and caressed her sleek neck. "If you had been with me, Bess, you would have seen something too wonderful to tell."

He moved back to the wooden fence and perched himself upon it. The cow followed the way a dog would. Joseph ran his hand gently across her back. "You have never been troubled the way I have been lately. There was such confusion among the different denominations when the revival ended. Each minister was trying to prove the others wrong, or at least to make people think they were wrong."

Bess nuzzled him with her tawny face as if she understood all that he was saying.

"In the midst of this word war I would ask, 'Which church is right? Or are they all wrong together?'" Joseph's hand moved gently down the cow's neck. "Bess, the Bible is a guide to strange and wonderful experiences." His voice held so much awe that Bess touched his hand with her cool, damp nose.

"The verse I read this morning was like a voice speaking. 'If any man lack wisdom, let him ask of God, who giveth to all men liberally, and upbraideth not, and it shall be given him." He was feeling the power that had moved him like a command, sending him into the woods to pray.

"Sometimes, when I'm certain no one can hear me, I *almost* pray out loud, but this was different; this was something I had to do." He stopped talking. The cow sniffed at his pockets, but he gave no notice. He was living again the awful power that had seized him, the astonishing influence that had bound his tongue, the thick darkness, the fear that he would be destroyed. This had been no imaginary power; it was an alarming experience from an unseen world. He was remembering with what strength he had called out for God to deliver him. Then the light—that wondrous holy light seen in the sky exactly over his head—how bright it was! As it descended, covering him, he had been entirely delivered of that awful spirit. He had never felt so free, so alive, so aware of what perfection really was. And the two Personages in the midst of that light! He would remember their bright glory forever. And the voice, "This is my beloved Son, hear Him." Joseph said the words aloud, softly, with his face turned heavenward. "I must tell somebody," he whispered. "I must tell someone, or I will burst."

He climbed down from the rail fence and put his face against the cow's neck. "I was told not to join any of the churches, because they are teaching incorrect doctrines. I have been called to do a special work for God, a work that will bring me heartache, loneliness, and peril, but it is for this reason that I was born. I'm not sure I understand all that I was told, but when the time comes, I will understand."

Tears came to his eyes, and he dashed them away. Should he tell his family? Would they believe he had seen a vision? Perhaps this was something to tell a minister. Sometime soon he would go to his minister friend and tell him.

Giving Bess a final pat he walked slowly toward the house, glad that only his father was there; he wasn't one to pry into the privacy of his children. No earthly splendor—nothing he had before seen or experienced—could compare with the vision or the voice.

A few days later young Joseph walked with his minister friend in the parsonage garden. The sun was warm, and white feather clouds moved across a sky that was bluer than the sea. Orange, saffron, and yellow crocuses bloomed along the cobbled pathway. Under a tall maple tree, where new leaves were announcing spring, tulips bloomed in riotous color. The whole world was awakening to new life, but at that moment the man and the boy were unaware of the beauty which surrounded them.

Joseph had just finished telling in all earnestness everything he had seen and experienced in the grove.

Unlike the earth, eagerly pushing life into new seeds, the minister's mind was closed to everything he had heard. Now as Joseph finished speaking and turned his eyes upon his friend he saw a face that registered only rejection. It was a handsome face crowned by gray hair that the wind had blown slightly askew.

There was a long pause in which neither of them spoke, then the minister's voice came harshly. "I am three times your age, Joseph. Believe me, I know there are no such things as visions and revelations in these days. Those ceased with the apostles, and they will never come again. We have the Bible with all the answers in it. You must choose a church—if not mine, then some other—but don't go chasing after fables that will set people against you and destroy you." His lean body seemed to grow taller and as unreachable as the clouds above.

"Sir," Joseph said in a kind of desperation, "I can't deny what I have seen and heard."

The minister put an arm across Joseph's shoulders. "It is blasphemy and of the devil. It is the sort of thing I will fight from my pulpit, for it is evil. Every minister will denounce it and you with it, if you continue to believe this folly. You must forget it—all of it."

"I can't forget it, Sir."

"Then I can't help you. You will be twice a fool and an enemy to all I stand for. There isn't a minister in Manchester or Palmyra who will support you. I dare to say every man, woman, and child will be against you."

"I will stand alone then," Joseph said in a kind of desperation. "If you had only been there to hear and see...."

"Have you told your parents?"

"No, Sir. I thought a minister should hear it first."

"Tell them. They should put a stop to this nonsense." At this moment he was in very deed a man of the cloth, immovable and determined.

"I must go now," Joseph said. "Please excuse me, Sir."

Joseph walked out of the garden without looking back. Other times he would have turned to wave, but not this time. There was a determined thrust to his shoulders, but blinding tears of disappointment and frustration filled his eyes. He was no baby—yet he was crying. When he reached the street he began to run, dashing his tears away as fast as they came. He had seen a light and heard a voice . . . he knew he had . . . and it was not of the devil. The whole world could declare against him, and it would not change truth. Why couldn't his friend see? If the devil had power, God would have more. "I heard the voice," Joseph said aloud softly. "And the words, 'They draw near me with their lips but their understanding is far from me. They teach the commandments of men, having a form of godliness, but they deny the power thereof.' " His friend was denying the power. "God does speak, and he will continue to speak. No matter what they do to me I can never deny that." Joseph set his feet steadily toward home. He must tell his parents. Would they too deny the power and make light of his experience?

That night when all members of the family had assembled for worship Joseph told them what he had told the minister. They listened with the gravest attention and believed him.

In small towns like Manchester and Palmyra news spreads quickly. Soon everyone had heard of young Joseph Smith's vision. Ministers denounced him in their sermons. Some said he was dishonest, some that he was mad, some that he was possessed with a devil. Joseph shunned the churches. He was a sensitive boy who loved people, but now many who had been his friends turned from him, their faces showing mockery or scorn. It was a frightening experience, for he was unprepared to cope with a public that had turned against him.

His family believed in him, loved him, and stood by him, but Joseph found it hard to endure the rejection of almost everyone else. Jerusha Braden and Cal Stoddard went out of their way to show him friendship, but that was because Cal was in love with Sophronia and Jerusha with Hyrum. The religious leaders were all his enemies. Each one tried to make him deny his experience in the grove, and Joseph began building a wall around himself. Under this defense he hid the bewilderment and wounds that were too deep for him to understand.

A few nights after Joseph's visit to the minister, Bess the cow had her first calf—a healthy little heifer. Young Joseph went with Alvin to see to the proceedings, and as at other times when he had assisted Alvin, he was aware that giving birth to new life does not always come easy. Birth, he thought, is like a new idea. It comes painfully.

The weaning of Bess from her calf came with difficulty too. Bess mourned the separation, and her bawling was a plaintive, lonesome sound. Two times they found her in the yard by the house, seeking for her calf, or perhaps courting sympathy from members of the Smith family. Both times it was young Joseph who led her back to the corral.

Alvin and Hyrum were making extra money assisting nearby farmers, as well as helping Father Joseph at home, and it was young Joseph's ambition to find extra work, but nobody seemed to want to hire a hand who was supposed to be mad or possessed with a devil. Time after time he applied where there was a need, only to be turned down and the work given to another. It was between seasons at the Knights' mill. It would be some time before the Smith boys would be needed there. Then Joseph got a job helping to sink a well for Martin Harris. The first night, because they were friends, he was invited to stay for supper. Mr. Harris wanted to hear about the vision, and to Joseph's great joy Martin believed the experience. The hour was late, but Joseph was coming home feeling free and happy.

It was very dark and extremely windy as Joseph ferried himself across the river and took a shortcut through the woods. It was a way he knew well, for he had traveled it many times before. The wind buffeted against him, making him walk slowly, and the lantern he carried shed a dim glow, for his oil was burning low.

Once he thought he heard footsteps ahead of him, and he stopped to listen. There was something or someone. "Hello," he shouted, but only the echo of his voice came back to him through the wind. Joseph thought nothing of it. There were no dangerous animals this near to civilization. It did seem a little strange that someone should be going in the direction of his house at this late hour. Perhaps it was Alvin or Hyrum coming home from somewhere, but if this were the case, why was there no lantern? Neither would venture out on such a dark night without one.

Joseph made his way slowly, steadying himself with his free hand and arm, picking his path. Then, as he passed through the last fringe of trees, his light went out altogether. Now it was indeed dark—too dark to distinguish the barns, the carriage house, or the corral, but candles burning inside the house guided him to his destination. The sky was as black and dark as the earth around him. Not even one star was visible.

Just before he reached the front door he stumbled into something—a wagon. Someone had unhitched and left the wagon parked in the yard next to the house. He moved forward, groping for the doorknob, and flung the door open. As he did so there was the sound of a shot. Half falling, in his haste to get inside, he closed the door as another shot rang through the darkness.

From all directions his family came running at the sound of the shooting. Some came from downstairs, some from upstairs.

110

"What is it, Joseph?"

"Are you all right?"

"What's going on out there?"

They all seemed to be asking questions at once, and Joseph's face was as puzzled as theirs. "I don't know," he said. "I guess someone is trying to kill me."

Alvin and Hyrum were dressed; the rest were in their nightclothes. Alvin started for the door and Father Joseph stepped in front of it.

"Stay here."

"He'll get away."

"He's armed, and it's pitch black out there. If he tries to get inside we'll handle the matter." Father Joseph spoke almost harshly as he turned the key in the door. "It's so dark a man could stand an inch away and it would be impossible to see him."

"He's sure to be gone by now," Hyrum said. "But I think we should light the lanterns and look anyway."

"We're out of lantern oil; there can be no light. Stay up if you like, listen for any unfamiliar sound, but stay inside. I'll wait up too for a while."

Twice they thought they heard something but decided it must be only the wind. They extinguished the lights and stood at the windows trying to peer through the night, but all they saw was darkness and trees blowing and twisting in the wind.

After a long time, one by one, all but Alvin, Hyrum, and young Joseph went to bed. These three waited, speaking in whispers, and listening until the light of a new day appeared in the east.

By morning the wind had worn itself out. The only sound now was of an awakening world. They opened the door and went out into the dawn. Alvin was leading. Then all three were moving as one.

"Oh, no! Oh, no! Oh, no!" it was Joseph's voice like a sob.

Bess, the favorite cow, was lying dead where balls from a gun had felled her. Stunned, they bent down to examine her. One ball had gone into her neck and one into her head. The beautiful tawny body lay on the grass with the head turned to one side. The body was cold.

Anger filled the eyes of the brothers. Poor Bess! Lonely for her lively calf she had come to be comforted by the only friends she knew. Now she was dead. Why? Why would anyone do such a terrible thing?

Young Joseph ran his hand tenderly down the sleek neck of the beautiful animal as he strove for self-control. "Those balls were meant for me. Somebody . . . wanted to kill . . . me."

"Who?" Alvin's voice shook. "Who, Joseph?"

"I don't know."

"Maybe we'll never know," Hyrum said. Then he raised his voice. "Father—get dressed! Come out here!"

The whole family came out. They searched for clues as to who the killer might be.

The grass was tall and needed scything. Underneath the wagon they found where it was down and matted. The person firing the shots had done so from underneath the wagon.

They never learned who had fired the shots, but they did discover that this was the beginning of real danger for young Joseph.

There was in the village of Manchester a clownish fellow named Ebenezer Horton, who had lived alone for years in a

112

tiny cabin in the woods near Manchester. Citizens of religion found this small, homely man dull but gay. He was a familiar sight at church suppers, husking bees, and various community activities, but whether he came or stayed people didn't care much, unless they could get him to perform the acts, without pay, that he put on almost daily at one of the taverns to earn enough money to feed himself and buy the simple clothes he wore. A nimble fellow, he could dance, somersault, and do improvisations. It was common talk that he had once been a performer of importance in one of the large cities, although nobody seemed to know where or why he had drifted into Manchester and stayed.

Young Joseph knew Ebenezer about as well as any of the other town's citizens, which wasn't really knowing him at all. And then one day Joseph, after being ridiculed by a student of the Bible, in desperation and rebellion wandered down to the tavern.

He arrived at a time when Ebenezer was putting on one of his acts. His coordination was perfect, his timing excellent, and Joseph joined in the cheering with honest enthusiasm. He even threw a coin, when the others threw theirs, to show his appreciation.

Ebenezer finished his act, picked up his money, and came to stand by Joseph. "I know you, son of Joseph Smith. How old are you, boy?"

"Does it matter?"

"It matters. I'm going home in a minute. Why not come along home with me?"

And Joseph found himself riding beside Ebenezer in a rickety cart pulled by a skinny, slow-moving old horse. As they rode along Ebenezer was no longer gay or clownish, but he was very kind to his horse, urging him forward in soft, gentle tones. Joseph found himself looking at the little man as if he were seeing him for the first time, and he liked what he saw.

The small cabin was very neat. Most of the furniture was homemade, and there were more than one hundred books in a case that went from floor to ceiling against one wall. The fireplace had been constructed with care, and near it was a chair and a table with books and a reading candle on it. The bunk bed, large enough for one man, was neatly made. There was a cupboard, and iron pots for cooking hung on the wall beside it. Joseph found himself suddenly at ease, as if he and the man had been friends for a long time.

Ebenezer brought slices of brown bread and cheese to eat and milk to drink. Then they talked. Joseph found himself giving Ebenezer an account of his visit in the grove, and the way the people of Manchester had received it. With his newfound friend there was no scoffing, no disbelief. He pointed to his books. "People's minds change, boy. Perhaps in a hundred years all religions will accept such miracles. Concepts change. Truth remains."

"Then you believe me?"

"I can't say I believe in visions. I have never had such an experience. What I am defending is your right to believe what you saw. When you are older you will learn how to keep criticism from hurting you. It is a common thing for people to fight anything that makes them uncomfortable, for most people are selfish and interested only in their own thoughts. What they want is for everyone to accept their ideas of what is right and what is wrong. If you had had your vision in a city where many persons are strangers and new ideas are not uncommon, I suppose hardly a voice would be raised against you."

From that day on Joseph and Ebenezer were friends. And Joseph began learning many truths. He found that sin and goodness were in all men, that no man is so good that he

114

cannot be better, and that no man is too evil to do acts of grace. He found that the bitterness of being misunderstood is less grievous after being discussed with a friend, and that a hurt is deepest when made by a friend. He found tormenters among the irreligious as well as the religious. He learned that truth is something to be faced, that it cannot be drowned in drugs, excitement, or indifference. While he was learning these all-important truths Lucy and Father Joseph watched, worried, and prayed. It was not so much what Joseph did, as what they feared he might do. He grew tall and comely, and few could match him. Would he become a Judas or a Paul? What was he doing when he came home in the early hours of morning? His keen mind was capable of carrying him to the heights or dragging him to the depths; and he had become almost a stranger, going his own way. They had no complaint about the work he did on the farm. He did it well, and more than earned his keep. It was the way he spent his leisure that worried them, for he had been their child of promise—the one they had counted on to go far and to give much.

Alvin, Hyrum, Sophronia, and Samuel all tried to reach him, but their activities were with their young friends in the church, and Joseph refused to go with them.

The truth of the matter was, Joseph felt as alone as Ebenezer in his search to discover what life was all about, but Ebenezer had compromised. He had found peace in books, in the things he made with his hands, in the nimble performing of his dance routines, and in the few friends who loved and understood him, as he loved and understood them.

Lucy and Father Joseph would have worried less had they known that Joseph's testings were being measured by their own goodness and the things he had been taught at home. Cheap girls lost their luster when compared to the shining inward beauty of Lucy and his sisters. Joseph was making up his mind about the true worth of many things. He was examining and concluding. Many a time when the family worried about him he was by himself in the grove, or he was in Ebenezer's cabin reading from his fine collection of books.

On July 18, 1821, another child was born to Father Joseph and Lucy. With a twinkle Joseph reminded Lucy of his dream, which was now fulfilled. They named the baby Lucy.

Alvin thought there had never been a baby like her; she noticed him first and preferred him above all the rest of the family.

"When little Lu outgrows her baby things you can give them away," Father Joseph teased Lucy. "We won't be needing them again."

"Oh, yes, we will," Lucy dimpled. "With Sophronia and Hyrum both in love, let's hope we have wedding bells and grandchildren."

Young Joseph was sixteen when Lucy was born. Mother Lucy had hoped the baby's birth would put a stop to his restlessness. It did help, but there was no outward sign of any change in him.

Perhaps there is no more critical person than one who must experience in order to discover. Joseph was almost a man now. In December he would be eighteen, and he began to look back on the road he had traveled since his fourteenth year. Some of the things he had done seemed so utterly foolish that he began to wonder if God loved him, for as he examined his life by his parents' standards he fell far short.

The experience he had had in the grove was often with

116

him. He had been called to do a work . . . but what kind of work? He was restless to be at it, but had he spoiled his chances altogether? He wanted to be done with frivolous time-wasting. He wanted to make preparation and put purpose into his life, but how was he to begin when he was in the dark as to what God expected of him?

On the night of September 21, 1823, Joseph sat at the window of his room where he often sat when he was troubled. He had come in early and excused himself from the family. The air was hot and sultry; there seemed to be no breeze at all. But the heavens were golden with stars, and there was a bright moon shining.

The weight of Joseph's sins seemed to overwhelm him. He prayed for cleansing and for a sign that God had forgiven him. He was not a weak man, but now, alone, where no human eyes could see him he let the tears fall until they wet the windowsill. He was feeling complete repentance, and his whole being craved guidance. After a time he arose and went to bed.

In bed, he went over his life again. He prayed earnestly for forgiveness, and for a divine manifestation that he might know the state of his standing, even if it meant rejection. His faith was strong. He knew that God would answer. Hadn't his prayer in the grove been answered when he had gone there for guidance? Then he had gone in all his boyhood purity; now he was coming to put himself entirely in God's hands.

How long he wrestled with his sins and prayed he did not know, but the hour could have been well past midnight. And then, as it had happened in the grove, he discovered a light appearing in his room. He sat up, his pulse quickening, his heart beating faster. He was trembling with both awe and fear.

The light continued to increase until the room was brighter than noonday. Then a personage appeared standing

117

in the air at Joseph's bedside. He wore a loose robe of exquisite whiteness. His hands and arms were bare a little above the wrists; his feet and legs were bare a little above the ankles; and his head and neck were bare. Not only was his robe exceedingly white, but his whole person was glorious beyond description, and his countenance was truly like lightning. The room was brilliant, but the brightness was more intense immediately around his person.

"Joseph Smith . . . my name is Moroni." At the sound of the voice Joseph found that his fear was gone and his whole being at ease.

"God has heard your prayers, Joseph. He knows and loves you as he loves all people, and he has a work for you to do."

Joseph was listening with rapt attention.

"Your name shall be had for good and evil among all nations, kindreds, tongues, and people. There is a book deposited in a hill which I shall show you, written upon plates of gold, giving an account of the former inhabitants of the American continent, and the source from whence they sprang. The fullness of the everlasting gospel is contained in these records, as delivered by the Savior to the ancient inhabitants. Deposited with these plates of gold are two stones in silver bows called the Urim and Thummim. When you see them they will be fastened to a breastplate. The possession and use of these stones was what set one apart as a seer in ancient or former times, and God has prepared these for the purpose of translating the records."

Joseph's full attention was riveted on that voice. If there were other sounds in the room he did not hear them.

Moroni was quoting prophecies from the Old Testament now. He first quoted part of the third chapter of Malachi, then he quoted the fourth or last chapter of the same prophecy with a little variation: "For behold the day cometh

118

that shall burn as an oven, and all the proud, yea, and all that do wickedly shall burn as stubble, for they that cometh shall burn them saith the Lord of hosts, that it shall leave them neither root nor branch." Then he quoted the fifth verse: "Behold I will reveal unto you the priesthood by the hand of Elijah the prophet before the coming of the great and dreadful day of the Lord."

The next verse he quoted differently: "And He shall plant in the hearts of the children the promises made to the fathers, and the hearts of the children shall turn to their fathers; if it were not so the whole earth would be utterly wasted at his coming." In addition to these he quoted the eleventh chapter of Isaiah, and the third chapter of Acts, twenty-second and twenty-third verses, precisely as they stand in the New Testament.

"Joseph," he said, "this prophet is Christ, and the day will come when those who will not hear his voice shall be cut off from among the people." He quoted the second chapter of Joel from the twenty-eighth to the last verse, and his eyes seemed to burn into Joseph's, they were so intense. "This prophecy will soon be fulfilled." For a long time he talked, explaining the scriptures; then he spoke again about the records written on plates of gold. "When you get them, Joseph, you must show them to no one, unless you are commanded to show them. If you do, you will be destroyed."

This time, while the angel talked about the plates, Joseph saw in vision the place where they were deposited. He saw it so distinctly that he knew the place when he visited it.

After this communication the light in the room began to gather around the personage. It continued to do so until the room was again left dark except just around him, when instantly Joseph saw a passage open up into heaven, and the

119

angel ascended until he disappeared. Moonlight was the only illumination in the room now.

Joseph lay marveling at what he had been told by this extraordinary messenger, when in the midst of his meditations the room again became light, and the same messenger was at his bedside. Again he related the same things. Then he informed Joseph of great judgments that would come upon the earth, desolations and famines, war and pestilence, after which he ascended as he had done before.

By this time the impressions made on Joseph's mind were so deep that sleep was impossible. As he lay contemplating what he had seen and heard, the room again became light, and a third time the messenger was at his bedside repeating all that he had said before. This time he cautioned: "Your family needs money, Joseph. You will be sorely tempted to use the plates for the purpose of getting gain. My son, you must have no other object in view in getting the plates but to glorify God, and you must not be influenced by any other motive except that of building the kingdom, otherwise you shall not get them."

As Joseph was left to ponder the strangeness of what he had experienced a cock began crowing. It was morning. His prayers and the strange interviews had occupied the entire night.

His father was stirring. Soon the whole household would be up and busy, for it was harvesttime, and the day would be filled with work. During harvest Lucy and the girls prepared breakfast early so that the men could be in the fields shortly after sunup. This morning the dawn held special promise for Joseph, for he felt cleansed and filled with wonder and amazement at what had taken place during the night. He was anxious to visit the place where the plates of gold were buried. Tonight he would go and bring them home. Imagine having in his possession plates of pure gold! That would give some of the doubting stalwarts in the churches something to contemplate, and they would be forced to believe in his visions if he had a material witness such as this as proof.

Joseph worked beside his father and Alvin. The yield was unusually good, and they would make money from this year's crop. Alvin was telling Father Joseph that he ought to buy the remainder of the Everston farm. "This is good land that joins ours, and if we don't buy it, we can't tell who our neighbors will be. We could build a house there large enough to accommodate the family." His face took on a sort of shine. "I could help lay the plans, and supervise, and work with the carpenters. You and Mamma deserve a special kind of home that will be a comfort to you when you are old."

His father gave him an indulgent smile but made no comment.

Although Alvin's mind was not on what he was doing, his fingers were deft and sure. There was no lost motion to his work. "The profit from this year's harvest will more than make a substantial down payment, even after we take out for our living. I hope you will give serious thought to what I am saying, Father."

It was plain to young Joseph that buying all of the Everston farm was something Alvin had given much thought to, and that it was very important to him. He was tempted to tell Alvin and his father about last night's happenings. He wondered what they would say if he were to tell them that buried in a hill not far away was more gold than they had ever seen. It couldn't be used to buy a section of land, but the people in Manchester were going to get a mighty big jolt. For some reason, the more he thought along these lines the weaker he got. His feet were moving now as though he had a

121

weight on each one. He became so weak he could hardly lift his hands. His tongue felt thick and dry, and black spots swam before his eyes. The admonition of the angel, that he was not to show the plates to anyone, passed through his mind. From some faraway place he heard his father's voice telling him to go home, that he appeared to be sick.

Joseph's head was swimming as he made his way to the fence that led homeward. By the time he reached the fence he was reeling and half blind. He remembered touching the wires with the intention of bending them so he could crawl through; then his strength entirely failed him, and he fell helpless and unconscious to the ground.

His first recollection was a voice calling him, "Joseph—Joseph!"

He opened his eyes and saw the same messenger standing in the air above him surrounded by light as before. Again the angel related all the things Joseph had been told the night before. "Return to your father, my son," he said. "Tell him the commandments you have received, and what you have seen and heard. He will believe you."

The angel's voice was still sounding in his ears as Joseph looked heavenward, but he was alone. The personage and the light were gone, and the tired, sick feeling he had suffered was gone too. He felt refreshed and strong. Always in his element at harvesttime he was again aware of the smell of earth, the feel of sun and wind. He was seeing the beauty and hearing the sounds all around him as his feet carried him toward the field. Father Joseph saw him coming and came to meet him. This was good. Now Joseph could converse with him away from the ears of his brothers.

It was a strange tale that Joseph told, but Father Joseph believed him. "You must go at once and do as you have been commanded. This is a divine work you have been called to do."

122

As Joseph neared the house little Lucy and Don Carlos came running to meet him. Lucy was a small, brown-haired cherub. It struck Joseph that time moved swiftly. How could this small girl be two years old? And Don Carlos was seven.

Joseph swung Lucy to his shoulder and took Don Carlos by the hand. At home he stopped long enough to wash his face and hands. He lathered them with coarse soap and warm water from a kettle, while the children watched his every move.

Mother Lucy asked why he had come in from the field.

He gave her a smile as he dried on the homespun towel. "I'll tell you later, Mamma, as soon as I can."

Baby Lucy dabbled small hands in the wash basin. "Tell Lucy too? And Don Carlos?"

"No, but if I see a wild flower I'll bring you one."

"And one for Don Carlos?"

"Maybe two for Don Carlos. Now whom do you like?" he asked with twinkling eyes.

"I like Amby." It was her nickname for Alvin.

He lifted her high, and she shouted with the joy of it; then she hugged his neck.

"You like me a little too, don't you?" he asked as he set her on her feet.

"No," her eyes were dancing. "I like Amby."

Joseph combed his hair, then he went to the box where his father kept his tools and picked up a lever.

His mother was really puzzled now, but his look reassured her. As she watched him stride off toward the Canandaigua road that led into the village, she felt assured there was neither danger nor wrong in what he planned to do, and she went back to her household chores with a light heart.

The sun was well up in the sky, and the air was warm with hardly a breeze blowing, but Joseph was unaware of it. After all these years he still favored his leg, but he had learned to walk for miles with only slight discomfort, and he could run with good speed. Today he walked swiftly. Green grass carpeted both sides of the road; wildflowers lifted bright heads to the sun; squirrels and rabbits crossed his path; bees buzzed from flower to flower, and grasshoppers plopped through dry weeds. All these things Joseph saw with his eyes but they did not register in his mind. The vision had been so vivid that he knew exactly where he was going.

Not far from the village was a hill of considerable size. It was the most elevated spot around Manchester, and Joseph had often climbed to the top of it, sometimes with friends or his brothers, sometimes alone. It was south from Palmyra, rising some one hundred and fifty feet above the surrounding country, and like smaller hills in the same region was a glacial deposit of the last ice age, marking the southernmost advance of the great ice cap which once covered the northern part of America. The face of the hill was covered with pine and spruce trees which made Joseph's ascent cool and comfortable. It seemed strange that plates of gold could remain buried in such a place all these years without being discovered. How wonderful it was that he, Joseph, should be the one chosen to find them. His was indeed a sacred trust. The angel had made that very clear, but after the translations were completed, after he had finished the work, perhaps he would be allowed to keep them. If this happened, his family would indeed be rich.

He was nearly to the top now, and ahead of him among the rocks he could see the exact spot. On the west side of the hill was a stone of large dimensions, and Joseph made his way to it. The stone was thick and rounded in the middle on the upper side and thinner toward the edges, so that the middle part was visible above the ground. This would be the rock!

Joseph looked all around to be sure he was alone; then he got down and began removing the dirt, certain that this was the place he had seen in his vision. He was as excited as a miner discovering a vein of precious ore. With the earth removed he could see where to place the lever, and now he worked swiftly. He fixed the lever under the edge of the stone and with a little exertion raised it up. There he beheld the plates, the Urim and Thummim, and the breastplate. With them was a sword and a strange-looking compass. The box where they lay was formed of stone and some kind of cement. In the bottom of the box two stones were laid crossways; on these lay the plates of gold and the other things. Joseph's eyes were shining, and his face was filled with wonder. Eagerly he reached into the cavity to remove the contents, but a shock like that produced by electricity rendered him powerless and caused him to withdraw his arm. Three times he made the attempt with like failure, only each time he reached the shock seemed harder than before. The third time he cried aloud in anguish, "Why can't I take them . . . why?"

A voice by his side replied: "Because you have not kept the commandments of the Lord."

It was the Angel Moroni, and his presence reminded Joseph of the injunction of the night before: "Have no other object in view in getting the plates but to glorify God." He remembered the wild dreams of wealth that had flashed through his mind. He had wanted fame . . . and ease for his family. Humbled, he knelt. Would he ever learn to put God ahead of his own selfish desires?

There was no reproach in the eyes of the angel—only

125

compassion. "Look!" he said. And as he spoke Joseph saw the Prince of Darkness surrounded by an innumerable train of associates. As this vision passed before him the angel said: "All this is shown, the good and the evil, the holy and the impure, the glory of God and the power of darkness, that you may know hereafter the two powers and never be influenced or overcome by that wicked one. Behold, whatever entices and leads to good and to do good is of God; but whatever does not is of that wicked one; it is he that fills the hearts of men with evil to walk in darkness and to blaspheme God; and you may learn from henceforth that his ways are to destruction, but the way of holiness is peace and rest. You now see why you could not obtain this record; that the commandment was strict, and that if ever these sacred things are obtained they must be gotten by prayer and faithfulness in obeying the Lord. They are not deposited here for the sake of accumulating gain and wealth for the glory of this world; they were sealed by the prayer of faith, and because of the knowledge which they contain they are of no worth among the children of men, only for their knowledge. On them is contained the fullness of the gospel of Jesus Christ, as it was given to his people on this land, America, and when it shall be brought forth by the power of God it shall be carried to the Gentiles, of whom many will receive it, and afterward will the seed of Israel be brought into the fold of their Redeemer by obeying it also.

"Those who kept the commandments of the Lord on this land, through the prayer of faith, obtained the promise that if their descendants should transgress and fall away, a record should be kept and in the last days come to their children. These things are sacred and must be kept so, for the promise of the Lord concerning them must be fulfilled. No man can obtain them if his heart is impure, because they contain that which is sacred; and besides, should they be

126

intrusted to unholy hands the knowledge could not come to the world because they cannot be interpreted by the learning of this generation; consequently, they would be considered of no worth, only as precious metal. Therefore, remember that they are to be translated by the gift and power of God. By them will the Lord work a great and marvelous work; the wisdom of the wise shall become as naught, and the understanding of the prudent shall be hid, and because the power of God shall be displayed, those who profess to know the truth but walk in deceit shall tremble with anger; but with signs and wonders, with gifts and healings, with the manifestations of the power of God, and with the Holy Ghost shall the hearts of the faithful be comforted. You have beheld the power of God manifested and the power of Satan; and you see that there is nothing that is desirable in the works of darkness; that they cannot bring happiness; that those who are overcome therewith are miserable, while on the other hand the righteous are blessed with peace in the kingdom of God where joy unspeakable surrounds them.

"I give unto you another sign, and when it comes to pass then know that the Lord is God and that he will fulfill his purposes, and that the knowledge which this record contains will go to every nation and kindred and tongue and people under the whole heaven. This is the sign: When these things begin to be known—that is, when it is known that the Lord has shown you these things—the workers of iniquity will seek your overthrow; they will circulate falsehoods to destroy your reputation, and also will seek to take your life; but remember this, if you are faithful, and shall hereafter continue to keep the commandments of the Lord, you shall be preserved to bring these things forth; for in due time he will again give you a commandment to come and take them. Your name shall be known among the nations, for the work which the Lord will perform by your hands shall cause the

127

righteous to rejoice and the wicked to rage; with one it shall be in honor, and with the other in reproach; yet with these it shall be a terror because of the great and marvelous work which shall follow the coming forth of the fullness of the gospel."

The angel paused. Joseph did not lift his eyes. "Stand up, my son."

Joseph stood, feeling the weight of his unworthiness. The angel's voice was compassionate and his love seemed to fill every fiber of Joseph's being. "Come to this place precisely in one year, and I will meet you here. You must learn to prepare your heart to receive the mysteries of heaven which are to be revealed through you. I will meet you here every year for four years. During these years you must prepare yourself by study and by prayer to receive the plates." Again the angel brought to light all the things that had been told on previous meetings, after which Joseph found himself alone on the hilltop.

After replacing the earth around the rock and being careful to cover the spot in such a way that other eyes would not be curious he went home pondering his strange experiences. Would his father say he had lost his mind, that he had imagined the whole thing? He wouldn't blame him for saying it. But the experience was real. He had seen the plates and talked face-to-face with an angel, not once but many times within a few hours. This was not something he had imagined. It was as real as the air he breathed, and he couldn't deny it even to save his own life. He knew now how Moses must have felt when he saw the burning bush, and like Moses he would do his best to carry out the commands. But was he man enough?

Just before reaching his own lane he stooped and picked four choice wild flowers, two for Lucy and two for Don Carlos.

128

There were times when young Joseph, like little Lucy, was sure he loved Alvin more than anyone. Alvin was wise, gentle, and understanding in almost everything he did. Life had been good to him. Few persons were ill at ease with him, and few envied him, for his interests lay in others. He had a quick mind, and he used it to dig deeply into realms both spiritual and material, but what he learned humbled him, for beyond each new truth there was so much more to discover that he never felt superior to his associates. He was a fine-looking fellow who kept his body clean and his person neat, without giving undue thought to himself; so no one envied him his good looks. He belonged to no church, yet he had an anxious concern for everyone. Young and old came to him to share their joys or to ask advice, and he probably carried as many of the villagers' secrets as did the ministers and those whose duties it was to be their "brothers' keepers."

Perhaps because Alvin approached things he wanted gently, he usually got his way. At any rate Father Joseph almost always came around to his way of thinking, and young Joseph wasn't at all surprised the day they made a down payment on the Everston farm and Alvin began working on plans for the new house.

They were taking on a very large debt, but all members of the family were for it. It meant that Hyrum, Samuel, young Joseph, and perhaps even William would be taking whatever jobs they could obtain in the villages of Manchester and Palmyra, but this was something the older boys were always doing, along with their regular farm work.

It was to young Joseph that Alvin went for help with his plans for the house. Alvin said Joseph had a head for planning, and it was true. He had revamped the barn without spending any money and made it easier for feeding, sheltering, and cleaning. He had enlarged the grain bins to hold an extra supply of wheat, and again he had done it without any outlay of money. Now he and Alvin began working on the intricacies of rooms, for this was to be no ordinary house. It was to be large, airy, solid, and well built without waste. There would be no lumber bought and no carpenters hired until every detail was drawn and accounted for. All their plans were approved by the Smith family before the blueprint was completed, and Mother Lucy had the final say after all suggestions had been made.

Sophronia's interest in the house was almost equal to her attention in cooking Sunday dinners for Cal Stoddard.

"Cal ought to be willing to work on the house without pay for a prize like you, Sophie," Hyrum teased her. And she retorted without even a blush, "Then we'll expect Jerusha Braden here to cook for carpenters. She'll find travel easy with the path you've worn to her door." Both young people wore the same look.

Soon the air was filled with the smell of newly sawed logs and lumber. Then came the hired carpenters and the sound of hammers striking nails. The building had begun.

Calvin and Jerusha did come to help. Also a distant relative of Cal's, an older man by the name of Stoddard, came asking for work. Alvin hired him over Cal's protest, for he was a good carpenter and a fast worker.

Alvin worked side by side with the carpenters and kept close watch on everything. He had never been so happy. "This is what I have always wanted for the folks," he would say to his brothers. "This will be the kind of place they have always deserved."

At the end of each day, when the Smith boys had finished with their jobs in town, long after the hired carpenters had quit Lucy would hear her sons' hammers ringing, and the air would be filled with song. Their voices

130

still blended as beautifully as when they were children singing in a cold barn.

Once Alvin told his brothers: "There is something about Cal's relative that I don't like, but he does his work so well that I have no complaints. Maybe it's because Cal warned me against him, but I have a feeling about him. I have no reason to doubt him, but I don't trust him. I have a strong hunch he is plotting something. I wish I knew what it was."

"Have you told Father?" Hyrum asked.

"No. I have no proof that he is planning trouble."

"Tell him anyway," said Hyrum the practical. But Alvin didn't. He could see no reason to worry his father over a phantom of the mind.

By day and by night Alvin drove himself, until he was so exhausted he could barely push one foot ahead of another. It was at these times, when he was bone-weary and his shoulders ached, that little Lucy was his comfort.

Their attachment for one another had always been strong. He had taught her to call for him when she wanted a drink in the night. She had taken her first step for him. He taught her to love the darkness, the moon, the stars. He gave her an "angel" to protect her. He taught her to love nature and to name the common flowers that grew in yard, field, and woods. She learned the names of birds and animals from pictures he showed her and from observations when she was his out-of-doors shadow. Before she could talk well she would try such difficult words as "rhi-noc-er-ous" or "rho-do-den-dron" for him. All these were more than words, for she knew them from pictures or by sight.

She was very often with him when he went to the village or to a neighbor's, and it was a common sight to see her walking primly along, holding his hand, or hoisted to his shoulders. He was a tall man, and now at two she barely reached his knee, but the bond between them was love that

131

came near to worship. Strangely enough Don Carlos was not jealous. He had a kinship with all the family, even as she did, and his lively imagination was sufficient to make most minutes of every hour an adventure in living. He was glad when she was with Alvin. When she tagged after him, she often spoiled his play.

The day the house was finished Alvin and little Lucy looked it over from bottom to top. It was really a finer house than he had hoped for, and now he lingered in the room that was to be his.

"This is Amby's room," he said.

"Lucy's room and Amby's," Lucy corrected solemnly.

He playfully tweaked one of her braids. "You're going to sleep with Catherine."

"No." Her eyes were merry. "Don Carlos will sleep with Catherine."

A fortnight later the family moved in. Alvin had asked Martin Harris to look over the papers; the deed was safely in the hands of an agent in Canandaigua, and the uneasy feeling Alvin had had at first gradually subsided. As long as they kept up the payments on the house, how could there possibly be anything to worry about? And they would keep up the payments; Alvin and his brothers would see to that.

Perhaps a month went by. Lucy and the girls spent the day polishing furniture, cooking, baking, and making the house as lovely as possible, for tonight the Isaac Stoals, the Martin Harrises and the Newel Knights were coming for an evening of fun and a tour of the house. The evening turned out to be the desired success. Isaac Stoal's two daughters were as lovely as Sophronia now, and the Smith brothers paid them special attention.

Later Hyrum questioned young Joseph about the oldest one, and Joseph replied quite seriously, "I've been teasing those girls for four years; now all at once they are grown up

132

and so am I. Tonight it was as if we had become acquainted for the first time."

Hyrum's look was shrewd. "And suddenly you are shy, awed, and very much alive."

Joseph's face wore a serious expression as he walked out of Hyrum's room. Over his shoulder he said, "They are two fine girls."

As he passed his parents' room the door was ajar, and without meaning to he paused.

Lucy was seated taking down her hair. "Everyone seemed to have a fine time. The meat was tender; the vegetables were cooked the way Sophronia likes to do them; and Catherine's pies were good, but I'd like to muzzle Martin Harris's wife. That woman has a tongue." And she mimicked Mrs. Harris: " 'I declare, Lucy, why do you need such a big house? I thought the old one did you quite well.' "

"It did do us quite well," Father Joseph reminded her with a gentle smile.

"That's not the point." Lucy's voice still held exasperation. "Nothing is ever quite right in her eyes. She'll manage to find fault with heaven if she's lucky enough to get there. And the way she treats Martin in front of everyone is shameful. He's such an understanding, patient man."

Young Joseph grinned as he moved on to his room. All in all the housewarming had been a great success.

The family never seemed to tire of hearing about Joseph and his visions. When winter began settling over the land, after the smaller children were in bed, they would have Joseph talk about his experiences with the supernatural. They all believed what he said. Had not Father Joseph himself had seven dreams, and often Mother Lucy's dreams had special meaning. It was easy for them to accept the visions Joseph had when he was awake. Was not the Bible filled with stories of people who had had such experiences? Then why not Joseph, who was always delving into spiritual things? Joseph, more than any of them, meditated over what he experienced and read, so why would not God use him?

They liked best to hear him tell about seeing the plates, the breastplate, and the Urim and Thummim. Since the angel had instructed him to tell his father, he supposed it was all right to tell the family. This was a grave load to carry alone, and it helped for them to know. He made it very clear to them that the secret must be kept, and he trusted them to keep it.

To Alvin, especially, getting the plates seemed a very serious business. Joseph often talked with him when the two of them were alone.

"How can I be sure I am keeping the commandments, Alvin? Goodness is instinctive with you. You should be the one to do this work. You seldom have a selfish thought. Your tongue is never on fire with hate or anger. You see the best in people. I see them as they are. To you all men are good; to me they are human and as imperfect as I am."

"In order to protect the plates you need to see men exactly as they are, Joseph. I know the truth about men too. By nature you are strong. I compromise. It seems better for me to picture a man the way he ought to be. Stop seeing me without faults. I have them, but when folks come to me for counsel, I try to see both what man is and what he may become."

"Sometimes I'm afraid when I think of what it will be like when I get the plates, if word gets out that I have them. I think of the danger. Is that cowardly?"

"I expect your life will be in danger many times. But knowing you, I'm confident you'll get the job done. I'd like
134

to be called to some great work and to feel that I am chosen."

Their conversations took many a turn, and each time Joseph saw things more clearly. It was almost as if Alvin were endowed with a power to point the way. Once Joseph said, "I don't know why, but I feel that in some way you are called to this work along with me." And he wondered if it were possible to love anyone more than he loved Alvin.

It was September 22. Father Smith and his sons were in the field again, but young Joseph was not with them. An hour ago he had quietly laid down his sickle and, without saying a word, they had watched him leave the field. Nobody questioned where he was going, but their eyes held a quiet glow and their hearts beat a little faster, for in their minds they were following Joseph up the hill that led to the spot where the plates were buried. Would the angel be there to meet him? What would Joseph have to tell this time? If only they could follow him, perhaps they would see and hear! At least they might see the light! But they worked on without voicing their feelings.

After a long time they saw Joseph returning. As he drew near they could tell that he had seen the angel. Some of the glow was still in his face, and his eyes were deep wells of thought. He joined the others in their work, but his mind was far away. Later they would hear from his lips what had taken place. Four years the angel had said. It would be four years before Joseph would bring the plates home. One year had gone. Three years more . . . what changes would three years bring?

It had snowed most of the day November 20 with flakes as large as popcorn, and the whole earth was beautifully white like a winter fairyland. Then suddenly, without any warning, the temperature dropped, the wind came in great gusts, and drifts began forming quickly.

The livestock, all but one cow, had been put in shelter early. Somewhere alone in that wild storm this cow was probably giving birth to a calf, and like as not they would both perish in the storm. This cow, aside from being their most valuable one, was the favorite of all the Smiths, for she was the offspring of Bess. Now grown and ready to give life to her own kind, she had been the wobbly calf Bess had sought when she had taken shots meant for young Joseph.

Alvin, Hyrum, young Joseph, and Samuel, equipped with lanterns, blankets, the means to build a fire, and what Alvin called his doctor's kit, were out on horses scouring woods, meadows, and hills. They were booted and dressed warmly, but even so, the wind stung their faces and chilled them, while snow half blinded them. The cow must be found before night settled.

Where would a cow go to seek shelter in a wild storm? They covered all the familiar places, and once Hyrum's voice shouted above the wind, "We'd better go home. We'll lose our bearings and we can't see with wind and snow fighting us at every turn." But they kept on riding and listening. Once they thought they heard a cow bawling, but going to the place where the sound came from they found nothing but wind whistling through swaying trees.

Minutes moved woodenly. Snow settled on them until they looked like snowmen riding white horses. To talk meant to shout, so for the most part they moved silently and miserably, eyes searching white surroundings, ears tuned for the sound of a cow's bawling.

They were almost ready to give up and turn back when they did hear a cow bawling, and they knew by the sound of it that in spite of wild weather, nature was having her way. The miracle of new life was taking place.

The Smith boys had often witnessed and assisted animals in bringing forth their young, but never in a blizzard.

The place the cow lay was partly sheltered by a hill that cut the wind but didn't keep out the snow. She had been in labor for some time, this Alvin's practiced eye saw at once, and she was covered with snow.

The boys worked quickly, freeing her from snow and covering her with blankets which they weighted down with stones to keep the wind from blowing them away.

Alvin worked with the cow, the others went into a ravine not far away, where the cow had probably tried to make it to shelter, and brought back stones. Trip after trip they made, until they had a small shelter where they could build a fire that the storm would not put out.

They unstrapped the tarps of firewood they had brought with them, and soon the red flames were warming away a chill that had seemed to penetrate the very marrow of their bones.

Minutes seemed like hours. Once Alvin said, "The calf's head is too big. I'm going to make an incision." Nobody asked, "Can you do that?" They knew he could. It was something they had seen him do before, to prevent the tearing of delicate flesh. Usually animals gave birth with ease, and seldom was this necessary, but Alvin knew what he was about.

Joseph brought the kit, and Alvin selected his instrument, holding the precision blade to the fire until it was sterile. The freezing weather cooled it quickly. With hands unmittened, he began working now, his fingers deft as any doctor's. He knew where the cut should be, and he made it well. Then, before their eyes, the calf's head appeared and the miracle of birth took place. They heard the sound of new life, and the calf stood on wobbly legs. Hyrum snatched up one of the blankets and covered the wet new body. "Bess is now a grandmother," young Joseph said softly.

Alvin sutured the incision. He had a way with animals, and the cow seemed to sense that it was a necessary procedure. The boys put out the fire. Alvin retied the equipment to his saddle and mounted his horse. They lifted the calf up to him. With the calf partly in his arms and partly on the saddle, he headed homeward. The cow, looking very strange under the blankets the boys had fastened around her, followed without protest, for Alvin was carrying her calf, still wrapped in a blanket.

With saddles lighter, minus blankets and wood, the Smith boys rode homeward, lighthearted in the midst of storm. Their mission had been accomplished.

With horses, cow, and calf all housed against the storm, the brothers thawed themselves by a roaring fire and talked over the day's happenings. Alvin, however, was strangely silent. Young Joseph, quick to observe, said he looked pale and asked if he felt all right.

"I could use a featherbed and a round of sleep," Alvin said.

Mother Lucy brought plates of steaming stew to the fire, and all the boys but Alvin ate hungrily. She stood holding the full plate and eyed him anxiously. "What is it, Alvin?"

"I don't know. Tired, I guess."

"Do you hurt anywhere?"

"I didn't intend to mention it, but my stomach has been upset all day."

138

"You're hungry," Father Joseph said. "You're bound to be. Make him eat. What he needs is something to warm his insides."

"I'd rather not," Alvin said. "If it's all right I'll just go up to bed."

"But you didn't eat much lunch," Hyrum said. "You should be starved like the rest of us."

Lucy's eyes looked so troubled that Alvin reached for the well-filled plate. "I can't fight all of you," he said with a rueful grin. "But I'll tell you in all seriousness, eating is not the thing I should be doing."

The plate was at last emptied, and Lucy took it to Sophronia to wash; then she came back for Alvin's good-night kiss. "Feel better?"

He gave her a small, crooked smile. "I feel as if I were all stomach." He kissed her and waved his hand to the others.

They watched him go up the stairs, and young Joseph said softly, "He won't spare himself. He's had a rough day."

"He'll be all right after a night in bed," Hyrum said, yawning. "I could use some sleep myself. Let's all go to bed."

Nobody was worried about Alvin. It was as young Joseph had said—he had had a hard day.

Father Joseph banked the fire, then he and Lucy followed their sons upstairs. A little later they looked in on the sleepers to make sure they were covered. Alvin was sleeping. They passed the stand in the hall and blew out the candle, said their prayers kneeling beside their bed, and soon they too were sleeping.

Sometime during the night Lucy heard low moans coming from Alvin's room. She hurried toward the sound and found Alvin bent double with pain. It was an alarming sight, for he was almost never sick.

She tried hot bricks to warm his abdomen, and when sweating didn't help she tried cold packs.

The family awakened one by one and gathered around his bed. Whatever ailed Alvin wasn't caused by tiredness or storm. This was something different.

He tried to make them all go back to bed. He would fight the thing through himself, he said with his gentle smile. But they all stayed. Minutes went by, then an hour. Alvin was very sick indeed.

Outside the storm raged; inside they watched Lucy try her remedies and did what they could to assist her.

Then Father Joseph left Alvin's room and came back fully dressed, bundled in warm clothing. He was carrying a lighted lantern. "I'm going for a doctor."

"I'll go for you, Father," young Joseph said. "This is no night for you to be out."

"I'll go," Hyrum said.

"Don't anybody go . . . please!" Alvin's words came through pain-pressed lips.

But Father Joseph was gone, his boots making a clumping sound as he went down the stairs. Before dawn he returned with a doctor but not their regular one, who was out of town.

The doctor made his examination without too much concern. He gave Alvin calomel and a depressant that was supposed to make him sleep. This sort of thing was not uncommon. He had probably eaten some tainted food, and if that were it the calomel would have him up as soon as it had time to act.

The doctor's casualness made their fears seem groundless. While it was still dark young Joseph, Hyrum, and Samuel went to do the chores. They divided Alvin's work among them and raced to see who would finish first. It had stopped snowing, but the wind tore at them and sent snow blowing everywhere. In places the drifts were shoulder high. They finished feeding the stock and did the milking with stiff, blue

140

hands. Their numb faces were windburned, and they laughed at Samuel trying to whistle with lips too stiff to pucker.

Young Joseph wondered if their apparent lighthearted-ness was a mask to hide their real feelings, for he was filled with apprehension. It was a feeling he couldn't explain—a kind of sixth sense. Mother Lucy sometimes got such feelings before some trial. But young Joseph had had them when nothing came of it, so now he tried to shrug off the foreboding. The doctor said it wasn't serious, and he should know.

By the time the chores were finished, Sophronia was ringing the breakfast bell. She and Catherine had cooked a breakfast of smoked pig and grits, but the only ones who seemed to eat it with relish were the smaller children and the doctor. Lucy was with Alvin and didn't come downstairs at all. Father Joseph sat with the doctor, but ate very little. And although young Joseph knew the food had been carefully prepared and was excellent, he couldn't seem to swallow over the dread that persisted.

The doctor left shortly after breakfast. He seemed confident that Alvin would be fine in no time at all.

But Alvin was not fine. He did sleep well into the forenoon, then pain with all its fury awakened him.

This time Hyrum saddled up and went for the doctor. Young Joseph would have welcomed the trip. The activity of fighting cold and drifts would have been relief for his tension, but Hyrum needed action as much as he. Young Joseph loaned him a muffler and watched him go, then he went to do what he could for Alvin.

Lucy welcomed Joseph's help. His hands were strong and gentle, wringing out cold cloths and applying them to Alvin's abdomen. Worry hung like a weight on Lucy too. Joseph understood this as he understood Alvin's suffering.

He knew so well what pain was like. Odd how Alvin's

141

suffering brought to mind those days when he had been almost out of his mind with pain. The thought kept occurring, what would small Lucy do if Alvin died? What would any of them do? Alvin was the dependable one. He kept their secrets, guarded their confidences, shared their problems, advised, loved, defended, and understood them. Why should such a one have to endure pain?

For three days Alvin suffered. He was examined by three different doctors, two from Manchester and a specialist from Palmyra. The doctor Lucy preferred was still in another part of the country, but these were good doctors. They did what they could, but there was no improvement. The specialist said he must be moved to a sanitarium where they could make tests, as soon as arrangements could be made for his admittance, which would be sometime during the late afternoon. He administered more of the depressant and left.

It might have been two hours after the physician had gone that Alvin awakened. His eyes were too bright, but the pain seemed gone, and he appeared to be entirely himself. Young Joseph was the only one with him at the time, and Alvin asked, "May I have a drink of water?"

Joseph had been half dozing while Alvin slept. Now he sprang up, overjoyed at the sound of the calm voice. "I guess we can afford to indulge you," he said jestingly. Then he noticed the over-bright eyes, the flushed face, and his heart caught. Alvin was very sick indeed.

The hand that reached for the water Joseph brought was far too hot. Alvin drained the cup. "I'm concerned about your future work, Joseph. Don't let temptation or persecution or the cares of this world keep you from accomplishing your divine mission." In his earnestness he raised himself to a sitting position, and Joseph gently pushed him back onto the pillow.

"Don't talk," he said. "Don't worry about anything."

142

But Alvin was up again, leaning on his elbow. "When things seem bad, Joseph, and they will, you must know that the One who watches over all of us will be protecting you."

Sick with apprehension, Joseph took the cup and went out to warn the family of Alvin's condition. They all wanted to go to him, but Father Joseph, fearful that so many coming all at once would upset him, suggested that they go to him one at a time, all except Lucy, who should go and remain. But when Lucy went in he asked for young Joseph. Joseph came praying, "God, don't let him die." Alvin was talking to Lucy in low tones, but Joseph in his anguish wasn't listening. When he looked again, Lucy's eyes seemed to be drinking in every detail of Alvin, as if she would memorize his image with a drawing so defined that time could never erase it. *She knows. Alvin knows.* Joseph's eyes were swimming. He is too young to die. He has only begun to live!

Hyrum came in and Joseph stepped to the wall, giving him room to come to the bed. Hyrum's eyes filled, and Alvin said lightly, "Cut that out . . . we've got things to talk over. I saw the gentleman in Canandaigua about our payments on the house. We are to make the final payment in three years, after the crops are sold. He extended our time a year, but it would be wise to see him as soon as this cold spell clears, and have his promise put in writing, because the papers we hold now don't give this extension of time."

"I'll remember," Hyrum told him huskily. "This is a dandy house we've built."

"It's a fine house," Alvin said proudly. "We've planned this house on good land for the folks to grow old in. Even Don Carlos wore skinned knuckles learning to drive a nail."

To every member of the family Alvin had something affectionate to say, and they left him, smiling through tears. Last of all Father came in with little Lucy. Her eyes spied

143

him, and with one bound she was on the bed and in his arms. Mother Lucy's hand reached to restrain her, but Alvin said; "Let her be."

"Amby . . . Amby!" Her voice was a caress as her small hands patted his chest and moved to gently touch his cheeks.

"You are Amby's favorite sweetheart." The love in the faces of these two was beautiful to see. He looked at his father, his warm eyes saying a tender good-bye, then with his lips against little Lucy's hair, he died. Without any change or noticeable pain, he died as quietly as if he had only dropped off to sleep.

There could never be greater sadness than that which filled the people in Alvin's room. It was difficult for them to realize that never again would they hear his voice, his laughter, never again feel his touch, or see him walking beside them. A hint of a smile was on his lips, as if in this farewell adventure he had glimpsed some joyous new experience. Father Joseph came to the bed and tried to take small Lucy from Alvin's arms, but she clung to him fiercely. For a moment he stood with stricken face, looking down at his son. Deep suffering and great love were shining through his tears. Then gently he forced little Lucy away. The child fought him, her reaching arms, her whole body begging Alvin to take her again, while she cried his name, "Amby . . . Amby."

Alone in his room young Joseph sat at his window looking out at the winter scene. He had fought back his tears in front of the others, but now with no one to see, he let them fall silently and unrestrained. The Smith household would never be the same with Alvin gone. He had loved the earth, every person and creature in it. Every blade of grass, every bud had held special meaning for him. The white snow

144

and Alvin had the same kind of purity. Why had he died when his kind of goodness blessed everyone?

For a long time Joseph stayed in his room. Sometimes he walked, his nails biting into clenched fists, while his soul probed the mysteries of death, searching for an answer to his loss. Time seemed to stand still. It seemed to Joseph that all motion, all living things should stop. Birth he understood, but not death.

The wind moaned through the stark trees outside his window. Covered with snow they looked dead, but they were living trees that would leaf in their season. They were as alive as the angel who came each September for a day to instruct him concerning things of the kingdom. Men would not believe that he actually talked face-to-face with the angel, yet their disbelief did not alter truth; he did see—he did converse—he did know there were kingdoms not of this earth.

Joseph knelt at the window, his eyes on the snow. The sun shining on it made it glow with dazzling brightness. Somewhere Alvin lived! Birth was a lifetime span on earth, and death was change. The putting away of an earthly body was the same as a Nautilus changing an old house for a new. "Alvin . . . " Joseph whispered, "wherever you are, God keep you!"

For a long time he sat alone with his thoughts, then he arose. A box must be made to hold Alvin's beloved body. Friends would be coming soon. The house would be overflowing, for no man had more friends than Alvin.

Winter continued cold and bitter. The new grave was covered with snow that did not melt for weeks on end. Then came the spring, and as new life awakened in earth and fields new hope was born in the hearts of the Smiths.

Alvin was thought about often and lovingly, for his face came to mind in all the familiar things that he had loved. Now he filled their hearts, not achingly but joyously. When they plucked the first blossoms of spring his eyes too seemed to catch the perfection and colors of the blooms, and he shared with them the delicate and varied fragrances. As they plowed earth and planted seeds his approving eyes were with them. They could speak his name now, loving what he had loved, seeing through his eyes new sights and sounds and an enlargement of soul because of him. His face seemed to appear to them through people too—a fleeting expression, a sudden smile, a certain bend to a shoulder—but this was not sadness; this was the expression of one they loved and held dear. Alvin was a part of them, and he would remain a part of them, constant as the sun and air that surrounded them.

Hyrum made his trip to Canandaigua, as he had promised Alvin that he would do, but the agent was away at the time. Later Father Joseph went. This time too the agent was out. The family supposed new papers had been signed but what actually took place was a verbal renewing of the contract with one who seemed to have authority, and Father Joseph returned to his family, assured in his mind that the farm was safe, for the acting agent's reputation was beyond reproach. Father Joseph's good friend Martin Harris had pronounced him trustworthy, and Father had a deep and abiding respect for Martin. He considered him smarter than most men, an industrious, rich man who walked humbly, accepting life's bounties gratefully. Martin, never boastful, was always willing to share what he had with a friend. If the Smiths were critical of him at all, it was in the way he overindulged his wife. Lucy often remarked with a toss of her head, "That woman can wheedle anything out of Martin, and the poor soul never seems to be aware that she has taken him in. He is blind where she is concerned, and she treats him like dirt, using her tongue with fire in it to gain the last word."

"It's a smart man who can hold his tongue under fire," Father Joseph reminded her with gentle good humor. He knew that deep down Lucy was a little jealous of Mrs. Harris—her fine clothes and the proud way she wore them, her shining black surrey with the matched team that was her own to drive wherever she chose to go, her fine house, and the hired help. Lucy was happy and content with her own house, but Mrs. Harris had a way of making the Smith possessions seem insignificant, and Lucy was never quite at ease with her.

The Smiths were careful to make each house payment as it came due. In order to do this Hyrum continued working in town, and after the crops were in young Joseph and his brothers went looking for town jobs, but work was scarce and rumors concerning Joseph were ripe in Manchester and Palmyra, for since his first vision in the grove ministers had been using him as their whipping boy. Most preached eternal burning for all souls who died outside the church. Most preached two places where souls went after death—heaven or hell. They had the Bible and claimed the canon of scriptures closed. There was no need for continued revelation, and as for supernatural visitations, these were of the devil and would damn a soul.

Little by little rumor began floating that Joseph walked and talked with angels. Perhaps Father Joseph, always open and unused to hiding truth, had told someone, but tales caught and people were saying, "Whoever heard of conversing face-to-face with angels in our day! And why should it happen to someone not in the ministry?" If this marvel were to happen at all, it would be to some learned scholar of the cloth who had made a lifetime study of the scriptures. And why should it happen at all, when the Bible contains everything needed for saving souls? If Joseph had come face-to-face with the supernatural, then he was as possessed as the witches of former days. If a devil lived in his body then death might be the only way to rid him of the evil spirit. And so as always, since his first vision in the grove, Joseph was faced with prejudice and hostility in his search for work. But he was determined to help with the payments on the new house and the land that meant so much to Alvin.

"I'll find something to do," he told himself doggedly, "even if it is no more than splitting rails that Samuel and William can sell to the villagers." And this he did until his muscles became like iron bands. He was indeed a striking figure. Odd that such a handsome young man with such calm and thoughtful blue eyes could be a living devil.

On November 2, 1826, Hyrum and Jerusha were married in Jerusha's home in Manchester. It was a simple wedding, but heaven seemed to surround them both as they were pronounced husband and wife.

Sophronia and Calvin were holding hands during the ceremony and dreaming of such a time in their lives but their hands were carefully concealed under Sophronia's muff.

As young Joseph took his leave after the reception he teased Jerusha about giving up the distinguished name of Braden for a common one like Smith.

"Hyrum isn't common," she retorted with a song in her voice, and Hyrum certainly didn't appear common as he looked on her with adoring eyes.

They moved to a small farm and a three-room cabin not far from the Smiths, and Hyrum didn't seem to mind at all leaving the family nest to make a new one of his own.

148

One warm summer day when other members of the family were busy with their various pursuits, Mother Lucy saw an old friend, Isaac Stoal, drive up in his light spring wagon drawn by a team of sorrel mares. She hadn't seen Isaac since Hyrum's wedding day, and she hurried to make him welcome and to ask about his daughters. After seating him in the parlor she went to the sawdust house and brought cool buttermilk in a pitcher. On her way back she asked Sophronia to fill a plate with some of the cookies Catherine had baked that morning.

While Isaac was enjoying the milk and cookies he told Lucy he had come to see if young Joseph would accompany him to Harmony, Pennsylvania, where he hoped to find a lost silver mine that was supposed to contain great riches.

"I especially want Joseph because he can discern things invisible to the natural eye," Isaac told her.

"You are wrong about that," Lucy said gravely. "Joseph has no greater powers of discernment than any other man. He'll give you a full day's work for his pay, and that is all he can do for you."

Isaac's smile told her very plainly that he was unconvinced, and she said with a certain urgency, "He can do nothing miraculous."

Isaac showed her the document that was supposed to hold a key to the buried treasure, then he asked where he could find young Joseph.

Lucy gave him time to finish his refreshment, then she put on her homespun bonnet, poured the remainder of the buttermilk into a tin pail, and walked with Isaac through the woods to where Joseph was felling trees and digging out stumps to make more farmland. He welcomed the cool drink, and she left them immediately to return to the house.

Joseph was happy to see his friend. He drank the buttermilk while they talked; then they both sat together on a log while he looked at the old document Isaac had thrust into his hands. He was giving his full mind to studying the map. The thought of silver deposits buried in the earth and waiting to be discovered excited him at first, but when Isaac told him fabulous sums had been coined and were just waiting for someone to remove it, Joseph was suddenly skeptical and said so.

"It's there," Isaac told him stubbornly. "I know it is. You've had visions and dreams a-plenty, and you'll be able to point the spot as easily as a man finds water with a divining rod."

Joseph shook his head. "All I can offer you in the way of help will be a strong back and willing hands. I have no supernatural powers. If you want my honest opinion I think the whole trip will waste your time and money, especially since you say you plan to hire other young men too. You will probably end up disappointed and disgusted."

"I've always liked you, Joseph. I reckon half the tales abroad about you are lies. Will you come?"

Joseph gave Isaac one of his rare smiles. "You're offering me adventure and a chance to get away from Manchester. I'll go with you for two months. If we find something, I'll stay on. If we don't, I think two months is long enough for you to be throwing money my way."

"We'll be boarding with a family named Hale," Isaac told him. "They have eight children, mostly grown. They're nice folks. Old man Hale's reputation around Harmony is better than most. He's got a fine farm, and he knows how to run it."

Joseph was only half listening. It would be good to be looked upon with friendly eyes and judged by his own merits. Isaac was a real friend and would present him in a proper light. He was taking other young men who were strangers to Joseph; these too could become his friends. Joseph's eyes took on a kind of shine. It wasn't that he would ever deny the work that he had been called to do, but he wanted desperately to be liked. Perhaps in Harmony he could be a plain son of the soil. Perhaps for a time no one would shun him or say that a devil possessed his soul.

"When do we leave?" he asked.

"As soon as I can choose my men."

"I'll be ready," Joseph said.

Stoal's men were on horseback, and he was driving his sorrel mares hitched to an overloaded wagon that contained camping and digging equipment, enough food to feed his men for several days, and personal luggage for each man. When he became tired of driving he would change places with one of the young men on horseback. They were averaging about three miles an hour.

The slow gait was especially enjoyable to young Joseph. His horse was his own, and a fast one, but the wooded land through which they were traveling was unusually beautiful. Pennsylvania was filled with mountains and plateaus. Joseph knew some of its history. William Penn had founded the state. He had sent a band of Quakers to America in 1661 and he had come himself in 1662. Joseph felt a certain kinship with Penn, for the man had been expelled from Oxford University in England because of his religious beliefs.

Penn's father, a wealthy English admiral, had loaned the King of England vast sums of money, then he had died before the debt was paid. To square things, the king had given William thousands of acres of land in America, and Penn set about founding a colony on the land. Because the people here could make their own laws and govern themselves they named it the land of brotherly love. Perhaps there would be less religious prejudice among Pennsylvanians where Dutch, Swedes, Finns, Germans, Scotch-Irish, and English dwelt together in apparent peace. It was something to hope for anyway.

By the time they reached Harmony Joseph felt at home with the "boys," and they liked him. He found himself laughing over their witty remarks, and they appreciated his own ready humor. Isaac Stoal was pleased at how well his boys got on together. Once he spoke about it to Joseph. "It proves I know how to pick my hands," he said. There seemed to be no discord among them even when everyone became bone-tired from traveling.

They were on the turnpike that led to Harmony now, and the road was becoming more crowded. There were riders on horseback, carts driven by oxen or horses, buggies, surries, homemade conveyances, and wagons. This was the road used by travelers going both east and west. Pittsburgh was the great manufacturing center, and it would continue to grow, for it was positioned where the Allegheny and Monongahela rivers joined to form the Ohio River.

"First fertile fields we come to on your left will be the start of Isaac Hale's land," Mr. Stoal told them.

"Another Isaac," Joseph teased him. "How do you suppose we can put up with another Isaac?"

"You'd best ask if he can put up with you."

It was plain to see that Isaac Hale was a prosperous farmer. His fertile acres showed great care in planting that would insure an abundant harvest. As they came nearer to the house they saw plump cows feeding in lush pastures. The

152

outbuildings were numerous, well built, and well cared for, and the fine house of stone and clay made the Smith house look small and plain by comparison.

Isaac Hale was as English as William Penn, a proud man who let it be known—after only a short conversation—that his progenitors were fearless men who had given their minds and brawn for the betterment of Kent as far back as the 1300's. However, in spite of his claim to English ancestors, his accent was as American as the Pennsylvania soil upon which he dwelt.

It was Isaac's sons Jesse, David, and Alva who unhitched the wagon and who, as soon as the saddles were removed from the horses, gave them feed and water before turning them into a nearby corral. It was Isaac Hale himself who showed them the well where they could refresh themselves, then led the way to the bunkhouse, pointing out which beds would be theirs to sleep on. He left after explaining that he would send his youngest son, Isaac Ward, to awaken them in plenty of time for their first evening meal.

Joseph was weary from traveling, but now as he lay on the bed that had been assigned to him his mind raced from one thought to another. No matter how tired he was, he had never found daytime sleeping an easy thing to do.

This Mr. Hale was no ordinary man. He was without doubt a person of influence in Harmony. It was in his bearing and in his way of speaking. Isaac Stoal had said the man was nearing sixty, but he appeared much younger. His movements were quick and graceful, his manner congenial and dignified. His sons respected him. Joseph placed the three older boys as somewhere near his own age, but he had an idea they would obey Isaac Hale as long as they remained under his roof. Yet the man was probably kind and fair. He had a good face with strong, rather handsome features.

From where Joseph lay he watched a lady come out of

the house. This would be Mrs. Hale; she carried her head high and was an imposing figure. She walked with such a queenly air that he knew he would be shy in her presence. She was carrying a bell which she now rang with a clear, mellow sound, and the young boy Joseph had seen when they rode into the yard came out of the barn and joined her. She sent him to the pump to wash his hands and then to the corncrib; when he came back with a bucket of corn he immediately set to work at the grinding mortar. She watched him work for a moment, then catching the full skirt of her dress in her hands with a graceful gesture she walked briskly into the house.

Joseph wondered sleepily what the young ladies were like. Isaac Stoal had said there were two. They would undoubtedly be unapproachable. He thought of Sophronia and Catherine with their calloused hands. Callouses would never mark the hands of the Hale girls. Not that he thought women's hands should be calloused. Perhaps someday their lot would be easier, and if he married he would do all in his power to lighten his wife's burdens. He hoped there would be the comradeship that his father and mother had—a close, intimate togetherness. For a fleeting moment he thought of Isaac Stoal's daughters; they were two nice girls. His mind moved sleepily. He liked them both, but if he married one of them he wasn't sure which one it would be. He turned his saddle-sore body into a more comfortable position and slept.

Six days went by. The diggers thought they had located the site marked on the map, but after careful digging they found nothing. Isaac Stoal, positive that the treasure was somewhere near, insisted that the work be continued. After assigning each of his crew a portion of digging ground he shouldered a fork and shovel and went to work at his own chosen spot. Unlike most employers he gave his men a break

154

in the middle of the day. They could lie in the shade or choose their own pastime for an hour, after they had eaten the lunch each one carried in his knapsack.

Joseph's muscles were hard and his body strong and supple from felling trees, digging stumps, splitting rails, and farming. He was tanned to a golden brown, and he did not know as he bent to his work that he made a handsome picture as the firm earth broke into clods at his feet. He decided that it was shrewd of Mr. Hale to allow Isaac Stoal to dig. This ground, that had never been worked, would be well plowed by the time Mr. Stoal had satisfied himself that his buried treasure was a myth.

The Hales were fine people—different, but he liked them. The sons were friendly, hard-working young men, quick to smile, and alive to everything going on around them. Mrs. Hale served the Stoal men their food in a room separated from the Hales' regular living quarters, but last night her sons had joined the diggers for supper, and their merry antics and light conversation had added zest to a carefully prepared, delicious meal. Joseph had not glimpsed the young ladies Mr. Stoal had said were part of the Hale household. Perhaps they were purposely being kept out of sight. If it were Sophronia and Catherine, he would want to be certain of the half dozen strange young men before introductions were forthcoming.

As Joseph's shovel moved in rhythm the sun became hotter, and insects flew out of the dry, unbroken top grass as if protesting his intrusion. He was sweating. Now and then he felt the sting of gnats through his thin, damp shirt. He drank often from the canvas water bag that was flung on the ground at his feet, or he would stop and wipe moisture from his face with a piece of homespun cloth that had once been a part of Sophronia's petticoat. He liked being in this virgin country, but the digging seemed such a waste of time.

155

Far away, like a distant speck, he could see the wooded area where yesterday he had spied a little cabin. He had ridden quite close to it yesterday morning. He was certain no one lived there, but it nestled in among a forest of pine, hemlock, and beech trees. Not too far from the cabin was a well with a dipper hanging invitingly from a chain. There was a good road leading to it from Hale's main house.

Now, with the sun pointing to midday, he decided to ride over there and eat his lunch on the way. If he found it truly abandoned, perhaps the Hales would allow him to sit on the stoop in the twilight sometimes, where he could be alone with his thoughts.

His horse was tied loosely in the shade of some trees where she could graze. He tightened the saddle girth that he had loosened that morning, gave her a drink by pouring some of the water from the canvas bag into a bucket that was tied to the saddle for that purpose, then mounted and set off in the direction of the cabin.

The cabin looked abandoned, but the forest surrounding it was breathtakingly lovely. The shaded coolness was a welcome relief after his strenuous morning in the hot sun. The trees were tall and their touching fronds stirred by a gentle wind.

He dismounted and tied his horse. As he walked toward the cabin he saw that the stoop was overgrown with ferns, grass, and dead boughs. Spiders had spun webs of intricate patterns across the front door and windows. He put his face to a window and peered in. The little house was furnished almost as if the occupant had taken a walk and would return soon. The furnishings were simple, home-constructed pieces—a table, some chairs, a fireplace with an earthen pot hanging in it. The house was built well as if skilled hands had constructed it to last down through the years.

Joseph walked to the well and lowered the wooden

bucket that was fastened to the end with a strong chain. If the water were cool and sweet, he would have a drink and fill his canvas bag; then he would return to his work, for he felt like an intruder on private property.

He cranked the wheel that lowered and raised the bucket. The water that came up was sparkling clear. He rinsed the dipper which hung by the well on a chain and drank thirstily. How cold and good the water was. He poured what remained in the wooden bucket into the horse's pail, giving Dancer a pat or two while she drank. In a tree above him a bluejay scolded while two squirrels eyed him curiously.

"All right," Joseph said with laughter in his blue eyes. "This is your special ground, and I'm leaving." He fastened the pail and water bag to the saddle, mounted, and had ridden to the edge of the road when suddenly he stopped, pulling Dancer back under the shade of a tree to wait.

Two horsewomen were coming toward him, riding sidesaddle at great speed. As they came nearer he saw that they were young. Their hair, which had been pinned up in the fashion of the day, was partly down now and flying in the wind—a beautiful sight! Their faces were flushed and merry, and they sat their horses with the ease of riders who had been in a saddle almost from birth. Arriving at the entrance leading to the cabin they made the turn and stopped by the old well where they dismounted, both laughing and both claiming to be the winner. They had seen Joseph watching the race, and he—unable to ride off—remained riveted to the spot, his face aglow with admiration. One of the young women beckoned to him, and he rode to where they stood.

"You saw the race," she said. "Who won?"

Joseph gave them one of his slow, deliberate smiles. These were the Hale girls, he was sure of it, and in all his life he had never seen two lovelier young ladies. They seemed

157

entirely unaware of their tousled appearance which made them even more attractive. Their eyes held his. They were interested in only one thing—which had won the race. The decision must be Joseph's.

Joseph dismounted, thoroughly enjoying the situation. In his eyes was a twinkle. "If I am to judge this contest," he said with mock seriousness, "it will be necessary for me to measure the noses of those two fine horses. If the noses measure the same, I'd say—fair and square—the winners are tied, and the purse should be equally divided between you."

He studied the noses of the horses gravely, then stooping he found two pebbles of equal size. With pretended seriousness he placed one in the hand of each girl, but as his fingers touched the hand of the second girl his heart reacted strangely. Their eyes met, held, locked. He saw a slow flush creep into her face. Could she guess how his heart was pounding?

"I'm Emma Hale," she said to hide her confusion, "and this is my sister Phoebe."

His voice held a strange tenderness as he said, "I'm Joseph Smith. I work for Isaac Stoal and board at your house."

"Then we will see you again." Her composure had returned now, and with it came his.

"I've never seen two better riders," he said, suddenly serious. "Someday, with a thousand yards headstart, I'd like a chance to race you."

"Perhaps tomorrow night?" Emma showed a dimpled cheek.

He wanted to say, "I'll be counting the hours," but the words came out a simple, "Thank you."

In that first searching glance by the old well they had become friends. After that they saw each other daily, sometimes only for short conversations but usually for walks and rides. Often they walked the horses at a slow gait while they talked. Occasionally they were out until long after the moon had risen in the sky. Joseph had never felt about any other girl the way he felt about Emma, and she had shown, by preferring him, that he was special to her. It was her mind even more than her beauty that held him. She was a woman of positive opinions without being arrogant. She was fair and honest, sensitive and gentle. Together their minds seemed to grasp fundamental truths. All his life he had been one to ponder, to delve, to go off by himself to think things through. Now he discovered that Emma did the same. About some things she made up her mind quickly, as he did. About other things she questioned and prayed for answers, as he did.

Alone, digging in the hot sun, he thought about her constantly. She was so lovely with her beautifully modeled cheekbones, her soft brown hair, and brown eyes that could express every emotion. Now that he had found her, what would life be without her? Yet over and over he asked himself if it would be fair to expect her to walk with him down the unpopular road he must travel, perhaps even into danger. And would the Hales permit her to marry him even if they understood that it was God's business that he had been called to do? They liked him, and of late he was often invited to sit with them at the family table. He was not completely at ease in the presence of Emma's mother, but her brothers accepted him as one of them. Phoebe—or Bea, as the family called her—was married and lived in Colesville. She had been home for only a short visit, but she knew the Knights—they were friends; this knowledge alone made her special to Joseph.

And so he worried and wondered how it would be when they knew of his visions and the work he had been called to do, and they would have to know soon, for time was growing short. He had already overstayed the digging time that he had promised Mr. Stoal, and he was sure his friend was about ready to abandon the treasure hunt as a lost cause. When this happened Joseph would be returning to Manchester, and he could not bear the thought of going without putting his love for Emma into words.

From Emma he had learned a great deal about the Hales and could understand why they were a proud family. Isaac Hale's ancestors had settled in Concord, Massachusetts, in 1635, and their descendants had gone to Connecticut and Vermont. Reuben, Isaac's father, had fought in the French and Indian War and the War of the Revolution. In 1770 Isaac himself had marched with Ebenezer Allen to Castleton, New York. If he hadn't, Emma had said with a teasing light in her eyes, "Canada would have taken the whole Mohawk Valley."

From his grandparents, Reuben and Phoebe Hale, Isaac had inherited land in Vermont. On September 20, 1790, he had married Elizabeth Lewis, first child of Esther Tuttle Lewis and Nathaniel Lewis, a Methodist minister. Nathaniel too had fought in the French and Indian and Revolutionary wars, and in 1780 he had started the first Methodist church in Wells, Vermont, holding meetings in his living room. It was in the same living room ten years later that Elizabeth and Isaac were married. Almost immediately afterward Isaac had brought his bride and her brother Nathaniel and his wife Sarah to Harmony, then called Willingborough. They had come by ox team over two hundred and twenty miles of almost impassable roads.

Emma's background worried Joseph more than a little. How would her mother, a Methodist minister's daughter, take to his experiences with an angel? Very probably she would

160

pronounce him a fanatic and have him thrown out of the house. And Emma—would she look at him with horror? Would she laugh? Or would she believe? With all his soul he prayed that she would believe. But fear gripped him. How could a girl with her upbringing believe such an account? And if she didn't, what would he do?

When the time was right he would tell her. She must know about the plates and all that was involved in bringing them forth. Translating them was to be only a part of his work. Exactly what lay ahead he did not know, but he was sure it would require the best of his manhood for the rest of his life. "I must tell her soon, and oh, please, God, let her understand."

It was a warm evening just before dark when the air smells fresh and all the world seems bathed in a mysterious magic. Joseph and the Hale young people had washed the supper dishes and laid two breakfast tables—one for the Hales and one for the work hands and Stoal crew. They had brought cream from the cold house for Isaac Ward to churn, since it was his turn, and now, after making sure all the family chores were done, Emma took off her apron and said matter-of-factly to Joseph, "Let's get out of this hot house and walk awhile."

Mrs. Hale looked up from her sewing as they walked through the living room. Mr. Hale stopped reading long enough to give an approving nod, for Emma looked like a cool flower in a full-skirted pink dress with a tight bodice that exactly suited her tall, slender figure. Her dark hair was done the way her father liked it best with a curl on either side of her lovely face. The tender admiration in Joseph's eyes seemed to hold Mr. Hale's gaze, and a look passed between them before Mr. Hale's eyes again returned to his reading.

Joseph and Emma walked—not caring where. A soft wind touched their faces as lightly as an infant's kiss. When they were away from the house and alone Joseph took her hand in his. The night and her nearness moved him tremendously. He had not known it was possible to love anyone as much as he loved Emma. He had made up his mind to tell her tonight, and now that the moment had come he did not know how to begin. Suppose when he told her she should turn from him in scorn—or fright? Suppose their friendship should end tonight? His fingers tightened on her hand.

She looked at him, surprised at the expression on his face. "What is it, Joseph? What is troubling you?"

He did not answer her at once. The air was filled with the sounds of night. In the grass near at hand locusts sang. In a tree above their heads an owl commenced whoo-whooing, but Joseph did not hear them.

Without realizing it, they walked to a spot that had been Emma's special retreat since childhood. Like Joseph, with his grove in Manchester, Emma had found a lovely place that seemed to be entirely her own. It was in a wooded area. Long ago, when she was quite young, she had coaxed her father and brothers to build her a bench and a table. The bench was light enough to move from one shady spot to another. In childhood Phoebe and her brothers had shared the spot with her, but even then they called it Emma's secret place. As she matured, this secluded area became more and more special to her. Here God and heaven seemed very real to her. Here she settled many a problem, read many a book, offered many a prayer. Sometimes she brought her sewing or her mending, and alone with only the birds to hear she sang the songs she

162

loved, or lived in her thoughts, as she discovered what manner of person she was.

Tonight it presented a lovely setting, with moon and stars casting silver shadows through the trees. They sat down on the bench together. Joseph wanted to take her in his arms, but he made no move to touch her, except that he had not let go of her hand. Her puzzled eyes were searching his face again. "What is it, Joseph?" And Joseph, with his heart crying for her to understand, began to speak with great earnestness. "Have you not thought it strange that in all our talks together I have not mentioned my future work?"

"I—I guess I took it for granted that you would be a farmer like my father and yours. But surely this is not what has put that look of trouble in your face."

"Emma, at the time of Christ's birth—do you believe the shepherds really saw angels and heard them sing?" There was an intensity in his eyes that held hers. "This is no ordinary question."

Emma felt the urgency of the question even though she was puzzled by it. "I have always believed the story, Joseph."

"Do you believe the virgin Mary saw an angel and heard the voice foretelling the strange birth of the Son of God?"

"Religion has always been very important to me, Joseph. I believe the story exactly as it is written in the gospels."

"And the other supernatural happenings recorded in the Bible—do you believe they were actual experiences of earthly men and women?"

"Yes," Emma said. "Surely you believe them too."

He nodded gravely. The moon was so bright she could see every expression on his face. Then, as his eyes held hers, he began telling her the strangest story she had ever heard. At first she was startled, but as his words unfolded she was strangely moved. In the days since their first meeting she had

163

come to know him very well. He was not one to exaggerate or make things seem different than they were.

He told her of his search for truth, his prayers, his faith, and the heavenly vision he had seen in the grove. He told her of the Angel Moroni, a personage he had seen not only once but several times, a heavenly being who taught him divine truths. He told her of the plates of gold hidden in the earth, and how it would be his work to translate them into a book. The sound of his voice blended with the magic of night and stars. She could not doubt his sincerity. It was all so very strange, and yet—other men had been called to do special work; why not Joseph? "The records written on plates of gold—what will they mean to those who believe them, Joseph?"

"Believers will see in them God's great love reaching down through the ages, bearing the same testimony as the Bible—that Jesus is the Christ, the Son of God, and that his plan of salvation has existed since life's beginning. They will show great things that God has done and will continue to do for his people."

He stopped speaking, his mind seemingly focused on some distant place. When his voice came again it was as if he were reliving past experiences. "If I could only help you see what it has been like to be instructed by a heavenly being. He has unfolded a story so wonderful that I ask myself if I will ever be able to translate the record correctly, even with the help of the Urim and Thummim. It is a story of the rise, decline, and fall of nations in the Americas, of records and abridgments these people kept that will make clear some of the issues Bible scholars now puzzle over." His fingers tightened on hers. "Do you believe babies go to hell if they die without being baptized, Emma?"

"I don't know. Ministers say they do."

"I've never believed it. There is no record in the Bible of

164

Christ baptizing babies, he blessed them. Can anything be purer than a baby? I feel strongly that their place in heaven is assured, that if I had a child I would consent to his baptism only when he was old enough to be accountable for his actions. That is why we need other records to clarify what men puzzle over." Did she believe him? She did! There was a kind of awe and excitement on her face. "Emma," his voice was suddenly tender with the love he had been holding back, "this work—translating the records—I hope you will want to have a part in it too."

"It is all so wonderful." She moved closer to him. "My family must hear the story. Will you tell them soon?" She was so close to him now that her hair brushed his cheek.

"I promise," he said. Then very gently and tenderly he kissed her. "I love you, Emma. With all my heart I love you."

"And I love you, my Joseph."

"Emma Hale Smith. Emma Hale Smith." Joseph did not speak the words aloud, for someone in the bunkhouse might be awake and hear him. Hours had passed since he had left Emma at her door. From where he lay he could see a stream of dim light shining through Emma's bedroom window. The burning candle meant that she too was unable to sleep. This had been a magic night. Wonderful Emma! How wise and good she was. How alive, vibrant, beautiful, desirable—and she loved him! The thought humbled him. How could Joseph Smith, common man that he was, be so blessed? That he loved her with his whole being did not alter the wonder of her love for him. And most blessed of all, she believed in his work—was willing to share it with him. They had talked long and earnestly and he had painted what their life together might be. He had pictured it without embellishments, and she didn't care. She was willing to face poverty, hardships, even persecutions so that they could be together. But was it fair to take this gentle, loving, wise woman down a trail that at best would be filled with peril and at worst might end in death?

The stars were bright in the heavens, and with his eyes upon them he prayed for wisdom and guidance, that he might bring no harm to the one he loved. It was a humble prayer of thanksgiving for Emma's love and understanding. He did not know how he could live without her, yet he wanted the best in life for her. And if someday they should marry . . . the thought set his blood to racing. He would cherish and protect her and do all in his power to bring her happiness.

A long time he lay praying and thinking. Emma's window became dark. The big house outlined in moonlight filled Joseph with a strange foreboding. Emma had said her parents must be told about the angel's visits and the plates hidden on Manchester's rocky hill. Joseph was almost certain they would reject the story. Yet Emma was right—they must be told. The Hales had every right to know of the work that lay ahead for him, before he asked permission to marry Emma.

If only I could speak with the tongue of angels and make them believe! But he knew he could not. At best he was ill at ease with them. There seemed to be a wall between him and them. He wanted to break through it, to be himself, to like them and to have them like him. Words that fell like raindrops when he was alone with Emma froze on his tongue when he was alone with them and made him feel stupid. Why? They were Emma's parents, flesh of her flesh—why then the wall? He didn't feel shy with Emma's brothers or with Phoebe. Then why with them? The answer did not come and he finally slept, but even in sleep he tossed and turned fretfully.

166

Only one day remained before Joseph was to return to Manchester, and still he hadn't told the Hales of his experiences with the angel.

"You must tell them, Joseph." Emma's eyes twinkled a little. "They know we are in love. Of course they would prefer one of the dandies in town for me, but as near as I can gather they plan to let me make up my own mind. They know I would make it up anyway."

"Thank God for your stubborn disposition."

The twinkle flashed again. "Someday when we are married and my stubborn nature exerts itself you won't be thanking God for it."

Darkness came too early. Joseph's hands, drying dishes for Emma, seemed to move at a snail's pace. Emma, on the other hand, seemed driven by a swift impatience, making the work vanish. At last there were no more chores to be done. She removed her apron and took Joseph by the hand. "Now," she said, "we're going into the living room, and you must tell them."

His face drained of color and she said, "Don't be afraid of them, Joseph. You have such a wonderful story to tell. You are a man called of God to do a work for him. There is nothing quite as important as that. They will be proud that you have been chosen."

Joseph's feet moved beside her leadenly. He knew what it was like to be rejected, laughed at, ridiculed. Too often he had seen friendly faces turn to hate. "I don't know how to tell them, Emma."

"Tell them just as you told me. They can't reject truth."

How mistaken she might be! Men had been rejecting truth since the beginning of time, but he didn't answer her.

He was silently praying that they would listen and believe, yet even as he prayed he was filled with doubt. Emma's parents had had their own ideas about religion long enough for their minds to become set, to conform to the pattern of the religionists of the day. Why then should they believe a story most ministers despised? Men who called themselves Christians were his greatest persecutors. They had given him no peace since his first vision in the grove. It was different with Emma. She had an open, questioning mind. New ideas fascinated her, and she weighed them, searching for new truths. She believed in Joseph and the work he had been called to do, and because she believed she felt that her parents would also believe. She was forgetting that most people drew conclusions too soon, shutting off the valves of truth. Unable to think beyond the rigid set of their own minds, they lived content with popular beliefs and established conclusions that would in no way ruffle the pleasantness of living. This was the thing he feared most for himself. He wanted his horizons to reach far and wide and deep. He wanted to see beyond the seed to the full flowering of an idea, but it wasn't easy. The easy way was to conform.

Emma's hand tightened on Joseph's as they entered the living room.

Isaac Hale looked up from the harness he was mending as they came in. "Did you finish your chores?"

"Yes, Father," Emma said.

The young people sat down.

Mrs. Hale was mending a garment. Her eyes looked up, and a swift glance passed between her and her husband. It was unusual for Emma and Joseph to tarry in the living room. Joseph caught the glance. They would be expecting him to ask for the hand of Emma.

The room became suddenly too silent, so that everyone present was uncomfortable. Then Isaac cleared his throat and spoke. "You are a hardworking man, Joseph. I've watched you digging for Isaac Stoal. You have never spared yourself. I like that in a man."

"Thank you, Sir."

"After a hard day at work you still find energy enough to help Emma. I like that in a man too."

"Helping Miss Emma is a joy, Sir."

"No matter how tired you are, you are considerate of your horse. That too is a good trait."

A glimmer of a smile appeared on Joseph's face. Mr. Hale was clearing the way for him. Now if all he had to do was to ask permission to marry Emma, it would be very simple. But it wasn't simple. They must be told of plates hidden in a rocky hill, plates he must bring forth and translate. And someday, perhaps in the not too distant future, he would be called to establish a church that would clash with many of the established denominations.

"Sir," Joseph said earnestly, "I love your daughter with all my heart, and with your permission I want to marry her, but first you must know certain things about me, for I am not like other men."

Mr. Hale raised an eyebrow. "In what way are you so different?"

"You undoubtedly know, Sir, that in ancient times records were kept on plates of gold or brass. Engraving on metal was an art practiced by educators and craftsmen trained in that field. Moses and his brother Aaron kept such records. Have you ever wondered about the Americas, the ancients who lived here—where they came from, how they lived, whether they kept records?"

"What has this to do with you and Emma?"

Emma's eyes were glowing. "Wait until you hear. It is so wonderful."

Joseph's eyes covered first Mr. Hale, then Mrs. Hale.

169

They had stopped their work to look at him. "Do you believe in angels? I mean do you think it is possible for a person to die and then return to earth for a short period in the form of a heavenly messenger, in order to call a man to a certain work and give him instructions?"

"How ridiculous!" Elizabeth Hale was so startled that her sewing fell to the floor unnoticed. "What is this absurd talk leading up to, and how can it possibly concern Emma and you?"

"I have been meeting with a heavenly being, not one time but many times. He has been instructing me concerning records of gold hidden in Manchester on Hill Cumorah. I have seen these records and touched them, but I have not been allowed to take them. Very soon though I will take them, for I have been chosen to bring them to the world—to translate them."

The faces of Emma's parents became incredulous. Mr. Hale's voice when he spoke sounded dry, almost harsh. "Go on, young man. I suppose this apparition—this once earth man—is going to give you these plates."

"Yes, Sir. In a little more than a year, if I am worthy, I will be allowed to take them."

Mrs. Hale took a deep breath and exhaled slowly. "Joseph Smith," the words came coldly, "you have lost your mind."

Mr. Hale's voice was stern. "Speak on, young man. If you have more to say we will hear the whole of it."

"I know it sounds unbelievable, Sir, but why? The Americas were peopled somehow. Men were here when Columbus discovered this country. You accept the Bible as a divine book. You believe its history. Then why not believe that nations rose to a high degree of civilization and culture in South, Central, and North America, and that records they

170

left support the claim of the Bible that Jesus is exactly what he claims to be—God's Son and the Savior of the world?"

Emma said with eyes aglow, "Is it not wonderful?"

Mr. Hale's tone was brittle. "If such a record exists—yes, I'll admit it is remarkable. The point is, I don't believe it."

"But it's true, Father. How can you help believing truth?"

"If such a record exists it won't be engraved in English, it will be in Hebrew, Egyptian, or some of the ancient hieroglyphics. If God wanted such a record translated he would call on someone skilled in languages. How many languages do you know, Joseph?"

"English, Sir. But God has supplied a means of translating."

Mr. Hale covered Joseph with cold eyes and his manner was like ice. "I agree with my wife. You have lost your mind. The God I worship works by law. There are probably only a handful of men in America capable of translating such a record, but there are a handful, so why would he call on you to do what you are not qualified to do? Such work would be given to a scholar trained in languages. You are a bigger dreamer than Isaac Stoal with his silver mine. I can't forgive you for filling Emma's mind with this nonsense."

Emma's eyes blazed suddenly. Then they filled with tears of disappointment and frustration. She got to her feet and stood facing first one parent then the other. "It isn't nonsense. Christians make the claim that the Son of God came to earth, lived, died, and was resurrected that man might be saved. Is it too much to ask that Jesus should have more than the Bible as a witness?"

Mrs. Hale stood up. "I'd say this whole thing is a kind of blasphemy. I think you had better not see Joseph again—ever!"

171

Emma's voice was low and controlled, the voice of one who has been used to respecting and obeying her parents all her life, but her hands were clenched into tight balls and she was using all her willpower to remain calm. "You are both unfair. Joseph has done no wrong. I believe him and his work, and I want a part in it. Last night I sat for hours thinking and praying. I have never felt so close to God before, or so sure of his love and guidance. I am not a child. I am a woman capable of making my own decisions."

Mr. Hale was on his feet too now and he spoke sharply. "Go to your room!" He walked to the front door and flung it open, his every gesture ordering Joseph out.

Joseph's eyes met Emma's. In one glance he covered her with love, tenderness, compassion, and a promise; then with quiet dignity he walked toward the door.

She ran after him, and he stopped. "I'll see you tomorrow before you leave for Manchester." Tears brimmed her eyes, spilled over, and ran unheeded down her cheeks.

"She will never see you again. We'll see to that." Mr. Hale stood stern and unbending.

"Please wait—Joseph—I'll go with you." She started to follow him, and her father caught her arm.

"If you go, Emma, you can never enter this house again. We'll disown you."

Joseph was out the door now and she called after him, "I love you." But she didn't follow him.

Joseph was both hurt and angry, and the feel of cool air did not stop the fire in him. He walked now as a man walks through a tempest. Why, when he was doing all in his power to obey the will of God, was life so difficult?

Without any thought as to where he was going, he went toward the little house where he had first met Emma. Reaching his destination, spent and still angry, he sat down by the old well where he had watered his horse that day and

172

relived the scene that had brought him Emma. The tiny house seemed stable and comforting surrounded by forest trees. With the moon shining on it it looked like magic silver. Odd that such a well preserved cabin should remain unoccupied. He pictured what it would be like if he were living in it with Emma. The little house would be filled with such love as it had probably never known before.

"I love her more than anything in the world," he told the stars. He touched the ground where she had stood that first day. It seemed almost sacred. What if he married her against the determined wills of her parents—would they really disown her? They would. He was sure of it. Emma had always been close to her parents and loved them dearly. Would his love be enough to make up for all she would be giving up? His people would welcome her as their own, but they were strangers she might not be at ease with. He thought of the dangers when the plates were in his hands. She would be in danger too. Could he ask her to leave family and safety for him? Yet how could he live without her? Through his mind her voice rang again. "I love you, Joseph." The way she looked, every gesture, all they had experienced together left him with the aching knowledge that he could never be a whole person again without her.

An owl hooted, and night wind stirred the trees. I must think of her happiness above my own. If she comes to me the decision must be entirely hers. He got up and began the long walk back to the bunkhouse. The hour was very late, but before he reached his destination he could see a light burning in Emma's room. She too was awake. She too was wrestling with the complications made by her parents. Joseph blew a kiss toward her window. "I love you, my darling. Blow, wind, blow, and carry the message to her."

The trip back to Manchester was one of heartbreak for Joseph, a heartbreak he dare not show for his companions, not knowing what Joseph's last night in Harmony had been like, teased him in friendly fashion for keeping his lovely lady out so long. They hummed the wedding march and in various ways kept alive the scene of his parting with Emma.

He had hoped he would see her again and had watched for some sign from her to the very last, a curtain moving at her window, a wave of her hand, a note, or Emma on horseback waiting somewhere along the road. There was nothing, and he took it to mean that she had made her choice and would never see him again. He had no way of knowing that Isaac Hale had ordered two of his sons to keep Emma in the house by force. He had no way of knowing that she had sobbed aloud as he rode away, and that his name had been on her lips as she struggled against the strength of her brothers to reach him.

Joseph was glad to be at home again with his family. There was work to do, and he welcomed it. He forced his body into a tiredness that made thinking an effort. Still he could not forget Emma.

The fall harvest was abundant. The wheat crop alone would more than cover the last payment on the farm. The larder was filled to overflowing, for Lucy and the girls had canned fruit and vegetables while the men smoked and dried meat. Now they were gathering beans and nuts. The year had indeed been rewarding with fat cattle and sheep feeding on the hillside and sleek pigs fattening for market.

There was a special reason for extra canning and supplies, for Sophronia and Calvin Stoddard were planning marriage early in December.

174

It was not only Sophronia who was happy these days. Happiness was in the eyes of all the Smiths as they went about their fall tasks. There were stacks of fragrant hay, the fences were strong, the buildings snug, and when Joseph was not thinking of Emma very often he was thinking of Alvin. There were times when Alvin seemed to be walking beside him with his farsighted wisdom that had made all this possible.

It did not occur to the Smiths that anything could be wrong. It crossed Joseph's mind once or twice to ask his father about the papers. He remembered how Alvin had cautioned them to have their papers in order. But he was busy and his heart was heavy. Everything seemed in order, so he promptly forgot the matter. If he had thought there was something to worry about he would have attended to it. But shortly after Alvin's death Hyrum had gone to Canandaigua to make the farm secure, and failing, Father Joseph had gone and returned with word that all was well. And so the days passed. Soon it would be Sophronia's wedding day.

If there was one man Calvin Stoddard had no use for, it was his relative, Mr. Stoddard, Alvin had hired to help build the Smith house in spite of Calvin's warning that the man was a swindler. Since then the man had called infrequently to talk with Father Joseph and to look around the premises admiring the improvements. Each time he came, if Calvin knew, he sounded a warning that the man meant no good to anyone who befriended him, but since his visits were infrequent no issue was made of the matter.

On December 2, 1827, Calvin and Sophronia were married in the Smith parlor with only the family and a few friends present. Joseph watched the ceremony with mingled feelings. He was happy for Sophronia and miserable for himself. He had never missed Emma more than at the

175

moment the minister said, "I now pronounce you husband and wife."

Calvin moved Sophronia to Fairport where he had been made foreman of a lumber mill, and the house seemed strangely empty. Work soon settled the family into its daily routine, however. Soon after the wedding Joseph began taking wheat to Colesville to be ground into flour. Ever since harvest they had been receiving orders for flour, some coming from as far away as Harmony. Days were short now and cold. The first deep snow had fallen on Thanksgiving Day, and many of the vehicles in Manchester had been converted to sleds.

One dark afternoon Joseph returned from Colesville with a load of flour, after a visit with the Knights, to find a letter from Emma awaiting him. His parents knew about Emma, although he hardly mentioned her. They knew by the hurt he carried in his eyes, by the way he forced himself to work beyond his strength, by his small appetite, and by his inattention at times when he seemed lost in thoughts so deep that they could not make him hear.

Lucy handed him the letter and saw his face blanch. He wondered if the family knew how his heart was pounding. Without a word he raced up the stairs to his room, tearing the letter open as he ran. He dropped on the bed, almost afraid to read the words. The paper rustled in his hands, and his mind cried, "Don't let it be bad news!" Then as he read his eyes took on a shine, while his heart was singing, "Thank God, oh thank God!"

"Dear Joseph: I must ask forgiveness for being so bold as to write you, but weeks have gone by with no word from you."

She told him how she had tried to see him on that last day he was in Harmony, with two brothers holding her while she struggled with them to free herself and go to him.

"Oh, my beautiful darling," he said aloud. "You are suffering as I am suffering."

Then the last part of the letter: "I love you, Joseph, and pray for you every day. If you should decide to come to Harmony, I shall be here waiting. I can't tell you what it has cost me to write this letter, but I feel if I don't write it, I shall never see you again."

His eyes had filled with joyous tears that fell unnoticed on the paper. "She loves me—misses me—wants me!" He touched the letter with his lips, then read it and reread it, before tenderly folding it and placing it in his pocket. I must speak to Father, he thought. He must send me to deliver a load of flour in Harmony. I will be ready to leave by tomorrow.

Father Joseph decided to go with Joseph to Harmony. The trip was an outing he needed. He was tired, for work had been heavy all that summer and fall. Before they were ready to start snow began falling, and the temperature dropped. The flour had been packed into a sled and covered carefully, so that no matter what weather they encountered on the way it would stay dry.

They mapped their journey carefully. Lucy sat with them writing down each stop where they would spend the night. Later, after everyone had gone to bed, she and Father Joseph talked about the trip and changes it might bring. Would Joseph bring back a wife? Hyrum and Jerusha were a contented, happy couple in their three-room cabin, and Sophronia and Calvin seemed just right for one another. Odd how marriage stabilized young folks and made them grow up. "We are growing old, Joseph." Lucy said. "But the years have been good. How grateful we ought to be for the many mercies of God."

Next morning early, after a warm breakfast, the men bundled themselves into heavy clothing and, with plenty of bedding tucked around them and warming stones at their feet, began the journey to Harmony. They were taking blankets and comforters in case they had to bed out along the way.

Lucy did not go back to bed. Later that morning, before most of the children were awake, Hyrum and Jerusha came driving in. Hyrum had come to help with the livestock and chores because of the storm. They had come to spend the day.

Forenoon sped by. Catherine had decided to take over the cooking, and the fragrant odor of baking filled the house. Don Carlos and little Lucy had spent the time in play. Now their voices and happy laughter reached the women inside the house. William, Samuel, and Hyrum were seeing to it that all the animals were sheltered, for the storm had worsened.

Jerusha and Mother Lucy were working on a quilt Lucy had in quilting frames. The room was warm and comfortable, and life seemed indeed rich. As they bent to their work Lucy's eyes touched Jerusha fondly. The girl was very special, everything Hyrum could ask for in a wife. Would Joseph's Emma be as good? Yesterday after getting the letter, Joseph finally talked to them. To hear him tell it there was nobody as wonderful, and he was a pretty good judge of women.

The sewing was going well, and the minutes were filled with talk and thoughts and dreams.

About two o'clock Lucy walked to the window and looked out at the white world. Who were the two men with Hyrum? They were walking toward the house, and they were in a great argument about something . . . she could tell by all the gesticulating and hand motions. As they came nearer she recognized Calvin's relative, Mr. Stoddard. Lucy disliked him heartily, for he had a way of prying into their affairs and pumping Father Joseph about intimate matters that were absolutely none of his business. Lucy was always on guard around him. He made her uneasy. Odd that he should be here now.

Presently there was the sound of feet stomping on the porch. Hyrum flung the door open, and his voice rose like angry thunder. "You men stay outside. There is not one spot in this house where you're welcome."

The women had never heard him talk to anyone in such a tone. They flung needles down and rushed to see what it was all about. He was inside now, slamming the door behind him. They had never seen him so angry. His eyes were like two burning coals.

"What is happening?" The two women cried at once.

Hyrum was looking at his mother now, and his face changed to gentleness, although it was plain to see that he was almost too angry to speak.

"Sit down, Mother. Sit down, both of you, and prepare for a blow." His voice seemed to come from a long way off. The women looked startled, and his face changed to one of weariness and pain. "Mr. Stoddard has stolen this house and land. He bought it today, and he has the deed."

For a moment there was not a sound in the room. It couldn't be true of course—there must be some mistake. Lucy heard Jerusha protesting now, but her own voice was still. It was like having a tornado suck the flesh off her bones.

The two unwelcome visitors had entered unbidden, and they stood towering over her with snow dropping off them and falling on the floor. Soon snow would be puddling around their boots where they stood. Mr. Stoddard's voice shook her to reality. "We have bought the place and paid for it. We now forbid you to touch anything on the farm. You are to pack up and leave and give possession to the lawful owners."

Hyrum pointed to the door. "Get out of here."

They continued to stand where they were.

"I'm going into Canandaigua and see the agent, Mother. He gave us the whole month of December to make the final payment."

"I'll go with you, Hyrum. There must be something we can do."

Mr. Stoddard's face wore a mocking smile. "Just what do you think you can do, Mrs. Smith? I hold a warranty deed to this property, all signed and recorded."

"You stole our house and land," Lucy's voice came shrill and unbelieving.

"Go ahead. Try to prove fraud if you can. Right after we finished building this house I offered Alvin a fair price for it. He wouldn't sell."

The devilish light on his face seemed to fill the whole room with evil. "I move slow and stay on the side of the law. You'll learn soon enough who owns this property." His crafty eyes covered first one Smith and then another. "I'm giving you notice now. I want you out of here by January. If you aren't out, I'll get a court order and have you evicted."

The men turned then and walked out.

Within the next few minutes every member of the Smith family—Samuel, William, Catherine, and the two small children were all in the room—every face was grave. What should they do? How should they move?

"We'll have to get Father and Joseph back here," Samuel said.

But how? The question was on each face.

"We can write letters," Lucy said, "and send one to every stop where they plan to stay. Surely one will get through to them."

"Then write." It was an urgent chorus.

Feverish writing stilled the agitation in Lucy. She

180

poured out her fright in words, and when the letters were written, signed, sealed, and stamped she was able to face her family with a calmness that quieted them to a point where thinking was possible.

Jerusha and Lucy put on their wraps. They would go with Hyrum to Canandaigua, stopping in Manchester to post the letters. There should be a rider leaving with mail before the day ended. Catherine, William, and Samuel would know how to take charge of things at home. The little ones would be in their care. She left no special instructions. She knew her young people. They were dependable.

In town they left the General Store with the assurance that a carrier would leave with the letters before nightfall. As they were about to proceed on their way to Canandaigua Lucy said, "We'll be riding right past Dr. Robinson's. I'd feel better if we could talk to him about all this."

Dr. Robinson was an old and trusted friend. He had been in another part of the county when Alvin needed a doctor. It was Lucy's firm belief that if he had been there, Alvin would not have died.

He was much more than a doctor. Many called him the listener, and that is exactly what he was. He had heard more confessions than the priests. He gave advice sparingly, and what he gave was sound. His tongue could chasten as well as bless, but he seasoned his words with kindness. It was said of him that he loved a sinner and flailed the sin. He could humble the proud without speaking a word. He guarded confidences as a miser guards money, and he seemed not to mind that he was overworked and underpaid. He went about ministering to minds and bodies wherever there was a need without being aware that he was old and in need of special care himself.

One room in his modest home was his "office," and now Lucy, Hyrum, and Jerusha made their way up the

181

snow-covered cobbled walk, feeling the sting of the wind and snow against their faces. As they walked some of the tension inside them lessened.

They climbed the porch steps and a tinkling bell fastened to the door announced their entrance.

In a moment the doctor himself appeared. At the sight of the genial, white-haired man Lucy sighed in relief. He was here! He would listen to what she wanted to tell him.

His shoulders seemed more bent, but he was intensely aware of life and his part in its turbulent motion. When he learned why they had come he helped the women out of their wraps and showed Hyrum where to hang his coat.

"It's a cold day," he said. "Stirs up the blood and makes us oldsters feel young like Hyrum and his pretty wife."

When they were all seated comfortably he sat beside Lucy and listened as she and Hyrum told their story. Now and then he interrupted with a question, but mostly he gave his full attention to all they had to tell him. When they had told all, he reached to touch Lucy's hand. "You are fretting, my dear, when you need to be calm. Maybe I can help. At least I can try."

He turned to his desk then and wrote for a considerable time. The scratching of the quill pen and the crackling of the fire were the only sounds in the room. At last he handed what he had written to Lucy for all of them to read. It explained the good character of the Smith family, their industry, their faithful efforts to secure their farm and home. It was a paper carefully prepared to foster confidence and respect, and it was prepared in such a way that no one could doubt the sincerity of its contents.

As they finished reading he took the paper from them gently, waving aside their grateful thanks. He had put on his warm topcoat, his muffler, and his boots. Now with the writing in his hand he said: "You must wait here. If patients

182

come my wife will hear the bell. She is to tell them I'll be back in about an hour." He was gone then, an old man facing the wind and the snow.

"If he had left us the paper we could be on our way." Hyrum's tone showed his anxiety to be off to Canandaigua.

"He knows what he is about," Lucy said. "You heard him say we are fretting when we need to be calm. An hour is not forever."

And so they waited. In just about an hour he came back. He had gone through the village and had obtained sixty signatures for his document.

"Now," he said with the simple dignity that was so dear to all who knew him, "you will have some weight to give the agent."

Lucy's eyes brimmed with grateful tears. Hyrum spoke his thanks tremblingly, and Jerusha, with the impulsiveness of youth, kissed his forehead gently. Was there ever anyone in all the world quite like Dr. Robinson!

There was nothing spectacular about the land agent's office. It was a modest room with bare walls and bare floor, a desk, and some chairs.

Although the Smiths had driven as fast as caution would allow, it was near closing time when they made their appearance, and the agent showed his displeasure. But as he read their document his attitude changed. What he was reading was not at all like what he had been told about the Smiths. He was at first surprised, then concerned, then enraged that a man like Stoddard had taken him in. With the reading finished he faced them with troubled eyes. "Mr. Stoddard was very convincing," he told them apologetically. "He said Mr. Smith and his son Joseph had run away, that

Hyrum was cutting down the sugar orchard, hauling off the rails and burning them, and doing all sorts of mischief to the farm."

Hyrum had been sitting down. Now as he stood up he seemed to grow taller than his six feet one inch. "What I want to know is how we can get our farm back. I'm Hyrum Smith and I have never cut down an orchard or destroyed anything useful. There isn't a farm around better kept than this one. According to my father the last payment isn't due until the end of this month. If you're the agent he talked with, you will remember he came to you shortly after we built the house to have the contract changed and get an extension of time for the final payment."

Concern deepened in the voice of the agent. "That land agent is dead. I'm the new agent. If such a contract was made by your father it must have been a verbal one. The contract in our files showed payments several months in arrears." His voice became even more gentle, but it was firm. "A verbal contract won't secure anything. It is worthless in a court of law."

The Smiths were silent. A verbal contract—how like Father Smith this would be. I should have gone with him and made sure we were secure, Lucy thought in desperation. Oh, why didn't I? Aloud she said, "Must we lose the farm? Isn't there anything we can do to get it back?"

"I'll get in touch with Mr. Stoddard, but he paid cash for a warranty deed. Come in Thursday, Hyrum, and we'll see what can be worked out." His tone was cordial but he seemed to imply that it would be useless to try, even with the document containing all the signatures, and he was very kind as he walked them to the door.

Oh, dear God, Lucy thought as they walked out into the stinging cold, if the farm is lost to a man like Stoddard how can I bear it?

184

The hour was very late, but Lucy lay wide awake in the big bed that was hers and Joseph's.

Hyrum and Jerusha had gone on home after returning from Canandaigua, and Lucy had found the children still up waiting to know the outcome of the trip. The little children had gone to sleep on the parlor floor, and she and Catherine had carried them to their beds and undressed them without waking them. But the older children had lingered on with Lucy as if bed were the last place they wanted to be. The house and farm had suddenly become their most cherished possessions. It had been Lucy who had finally urged her sad brood to bed, and now she too lay wide awake staring into the darkness.

Almost as if she were punishing Joseph for his carelessness, his empty pillow lay untouched beside hers, and she was rigidly careful to stay on her half of the bed. She wanted no contact with the spot that usually held his body. She blamed him. How could he have neglected to secure this house of all houses—this house filled with rooms Alvin had planned and helped to build? She recalled Alvin's walk, his voice, his laughter, his eyes that could speak volumes in a glance. She saw his face with all its changing moods. His presence filled her whole mind as she remembered that this was the house he had planned for a place that would bring them joy in their later years. They were too old now to begin rebuilding an inheritance. How could Joseph have been so careless with what Alvin had planned for them? She found herself recalling misfortunes that had happened in other years, misfortunes that could have been avoided if Joseph had used common sense instead of expecting everyone to be honest because he was.

She cried then, deep sobs of anguish, until her eyes were

swollen shut and her body exhausted. When she could cry no more she began to see that the loss of the house had been her fault too. Did she not know Joseph's weaknesses as well as he knew them? Why hadn't she gone with him to make sure the contract was in writing? She knew the law, and she was aware that there were scoundrels in the world. As dawn began lighting the windows she moved over to Joseph's side of the bed. He would be hurt beyond measure when he learned about the house, and he would blame himself.

Suddenly Lucy was remembering Joseph's tenderness, his faithfulness, his hard work, his gentleness with her and the children, his faith in the goodness of everyone, his honesty. How could she have been so angry with such a good man? She pressed her face into Joseph's pillow. No matter how disappointing this experience might be they would face it together.

By Thursday the snow had deepened. Early in the morning Hyrum left on horseback for Canandaigua to meet with the agent and possibly Stoddard. That night, shortly before his return, the two Josephs came home. One of Lucy's letters had reached them when they were fifty miles from home. Fifty miles through drifts and storm over treacherous roads had been a long and difficult trip. The men were beside themselves with worry. It would do no good, they told one another, for Hyrum to meet Stoddard in Canandaigua. Since he had schemed and planned to get the farm he would hold it at all odds. This was something for the law. Father Joseph blamed himself, just as Lucy knew he would.

While the family was holding conference, trying to decide what to do, Hyrum came riding up the lane. He tied his horse under shelter, and all the Smiths gathered around him as he came in to hear what he had to say.

"When I got there," Hyrum said, "Stoddard hadn't made an appearance. The agent sent a message, stating if he didn't come he would fetch him with a warrant; I spent the morning waiting. When he came, the same person he brought with him here was with him there—a sort of bodyguard for his protection."

"Yes," William said, clenching his fists without humor. "Someday I'll meet that man."

Almost as if William hadn't spoken, the family's attention was turned toward Hyrum.

"The agent didn't spare words. He told them the course they were pursuing was disgraceful and urged them to let the land come back into our hands. You should have seen Stoddard sneer then. 'We've got the land, and we've got the deed, so just let Smith try to help himself.' Finally, though, he agreed that if we can raise a thousand dollars by Saturday at ten in the evening they will give up the deed."

"A thousand dollars!" Father Joseph and Lucy spoke as one. Then Lucy's tone matched the desperation in all their faces. "It's robbery. Until the crops are all sold we'll be scratching for pennies." They had skimped and planned and saved to scrape together enough to make the final payment, a third of that amount, and they were still counting on wheat money to make that.

"I'd sooner give the farm away than to let that thief have it." Father Joseph's voice rose in weariness. His shoulders drooped from fatigue, but his anger was for himself, a kind of self-loathing.

Lucy spoke quietly to Catherine. "We have a hungry family on our hands. Light a taper in the kitchen and we'll feed them. We can't improve our situation tonight. All this can wait until tomorrow." She took Hyrum's damp coat

187

from him, and following Catherine she hung it on a peg by the kitchen stove. He would be riding home after supper, but at least it would be warm when he put it on again. She looked out at the storm. It was raging as fiercely as the one in her heart. Hyrum's mare was still saddled and tied in the shed to a tethering rod. A well cared for horse had few problems, but humans—it seemed they had more burdens than they could bear.

Although Father Joseph knew it was hopeless without his house and land as security, he tried several places to get a loan. It was useless. Then he approached friends and neighbors. They were sympathetic and kind as they refused him.

Hyrum offered his land and little house as security, but since they were only partly paid for his equity was not enough to secure a loan. Then Father Joseph remembered an old Quaker friend who had always admired their house and land. Should they sell to him if he had a thousand dollars to meet Stoddard's price? At least if he bought it they could continue to live here and benefit from crops and livestock and household goods. His eyes were deep wells of hurt in his haggard face as he talked this over with Lucy.

And so it was decided that if the Quaker had a thousand dollars ready cash they would see what kind of deal they could work out with him.

"This time I'll go," Lucy said. "You are half sick with traveling and worry."

He tried to talk her out of it, but she was firm, and in the end he gave in because they both knew that she could make a better bargain, and that whatever agreement she made would be a sound one.

188

Father Joseph went out to saddle up for her; his shoulders were bent, eyes on the ground. Lucy felt her heart wrench at his suffering. She didn't think of him as a weak man—only a good man who trusted in a world where all men were not good.

She packed herself a lunch, changed to a clean frock, slipped into a riding skirt, warm coat, hood, and mittens, and armed herself with a rifle. It was a several-mile trip, but she knew the way. Most of it would be through forest, and if after night she lost her way in the dark, the horse would know his way home.

By the time she was ready the horse was ready; attached to the saddle were water bags, grain, lantern, matches, and a blanket. They always carried lantern, matches, and an extra blanket in a storm, even when they were going no farther than Manchester.

Father Joseph's face was full of misgivings as he walked with her to the shed and anchored the rest of her belongings, for they both knew it would be well after dark before she could return.

In spite of the confident face she bent to Joseph for a parting kiss, Lucy dreaded the trip. The long ride on this cloudy day would be a lonely one. Snow had been falling intermittently all night, and it looked now as if a real storm might begin within minutes.

She rode to the end of the lane and looked back. Father Joseph was still standing watching her go. She waved, and he waved back. He would stand like that until she was out of sight.

With the farm far behind her Lucy began to enjoy the feel of falling snow and the chill of the wind on her face. A long time later she rode without incident into the farmyard of their Quaker friend.

The old man welcomed her with surprise that she had

189

made the trip alone on such a day. He hung her wraps on a peg near the fire and led her to a chair near the fireplace, gave her hot tea to drink, and listened to all she had to tell him. He knew the man Stoddard, a greedy man feeding on other men's fat, and his anger blazed with hers at the telling.

"And so," Lucy finished, "we are offering to sell you our beautiful house and land, since we have no security to offer you on a loan. And we hope when we are able that you will sell it back to us for a reasonable amount. We know you will let us keep our crops, livestock, machinery, and all our belongings."

"Lucy," there was hopelessness in his tone, "why didn't thee come sooner? If thee had come earlier, my child, thee would have found me with fifteen hundred dollars in my hands. Now it is gone. I just paid it all out to redeem a piece of land for a friend in this immediate neighborhood."

Disappointment covered Lucy. She had been so sure of his help. Where would she turn now? What would she do?

He came to her and touched her drooping shoulders gently. "I have no money, but I will try to do something for thee. Thee may tell Joseph I will see him soon, and if I can help him I will bring the good news to him." The wrinkled face was kind and gentle as he spoke.

"But we have only until tomorrow night at ten o'clock!"

"Perhaps it will be time enough. I know someone—a Mr. Durfree. I think he may take thy house and land. I will ride at once and talk with him."

"Will you be gone long? Shall I wait here for his answer?"

His eyes twinkled a little. "Unless thee plans to spend the night in bachelor quarters with a harmless old man, I would advise thee to ride home as soon as thee can."

190

He walked to the peg where her wraps were hung and helped her into them. Then he went for his coat. "If Mr. Durfree can't help thee I'll ride to Manchester and tell thee so. Unless I come, Joseph is to meet me here tomorrow morning. I'll go with him and introduce him to Mr. Durfree." He cupped her chin with time-worn hands, a friendly gesture, nothing more. "Thee is not to worry. Thy trouble is bad but not hopeless. Believe, child, and everything will come out right."

Was it the kindness in his voice, or her disappointment, fatigue, and despair at the thought of losing all her material possessions? Suddenly she was sobbing in her old friend's arms, while he consoled her gently. At long last she smiled through her tears. "Thank you. It's just that . . . life . . . seems pretty hard . . . right now."

He walked with her to her horse and helped her mount. "Take care, on the ride home. And may God be with thee."

Next day one of Mr. Durfree's sons, who was high sheriff, made a bargain with Father Joseph for his house and land. He would take it for one thousand dollars cash and let them remain as tenants. Not by any outward sign did Lucy show her heartbreak, for Joseph's hair seemed to grow whiter daily, and the hurt in his eyes was pitiful to see. But in her heart was bitterness toward all men like Stoddard who fattened their purses at the expense of others.

Christmas came and went, a halfhearted celebration for everyone in the Smith family except little Lucy and Don Carlos.

With the loss of the farm it seemed to young Joseph that all of life had gone wrong. More than anyone, except his parents, Joseph felt the blow, for he had helped Alvin plan the house and had listened to his dreams of a secure future for Lucy and Father Joseph. Without saying so, Joseph

191

thought his folks had acted too hastily in selling out for such a ridiculous price. His heart told him there should have been some way to save the house and land. True, they had saved the stock, their personal belongings, and a future in shared crops for a limited time. Then what? Where would they go? What would they do? Heartsick and discouraged, he forced himself to think of the one thing he wanted above all else—Emma Hale. If God would see fit to grant him Emma for a wife, then no matter what material hardships were in store they would be as nothing compared to the joy of her companionship. He must see her soon, for he missed her as if she were already a part of himself.

With the farm sold, young Joseph had gone to work for Isaac Stoal again, this time helping to repair some buildings, but there was the flour still to be delivered, and Joseph spoke to his father about it. Must he delay longer? Could he not be on his way to make the deliveries? Isaac Stoal understood and wanted him to go. And Father Joseph, knowing what was in Joseph's heart agreed to a speedy departure. This time young Joseph made the trip alone.

He went first to the Knights to have some wheat made into flour. Here he learned that he could see Emma without making a visit to the Hales. She was in Bainbridge visiting friends—or maybe it was relatives. Newel Knight had met the people and could direct Joseph to their home. He would make a map with directions to follow. The trip from Colesville could be made in less than a day.

Joseph rested at the Knights one evening—just long enough to polish up the sleigh—then set off with his map for Bainbridge. Would Emma accept him? Were they to be married? The trip seemed unending as he urged his team and sleigh toward Bainbridge. He was jubilant that he did not have to face the Hales before he had a chance to talk with

Emma, although he had prepared himself to use strategy to see her.

He had no eyes for fields white with winter snow, as he urged his team onward. He was unaware of icy wind that reddened his face and numbed his mittened fingers. He followed Newel's map with ease, making each turn along the way without any backtracking. Soon he could see the house with smoke rising from the chimney like a sign of welcome.

Now that he had arrived he found himself feeling suddenly shy. Emma's letter had said that she missed him, but did that mean she would be willing to give up family for him? Was he being too hasty in coming? Should he have written first?

He climbed stiffly from the sleigh and tied his horses. Presently he was standing at the front door. His knock sounded almost too loud, and he waited with pounding heart for an invitation to enter.

The door was opened by a strange young woman, and beyond her Joseph could see Emma. She was sitting in a chair beside a window with a book in her hands. At the sight of her his heart seemed to stand still and then commence the wildest beating. How beautiful she was!

"Yes?" The young woman said, looking at him.

"I have come to speak with Emma Hale if I may."

At the sound of his voice, Emma dropped the book and swept her skirts above her ankles in order to run faster to the door. "Joseph!" She spoke his name like a caress. "Oh, Joseph!"

Now he was holding both her hands in his and looking deeply into her eyes—eyes that were as shining and bright as his own. Without letting go of his hand she introduced him to the Stowell Family. By and by the Stowells left the room, and they were alone.

He took her in his arms then and said all the endearing words that had been locked in his heart for so long.

"Don't leave me again, Joseph. Please, never leave me again," she said with her lips against his cheek.

"Then you will marry me?"

"Yes, Joseph. All I want is to love you and to be loved by you." Their lips met then in a kiss they would always remember.

Strangely enough, it was Mr. Stowell who convinced Emma that she should marry Joseph without going first to Harmony to get her parents' consent. "You say you love Joseph as you will never love anyone else, Emma, and you know the man your father has his heart set on your marrying."

"I know," Emma said. "I'd never be allowed a contrary thought while his critical eyes blamed me for my imperfections." Then she lifted herself to her full height. "I'd rather be dead than to marry *that* man."

"You know your father's strong will, Emma. Are you brave enough to defy him?"

"I'm brave enough," she said.

On January 22 Emma and Joseph went to Squire Tarbell's house and were married. The Tarbells were also friends of Emma's, but the wedding was not at all like the one she had dreamed and planned for herself. Her shining eyes told Joseph that it didn't matter, and he was satisfied, although he knew this would be one more reason for the Hales to dislike him. He had never been so filled with pride or so happy. How, he marveled, had he ever managed to rate such a prize for a wife?

"Beloved wife Emma," he whispered as the ceremony ended. And in his heart he added fervently, "Please God, give me wisdom that I may always keep her as happy as she is right now."

Part 3

The trip back to Harmony began two mornings after the wedding. Joseph and Emma spent their first night in Bainbridge and their second night in Colesville.

The next morning Joseph loaded the sleigh with the barrels of flour he had bargained to deliver to a purchaser in Harmony, and they were off on the dreaded mission of telling the Hales they were husband and wife. He knew it would be easier to establish relations with an enemy country than to face Emma's parents, and far easier to turn the sleigh in the direction of Manchester and inform them by letter, but this he decided would be a coward's way out. They must hear the news from him for Emma's sake. She was their daughter, and he hoped whatever bitterness they might have would be turned against him, not her.

It was Sunday afternoon when they drove into Harmony. Emma had been her gay, happy self until after they had delivered the flour, but when they were nearing the Hale farm she grew suddenly quiet beside him.

He glanced at her, pink cheeked from the wind and lovelier than any woman he had ever known.

"Cold?" His eyes caressed her.

"No." She attempted a smile. "Just scared. Isn't that foolish?"

His arm encircled her, and his voice was half sober, half teasing. "I've been trying to rehearse some appropriate lines ever since we left Colesville, Emma, but I can't seem to get the words over my Adam's apple."

Their eyes met with understanding. They laughed, but it was feeble.

Joseph had never been one to turn his back on a difficult situation, but as he moved the horses into the Hale lane he wished he could head them toward Manchester . . . and fly! Instead he kept them moving toward the hitching post for visitors.

Since it was Sunday all members of the family were undoubtedly at home. Suppose they manhandled him; should he fight back? Would it be fair to Emma to fight her father or her brothers? He could handle himself pretty well, but if they all pounced on him at once—what then? He was no coward, but there should be better ways to settle things.

He tied the horses and helped Emma from the sleigh.

At another time Emma might have let go Joseph's hand and raced up the front steps to greet her family, but not today. Now, with one hand she held her full skirts primly, as any well-bred lady would, but the hand that clutched Joseph's was trembling.

He said in a low tone, "You'd better let me do the talking. Should we sound the knocker or walk right in?"

While they hesitated, the door was flung open by Mr. Hale. He seemed to fill the whole doorway, and immediately behind him stood Mrs. Hale. They seemed not to see Emma. It was Joseph they were looking at.

"I suppose a thank-you is in order for bringing our daughter home," Mr. Hale said. "I also hope you will pardon us for not asking you in."

"We are married, Father." Emma hadn't meant to say it, but the words came tumbling out. "We were married in Bainbridge. Joseph wanted us to wait and have the wedding

196

here, but I knew you would never let us. It was I who talked him into it."

For a moment the air around them seemed not to move. Their pounding hearts almost could be heard in the silence. Then as the full import of her words became reality the faces of Emma's parents grew ashen. Joseph spoke through the stillness.

"I love your daughter." He straightened to his tallest height and stood with unbowed dignity. "I will do everything I can to make her happy and to keep her happy."

Anger blazed in Mr. Hale, although he was trying with a sort of inner strength to hold it in check. "You love my daughter? You have destroyed her! Come in, come in, we can talk without letting the cold air in."

As they entered his arm reached for Emma . . . almost roughly. "You know the plans we've made for you. The most up and coming young man in Harmony has asked to marry you. With him you would have had a life worthy of a Hale."

"But I don't love him, Father. The truth is I dislike him immensely."

He pushed her to the sofa, and Joseph sank down beside her. Elizabeth Hale found a chair near them, but Isaac stood towering over them. "Love," he almost shouted. "Do you expect to find love with this—this dreamer—this religious blasphemer?"

"I *have* found love with Joseph. And I'm his wife. Nothing you say can change that."

"I know—I know." Mr. Hale took a few turns about the floor and stopped in front of Joseph. "How do you intend to support her? In poverty? She could have married an idol of all the young women in Harmony."

"I can understand your disappointment, Sir. I don't know this man you wanted for Emma. I only know what she told me—that he doesn't love her for herself, that he wants her because marrying a Hale will bring him prestige. He wants a beautiful wife, someone to own, to preside over his house. But when they are alone, Emma says he never listens to a word she says. He only hears himself. She told me any woman who lives with him will be a bowing doll. With me Emma may not have what she is accustomed to, but I'll do everything I can to make our life together something special for her. I want her to be the woman God intended her to be."

"All right," Mr. Hale said. "Now I'll give you a challenge. You say those records you plan to get are gold. Would you be willing to sell them to give yourselves a good start in life?"

"No, Sir."

"Then will you forget this devil's folly and go to work with hands and brain to support her?"

"I'll work for the best livelihood I can as long as it doesn't interfere with what I know I must do. I'm sorry, Sir, but you asked, and this is my honest answer."

"So you'll bring her down to poverty and disgrace."

Joseph's eyes met his sincerely. "I don't know. We've talked about all this. I honestly don't know what lies ahead."

"And yet you married her." Mr. Hale's tone was bitter. "For this I can't forgive you."

"I'm taking her to live in Manchester. The Smiths have a way of helping one another, and they will love Emma as their own."

Thus far Elizabeth Hale had not spoken. Now she got out of her chair as if all the weight of the world were on her shoulders. "Come, Emma, I'll help you pack. How you could have done this to your father—to me—I can't understand, and I can't forgive you for it. You'd better leave this house before your brothers come home. I'm sure they won't forgive you either."

198

Joseph had hoped Emma's people would forgive her once the shock of their marriage had diminished, but they had been in Manchester with his family only a few days when Emma got a letter saying she had disgraced them and was no longer their daughter, and that she need never come home again. Emma read the letter, put it aside, and read it again without comment.

Later, when Joseph wanted to talk about it, she said, "Father rules the family. With you I am happy. Away from you I am miserable. Someday they may forgive me, but until they do you are all the family I need."

These were brave words, but he was not deceived. He knew in what great esteem she held her family. Many times he had seen the closeness and love they had for one another, and he knew what she was giving up.

Each day he tried to make it up to her, showing his appreciation by an extra polish on a bright red apple, a bird's egg from an abandoned nest, a pretty rock, anything and everything that he thought would interest her. It was his nature to be gentle and considerate and attentive, and their companionship and the understanding they had for one another became very precious to both of them.

She endeared herself to Lucy, especially, for she had been trained to cook and sew, spin and weave, and do all manner of housework. She would pitch into the most menial tasks as though they were her own special duties. She made work so appealing that the younger children begged to help, and her patience seemed unending.

Father Joseph marveled at the things Emma could do. "It does beat all," he remarked to Lucy, "how a girl brought up with everything can face up to work the way she does."

Lucy only smiled, for she too had been a girl brought up with everything. Yet in her own way she marveled also. How could Emma work so hard yet manage to look so lovely? She was every inch a lady, and Lucy knew that young Joseph had found a prize. For the young couple life moved joyously. There was love and laughter, long talks and comradeship. It wasn't all bliss and contentment, of course; life in a household never is. But Lucy, writing to Sophronia about young Joseph's marriage, described it with appropriate words: "They have enlivening bonds."

That spring Hyrum and Jerusha walked with a new light in their eyes. In September they would have a baby. Lucy wrote Sophronia and Calvin the news, and it wasn't long before a package came—a handmade dress with delicate lace trim.

I've been making lace to keep myself busy when Calvin is off working. We have hoped we would have a special need for it, but so far we haven't. Tell Jerry I'll be sending more little garments soon, and I suppose, Mamma, you and Catherine and Emma will be helping her make baby clothes too, so she'll be lucky if she gets to do many for herself.

Tell her not to buckle in like so many expectant mothers do. Why women feel they must hide their unborn children under corsets of bones and stays and never mention the baby in mixed company seems all wrong to me. A legitimate baby should not be whispered about, especially when the moment it is born it is visited, gifted, and spoken of as a blessed event. So tell Jerry to carry Hyrum's with pride, and to speak of it whenever and wherever she chooses.

If we ever have a child, and it is our one great hope, I shall disgrace the whole town, because no child of ours will ever be carried under bones and stays. We are a new generation of women, Mamma, and it is high time we asserted our rights and changed a good many things that need it. A healthy baby needs freedom to grow. You tell Jerusha that.

"Amen," Lucy said reading the letter for a second time. Then her eyes twinkled a little. "Maybe it's good we have

200

always been too poor to afford those unmentionables. All my children have had freedom to grow. They have been carried by your standards, my girl. Do you suppose some of your ideas could have originated at home?"

Young Joseph and Emma enjoyed tramping woods and fields together, and often their feet carried them to hill Cumorah.

The first time they climbed the hill the moon had been silvery white, and the stars had shed a light almost like day. Joseph showed Emma the rock under which the plates were hidden, and she touched it with a kind of awe, for the whole place in moonlight seemed unreal and tinged with a kind of holiness.

Very soon now Joseph hoped the plates would come into his possession, and Emma too was feeling the suspense and the responsibility of what lay ahead for him.

As the month of September approached, their excitement grew until the very air they breathed seemed charged with a kind of breathlessness. Would they indeed get the plates this September? Would Joseph's work really commence now?

On September 16 about noon Hyrum came riding in. Emma saw him first and knew by the way he carried himself that the baby was already here and that everything was fine.

She called Mother Lucy who alerted the household, and everyone went out to meet him.

"It's a girl," Hyrum said, grinning. "The greatest little girl that has ever been born."

"When was she born?"

"How much did she weigh?"

"Have you named her yet?"

The questions came like a chorus.

He laughed. "How about a drink of cool buttermilk? I've been up all night."

"Then have some dinner. We're about to eat," Mother Lucy said.

"No, just some buttermilk."

They followed him into the house for details. He held small Lucy while he enjoyed his drink, and the others listened with fascination to what he had to say.

"We named her Lovina. We thought you would be happy, Mamma, to have a child named for the sister you thought so much of. Jerusha's mother was midwife, and she let me stay the whole time. Jerry pulled on my arms until they are sore. The birth was pretty bad for her, but she was a real trouper. I think every father should see his child born. Now our problem is keeping Jerry in bed. She says she feels good and wants to get up."

"Well, you keep her in bed," Mother Lucy said. "Make her lie flat, and don't let her up until her tenth day. That's when the bones go into place."

"We've told her that. She says Indian women have their babies on the march and go right on marching."

"I'm sure they do," Catherine said.

"Well, you keep Jerusha in bed," Lucy said again. "If you need me, Hyrum, I'll go over and stay."

"We don't," Hyrum said. "All the Bradens are there. They are staying the full ten days. Lovina is their first grandbaby, too, you know."

"I know." There was a kind of hunger in Lucy. "The other grandmother will get to bathe and diaper her and do everything for her first."

202

Everyone laughed.

Hyrum's eyes were twinkling. "I feel downright sorry for you, Mamma. You've never had a chance to do any of those things."

"Oh, go along, all of you," Lucy said. "When can we see the baby?"

"This afternoon if you can elbow your way through the Bradens. And don't be surprised if Jerusha meets you at the door carrying the baby herself."

"Tie her down," Lucy said. "I'm serious. If moving about doesn't hurt her now, it will make her old when she turns middle-aged."

Hyrum's face took on tenderness. "You should see Jerry with the baby. You'd think ours is the only baby with perfect eyes and ears and toes. But then . . . " his eyes held a glow, "everything about Lovina *is* perfect. She's like a miracle. I don't see how anyone can look at a baby and not believe in God."

This year the crops on the farm were more abundant than usual, for all the Smiths had worked exceptionally hard. The bargain they had made with the new owner was to work the farm on shares. This year there would be a profit, for the yield was more than one third greater than last year, which had been a good year.

On September 21 Isaac Stoal and Newel Knight surprised the Smiths with a visit. They were driving a team of well-matched geldings hitched to a spring wagon belonging to Newel. The whole family came out to admire the new vehicle, but it was the horses that impressed Emma.

"They're beautiful," she said. Her practiced eyes moved over their smooth lines while her hand stroked the neck of one gently. "How I would enjoy driving such a team."

Newel looked at young Joseph. "We'll be here a couple of days if you can put us up. The two of you are welcome to take the wagon and team any time. The horses are spirited, but they handle well." His eyes met Emma's. "Drive them whenever you like."

Emma thanked him with a grateful smile.

The next afternoon Joseph needed a tool in Manchester and went by himself to buy it. It should have been a quick trip, but well after dark he had not returned and all the family became apprehensive. Emma, sick with worry, made trip after trip to the road and back, searching for some sign of him. The men had finished the outdoor chores, small Lucy and Don Carlos were in bed asleep, and the rest of the household had gathered in the living room when Emma excused herself. Without telling the family, she had made up her mind to ride into town and look for him.

Upstairs in the room she and Joseph shared, she was putting on her riding habit when he came walking in.

One look at his face and the scolding words she was about to utter died on her tongue. He looked haggard and pale, but his eyes were bright with excitement, and suddenly she knew Joseph had been with the angel.

He caught her to him and held her. "Tonight is the night, Emma. Tonight we will bring home the plates." Awe was in his voice. "No one must know when we leave the house. We must go downstairs now and act the same as on other nights."

"But they will want an explanation. They will want to know why you have been gone so long. Let me go down and tell them that you don't feel up to seeing anyone tonight. I'll fix you some supper, and when they know you are home and all is well they will go to bed. Later we'll slip out of the house and take Newel's team and wagon. The townspeople

204

won't recognize the strange vehicle, and we'll be less apt to be followed."

Joseph kissed her, and there was admiration in his glance. "You think of everything," he said. "If you get a chance, bring the lantern from its peg in the kitchen and put it where we can lay our hands on it in the dark."

The hour was very late. Emma held the lantern while Joseph harnessed the team. The whole earth seemed silent. The house was dark. Off somewhere a dog barked, and the sound seemed eerie and unnatural in contrast to their stealth.

Joseph whispered, "You forgot to bring a wrap, Emma."

"Yes," she said.

There was a tow frock in the barn hanging on a peg. He brought it and tossed it into the wagon bed. "In case you get chilly." He went for a crowbar. "We're ready now." His voice was low. He lifted her gently to the wagon seat and handed her the reins, then he walked, guiding the horses carefully, in order to make as little sound as possible. Once they reached the road Emma moved over. "You drive," she said.

"Are you sure you want me to?"

"I'm sure."

He climbed into the driver's seat and took the reins.

A soft wind was blowing. The moon was golden and round like a shining ball, and the stars were bright in the sky. The horses moved at a trot and in unison. They needed little guiding, and Joseph held the reins in one hand. His free hand went around Emma. This was the night he had waited for so long. How grateful he was to have Emma sharing it with him, yet he sensed their danger if someone should see them and discover what they were about. Had he done right to bring her on this strange mission? Yet how could he have left her behind? Her interest in the work was almost as great as his. Emma seemed to read his thoughts.

"Are you afraid, Joseph?"

"We must make sure we aren't followed," he said.

They skirted Manchester, following a devious route to Cumorah's hill. They stopped quite close to the hill in a sheltered spot where the team and wagon could not be seen from the road, and he handed the reins to Emma. "Will you be afraid to wait here alone? I think I should go the rest of the way without you."

"I understand, Joseph, and I won't be afraid. You take the lantern. It will only lead some traveler to me, and you'll need it to help you find your way down the hill with the records."

He knew she spoke wisdom. The light could bring some stranger to her, and he would need it to get the records and to guide him through the rocks.

"I'll let the horses graze, if they want to eat with bits in their mouths."

He took the crowbar from the wagon bed and, without realizing it, he took the tow frock too.

"Be careful, Joseph. I'll pray that everything goes right for you."

He left her, climbing swiftly, feeling the uneven ground beneath his feet, remembering other times that he had met the angel on Cumorah's hill, but this was different. Tonight he would bring home the plates.

He made the ascent without great effort and went immediately to the rock. The night wind touched his face and flickered the lighted wick in his lantern. The very air was charged with expectancy as he stood alone at the top of the silent hill.

Presently he discovered a light appearing. At first it

206

seemed to be only one of the stars, then it descended from the heavens like a meteor. Joseph's heart beat faster as the light continued to increase until the earth around him became like day. Was Emma seeing the light too? He hoped so! Then he saw Moroni as he had seen him at other times, clothed in a robe of exquisite whiteness.

Again, as on the other occasions, Moroni spoke of Joseph's work, warning him that his name should be had for good and evil among all nations, kindreds, and tongues. Almost as if he were speaking for the last time, he reviewed again judgments that were coming on earth—desolations by famine, war, and pestilence, adding the caution that Satan would tempt him to use the plates for the purpose of getting rich, but that he must have no other object in view but to glorify God, and he must not be influenced by any motive other than that of building the kingdom. "Remember, Joseph, the records will be your responsibility. *You must show them to no one.* If you do you will surely be destroyed. There will be witnesses, but you cannot choose them. It is I, not you, who will say who these witnesses shall be."

Almost without effort then Joseph pried up the rock, and there before him lay the plates, the sword of Laban, the compass, the breastplate, and the Urim and Thummim. He bent to take them and again heard the words of caution. "Show the records to no one."

Now Joseph found himself alone with only the small flickering light of the lantern to guide him. Remembering the angel's warning, he wrapped the contents of the stone box in the tow frock, then with the lantern to guide him, and carrying his bundle with the greatest care, he descended the hill. Even so, he walked swiftly, for his heart was light. This was the time he had waited for so long, and his joy was full.

As he neared Emma his feet came to a sudden halt. He could not show the records to Emma. How could he tell her?

207

Her disappointment would be great, perhaps as great as his joy at receiving them. What must he do? His feet lagged. Lifting the lantern he blew out the flame and proceeded the rest of the way in the light of early morning.

As he reached the wagon he could see Emma's face in the dawn. "You got them!" she said. "Oh, Joseph, let me hold them . . . let me see them."

His regret was reflected in his voice. "How can I ever tell you? Oh, Emma, the angel said I am to show them to no one. It was a command with a warning that if I do I will be destroyed."

"You mean . . . I can never . . . see them?"

His concern increased. "Perhaps you can never see them."

"May I touch them, Joseph?"

He brightened. "Of course you may touch them. There was nothing said about touching them. You may even hold them as long as they are wrapped." He lifted them up to her and watched her hands move over them. She was seeing them with her fingers—the way a blind person sees. With her examination finished, she very carefully handed the bundle back to him.

"I'll drive home," she said. "Oh, Joseph, is it not wonderful—is it not truly wonderful that the Bible will soon have another witness that Jesus is the Son of God, the Savior of the world? And the best part is, *you* have been chosen to translate the book by the power of God!"

The sun, like a fireball, had appeared in the east when Joseph and Emma drove in at the farm gate. As they approached the outbuildings Mother Lucy came around the side of the carriage house. Her face wore a strange expression that told them she knew where they had been and suspected what they had brought home. She stood waiting until Emma brought the horses to the spot where Joseph would unhitch

208

them, and as soon as the wagon stopped she came up to them.

"I heard you go out last night," she said. "At first I thought that something was wrong at Hyrum's, and that you were going there. Then I remembered the date, and I *knew*. Mr. Knight and Mr. Stoal decided to get a real early start. They're going to take a load of wheat back to Colesville."

"Did they mind that we took the team?" Joseph asked.

"No. But William kept insisting that I call you down for breakfast so you could visit a little before the men left. I had to tell them you had their team and wagon." Her eyes twinkled at the remembrance. "They think you were prolonging your honeymoon." She paused with her eyes on the tow frock Joseph held. "You got them! Please, Joseph, let me see them."

Again Joseph found himself apologetic, explaining the angel's command.

"But you may touch them, Mother Smith," Emma said. "Joseph let me do that."

"But not here, Mother," Joseph told her. "In the carriage house with the door closed. No one else must know we have them."

Emma held the tow frock while Joseph tied the team to a hitching post, then she handed the bundle to him, and he handed it to Lucy while he assisted Emma to alight. The three of them entered the carriage house and closed the door behind them.

Just as Emma had done, Lucy examined everything with her fingers. She was especially interested in the feel of the records. After a time she said, "I'd say the plates are . . . about eight inches long . . . six inches wide . . . and not quite as thick as common tin. They are bound together . . . with three rings running through them. The volume is about six inches in thickness . . . and a part of it seems to be sealed. You saw them, Joseph. Are they truly made of gold?"

"Yes, Mother, thin sheets of the precious metal."

"They must be very valuable."

"Yes. And that brings up a question. Do you have a chest or trunk that fastens with a key?"

"No. Hyrum does, but we don't."

"I should have seen to it," Joseph said. "We can hide them for a day or two, since no one knows we have them. I'll have a chest made, but you and Father will have to lend us the money for a short while until the crops are sold."

Lucy's eyes met Joseph's as he took the bundle from her hands. "The cabinetmaker who made Sophronia's furniture could make you a fine chest, and we could pay him as she did—half in produce and half in cash—but Joseph, there isn't a penny in the house."

"You mean we have no money?" Emma was looking as worried as Lucy now. Joseph said, "Stop fretting, both of you. We'll hide everything here in the carriage house for the time being. They will be safer here than in the house. One of you stand outside the door and warn me if you see anyone."

"I'll guard," Lucy said.

Joseph began digging a hole in the earth floor. When it was large enough he buried the bundle and covered the floor with straw so that it looked the same as it had before.

Joseph smiled. "Well, they're back in the earth again. No telling how long they were buried before I got them. I guess a little longer can't make much difference."

Isaac and Newel were about ready to leave when Hyrum came riding in. He had remembered the date and had come to find out if young Joseph had the records.

Finding Newel and Isaac there, he persuaded them to spend a day or two longer in Manchester. He had wheat ready for milling and wanted Newel to take it to the mill, thus saving him a trip to Colesville.

Another time young Joseph would have been glad for a chance to prolong his friends' stay, but now that he had the records he was anxious to get started with his work. Yet being a good host he knew he would do what he could to make their visit a pleasant one.

At the first opportunity Father Joseph and Hyrum took young Joseph aside. "Do you have the records?"

"Yes."

"May we see them?"

Again Joseph found himself explaining. They could handle them, but they could not see them. And once more he was in the carriage house with Father Joseph and Hyrum examining the plates through the tow frock.

"They aren't safe here, Joseph," his father said. "Once word gets out that you have them there will be those who will tear this farm apart to find them."

"If we don't tell anyone we have them, who is to know?"

Father Joseph's gaze followed the straw on the carriage floor. "You have been meeting the angel every year for four years and other times too. Lots of folks will be figuring the date. For one, Martin Harris knows. He's known for a couple of years."

"You were to tell no one, Father."

"I haven't talked. He confronted me with the story. Most of what we know was spread abroad after you told the preacher. And you've talked other times too—you've told the Hales—"

"Stories leak out," Hyrum said. "I haven't talked. I don't think anyone in the family has, but 'Joe Smith's gold bible' is common talk."

"What about Newel and Isaac. Do they know?"

Father Joseph moved to the door where he could watch the house. "They were teasing Lucy about you and Emma not knowing when the honeymoon was over, but I got the feeling that underneath their banter was an undercurrent of waiting. They are our friends, Joseph. You have nothing to fear from them."

Young Joseph was remembering the angel's words. "You are to tell no one." How many of the townspeople knew that this was the year and the time when the plates would come into his hands? There were those who would destroy him for the records, and not only him but his whole household.

"Do you have a chest, Hyrum—one with a good strong lock and key?"

"Jerusha has it filled with linens. She isn't going to want to part with it for very long."

"Just until I can have one made."

"With guests in the house, won't bringing in a chest cause questions?" Hyrum asked.

"If I should send word by one of the family that I need it, would you bring it to me at a moment's notice?"

"You know I will. And let's hope it will be at night under cover of darkness."

Joseph took the bundle from Hyrum's hands. "If you two will put the floor back exactly as it was I'll take the records and hide them in a new place."

Twenty minutes later young Joseph joined the family and his friends. He received inquisitive looks, but no one voiced a question.

Stray horses were not often seen in Manchester or Palmyra. If one was found it was a law that a hickory withe

212

be hung around its neck to show that the animal had not been stolen by the finder, and that the owner was being sought.

It might have been an hour after Joseph came back from hiding the records that William found a stray.

Emma discovered him with it when she walked down to inspect the carriage house floor to make sure it looked normal and above suspicion, even though she was certain Joseph's bundle was no longer there.

William was on the horse, in the corral, riding bareback at a fast gallop. Emma saw at a glance that this was no ordinary animal. Lifting her skirts, she went flying with all speed to the corral fence for a closer look and to find out how William had come by such a horse.

Emma climbed to the top of the fence and sat there watching William ride. The horse was an English chestnut, fifteen or sixteen hands high, a gelding. Emma could only guess at his age—possibly two or three years old—and it was plain to see that he had been tutored by a careful trainer. One thing was certain: this was someone's prize horse. As William came up to her he reined in.

"Did you ever see such a horse?" he said.

She saw the hickory withe he had fastened on him. "Where did you find him?"

"He found me," William said. "I was walking home from town—had turned into my own lane, in fact—when he came up and nuzzled me."

Emma was admiring the head. It was light, lean, and well set on the arched neck; the ears were soft and beautifully shaped, the eyes full, the nostrils dilating. The body, the shoulders, the back—every part of him was beautifully proportioned. Emma dropped into the corral, felt the soft skin, admired the silky hair, and noted the veins

213

under the skin that told her this was indeed no ordinary horse.

"He glides with a motion as even as a song," William said. "Here, let me show you." And swinging himself easily to the horse's back he was off.

Emma watched, and her admiration was twofold, as much for the rider as for the horse. With Emma for an audience he moved the horse into a smooth gallop, then with careful precision he began what looked like clowning, but Emma knew the hours of practice he must have spent on every kind of steed to ride the way he was—backwards, sideways, then standing up, his balance timed to the even gait of his horse. Then he came up grinning and riding properly, the way a horseman should.

"One of these days you'll kill your fool self," Emma said, but her eyes told him he was great. "It's plain you'll be making a real effort to find the owner."

"I wish I could keep him," William said wistfully. "My worry is that he'll be claimed by a thief."

"Then put him in the barn. We'll keep our eyes and ears open and wait for the true owner to make himself known. It's odd that he had no saddle on when you found him."

"Only a bridle, and it was dragging the ground."

It was noon that same day. The air was filled with the fragrance of beef and vegetables.

Family and guests had just about finished their meal when a knock sounded on the front door. Emma and William exchanged glances; this could be about the horse, but it could also mean trouble for Joseph. Involuntarily every adult at the table stiffened. Young Joseph half arose from his chair, but a touch from Emma made him sit down again.

"I'll go," Father Joseph said. "All of you stay."

"I'm going with you, Father," Samuel said, and he got up and followed him.

214

The room was strangely silent. Everyone except Don Carlos and small Lucy had stopped eating. Nobody spoke. Then they heard Father Joseph's voice, friendly and warm, another voice, and a low chuckle. These were not sounds of danger.

A moment more and Samuel came in grinning. He pushed his long, lean body back into his chair. "A widow in Macedon wants some work done on a well. A friend of Father's, Mr. Warner, is at the door. He thought maybe some of us would want the job. I don't, do you, William?"

"Not this week." He glanced at Emma. He had to find the owner of a stray horse.

"I'll take the job," young Joseph said. "Fixing a well is something I can do."

"But you can't," Emma said. "That is, you had better not leave Manchester right now."

"It will be a way to pay . . . for something . . . we need." He got out of his chair. "If Mr. Warner will give me directions to the widow's place I'll go in to Macedon early in the morning."

That night, after they had gone to bed, Emma told Joseph about the stray horse.

Early next morning, after a good breakfast, young Joseph started for Macedon. Emma went with him as far as the barn, to show him the stray and help him saddle his horse.

"That's a fine gelding," Joseph said. "Tell William to give it special care. The owner is bound to turn up today."

When he was ready to leave he took her in his arms and kissed her tenderly. "Be careful," he cautioned. "Don't talk with strangers, and don't let any inside the house."

"What about friends?"

He cupped her chin with his hands. "Just be sure they

are friends." He kissed her again and mounted. She watched him ride off down the lane to the main road, watched until he disappeared from sight, then she walked thoughtfully back to the house. Must they always live in fear now until the translation was completed? If this were God's work, why were they afraid? Would He not protect them and the records until the task was done? And it wasn't a task really; it was a privilege. They had been chosen to bring forth truth written in ages past, and from these pages of history new faith would be born.

The rest of the family was up when she reentered the house.

The busy morning wore on. The men and boys, accompanied by Isaac and Newel, finished the outdoor chores and came in for breakfast. After breakfast Mother Lucy made golden loaves of bread. Emma and the girls took over household tasks, and by nine everyone was in the parlor enjoying a leisurely visit. At another time Father Joseph and his sons would have been in the fields, but today they were taking off to spend time with Newel and Isaac.

Emma was sitting by a side window facing the road. Suddenly she saw more than a dozen men enter the lane that led to the house. They were armed with sticks and clubs and they walked like men with a purpose.

Her warning cry brought everyone running. One look and guns were taken from the wall and loaded. Don Carlos and little Lucy were herded to the back part of the house with Catherine to tend them, while Emma and Mother Lucy joined the men watching at the window.

"The man leading the group is Willard Chase. He's a churchman with the reputation of being a forthright citizen."

"Don't forget, Father, churchmen are Joseph's worst enemies," Emma said.

216

They waited. The men were close now, and the crunching sound of walking feet could be heard.

"All of you move back where they can't see you from the window," Father Joseph said. "And don't make a sound."

The walking stopped just short of the porch. "Joe Smith . . . " It was Willard Chase's demanding voice. "Come out on the porch, Joe Smith."

"I'm going out there," Father Joseph said. "The rest of you stay, unless you see I can't handle them."

"Be careful," Lucy said. "Oh, please be careful."

Father Joseph, gun in hand, walked out on the porch. He was a dignified, quiet figure standing alone with the wind rumpling his white hair. "Joseph isn't here," he told them in a friendly, low voice. "He left early this morning to work in a distant town."

"We don't believe you," Willard Chase said, and a sneer spoiled the looks of his rather handsome young face. "He was seen on the Hill last night, and the word is out that he got his gold bible. Everything of value—gold, treasure—buried in that hill belongs to the people of Manchester, and we've come to fetch it."

"Go home, men. Joseph is not here."

"Do you deny that he brought a gold bible from the hills last night?"

Father Joseph said nothing, but he seemed to stand taller.

"Come on, men, let's search the house. The old man knows it's in there someplace."

"Stand back," Father Joseph said. "I swear there is no treasure in my house, gold or otherwise. But you won't tear this place apart—now or ever!"

Willard Chase pointed to a man in his party. "Do you know this man?"

217

"Is he someone I should know?"

"He's a conjurer. We sent sixty miles to have him brought here. He knows Joe Smith brought something valuable down from the Hill. Stand aside, old man. We're going to search your house."

A conjurer! It was all so ridiculous that Father Joseph and the tense ones waiting inside the house wanted to laugh, but they didn't, for the men were charging full force onto the porch.

It was then that the door opened, and Isaac, Newel, Samuel, William, and the two women came out armed and angry.

Willard Chase and his men stopped. They hadn't planned a battle or a murder.

"Get off the porch." Samuel's voice was sharp. "Get off our land—all of you, or take the consequences. You'll have to kill or be killed if you cross this threshold."

For a moment Willard Chase and his men hesitated. They would have left the porch, but at that moment small Lucy came running out, laughing because she had gotten away from Catherine. Before anyone could guard her one of the men swooped her up. "Now," he said, "tell us where Joe Smith has gone."

"He's in Macedon," the child said, struggling to be released. "Please—put me down."

"Lucy," Emma's face was white and strained. "You shouldn't have said that."

Willard Chase turned. "Come on, men. We'll get Joe in Macedon."

Willard and his band would go to Macedon. All the Smiths knew it; Isaac and Newel knew it. Joseph must be warned.

A good horse was needed—a fast horse that would be sure to arrive in Macedon ahead of Joseph's enemies.

218

Emma's eyes met William's, and William got the message—his stray!

"Saddle him quickly, and I'll go," Emma said. "I'm the least likely to be followed, and—" her eyes were imploring, "I don't think I could stay home, not knowing what was happening to Joseph."

They knew her anxiety and didn't protest. William left to get the horse ready and Emma went upstairs to put on her riding clothes. The rest of them just waited—a worried group gathered on the porch.

In a few minutes William came with the horse.

"Better take a gun," Newel said.

"No, I could never shoot anyone. They'll have to get mounts before they can leave Manchester, so I'll be ahead of them all the way."

"Unless you are stopped by the owner of the stray," William said as he helped her mount.

"Don't say it, William. All of you pray I'll reach Joseph before they do."

"You've got your directions—the woman's name is Duprae." Father Joseph's eyes looked worried. "Be careful."

She nodded, then she was off, feeling the speed and the rhythm of her horse.

Few women could ride better than Emma Hale Smith. She loved a good horse, and riding had always been her great delight, but today the ride held no joy—only urgency. Behind her fifteen men would be riding, fifteen men bent on bullying Joseph out of the sacred records he would guard with his very life. Emma didn't know where Joseph had hidden the records; none of the Smiths except Joseph knew that. She only knew they had been moved from the carriage house, and that Joseph would die to defend them.

Out on the main road traffic slowed her. Sometimes she had to pull her horse to a walk before she could go around a wagon or a cart. At these times she looked behind her, eyes straining for a sight of Willard Chase and his men. Was this the only road to Macedon? Was there a shortcut? If only she could leave the main road. Suppose the horse were recognized by someone? Terror gripped her at the thought of being stopped. Whenever she could she raced her horse. When she was forced to pull to a slow gait her heart kept on speeding so that the delay was almost more then she could bear. At last she came to a fork where the road to Macedon became only a trail through dense woods. Now terror gripped her again. Suppose they found her here. What could she do? Fifteen men—what they could do to her with no friend near to hear her screams! The thought made her head throb and her tongue dry. "Go—horse—go! And please, God, protect me."

She felt closed in with trees on every side. The frightening thought came that if the men were near she wouldn't know it. Thick trees would shut them from view. Her ears strained to every sound. Once a deer crossed the trail behind her, and her body froze at the sound. Afterward, when she knew what it was, she wiped cold sweat from her forehead and discovered she was crying. "Go—horse—go. And dear God, let no animal come near." If the horse should stumble, if she should be left alone to plod the thick trail alone would she ever make it on foot to Macedon?

At last, after what seemed forever, trees became thinner. Now she could speed. As she raced forward she passed an abandoned lumber camp. The buildings were old and rotting in the weather. It made her wonder if at some future time the thick forest would be gone. Once the lumber camp must have

220

been surrounded by trees. Had the trees died, or had men cleared the land so that only the rotting camp remained?

Then the woods were behind her. Before her lay the fields of Macedon, and a few miles beyond she would find Joseph.

Joseph was making progress with the well. He would have it in good running order in plenty of time to return to Manchester by nightfall. He whistled a gay tune as he repaired the wheel that lowered and raised the water bucket.

Suddenly he became aware that a woman on horseback had turned in at the gate and was riding toward him at full gallop. As the rider came nearer he recognized Emma.

She pulled the horse to a stop almost at the spot where he was standing. Her face was flushed, and the horse was wet with sweat, which meant that she had been riding hard for a considerable time.

"Joseph—come with me." Words tumbled from her lips. "It's Willard Chase and fourteen men. They plan to force you to give them the plates. They're on their way here now! Come on—hurry!"

"I'll tell Mrs. Duprae I'll finish her work later." He spoke over his shoulder on his way to the house. "My horse is in the barn. Start bridling her. I'll be back to put the saddle on."

"Hurry . . . please hurry!" She called after him as she moved her horse forward toward the barn.

Joseph didn't discount the danger to himself or Emma. How far behind the men were he had no way of knowing, but he knew they must not find them here. They would be no match for fifteen men.

As they rode out the front yard Mrs. Duprae was standing at the door. She waved and they returned the wave. Joseph had told her what to expect. She would lock the doors now and keep out of sight. It was unlikely the men would break into her house, but if they did she had promised to hide and make no sound at all. Joseph felt certain they would leave if they found no one at home.

It would take Willard and his band awhile to find out where he had been working, but Macedon was small; neighbors knew things, and they talked. There would be those who would know where a stranger had gone to mend a well.

"What shall we do?" Emma asked.

What indeed ought they to do? Joseph knew the woods would be no place to encounter Willard Chase and his men. They must get out of sight somewhere and hide until they could put distance either ahead or behind their enemies. In order to do this they had to know where the men were—to see them without being seen.

"Joseph," Emma said, "if we could make it to the abandoned lumber camp we could hide there. I'm sure we could see the men pass there. If they should be on their way to the Duprae farm we would have a long start ahead of them back to Manchester."

Joseph knew it was a good plan, perhaps their only chance to return home safely. But there was danger in the plan too, for it was open road most of the way. He was fairly certain an encounter with the men would do him no real harm, since it was the plates they wanted, and he was the only one who knew where they were hidden. But he was just as certain they would force Emma to go with them in order to bargain her safety against their getting the records, and if they tried this they would have to kill him first. Perhaps they should knock on the door of some strangers and ask them to shelter Emma for a fee.

She was against this. "What makes you think I would be safe in someone's house? They could find me there the same as anywhere. Let's try for the camp. My horse needs to cool off and rest, and so do I. There will be clear running water in the mill ditch back of the shanties, and I'm thirsty." She put her face down and caressed the neck of her horse. "You're thirsty too, aren't you Willow Withe?"

Silently they rode with only one purpose in mind—to make the abandoned camp ahead of Willard Chase and his band. Always they watched for their pursuers. That many riders would stir up enough dust to be seen at a great distance.

They reached the camp without a sight of the Chase band. Perhaps the men had decided against a trip to Macedon, knowing they could waylay Joseph on his return home, or perhaps they were waiting for him in the thickest part of the woods, knowing he would hardly dare to leave the beaten trail.

The ghost camp consisted of a number of dilapidated shanties and a log millhouse with part of the roof gone. Near the big ditch, where the flow of water was shallow compared to what it had been years ago, was the skeleton of a rotting barge and the remains of hewn and fallen logs in the process of decay.

The horses were tied behind the millhouse in a sheltered spot well hidden from the road where they could eat the wild grass that was beginning to dry in the September sun. As soon as Willow Withe had cooled they would give him a drink.

With the horses cared for Emma dropped full length to the bank of the swirling water and drank thirstily.

"Sweet, pure water," she said as she got up. "I'm a new woman now."

Joseph was appraising the old buildings, and now they both glanced quickly around them for the best spot to hide

223

in. It must be where they could observe the road from both directions but where they wouldn't be seen.

The shanty they decided on was leaning and filled with dust. Joseph had to clear spider webs from the door before they could enter. The remains of a rusted stove, half a table, and a broken chair were of a past that was now history. He inspected the rotting boards of the floor to make sure they were safe and free of snakes. Two squirrels scampered out the door as they entered and scolded them from the roof of a neighbor shanty.

Joseph placed himself beside an opening in the wall that had once been a window. Emma turned the broken chair on its side, and sat down near him. If the men were coming, why were they not here by now? True, it would take them a little time to get horses for they would hardly attempt a trip to Macedon in any vehicle that would slow down their mission. "I think they are waiting for you somewhere in the woods, Joseph."

"You could be right."

"What will we do?"

"You look tired, my love." He spoke with tenderness, but his eyes appraising her held the hint of a twinkle. She had lost most of the pins from her hair; her face was dirt streaked; and her clothes—usually tidy and clean—were soiled. "We'll stay here and wait," he said.

"And if nothing happens?"

"You're positive they said they would come to Macedon?"

"I'm positive."

"It would be much simpler for them to wait for me in Manchester," he said.

"In Manchester you have your family and Isaac and Newel to help you. They saw some determined resistance this morning." She got up and stood with him at the window opening.

He kissed her. "I imagine Willow Withe has cooled off enough for a drink. You stay and watch the road while I lead him to the ditch."

"I'm thirsty again too, Joseph."

"I'll bring you one."

"In your shoe?" she asked, laughing at the thought of it. Then she remembered. All the Smiths always carried a canvas bag fastened to their horses' saddles whenever they went even as far as Manchester. His was empty now she knew. He would have given her a drink when she first mentioned being thirsty if it hadn't been. She had come poorly equipped in her haste to get away, but she knew how important it was to have water and a blanket. What a godsend Joseph's blanket would be if they had to spend the night here.

He brought the bag filled with water, and she drank again. Afterward she dampened a handkerchief and washed her face and hands with it. Then she took the remaining pins from her hair. At all times Emma was beautiful, but to Joseph she always seemed most lovely with her thick, dark hair falling to her waist. It was the way she had looked when he first met her, and there was something very like a little girl about her with her hair down, although Emma was a woman with a woman's wisdom and reactions. Often Joseph was humbled in her presence, wondering how he could have been the man blessed to win her. She was his dearest friend, as well as his adored one, and she had endeared herself to his family in a way that made them her their own. She seldom mentioned her people, but he knew she missed them. She had taken Don Carlos to her heart as a kind of substitute for her own smallest brother. His eyes brushed her now, lighted by his great love for her.

Ten minutes went by. Suddenly Joseph and Emma

stiffened. Down the road from the direction of Manchester there was a great cloud of dust. Involuntarily Joseph reached for Emma's hand. They watched the cloud of dust come nearer. Soon they could make out ten riders on horseback. Nearer and nearer they came. The rider in front was Willard Chase. Joseph and Emma ducked down, making sure they could not be seen from the road. Willard Chase and his men were riding hard, and they were armed with guns and clubs.

Joseph's hand tightened on Emma's. He was so silent that Emma looked at him questioningly. "Are you praying, Joseph?"

He looked down at her, love shining in his eyes. "My heart is praying for our safe return to Manchester." His voice was very gentle.

"Did you notice that only ten men rode by? Where are the others?"

"Waiting for us in the woods probably. But we must go at once . . . it is better to meet five men head on than to fight ten."

This time as they rode toward home they knew danger might be just ahead of them in the dense woods.

It didn't seem possible to Joseph and Emma that they could have come all the way through the woods with nothing happening. The ride had been a nightmare all the way. Every unnatural sound, every movement of animal or bird had sent a chill creeping through them. They were so tense when they arrived where traffic was heavy that their nails had bitten into their hands and they were trembling from strain. As they began to relax their faces took on color. Emma flashed Joseph a smile, but her teeth were chattering.

As they rode through Manchester they met Samuel

standing at the entrance of the Canandaigua road that led homeward. "I came to warn you. There are men in the grove near the land that leads to the house. Father spotted two; there may be more."

Joseph looked grave. "Emma," he said, "I want you to go to Martin Harris's and spend the night. They will be proud to have you, and I can't risk any harm coming to you. Samuel, you take my horse and ride with her. Take care of her. I'll go the rest of the way on foot. They won't be expecting me to come in walking; it will be the best way."

Emma started to protest, then thought better of it. Instead, her eyes twinkled. "Mrs. Harris loves to gossip. She is bound to think we've had a quarrel if I go to spend the night without you."

"Good," Joseph said grinning. "Tell her I walloped you." He got off his horse and handed the reins to Samuel. Then he went to Emma and she reached for him. They held each other in a tight embrace. "Oh, Joseph, I love you so much." Their lips met. Her eyes were wet with tears. "Be careful, Joseph."

"I'll be fine," he said.

"Of course," she said, smiling, while tears ran down her cheeks. "You are practically indestructible."

Samuel and Emma rode away then. Once she turned and blew him a kiss. He returned the kiss and waved, then stood watching until they rode out of sight.

With Emma on her way to Martin Harris's and Samuel riding to protect her, a great weight seemed to be lifted from Joseph's shoulders. He was positive that Willard Chase and his men would attempt to finish what they had started, so he walked warily with his eyes constantly on the alert for anyone who might try to start something. The hour was approaching seven, but after sunset there would be a long twilight. He needed the chest from Hyrum's. He must remove the records from their secret hiding place, which was unsafe, and put them under lock and key where he could guard them.

The sky was blue, and the feel of fall was in the air. He walked swiftly. The slight limp seldom bothered him anymore unless he was on his feet for hours at a time. In fact, it had been a long time since he had thought of his leg at all. Work with Isaac Stoal and labor on his father's farm had toughened him, given him powerful shoulders, a healthy body with strong muscles and no fat. He was a handsome figure as he swung along with his keen eyes awake to everything around him.

Before he reached home he was surprised to see Samuel come cantering up. He pulled to a stop. "We met the Harrises in their surrey. They were happy to have Emma, and she went the rest of the way with them. I told her to stay there until some of us came for her."

"Good."

Samuel was leading Willow Withe, and Joseph mounted him. They rode side by side, ever watchful. Joseph was doing some mental planning. At last he said, "Why don't you ride to the house and send Don Carlos to Hyrum's? Hyrum promised me a chest with a lock and key until I can have one made. Our enemies will hardly stop a boy. Tell Don Carlos what I want of him, and tell him to accomplish the errand with all speed."

"Aren't you coming now?"

"The records aren't safe where they are. If those prowlers Father saw are still searching, they could discover them."

"You didn't hide them in the woods?"

228

"Yes, I did," Joseph said. "When we get to the lane, you take Willow Withe with you. A horse can't go where I'm going."

They reached the lane and Samuel said, "If you'll come to the house with me, I'll go with you."

Joseph dismounted, and Samuel took his horse. Then Joseph said, "Why don't you meet me? Remember the birch log where we sat and skinned rabbits last month? The plates are hidden near that log. I'll get them and come home by way of my retreat and make a straight dash for the house from there. You should meet me somewhere between the log and the house."

"I'll find you," Samuel said. "Be watchful. When you hear my birdcall, answer, so I'll know where you are."

The hiding place was east of the house. Joseph was so familiar with the spot that he could almost find it with his eyes shut. Near the log he had mentioned was another one. It was hollow and decayed except for the bark, which in a measure was sound. Yesterday Joseph had taken his pocket knife and cut the bark on the old birch log with special care, turning it back and enlarging the hollow until it was big enough to hold the wrapped package. After putting it in the cavity he had replaced the bark, then he had covered it with vegetation and a tree branch in order to conceal it as much as possible, but he couldn't be sure the camouflage was good enough to deceive the eyes of trackers, if such were about.

He went cautiously, his ears and eyes alert to every sight and sound around him. If there were trackers, they would take every precaution not to be discovered, and they would be able to walk with almost no sound at all. Joseph could not afford to be careless.

In some places birches grew close together, in other areas the trees thinned, leaving barren spaces where a traveler could be easily spotted. As much as possible Joseph skirted the open spaces, but he could not help wondering if he had been seen.

It was very beautiful in the woods among the silver birches, pines, and hemlocks. Wild flowers and ferns made a colorful carpet for his feet. Birds, startled by his intrusion, flew over his head, singing or scolding. Squirrels eyed him curiously. The air was alive with wildlife and growing things, but Joseph saw and heard only with his senses for his mind was bent on one thing—to get the records and make certain they did not come to harm. He prayed for guidance. If there were trackers in the woods he hoped he would see them before they saw him.

At last he came to his secret hiding place. The trees were thick here, and it was very quiet. He paused, his ears and eyes straining for any human sight or sound. All was silent save for the usual noises of the forest. He walked with caution to the log, then he bent and carefully turned the bark back, feeling for the bundle. It was safe. He lifted it up and started for home, going as swiftly as possible. His danger was very great now. If his enemies had followed him they would strike now, for the plates were in his hands. Had he been foolish not to wait for Samuel? Every sound seemed amplified a hundred-fold. He came to a windfall. Ahead of him was a log. He jumped it nimbly, and a man sprang up from behind it, striking Joseph a glancing blow on the head with his gun. The blow hurt but did no other harm. Then it was man against man.

Joseph knew how to use his fists and his weight to good advantage. The records lay on the ground out of reach of the attacker, and Joseph was using skills he had learned under careful tutoring at the Knight home. Friendly combats with his brothers had kept those skills sharpened through the years. It was flesh against flesh, but his enemy was not trained. Joseph's movements were controlled. He was waiting

230

for a chance to use a certain wrestling hold, while he dodged and outmaneuvered the blows of his opponent and delivered some skillful punches of his own. His feet, his hands, his body moved like a timed machine. The fight was unequal— the skilled against the unskilled; but his attacker was bull-like and strong, and he bellowed with an unnerving sound. Joseph knew he must do more than down him; he must use the one wrestling hold he knew that would throw him and wind him so that he would be unable to follow and attack again. He moved, he watched, he waited, then with one deft and careful hold he lifted the man and hurled him to the ground. The big body didn't move. Joseph had done him no lasting harm, but it would be some time before he could get up.

He hid the attacker's gun under a fallen log, since he had no intention of using it and it would be added weight to carry. Then he picked up the records and walked away. Soon he was running as if the fight had not occurred.

Two hundred yards farther on he was attacked again. This time Joseph was panting hard when the fight was over. His face was bruised and his clothes were torn, but no harm had come to the sacred records. Were there three others? Had Samuel run afoul of them? Was this why he had not met him as planned? He trilled the birdcall and listened, but Samuel gave no answer through the forest's silence. Wherever the growth was dense he trilled and listened in vain for the answering call. What ought he to do? There was still a considerable distance to cover, and an enemy could sneak up on him from almost any direction. Suppose all three should attack at once—what then?

He moved slowly and with great caution. He inhaled deeply until his heart stopped its unnatural pounding and his breathing became normal. What would he do if he had to fight three men at once? Could he even win over one at a time now? And if they were trained. . . . The last man had not been easy to overcome. If they succeeded in wresting the records, would he ever get them back? And if they killed him, would the angel protect the plates and prepare another to translate them? His ears strained for Samuel's soft, fluted call while he breathed to conserve every ounce of his strength.

He was in a well-known part of the woods now. Here every tree seemed a familiar friend; still there was no sign of Samuel.

It occurred to him that he could hide his package here, but on second thought he decided against it. If he were being watched, to leave the records unguarded would be utter folly. Now he was in his own part of the grove, the place where he went often to pray and meditate, to be alone, to solve his problems. Ahead was ground the Smiths were clearing. It was like an amphitheatre with trees growing thick all around it; beyond was open country, and a little farther on was home.

He was about to enter the cleared area when he saw something or someone move in the thick growth of trees across from him. Was it a deer? Animals seldom ventured this near except to search for food or water in times of drouth. He moved backward into his own grove and stopped to listen. In order to get home he had to cross the cleared area, back into trees, then open country and home. Was it Samuel that he saw? He trilled and listened. Silence was his only answer. Should he hide the plates or keep them with him? If he had been seen, his bundle would have been seen also, and to try to defend it in the clearing would be most difficult. Perhaps it would be safer in the thick familiar tree growth for night was upon him; very soon now it would be dark.

Without making a sound Joseph placed his bundle on the ground, hiding it in the underbrush where four trees grew almost together. Satisfied that it was well hidden, he moved through the trees as soundlessly as he could, then he walked

232

boldly out into the clearing several feet to the left of where the plates were hidden. Nothing happened. He kept on walking.

Now he was in the cleared area with the tree growth fifty or sixty feet behind him.

Suddenly, out of the thicket a man came charging. He was a tall man, muscular like Joseph and powerfully built. Joseph knew him. He was one of Manchester's esteemed ministers. The two men eyed each other. In the reverend's hand was a bullwhip.

There were ministers in Manchester whom Joseph admired and respected. Such a one was his mother's minister who had conducted Alvin's funeral with dignity and sincerity. He had stood at Alvin's grave with tears in his eyes, and words of comfort and strength had come from his lips. He had made Hyrum's and Sophronia's marriages seem like holy sacraments, but there was no resemblance between him and the man Joseph was sizing up. This man frightened his congregation into serving a God of terror, even as he set himself up as an example of perfection. We must get this over, Joseph was thinking. We must get it over while there is still light enough for me to see.

From across the clearing came the voice that was meant to frighten. "That bundle you were carrying, Smith, is Manchester property. Get it." The whip hissed, but Joseph knew it was only a warning. It would hit a length away.

Like Joseph, the man was muscle and sinew without fat. They were a match in size. The minister had a handsome face that he would guard. Lucy once remarked that his slick dark hair brought more single women to his congregation than any other church in town. There were other things Joseph had noticed at various times. He didn't like soil on his person or his clothes, and his hands were perfect with smooth, oval nails, these too he would guard. He was older than Joseph, but Joseph had a tired body, bruises, and a swollen face. If the man were trained in boxing or wrestling, or if others were in the trees waiting to assist him, the outcome could be pretty bad.

Silence was making the reverend angry. He held the whip as if it were a familiar friend. Then again it whined through the air. "For the last time, Joe Smith, where have you put those records?"

Joseph dodged the blow. Instead of running as the minister had expected him to do, he moved forward, his eyes intent on the arm and the whip. Again the whip came, and again Joseph dodged it. This was no game. This was power wielded by a powerful man.

Joseph's feet moved deftly, but night was coming on. He had to see the flex of the muscles in the arm and the way the wrist and hand and fingers moved in order to tell the spot where the whip would land. But it was getting dark. He had to get the whip or suffer a terrible beating. Inch by careful inch he moved himself forward while the whip whined. It was moving with a kind of awful rhythm with the reverend being forced backward as Joseph moved forward. But now it was too dark to see. The whip caught his left arm and his sleeve became crimson with blood.

The reverend taunted him. "Your luck has changed, boy."

Joseph didn't answer. He was straining through the darkness, trying to see. The whip was hitting him now as often as it missed, and he was feeling the cuts in his flesh. Blood flowed from his wounds until his shirt became wet and clinging, but he was forcing the reverend back into trees, far away from the records, where a whip would be a useless thing.

They reached the wooded area and began to grapple, their bodies moving with planned precision. Then, with one

234

strong lunge—a lunge Joseph had perfected as a boy—the whip changed hands. Joseph stood at the forest's entrance with his opponent in the clearing. What the minister didn't know was that he was in no condition to use the whip now that he had it, and he wouldn't have used it if he could. Three bouts with the enemy had all but done him in. His head reeled, and he was so dizzy that the whole earth was whirling. His ears rang, and there was a buzzing in his head. Both men were panting. And then the reverend came charging again. With the last ounce of his strength Joseph landed a blow to the preacher's face and one to his stomach. Then while the reverend's knees were buckling he pushed his face into the dirt. Maybe this was the one and only time it would be dirty, but it would be dirty now.

The preacher was getting up and Joseph moved back out of his reach, supporting himself by leaning against a tree trunk. He was glad for the darkness that hid his weak condition. Striving to control his voice and make it strong he said: "I have the whip now. If you think I don't know how to use it why don't you stay three seconds longer and find out. Even in the dark I can spoil your handsome face." He began to count then: "One . . . two . . . three."

The reverend didn't tarry. If he had, Joseph would have lost the fight. When he was well out of reach he turned once again and called back: "Our fight has just begun. Before we finish, ministers and Christians alike will be out to get you. And we'll have those records."

With the minister gone, Joseph sank to the ground, resting his head against the tree trunk, wondering whether he could make it home. If there are more waiting to fight me, they can kill me and take the records, he thought. And rising, he walked with uneven steps to the place where he had hidden his bundle. Taking it up he began the slow and painful walk home.

It was Lucy who found him leaning against the door, too weak to open it. A cry of dismay came through her lips that brought the family running. Samuel's eyes filled with quick tears when he saw Joseph's condition. He and William helped Joseph to the kitchen into a chair, and began cutting the shirt away from his torn body and arms. Tears were running down Lucy's cheeks as she hastened to heat water on the iron stove. It must be sterile to wash his wounds.

Father Joseph, Newel, and Isaac rushed from the house to search the woods for Joseph's enemies, while the others stood helplessly watching and hoping for a chance to assist Joseph in whatever way they could.

"It's my fault," Samuel said in a dazed voice, as if he couldn't believe what he was seeing. "If I had come as I promised, this wouldn't have happened."

"If you had come, we could both be in this fix," Joseph said, wincing as they pulled the shirt from his wounds. "But why . . . didn't . . . you come?"

"At first we couldn't find Don Carlos. He was hiding in the haymow waiting for you to come home. He had seen the men looking for you. In fact, they stopped Don Carlos to ask about you. They said they were your friends. Don showed them the part of the woods where you usually go, and then it came to him that maybe the men were out to harm you. He knew you and Emma would ride into the barn, so he hid in the haymow to warn you."

"But you did send Don Carlos to Hyrum's."

"Yes, after we found him. I started out to help you and met your friend the reverend. He said he had come looking for you to warn you that enemies were in the woods to harm you, and asked your most likely route home. I told him, Joseph. I believed him."

236

Joseph winced again as Lucy began washing his cuts. "Ministers are my worst enemies. I thought you knew that."

When Joseph's wounds had been washed, oiled, and bandaged he felt much better. He was helped to his room and to bed. By lying quietly, he found that he could be almost comfortable.

Father Joseph, Newel, and Isaac came back from their search. They had found no one.

Willow Withe's owner came for him, and William got a reward—or at least money enough to pay for his keep. He belonged to a wealthy farmer in Palmyra, someone Martin Harris knew. How he came to be in the Smith lane would always remain a mystery.

A trip to Hyrum's was always welcomed by Don Carlos. Jerusha kept a neat house, and since she took great pride in housekeeping and cooking there were always scones, a molded pudding, or something good that made the visit a happy event. Today might be different, with Jerusha in bed, but he would see the baby, and with the Bradens there taking care of everything, they might offer him a tea cake or a biscuit.

When Don Carlos arrived Hyrum was at tea with Jerusha's two grown-up sisters. There were no other Bradens there.

Hyrum was in the act of raising a cup to his lips when Don Carlos walked in and touched him on the shoulder.

Without waiting to hear one word he put the cup down, sprang from the table, caught the chest that stood in one corner of the room close by the bed where Jerusha lay, and turning it upside down he emptied its contents on the floor. Then he left the house with the chest on his shoulders.

The astonished women jumped from their chairs. "Has he lost his mind?" asked one.

A look passed between Don Carlos and Jerusha, a look of complete understanding. Then Jerusha's merry eyes touched her sisters. "Don't worry about Hyrum. He just thought of something he has neglected, and it's like him to fly off in a tangent when he thinks of anything in that way." Then she called Don Carlos to the bedside, and turning back the covers she showed him Lovina. He touched the baby's tiny hand with a finger, and she grasped it. "I guess she's the smartest baby in the world," he said, feeling the grip of the small fingers. And Jerusha agreed. "Stay and have some tea," she said. "We have beans and ham and cake." Later she called him to the bed again. Her voice lowered so that only he could hear. "Hyrum left with the team and wagon just now. The chest will soon be there. Be very careful as you ride home."

Emma was escorted home from the Harrises by all the men in the Smith family and Newel and Isaac. The saddled brigade was quite impressive, for the men rode so that her horse was completely surrounded on every side. One look at their serious faces and she knew that the danger was real. From this moment she would live in fear for her life and for her husband's.

Joseph's wounds healed quickly. The plates were locked in the chest, and some member of the Smith household was always on the lookout for the approach of anyone who might prove to be an enemy.

If Joseph lived in fear he gave no sign. He went about as soon as he was able, taking his place as a helpful member of the Smith family, working wherever he was needed, inside or out of the house, but he did not venture away from the farm

238

alone, and he was always watchful. If anything, he was even more tender with Emma, as if he were trying with kindness and love to compensate for bringing her into his troubled life. This worried Emma. Did he not know that being by his side was her joy, and that no other place on earth would do for her? His problems were her problems. His concerns were hers. She would share whatever was good or ill with him.

The thing that puzzled her was the fury of the men who, like Joseph, claimed to be working for God. How could Joseph's visions with an angel arouse such hate, when they too believed that they had been divinely called? They claimed Joseph possessed a devil, yet their very actions toward him and his cause were like the breath of evil. It was as if they were so important that they could tell God what should or should not be brought to light. God was eternal goodness, eternal love, all knowledge, all wisdom, and much more. He did not destroy, yet those who claimed to know Him were tearing Joseph down and saying it was the will of heaven.

Joseph's calmness amazed her. "It is man's nature to fight what he doesn't understand, Emma. Over the years many have come to believe that the Bible is all we need. They read the word of God but fail to listen for his voice. With their minds and hearts closed to his constant presence they say he does not speak. My claim of personal communion strikes at the very foundation of what they believe is truth, yet someday I believe every church will accept divine revelation, and that many will know God as a personal friend and commune directly with him. When this happens the written word will point the way until man can walk with the source of all wisdom and be led by his eternal presence."

The animosity of the clergy was not altogether due to Joseph's claim of angel communications. There were other factors. There were sermons which Joseph termed limiting

239

concepts being preached from the pulpits. Joseph called these delusions and deceptions. He didn't accept the concept that man was an abominable sinner doomed to disease, destruction, and death. To Joseph, man was a miracle created in the image of God and alive with the life of God. He didn't believe man was accountable for Adam's sin. "The only sins I expect to pay for are my own," he told Emma.

He openly challenged infant baptism, and he did not believe in eternal damnation. His very nature rebelled at the thought. The God he worshiped was a God of love—merciful and forgiving.

He didn't believe that salvation was for a few who were lucky enough to find the door of heaven, and he didn't believe that every ordained minister was called of God. He weighed everything he heard and everything he read, accepting what he believed to be truths and discarding what seemed to be false doctrines. He remembered the promise of the angel that the priesthood would be revealed by the hand of Elijah before the coming of the great and dreadful day of the Lord. He didn't go out of his way to clash with the clergy, but when he was confronted with ideas that he couldn't accept, he spoke his mind. Although his voice was usually calm and without malice, his answers often sparked controversy.

There were those who wanted to get hold of Joseph's golden "bible," as they called it, in order to sell it. Others wanted it simply to satisfy their curiosity that such records existed. But more dangerous than these were the agitators who believed that the plates were wicked and must be destroyed, that Joseph was in direct communion with Satan, and that the only way to destroy the evil in him was to kill him. There were a few who believed in the divinity of the records and were Joseph's loyal friends—Martin Harris, the

240

Knights, the Stoals. Joseph and Emma loved them for their concern and help.

Joseph was anxious to begin translating the records, but with the harvesting of crops and the multitude of chores to be done before winter there was no time to begin it. There was more work now than there were hands to do it, for in order to make ends meet they had to work longer and harder. It galled all the Smiths to work for their landowner, when by every right the farm should belong to them.

It was midafternoon of a sunny autumn day. Joseph, Samuel, and William had been sacking and storing wheat since early morning, and they were bone-weary. Some of the wheat they would sell for seed, some for flour, and some they would keep for their own food supply and planting. They were stacking the sacks in the granary as they filled them, which made the job backbreaking.

Suddenly half a dozen men came riding up the lane. They were strangers, and they were carrying clubs. Dismounting simultaneously, as if their timing had been rehearsed, they rushed toward the granary door, caught hold of Joseph, and began dragging him. He struggled loose, and he and William fought them, using every skill they knew. Samuel raced for the house for guns and any help he could bring. It was six against two.

A club struck Joseph a glancing blow, and there was laughter.

"We're here to break your bones one at a time."

"We'll drag you behind a horse until your skin falls off."

They were all on him, holding him in a grip he couldn't break.

"If you want to live, Joe Smith, you'll give us your gold bible."

They clawed at him and mauled him, while fighting William off. The two Smiths struggled until they had no more strength left. Their clothes were in shreds, their bodies sore, their faces bleeding.

All this happened in the short time it took Samuel to speed to the house. Now he was racing back, and with him came Father Joseph, Lucy, Emma, and Catherine, all armed.

A bullet whined and Father Joseph shouted, "That's a warning. We know how to shoot and hit what we shoot at. Get off this land, and don't come back."

It could have been the guns, or maybe they were above fighting women. Whatever it was, the men mounted their horses.

"We'll finish you off another time, Joe. And we'll have that bible."

William and Joseph were panting hard. William started a painful walk back to the house, but Joseph made his way to a grain sack and sat down. He was angry and rebellious. One eye was swollen shut, his lips were cut, there were claw marks on his cheeks, his head was skinned in a spot above his right temple, and he had been clubbed until every movement was pain.

They begged him to come to the house, but he wouldn't. "Go along and let me be," he said gruffly. He didn't even want Emma to touch him. And because they didn't know what else to do, they left him. Joseph sat defiant and grim. If an angel could deliver records he could also protect them. If this were God's business, why didn't He show a little concern and keep these devils off the land? Why must it be his and his family's business to do all the protecting? He was fed up with floggings and clubbings and clawing.

His eyes moved over the land—Alvin's land. He looked at the house with a kind of hunger. Were those records worth risking all their lives to protect? He put a hand to his throbbing head and touched his swollen eye. Those plates

242

would bring enough to buy back the farm, and with them out of his hands life would be simple. He and Emma could settle down to quiet living the way Alvin had planned it. This would be a place to raise healthy children—his children and Emma's. Why not do it? Why not put an end to trouble and danger?

He got up then, still grimly defiant, and walked toward the house. All he could think of was the farm, the house, and his longing to possess them and be free of trouble. But as he walked Emma's face kept coming into mind. It didn't make him proud that he had hurt her. But his feelings of guilt went deeper than her tears, for his heart told him, "You are a chosen instrument of God."

"But I don't want to be chosen. I want to be as other men, accepted by my fellows, free. I want a family to rear on land where Alvin walked and dwell in the house we built together."

"And the sacred records? If you let them out of your hands, what will become of them?"

"Why are they so important? We have the Bible which most religious thinkers claim is enough for time and eternity. Even if there is need for more light, why must I be the one to bring it? Why not someone else? The plates are very valuable. Is it wrong to desire riches?"

"Of course not, but it is wrong to steal to become rich."

"Would it be stealing? The records belong to no earthly man, and I'm not going to destroy them. They will still be around for some scholar to translate."

But Joseph knew this might not happen, for had he not been prepared for this special work over a period of years? The angel claimed the records had great spiritual worth. Would this theft rob posterity of knowledge that might never come again? Were not the records supposed to make plain some obscure writings in the Bible?

The words of the angel troubled his mind almost as if the holy vision were being repeated: "Now you have the records in your hands and you are but a man; therefore you will have to be watchful and faithful to your trust, or you will be overpowered by wicked men. They will lay every plan and scheme possible to get them from you, and if you do not take heed continually, they will succeed. While they were in my hands I could keep them, and no man had power to take them away, but now I give them to you. Beware, and look well to your ways, and you shall have power to retain them and translate them."

Penitently now, Joseph walked into the house. Where was everybody? The menfolk had gone back to sacking and stacking wheat, where he ought to be, but the women? Usually the house buzzed with their activities. Even the children had vanished, and Joseph found himself entirely alone.

He changed to his work clothes. He was about to leave for the granary when he felt a great urge to open the chest. He had been very careful to keep his promise not to show the plates, but now that he was completely alone, this would be a good time to handle them, for up to now he had had no chance to thoroughly inspect them. He walked to the door and locked it; this would give him time to put them back if someone wanted to come in. He unlocked the chest and lifted them out, removing the cloth they were wrapped in. The sunlight through the window made them brilliant, as if each sheet had been newly polished. They had the appearance of being a book, for they were held together by three rings. He began turning the sheets the way one would turn a page in a book, and they gave forth a metallic sound. To the touch they were a little thicker than common tin. He studied the engravings. They were very small characters filling both sides of each sheet, with lettering painstakingly and skillfully

244

done. A part of the volume was sealed, and Joseph remembered that the angel had said these would come forth and be translated by someone else at a later date in history.

The writings were probably Hebrew or Greek or Egyptian. Joseph was not familiar enough with languages to know their origin. After a time he got a clean pillowcase and wrapped the plates in it; then he put the bundle back into the chest, and picked up the breastplate. It was converse on one side, convex on the other, and extended from the neck downward as far as the center of the stomach of a man of extraordinary size. Joseph was no small man, but the breastplate had been worn by a man or men of much larger build than he. It had four straps; two of these went back over the shoulders, and the other two were fastened at the hips. They were a little less than the width of two of Joseph's fingers, and they had holes in the ends of them for convenient fastening.

The Urim and Thummim were fastened to the breastplate. They consisted of two three-cornered stones set in the rims of bows that looked like silver. The stones were transparent, like diamonds, and the bows resembled spectacles. Although they were fastened to the breastplate they could be removed. Joseph took them in his hands. As he examined them he had a strange feeling of going back into time, to the days of Moses, Aaron, and the prophets. He remembered reading that priests of the Aaronic order instituted in the time of Moses wore distinctive robes. One of the vestments was the Ephod, a garment covering the breast and back, fastened to the shoulders. Attached to the Ephod was a breastplate of linen which served as a sort of pocket in which were carried two sacred stones. Those who had such stones were called seers. A seer was greater than a prophet, for he was a revelator, given to know things of the past and also things which were to come.

A strange excitement moved through Joseph. Was he perhaps looking at stones that had once been handled by Aaron, the brother of Moses, or some ancient seer of generations ago? As he looked at them a very odd thing happened. He felt a sudden sensation like heat in his breast. It was not a frightening sensation, but the warmth moved through him, tingling his body, and his heart began pumping very fast. He had not been trying to know the future. In truth, it had not occurred to him to make use of the Urim and Thummim for his own benefit at all, but suddenly, without knowing how he knew, he was made to realize that within a few hours a mob would come to the house looking for the records.

Oh, no, he thought. Not again. A mob meant many, and six had all but finished him and William. He touched his swollen eye, his broken lips, the raw spots on his head, the sore places on his body. And what about the plates? They were not safe in Hyrum's chest, which was light enough that a man of ordinary size could carry it off and could be unlocked without the help of a locksmith. He must hide them so they couldn't be easily found. But where? He went from room to room searching for a hiding place. Drawers, cupboards, closets—these were sure to be ransacked. He went downstairs. In the parlor he stood beside the fireplace, his eyes moving from spot to spot. Then he glanced down at the hearth—a portion of the hearth could be taken up. He could bury the plates and the breastplate there and relay the hearth without too much trouble.

He went for his tools, and had barely begun to work when the family came in. Hyrum was there too. No one showed surprise that he was tearing up the hearth.

Emma stooped down to kiss him on the top of the head; then she squatted to watch him pry up a board. The rest of the family stood close, watching too, and Emma said: "We

246

were worried about you Joseph. You were so—obstinate—so untouchable."

Hyrum picked up a tool and commenced helping with another board.

"The women rode over in the wagon after me when they couldn't stir Father or William or Samuel to action. I told them it was unlikely the mob would come back today, and that you were tough enough to last, but I came along anyway. I told them they had no cause to worry."

"They had cause to worry." Joseph said.

"Hey," Hyrum said, suddenly becoming aware of what they were doing. "Why are we taking up the hearth?"

Joseph told about his experience with the Urim and Thummim.

"It's a good hiding place," Hyrum said. "What made you think of it?"

"I had to think of someplace. Let's hope it's as safe as we think it is."

"I'll stay," Hyrum said. "I hope you're wrong. . . . I hope there won't be any trouble . . . but if there is I want to be here."

The hearth looked the same with the treasures buried under it.

Supper was over and the evening chores inside and outside the house were done. Don Carlos and small Lucy were sleeping in their beds; other members of the family were in the parlor, pretending to relax while they listened to every sound that might announce a mob. William had joked a little about hobbling out to join them. Joseph sat with his head in his hands, wondering what he would do if they descended on him. He had had his fill of trouble.

While they waited they made tentative plans as to what they would do to keep the enemy out of the house. Mother Lucy's brother, Major Mack, and his men had used a simple strategy once which had worked. Young Joseph thought they might try it, for the very thought of fighting the enemy in his and William's battered condition was revolting to him, and he knew William felt the same way.

The candle was burning low. Twice Samuel threatened to go upstairs to bed, but when nobody seemed to care one way or the other he stayed.

Once Father Joseph said, "Hyrum, you had better go home to your family. Jerusha will be worrying about you."

But Hyrum didn't go.

Heads began to nod. Surely Joseph was mistaken. At this late hour there would be no mob.

And then they heard the sound of stealthy footsteps. Lucy snuffed out the candle, and they moved silently to the window where they could see the forms of creeping men. They waited until the first foot touched the porch and the attackers were about to flood onto it. Just at that moment young Joseph threw the door open and hallooed as if he had a legion at hand. At the same time Hyrum gave words of command with great emphasis, while the whole family burst out of the house screaming with such fury that the mob fled.

Their plan had worked! Or had it? Would the men come back? Presently there was the sound of galloping horses. Sleep was impossible now. The men took turns watching at the windows. Night ended and daylight came with nothing further happening.

The Smiths were feeling poverty's pinch. In spite of all their labor, much of the harvest had gone to the landlord, and it was only by the most careful managing that they were able to meet expenses. There was meat in the cold house— half a beef, a porker, venison, hams and bacon. These were hanging suspended by wires from the ceiling, and they were kept cold by blocks of ice packed in sawdust that lined the cold house walls. There was corn in the granary, flour, and

248

bins of grain for next year's planting; but the Smith family was large, and much of this would have to be sold for necessities. The women canned, dried, and preserved fruits and vegetables; there would be no hungry stomachs, but after a year of hard work, it did seem there should be something more to show for it.

And the work seemed never to end. The spinning wheel was seldom idle. There were few evenings spent in fun and leisure. Hands carded wool, knitted, sewed, mended. Old garments too worn to wear were made into something else. By ingenuity, hard work, and imagination the Smiths were able to make a neat appearance among their fellows, but young Joseph especially felt the pinch, for he knew Emma's desire, like his own, was to settle in a place of their own as Hyrum and Jerusha had done. Emma didn't complain, but the longing was in her eyes often of late when they visited at Hyrum's. He knew it was a man's place to set up his own household, but where would they go? It cost money to move, and they owned almost nothing. Even Emma's clothes were what she had had before marriage, and this hurt him too. Emma loved beautiful things, and he wanted to supply everything beautiful for her. He didn't mind cobbling and resoling shoes for himself and other members of the household—they were used to skimping—but he minded it for Emma. Each week he shined their shoes with polish made of soot and oil, but there was a lump in his throat when he saw the fashionable shoes for women displayed in the stores, for he could imagine Emma dressed as she deserved to be. It hurt that he could provide only the meager necessities.

The weather was growing colder. Small Lucy and Don Carlos undressed in front of the fire, then raced for their beds. The other members of the Smith family undressed in their rooms in great haste and climbed into feather beds, tucking covers to their chins and enjoying the luxury of bed warmers or heated rocks until they cooled.

One windy night in November Emma and Joseph were making quick preparations for bed. Emma had put hot coals in the bed warmer and thoroughly warmed the covers before Catherine came to claim the warmer. Near the foot of the bed, underneath the covers, were two heated rocks carefully wrapped, one for Joseph and one for her. Now, with a quick look to make sure Joseph didn't see her, she slipped something under his pillow and climbed into bed. She slept next to the wall, and it was Joseph's habit to snuff out the candle they always kept on the nightstand by the bed. Tonight Emma said with a mischievous toss of her head, "Leave the candle burning for a little while. There is something I want you to see." Looking puzzled, he climbed into bed beside her, and she kissed his cheek. "We have a secret to share," she said gently. "Reach your hand under the pillow, and you'll find something there."

He reached and brought out a tiny knit stocking for a very small baby. She watched the expression on his face almost breathlessly. Would he understand and be glad?

For a moment he turned it in his hand, and then as if suddenly comprehending the message that it bore, his eyes grew warm and tender as they caught and held Emma's. "You mean we are going to be parents?"

She nodded. "Are you glad?"

He caught her to him and held her as if he would never let her go. "She will be a girl exactly like you, my Emma."

"No, he will be a boy exactly like you."

They laughed because the moment was so wonderful.

"I was afraid you would think we couldn't afford him," Emma said with her lips against his cheek.

"We can afford her, even if she is twins," Joseph said. "I could take two like you."

250

She didn't answer, and presently he said, "Imagine our child with the blood of the Smiths and the blood of the Hales in her."

"Well," Emma said, "we'd better not imagine her with anybody else's blood." Then she grew serious. "Joseph, do you suppose my folks might see us now? Do you think they might love our baby?"

"You must write them tomorrow, Emma. Remind them of the blood of the Hales, but don't mention the blood of the Smiths."

"I hope he'll look exactly like you, Joseph. Someday my folks must know what a fine and precious husband you are."

Emma was soon asleep in Joseph's arms, but sleep was far from Joseph. More than ever now he wanted to leave Manchester. He didn't want his child to hear ugly rumors about his father. Joseph had not extinguished the candle, and Emma's face so close to his own was the most beautiful face in life to him. He still marveled that she preferred him above all other men when she could have had her choice of many in Harmony. She was a gentlewoman, reared to be the mistress of a beautiful home, surrounded by luxuries, yet here she lay in a common homespun gown, content to be near him.

Oh, God, he thought, if only I could give her what she deserves, but I can give her only love and tenderness, and sometimes I don't even measure up to that.

He thought of the records. He should begin the translating. Would he ever be able to translate in Manchester among so many enemies?

"Show me the way," he prayed. "Show me what I ought to do."

Emma wrote her parents, as she had often done before, and this time she wrote with a prayer in her heart that they would answer, for they had ignored all her letters each time she had tried to make reconciliation. She told them they were to be grandparents in June, and her special plea that they would allow her and Joseph to come and stay with them, at least until after the birth of the baby, was soul-touching, even as it conveyed her love for them.

She gave Joseph the letter to read, and his gentle comment when he finished was: "Unless their hearts are stone, Emma, I'll wager you have won your case." Then his tone took on real concern. "Even if they ask us to come, our problem still remains. Where will we get the money to move? We can't move and let them support us, and if I'm translating I won't have time to work and earn our keep."

"We'll get it somewhere," Emma answered with more confidence than she felt.

Days went by and there was no answer. Emma's eyes became brooding and sorrowful. "Why must they hate us so much that they refuse our baby?" she burst out one evening when they were alone. Then her words stopped as hurt deepened in Joseph's eyes, and she caught him to her as if she must prove again how much his love meant to her.

Joseph knew he could translate. He had tried it, and he could. Now he was chafing to find time and a safe place to work, but mobs continued to storm the premises. The plates were removed from their hiding place, and the hearth relaid again. His odd jobs had paid for a strong box with a good lock, but his worry remained, for the only box he could afford was light enough that a man could carry it off. Emma had promised to act as his scribe, but it was hard for her to take the time from household tasks that needed to be done, for the women were making garments for the baby without slackening their regular chores. The translating was moving slowly.

One day the children brought in a box to play with that Joseph eyed with interest. It was strong and sturdy, and the right size to hold the plates without the breastplate.

"Where did that box come from?" he asked Don Carlos.

"You know that old cooper house across the Canandaigua road from here? We got it there. There's not much in that dirty place except some flax and a few barrels and staves."

"Stay out of there and play near the house," Joseph told him.

"It's a—abandoned," Lucy said, using the big word with pride.

"Abandoned or not, stay out of there. And don't tear up that box. When you finish playing with it, take it back where you got it. It belongs to the coopersmith, and he may want it for something. He may start working in the cooper house again when the weather warms up."

"He won't," Lucy said. "It's full of cobwebs."

Joseph smiled and ruffed her hair. "The old cooper house is not a fit place to play," he said as he left them.

Whenever Joseph and Emma had leisure and conditions permitted, they did work at the translating. He hung a quilt across the middle of the room, a kind of wall, with a table and chair on one side and the bed on the other. Emma would sit at the table and write, while he sat on the bed. In this way she couldn't see the plates, but she could hear the metallic sound whenever Joseph touched them.

"Our first step," he told her, "will be to make facsimiles of some of the characters we've translated, which I think are reformed Egyptian. We'll send them to some learned men and get them to authenticate our translation."

Emma agreed, wondering how they could ever make any

253

headway, with strangers and mobs appearing any time of day or night bent on destroying both Joseph and his work.

"I keep thinking of Martin Harris," Joseph said. "He often goes to New York on business. I'm sure he wouldn't mind taking copies with him."

Again she agreed. Martin had tact and poise, and he seemed to be at ease with strangers. "Did you ever think of asking him to be your scribe, Joseph? He can't be very busy in winter with all the hired hands he keeps the year round."

The more Emma and Joseph thought about Martin, the more certain they became that he would help. Since it appeared that Emma's folks wouldn't have them perhaps the Harrises would invite them to stay with them. Their daughter was soon to be married; maybe Emma could help with her trousseau. Mrs. Harris wouldn't be easy to get along with. She was a peculiar, prying woman who seldom did a favor without turning it to her own ends, but Emma told Joseph: "It will be only until you can find work in Palmyra and rent a house for us." Her tone conveyed to him how much she longed for a place, any kind of place that she and Joseph could make into a home.

He didn't remind her that a job would mean no time to translate, and that the records would be no safer in Palmyra than in Manchester. At this point he wanted what she wanted.

A night or two after this conversation, Joseph again received the strange warning that the records were in danger, and heeding the warning, he took them from the strong box and carried them across the Canandaigua road to the old cooper shop. The box the children had played with was there among the old barrels and staves that Don Carlos had spoken about. He climbed the rickety ladder and laid the plates in a quantity of flax that was stored in the shop loft. Then he nailed the box shut with an old wooden lid he found in the debris. This done, he tore up the floor of the shop and put the box under it, carefully relaying the floor again.

At nightfall the mob came and commenced rummaging around outside the Smith house and all over the premises. The Smiths stood guard at the windows, ready for whatever might come, but the mob made no attempt to enter the house. After an hour or more they went away.

Next morning the Smiths examined their place for damage and found none, but the floor of the cooper shop was torn up and the box shivered to pieces. Joseph climbed to the loft. The plates were safe. The flax and everything in the loft was undisturbed, but now Joseph and Emma were determined to leave Manchester.

It was Mother Lucy who went to see the Harrises. The family decided she needed a change of scene, for she was showing the strain of mobs, anxiety, and overwork. More than any of them, she needed something new to think about.

"Besides," Joseph told Emma, "she understands Mrs. Harris, and in that family, whatever Mrs. Harris says goes."

Lucy came home in a glow. She had seen many who had been her neighbors and close friends when she lived in Palmyra.

Her trip had been partly successful. Martin had seemed pleased that Joseph wanted him for a scribe and promised to get his business and everything in order, ready for whatever plan Joseph might have. But their daughter was having romantic problems that might end her engagement. The parents were so upset that Lucy's good sense told her it would be unwise to approach them about the young Smiths staying with them at this time.

This was another disappointment for Joseph and Emma, and another closed door.

Tuesday dawned bright, cold, and clear. The air was raw, and the men's fingers felt almost frozen inside their mittens as they did their outside chores.

Christmas was less than a month away, and Joseph was beginning to feel that the winter would pass with little of his work accomplished. He pondered his situation while he milked and checked the livestock to see that they were all in shelter, for this was the time of year when storms could descend without warning. He was cold, rebellious, and miserable, but he was watchful too, and that is how he happened to see the covered wagon drawn by four fine horses turn off the Canandaigua road and enter their lane. He could think of no one he knew who would be driving such a finely matched pair, so he picked up his filled milk pails and made quick steps to alert everyone in the house. If this were trouble coming, there would be little time to prepare for it.

He had almost reached the house when Emma flung open the door and raced coatless down the steps. She hardly saw Joseph as she flew past him toward the wagon that was approaching the house. He set the milk pails down, only half comprehending what was going on; then he was racing after her, but by now she was far ahead of him.

A young man jumped nimbly to the ground, and the next thing Emma and the young man were locked in each other's arms. It was Alva, Emma's brother. By the time Joseph reached them Emma was crying and laughing at the same time, her actions showing how very much she had missed her family. Then Joseph and Alva were clasping hands in a warm handshake, and Alva said: "The folks sent me to bring you both back to Harmony. I have come to move you, and we won't take no for an answer. We want you home for Christmas."

Emma's eyes were like stars as they met Joseph's. "They want us."

Later Joseph asked Emma, "How did you know it was Alva in the wagon?"

"I didn't," Emma said, "but I recognized the team, and knew some of my family were in the wagon. Isn't it wonderful! Everything will be fine now. You'll see!"

And Joseph, watching Emma's joy, hoped the move would be as good as the dreams in her shining eyes.

The Hale wagon was more than adequate to hold Joseph and Emma's meager possessions, but there was still the problem of money to pay for lodging and for their keep after they were established at the Hales', for Joseph refused to allow others to support them. If he tied up his daylight hours earning money on which to live, there would be no time for translating, and this was his main object in leaving Manchester. He took pains to impress it upon Alva that translating the plates was to be his special work throughout the remainder of the winter.

As they talked it became clear to him that Alva thought little of his plans. If Joseph truly had an authentic record, it was Alva's belief that he should turn it over to some language expert. He intimated that the Hale family thought Joseph was laboring under some grand delusion—or an evil spirit— and although Alva refrained from being unkind, Joseph was quick to discern Alva's true feelings.

One thing Joseph was firm about—he must see Martin Harris before leaving Harmony, for he had to know if Martin would be willing to go to Harmony to be his scribe. Alva assured Joseph that if Mr. Harris wished to come to Harmony he could board and room with the Hales. The bunkhouse was seldom full at any time, and in winter there were always several empty beds. As for food, it was always plentiful.

The following day found Joseph and Alva riding horseback along the road that followed the numerous acres which made up the Harris farm. Mr. Harris had some of the best wheatland in New York State, and Joseph found himself looking at it with a kind of longing, for he couldn't help comparing his nothing with so much plenty. Without wanting to do so, he found himself thinking again of how hard Alvin and all the Smiths had worked for ground that his father's carelessness had lost them overnight. It was good that Alvin would never know of his family's poverty. Yet the fertile acres reminded Joseph of his blessings too. Emma was his greatest. In his mind's eye he compared her to Mrs. Harris—the proud, demanding, sharp-tongued woman who often made Martin's life miserable. Although she had no reason to believe herself above her husband, she had a knack of making him feel inferior, and whether intentionally or not she often humiliated him before his friends. Martin, on the other hand, was most patient with her, supplying her demands whenever he could and, in spite of all her faults, appeared to be genuinely fond of her. They had little of the deep and tender understanding that Joseph and Emma shared, and it seemed to Joseph that Martin's whole family looked upon him as the source of supply for their unending material desires—nothing more. And it was a shame, for Martin's mind was one few could match. He was wise and understanding, a man respected and well liked by almost everyone.

Alva and Joseph rode along almost in silence, for the two were not kindred spirits. Their only common interest was Emma. Near the end of their trip Alva—used as he was to fine surroundings—showed genuine admiration for the Harris barns, carriage house, and granaries, for they were large, carefully constructed, and in excellent repair.

"Your friend Martin Harris is not a poor man."

"But he wears his riches with humility," Joseph answered thoughtfully.

They came to the house. It, too, was large, constructed after the pattern of fine New Amsterdam city houses. Joseph was welcomed cordially by Lucinda Harris, who explained that her father had gone in to Palmyra; she said they would probably find him at the bank or the tavern across from the bank, or they might overtake him, as he was driving the surrey and had been gone about twenty minutes. She tried to get a promise from Joseph that they would stop back for tea and a chat with the family. Her mother had gone into town in her own conveyance much earlier in the day to attend a gathering of women and a fashion show, but she would most certainly want to see Joseph.

He thanked her warmly, explaining why they must leave Palmyra and return to Manchester as quickly as possible to get things ready for their move to Harmony.

"It is what Emma has been wanting for a long time," Lucinda said. "How happy she will be to see her family again!"

And Joseph and Alva agreed.

The search for Martin had not been as easy as Lucinda had anticipated, but on their second trip around they found him in the general store with half a dozen men visiting congenially around a stove, discussing Martin Van Buren's chances of becoming governor of the state.

Mr. Harris insisted on taking them across to the tavern and feeding them. "It will be a good place to air our minds," he told them.

Alva was drawn to Mr. Harris exactly as Joseph was. He was a kindly, soft-spoken gentleman. True, he was a farmer,

259

but he was much more, for his eyes were the eyes of a dreamer and a scholar. These were the characteristics in Martin that all the Smiths held in such esteem.

Yes, he would go to Harmony. It was the time of year when he could easily get away. His house was in order, and he would come directly after Christmas.

Joseph's joy was boundless. And then at parting Martin insisted upon giving him fifty dollars to help out on the trip. At first Joseph wouldn't take it, but Martin insisted. "My boy, I believe you have been called by God to do a divine work, and I'm proud that you are giving me a chance to have a part in it. Take the money. In a small way it shows my faith in you."

Joseph tried to hide his emotion, but his eyes filled, and he wiped the tears away quickly as he said good-bye. The fifty dollars would give him and Emma a start at being self-sufficient.

There were delays on the trip to Harmony. A storm kept them marooned at the Knights in Colesville for a few days. Then, as they traveled on, in some places roads were so snowbound that they had to shovel their way through drifts. It was a tiring trip, but there were few complaints. They had hoped to be home three or four days before Christmas, but it was Christmas Eve when they drove into Harmony.

The house was ablaze with light, and as they rode up to it they could hear music and laughter. A party was in progress.

As Alva drew the horses to a stop the music ceased, the door flew open, and Emma's family and friends came flooding out to greet them. Emma had forgotten how beautiful women dressed in the latest fashions could look.

The men too were something to see in their holiday finery. For a moment her throat caught at the contrast—but only for a moment; then all were talking at once as they moved into the house. Emma's shining eyes told Joseph how very much she had missed being a part of all this.

Joseph and Alva spent a little time by the fire warming themselves, then they went out to take care of the team and unload the essentials. Joseph had brought a supply of staples from Manchester, and the Knights had added more rations. In the freezing weather these would keep until they were unloaded later, but the sight of them gave Joseph a feeling of independence. For a time at least he and Emma would be self-supporting.

It didn't take long to do what had to be done. He carried their clothes wrapped in a canvas bag up to the room that had been Emma's—the room they were to share—and hung them in the closet. How elegant the furnishings were. He could tell that nothing much had been changed, for the room still looked like Emma. A smile touched his lips as he pictured himself sleeping in the four-poster bed with the ruffled canopy top and the matching spread. But the smile vanished almost as it came. Before they entered into the festivities they would have to wash and change, and what could they wear that would be presentable? They would be neat and clean but strangely conspicuous. He didn't mind so much for himself, but oh how he wished he could wave a wand over Emma and change her into a modern Cinderella just for the night. Well, he couldn't, and he had better let her know that her Sunday best was hanging in the closet.

He went downstairs and paused at the bottom of the landing, searching for Emma in the friendly, happy crowd.

He couldn't see her, but his eyes focused on the tree. It was in the room they had ordered him out of, the room where he and Emma had brought the news of their marriage.

It went from floor to ceiling—a most beautiful tree aglow with what must be hundreds of little candles in tapered holders, in all the colors of the rainbow. There were gossamer angels that seemed to float on cobweb wings, and bright colored ornaments delicate as snowflakes. Under the tree it looked as if Santa had dumped his entire sleigh load. Somewhere there Emma had placed their humble gifts for each other and for the Hales. Joseph drank in the beauty of the tree. Christmas was only a few hours away, and Emma was with the family she loved. This was what her heart had been crying for, and he must in no way spoil her happiness. The room was alive now with people, but where was Emma?

While he stood there a little boy of perhaps four years came up to him. "Are you Emma's buffroon?"

"No." A smile touched Joseph's lips. "I'm Emma's Joseph."

"Oh," the child said. "I like you." He caught Joseph's hand and hugged it, then he danced away.

So that's what they think of me, Joseph thought. A buffoon. His eyes twinkled suddenly. The way the child had said it made it sound like something very nice.

Almost as soon as Alva and Joseph went out to take care of the team and to unload what had to be unloaded, Emma found herself facing relatives who asked blunt questions. Was she happy? Were Joseph's people weird? What was it like to live with a religious fanatic? She felt trapped, like a bird suddenly made captive. It was her sister Phoebe who rescued her.

"Come upstairs, Em. Eric and I are in my old room for the holidays. Let's fill my pitcher with warm water, and you can sponge off in my washbowl. I know you must be tired after traveling so far in the cold."

The two sisters had always been close, but as Emma's eyes met Phoebe's understanding ones she was more than grateful. Her smile encircled the room, then excusing themselves, the two sisters gracefully climbed the stairs.

Out of earshot Phoebe said, "Don't let what they say worry you, Em. You should know by now we're a tongue-wagging family. If you're happy, that's all that matters to any of us. At least that's all that matters to Eric and me."

"I'm happy."

"I believe you. Maybe you don't know it, but I've always liked Joseph."

"With all my heart, Bea, I hope the family will come to know what a wonderful man he is."

Phoebe took her porcelain pitcher from the marble-topped commode. "I'll be right back. Stretch out on the bed if you like while I go for warm water."

"You look so beautiful, Bea. You shouldn't be doing menial tasks for me." But she gave her a grateful smile and settled back on the bed. It felt good to relax. If she could have her way, she would simply undress and go to bed, forgetting all the merrymakers downstairs.

Bea came back with water and filled the gleaming porcelain washbowl.

With a little sigh Emma forced herself upright. "If Joseph has brought our clothes up, I'll get a fresh dress." But instead of going, the girls sat on the bed and talked. Soon Emma was launching into the story about Joseph getting the plates, and their struggle to keep them safe.

The water cooled in the washbowl, and she forgot that she was tired.

At last Phoebe went for more warm water, and Emma went to her room to select a dress. The room, the familiar

263

surroundings, family—all these were suddenly very dear to her.

Back in Phoebe's room once more she began to wash. Bea touched the dress so carefully laid out on the blue ruffled spread. "This dress, Em, you had it before you married Joseph. Haven't you had anything new—anything pretty since . . . ?" She looked over the clean undergarments. "Haven't you had *anything* new?"

Emma stepped out of her soiled garments. "Material things mean a lot to you, don't they, Bea?"

"I don't know." Bea's face became thoughtful. "It used to be that you were the one who bought clothes."

"I know." Emma finished washing and began putting on her clean underthings. "With Joseph the material seems less significant, because with him I have found something that means much more."

"I'll fix your hair," Bea said.

Emma finished putting on her underclothes and sat down at the dressing table. Bea took down her long hair and began combing it carefully. "I'm waiting to hear why clothes are not important to a woman, especially one as pretty as you are."

Emma dimpled at the compliment; then she was serious. "That lovely dress you are wearing now, Bea, makes a rustling sound when you walk. Would it give you pleasure if you were the only one who would see it?"

Bea was winding a curl over her finger. "I think so, Em. I like pretty things."

"But your greatest pleasure," Emma insisted, "is having heads turn, to know you are lovely to look at. That knowledge makes you feel important."

Bea's amused eyes met Emma's. "So . . . ?"

"With Joseph I get the same feeling in a different way. Clothes are still important to me, but other things are more important. We look at a sunset together, and suddenly it becomes more than radiant colors in the sky. I begin to feel the whole universe in motion and a togetherness with Joseph that makes us one." She paused, hardly noticing that Bea was shaping her hair into the latest style. She only saw that she was listening intently.

"You can't imagine what it's like to live with a man like Joseph, Phoebe. Through his eyes a bird's egg becomes all of creation. A flower becomes all the beauty that exists on earth. When I'm with him everything seems in tune. It's that way even when his opponents harass us. I am still positive of his love, and I know that at the core of things, everything is right."

Bea studied Emma's face in the looking glass for a long moment.

"You may not be able to convince the folks that yours is a good marriage, but you have convinced me. And thanks for reminding me that there is more to life than wearing the latest fashions. Now, put on your dress. With this new hairstyle you're going to be the prettiest lady downstairs. And I dare you to say it doesn't matter to you."

Emma's eyes were suddenly like two stars. "It matters . . . it matters because I want Joseph to be proud of me."

Christmas for Emma was a day to remember, with all the members of her family together. Last night there had been friends—outsiders, today they were the Hales—a unit. Joseph, feeling a little out of it all, took pleasure in Emma's happiness and made himself as agreeable as he could. He ignored subtle jibes that were not heard by Emma, remarks that made him know that only Bea and Eric accepted him wholeheartedly into the family.

They spent half the morning around the Christmas tree singing carols and opening presents. Joseph's gift to Emma was a little silver thimble. How small it seemed beside her lavish gifts from the Hales, yet she received it with tender thanks that gave him pleasure.

She had woven some of her hair into a watch-fob for him—a gift he would always treasure. She didn't seem to mind that the small gifts from them for her family were homemade (with the help of Mother Lucy and Catherine). Among the gifts were some of Mother Lucy's oilcloth paintings which she gave with real pride. Joseph felt a secret satisfaction that the Hales were impressed by his mother's artistic skill.

"Isn't it wonderful, Joseph?" Emma said when the day ended, and they were getting ready for bed. "Here we are, at home in my old room, with persecutions and trouble all behind us. And my family likes you."

In bed he held her in his arms tenderly. Not for anything in the world would he spoil her pleasure.

Two days after Christmas the day began dark and murky, indicating a heavy snow by nightfall, for the temperature was dropping rapidly.

Immediately after breakfast Bea and Eric announced their decision to leave for home.

"But you can't," Father Hale said. "That's a hundred-mile trip. Stay here until the weather clears."

"We came equipped for storms." Eric's voice was mild, but his eyes were determined, and Joseph watching sized him up. Here was a man! He was slight in stature—five feet eight or nine inches in height—a kindly man with a sparkling personality . . . and more. There was steel in him. He knew his way. He could be led but never pushed. There was an honesty and naturalness about him that made one trust him,

266

but he would never be imposed upon. And he adored Bea. Who wouldn't? She was very much like Emma.

"We can't afford to be trapped away from home for an indefinite stay," Eric was saying. "And we can weather anything short of a blizzard. You know yourself that December storms often last a long time."

When persuasion failed, Eric and Bea began getting ready for a quick departure, and all the family helped. Emma went with Bea to pack. The men put on coats and boots and went to harness up. By the time the buggy was brought to the door for loading, snow had already begun to fall.

Mother Hale added a warm quilt to their supply of bedding, putting in a store of food and heated foot warmers.

It wasn't easy saying good-bye. Bea and Emma, standing close to Joseph, held one another for a long moment.

"I'll see you when the baby comes," Bea said in low tones, for a lady didn't speak of an unborn child in a mixed crowd, even if the men were her father and brothers, but her eyes covered both Emma and Joseph. "And I'll make a baby dress with needlework so fine it will be the envy of all the parents in Pennsylvania."

Emma kissed Bea, then she glanced at Joseph. Would he think Bea's remarks were unladylike? But Joseph's eyes held only approval.

Then Eric gently assisted Bea into the buggy. There were tears and farewells.

"You may have to change those wheels for sled runners," Father Hale said.

"I can do that if I have to," Eric answered with a grin. Then they rode away, and all the Hales stood watching until cold drove them into the house.

For a few days the weather held, then it broke in blizzard proportions that lasted more than a week. When it ended drifts were piled high, and Joseph knew Martin Harris would not be coming before February at the very earliest. All roads were impassable.

Emma spent a part of her housed-in time rummaging through some of her old belongings. She came upon a small red morocco trunk and suggested to Joseph that it would be just the thing to hold the plates and Urim and Thummim, for it was light and could be lifted easily. In fact it was small enough to be placed on top of their bureau, and it had a key. Joseph accepted the trunk gratefully.

They fixed one corner of their bedroom for his work, separating it from the rest of the room by hanging up a quilt for a screen. Behind this he put a chair and a small table. Now he had privacy to do his work, and commenced copying some of the characters that were engraved on the plates. He copied a considerable number of them and translated some by means of the Urim and Thummim.

Emma was fascinated. Working in the bedroom with only the screen between them she carded, sewed, knitted, or did whatever her hands found to do while Joseph worked. She could hear the sound of his quill pen as he wrote. Sometimes there would be the metallic sound of Joseph turning pages. Although she was not allowed to see the records, she could hear, and her ears became so trained that she learned to see in her mind what her ears heard.

There came a day when Joseph showed her pages of some of the characters he had written—neat facsimiles of the engravings on the plates. To Emma they looked a little like Chinese writing.

Daylight came slowly and the cold continued, but as was their custom the Hales arose early, for there was milking and feeding of livestock as well as fires to build throughout the house, and numerous other chores. The women, too, were early risers, for breakfast was served never later than seven in wintertime, and much earlier in spring and summer.

Isaac Hale was making use of the foul weather to mend harnesses, fix farm implements, wagon wheels, fences, and everything that needed repairs. These things were done with the help of his boys.

Although Joseph had made it quite clear that his reason for coming to Harmony was to translate the plates, he found that Mr. Hale and Emma's brothers expected him to spend time helping with chores and repairs. And Emma, overly anxious that Joseph should be well liked by her family, urged him to shoulder work that kept him away from his translating. "Until Martin gets here." So again, as in Manchester, Joseph felt frustrated. This was putting off important work for what seemed of little value, since there were more than enough hands without his to do what needed to be done.

"They are going to have to understand, Emma," Joseph told her with a gleam in his eye, "that I shall help only until Martin gets here. I came here to translate, and that is what I intend to do."

"That is what I want you to do," Emma told him, and she thought she meant it.

One day Emma found herself alone and idle in her room. She picked up her sewing with restless fingers, sewed a few stitches, and put the work down. She was not in the mood for sewing; in fact she was not in the mood for much of anything.

She missed Catherine's good-natured chatter. She had thought there was nothing in Manchester to miss, but today she was seeing in fancy Mother Lucy painting with pains-taking care on an oilcloth. She could hear Jerusha's laughter; Jerusha was a happy person, not because Hyrum was a better husband than most—although he was a good one—but Jerusha's happiness came from a contentment within herself. She was happy just to be a part of the whirl and motion of living. And now with baby Lovina, life for Jerusha was complete and full. Hyrum too was finding the baby a fascinating adventure. Lovina was so perfect. . . . Emma's eyes softened at the thought of her. Would their baby be as beautiful? June seemed far away. If only she could move time ahead. How wonderful it would be to hold Joseph's child in her arms. She liked to tease Joseph about the sex of their child, but actually it made no difference to her—a son like Joseph, a daughter like Lovina, or one of each if the Lord were willing.

She got up and walked listlessly. She could go talk with her mother, but all morning she had listened to complaints, mostly about Joseph. She had made the mistake of mention-ing the facsimiles of the engravings he had made, and Mother Hale had been antagonistic. Joseph, she said, was fooling with something of small worth. With a baby on the way and a wife to support it was his duty to forget trifles and settle down to earnest living. Take Eric; he had bought himself a fine piece of land and was well on the road to getting it paid for, while Joseph had no goal in mind. He was proving himself as worthless as she had told Emma he would be. It was this last remark that had brought Emma to her room.

She paused now in her walking. She was standing in front of the bureau. Opening the drawer in which she had the baby's clothes she began taking out the things one at a time. Sophronia had made this little dress from cloth she had woven. How dainty it was, with tucks and handmade lace. This one was from Jerusha. She had planned it for Lovina;

then with her impulsive bigheartedness she had placed it in Emma's hands. "Lovina doesn't need it, Emma. She has enough for herself and half a dozen brothers and sisters." There were lovely things made from cloth Mother Lucy and Catherine had helped to weave. How fine and useful everything was. They were all different, with tucks or embroidery, smocking, drawn work, or sheering. Sophronia, Catherine, Mother Lucy, Jerusha, and even small Lucy had helped make them. Some were finished with crocheted or knitted laces and insertions. Sophronia had given her yards of laces in different patterns, and Mother Lucy had come upon some fine dainty work she had saved for "sometime." There were dresses with slips to match, tiny shirts soft as down, bellybands and diapers of spun cotton. Jerusha had given a party to get them hemmed. So many stitches made by friends! Emma lifted one of the dresses and tossed the skirt over her shoulder. When Joseph carried the baby the dress skirt would reach below his waist. The dresses were all so beautiful and so long. There were a dozen pairs of soft knitted stockings; some she had made—the rest were gifts from relatives and friends. There were soft quilts, mostly gifts, and two small blankets soft as rose petals, gifts from Isaac Stoal's two daughters. Was ever a baby's layette more perfect than this one? She put the garments back, touching each one lovingly, seeing the friendly faces of the donors. There had been wonderful times in Manchester, and so many happy memories! She closed the drawer slowly. Every needful thing was here. Feeling all warm and at peace, she went out to find her mother.

As soon as the two of them were together Mother Hale started in on Joseph again. This time she reminded Emma of all the young men she could have married, naming them over one at a time. Emma liked most of these young men. She was glad they were busy and successful, but Mother Hale's digging at Joseph was too much, and she lashed out angrily. "Stop it, Mother. I married Joseph because I love him; because he is more right for me than anyone I know. Why do you always measure success in terms of money?"

Instead of answering her, Mother Hale came at her in another way. "How do you know Joseph has ancient records? Have you seen them?"

"I've handled them."

"But you haven't seen them." Mother Hale said with a kind of triumph. "How do you know he isn't fooling you with some great hoax?"

"You are just trying to hurt me, Mother, or else you don't know Joseph at all."

"I know his kind. Do we keep our valuables hidden away and create some great mystery about them? Your father is a very successful man. We display our treasures, and we're happy to share them with friends—even strangers."

"Joseph's work is different. The angel told him to show the records only to those persons he will name at some future date."

The two women were standing by the stove. Mrs. Hale was stirring soup, and she stirred it now with vehemence. "This angel business—I don't believe in it at all. Have you seen Joseph's angel?"

"No, but I saw the light the night Joseph got the records."

"If you saw a light, it could have been one Joseph made to fool you. You show me the records, and I'll believe he has them. But even if he has them he has no business with them. If they are what you both claim, he should sell them. It's possible they would bring enough for you to buy a business or a farm. I'll wager his laziness will keep you living off others for the rest of your lives."

Words flew to Emma's tongue, but she didn't say them.

Instead she ran to her room and flung herself down on the bed, breathing hard. "You're unfair—unfair—unfair!" She pounded the covers with clenched fists until her anger spent itself, then she lay still staring at the pink canopy and wiping away tears.

After a time she began to remember how anxious she had been to come to Harmony, and how much she loved her people. Christmas had been wonderful, but now, with days falling into routine, nothing seemed to be going the way she and Joseph had planned it. Without the cooperation of her family, how could Joseph finish the work he had been called to do? Were her people never to understand that he had not asked to do it, that he had been called? And translating the records was only a part of God's plan. The rest would unfold, not as Joseph willed it but as God willed it.

Her mother had said, "Show me the records, and I will believe." Would it be so wrong for her to see them if seeing would make her believe?

The house was very quiet. The red morocco trunk was on the bureau, and she knew where Joseph kept the key. In Manchester she had handled the plates many times. They were always wrapped in a pillowslip or a covering. She had dusted around them, even helped to hide them, and not once had she been tempted to look at them. Now she was hearing her mother's words and staring at the trunk. Why would it hurt to lift the lid and take one small peek? Who would know if she carried them to her mother and said, "See for yourself. These prove Joseph's claims are true." They *were* true; she would bank her life on it. Joseph had never deceived her even in small things, and he had defended the contents of that trunk with his life in spite of hurts and injuries. Her fingers touched where the lock was. She inserted the key and was about to lift the lid when the thought came, If you look, God

273

will know, and you have never deceived Joseph. There has always been truth between you.

She moved away from the trunk, but the desire to use the plates to prove Joseph's integrity did not leave her. She wanted her family to believe in Joseph, to esteem him as she did. She wanted a place for him in the family circle, with her own place back as it had been before she married him.

Again she found herself standing before the trunk. Was it really so important—all this secrecy about the records? She was Joseph's wife. If a husband and wife were one in the sight of God, was not this her work as well as Joseph's? And if it were her work, should she not be privileged to share in it completely and view the records? But even as the thought came she knew it was beneath her. As Joseph's wife she did not have a rightful claim to everything that was his, and she knew she could never again claim the exact place in the family circle that had been hers before marriage. Life had changed, and she had changed with it. Her loyalty did not belong to her family now; it belonged to Joseph.

Suddenly she was remembering the disappointment that had been in Joseph's voice the night they had brought the plates home, when he had told her he could not show them to her. In her mind she saw again the tender concern in his eyes and the look of love on his face. Now she no longer wanted to touch the trunk. Joseph had suffered every hurt to obey the angel's instructions, and his work had hardly begun. The faith they had in each other was the one shining thing that gave him the courage to keep going. It was the foundation of their love. It was what Joseph came back to when his burdens were almost too heavy to bear. In her heart she knew the records were more important than material wealth. But Joseph had pride. It wasn't easy for him to put God's work ahead of his desire to labor for fine surroundings, a nice home, and every good thing that would lift them in the

274

eyes of their fellows. As if scales were falling from her eyes, she saw that she too had been called. Her part was to keep the vision of Joseph's divine work in her mind and heart so that when he became discouraged she would be at his side to lift him up and keep him going. Her place was to comfort him, love him, and remind him that even if the whole world turned against him she understood and believed and held him in high esteem. She must assist him and stand with him even if it meant breaking away from her family. A look at the plates might be a harmless act in itself. The wrong would be in deceiving Joseph.

She sat on the bed with square shoulders now, comparing her marriage to that of her parents. And she knew that in spite of all the beautiful things her parents owned, and the many years they had lived together, she would not exchange her marriage for one like theirs.

Perhaps Martin Harris's greatest charm lay in the fact that although he had various gifts, not the least of which was making money, he was such a humble man that only a few envied him his possessions. He was a thinker, but he did not flaunt his learning. He was a peaceable man. Some said Mrs. Harris led him around as if he had no mind of his own, but they said it jestingly, for Martin was genuinely liked by persons of all ages. He arrived in Harmony in February, and the Hales were soon calling him by his first name. This was a help to Joseph. If the Hales had not welcomed him, work on the records could not have been done in the Hale house.

Joseph began translating in earnest now, and Martin proved to be an enthusiastic scribe. Outdoor living and clean habits had given him a healthy body, and he could write untiringly hour after hour. The writing seemed a welcome

275

change to him after the strenuous farmwork he was used to. He sat on one side of the quilt screen, and Joseph sat on the other. Emma was fascinated, watching Martin's quill pen move on the foolscap paper as he listened to Joseph's voice.

After three weeks of writing Martin received word that Mrs. Harris needed him at home. Both men were disappointed that the translating had to be postponed when it was going so well, until Joseph thought of the facsimiles he had made with such painstaking care. He had the translation for these now. Perhaps Martin could show them to a language interpreter.

"I'll take them to New York City and get signed papers that will prove the correctness of the translations," Martin promised. "And I'll be back in a fortnight to write for you."

Joseph and Emma were jubilant. If Martin returned with signed documents they would prove beyond question Joseph's claim to ancient records and his ability as translator.

"While you're gone, I'll help the Hales in the fields. It will soon be time for spring planting. But we'll be counting the days until you are back with us, not only for your help but for the good news we hope you will bring us."

"It's bound to be good news," Martin said, and they parted with great expectations.

It was a warm Sunday filled with the promise of spring. Mr. Hale, a churchgoing man, had taken his family—except Joseph and Emma—to an all-day meeting and an evening of visiting with friends.

The first few Sundays after Joseph and Emma came to Harmony they had gone to church with them, as two sore thumbs, for the Hales were proud people. The Smiths were neat and shining clean, but the Hales felt piqued that Joseph had refused their offer to buy what they considered suitable church attire. Then too, Joseph caused a stir, as rumors of his "gold bible" became common gossip.

If the church had satisfied Joseph and Emma, if they had felt a close communion with God there, they would have kept on going, but the terrifying sermons, the minister's apparent anger toward heaven and his congregation, made it impossible for them to identify what they heard with the God they had come to worship. It was a relief to everyone when they announced their intentions to stay home.

Today they had spent a restful morning, and now they were on the porch enjoying the afternoon sunshine. Presently they saw a black surrey driven by two fine horses, rounding a bend in the lane that led to the Hale barns.

Emma sprang out of her chair. "Isn't that Martin Harris?"

Joseph took a second look. It *was* Martin. He caught Emma's hand, and the two went racing toward the barns, confident that the news Martin had would be good. Joseph found himself contemplating his next move. Should he send the signed documents proving the authenticity of his records to the newspapers in New York, or have them printed in less important papers? At best news traveled slowly.

As a rule Martin's movements were swift and youthful, but today his age was showing as he climbed from the surrey. His handshake was warm and his greeting cordial, but there were shadows around his eyes.

"Are you all right, Martin? Is everything all right at home?"

"Everything is fine at home."

"And the engravings?" Emma asked anxiously, as if she couldn't wait. "What about the translations?"

Martin's face became grim, and Joseph felt his heart turn over. Something had gone wrong. He waited, fully aware that this would not be the good news he had expected Martin to bring back.

"We had better unhitch and get the horses fed, son," Martin said. "It is not a pretty story that I have to tell, but it will merit your full attention."

Emma, quick to sense Martin's meaning, said, "If you will promise not to leave me out of the telling I'll go and fix you some dinner, Martin."

The men nodded, and Joseph, making light banter that he did not feel, told her, "We'll talk about Martin Van Buren, the new governor. Rumor says he will resign and be succeeded by Enos T. Thorpe."

She tossed her head because she was a Van Buren fan, and Joseph watched her curls bob as she went hurriedly toward the house. He knew her disappointment was as great as his.

Martin finished his dinner of vegetables, corn bread, chicken, and pie. Emma and Joseph had eaten the same earlier that day.

Martin felt better now, and the story he had to tell seemed a little less grim. The three of them walked out on the porch and took easy chairs close together. Later Emma and Joseph would wash up Martin's few dishes, for they were careful not to leave clutter anywhere in the Hale house.

The sun was warm and bright. Emma put her hand in Joseph's, and his fingers closed around it. They both knew that Martin had not succeeded in getting the signatures, but here in the sunshine, with the beauty of the day enfolding them, adverse news would seem less grim. They were grateful that Martin had given them time to face it. Now it would be just one more disappointment that they must face together.

Martin's eyes were both gentle and serious as they rested first on Joseph, then on Emma. "I took our work to Professor Anthon, for I had been told he was the best in the

278

city, highly celebrated for his literary attainments. He told me the translation was correct, more so than any he had seen translated from the Egyptian. I next showed him the copies you sent that were not yet translated, and he said they were Egyptian, Chaldaic, Assyriac, and Arabic, and he said they were true characters. He wrote out a certificate stating that they were true characters, and that the translation, as far as you had gone, was also correct.''

Joseph's eyes began to shine, but Martin's face became weary. "I took the certificate, and was putting it in my pocket when just as I was leaving he called me back and asked how you had discovered the ancient records. I told him an angel of God had revealed the hiding place. Then he said, 'Let me see that certificate.' I foolishly handed it to him, and he tore it to pieces, saying there was no such thing now as the ministering of angels, and that if I would bring the plates to him he would translate them. I told him that part of the plates were sealed, and that I was forbidden to bring them. Then he said, 'I cannot read a sealed book.' I left him, and went to a Dr. Mitchell, who sanctioned what Professor Anthon had said respecting both the characters and the translation, but he too refused to give me a certificate. He said a certificate from him would do no good since by reputation he was not learned, but if I would bring him the records he would translate them correctly.''

"You did your best," Joseph said. "I'm more than grateful to you.''

"There is more," Martin said. "I was so disappointed when I left Dr. Mitchell's that I walked until the day was spent, and I found myself sitting on a log down by the Hudson River. Cold as it was, I must have dozed and dreamed, for I heard a voice telling me to read the twenty-ninth chapter of Isaiah. Get your Bible, Joseph, and tell me what you think of that chapter.''

Joseph went for his Bible, found the chapter, and commenced reading aloud. He read the chapter through while Emma and Martin listened, then he went back and read from verses eleven through eighteen again:

And the vision of all is become unto you as the words of a book that is sealed, which men deliver to one that is learned, saying, Read this, I pray thee; and he saith, I cannot; for it is sealed:

And the book is delivered to him that is not learned, saying, Read this, I pray thee: and he saith I am not learned.

Wherefore the Lord said, Forasmuch as this people draw near me with their mouth, and with their lips do honor me, but have removed their heart far from me, and their fear toward me is taught by the precept of men:

Therefore, behold I will proceed to do a marvellous work among this people, even a marvellous work and a wonder: for the wisdom of their wise men shall perish, and the understanding of their prudent men shall be hid.

Woe unto them that seek deep to hide their counsel from the Lord, and their works are in the dark, and they say, Who seeth us? and who knoweth us?

Surely your turning of things upside down shall be esteemed as the potter's clay: for shall the work say of him that made it, He made me not? or shall the thing framed say of him that framed it, He had no understanding?

Is it not yet a very little while, and Lebanon shall be turned into a fruitful field, and the fruitful field shall be esteemed as a forest?

And in that day shall the deaf hear the words of the book, and the eyes of the blind shall see out of obscurity, and out of darkness.

Joseph paused in his reading, and Emma said in a voice filled with awe: "Do you think it means us, Joseph? Can we dare say this is a prophecy concerning our records?"

Joseph's eyes were alive as he answered her. "This is a part of the Bible that the angel quoted to me." His voice became warm and gentle. "Thank you, Martin, for bringing it to my remembrance. It may be that our book will be rejected by the world until that time in history when the Jews are gathered back to their own country as a fruitful and prosperous nation."

The work of translating began in earnest again with the return of Martin Harris, much to the annoyance of the Hales, for it was spring planting time, and although there were plenty of men to do the work, all the Hales except Emma were of one accord: Joseph should be in the fields helping.

Relations between Joseph and the Hales became so strained that Emma found herself trying to see all sides as she endeavored to keep the peace. The results were not good. Joseph felt he should use every available minute to translate while he had Martin to write for him. Emma thought they should do enough work to earn their keep, yet in her heart she felt that Joseph was right, for if he were ever to finish the manuscript he was obliged to keep working, and her father's year-round farm hands were often idle at the bunkhouse just waiting to be assigned work. Why, then, all this fuss?

The situation was hard on Joseph. It was his nature to share whatever he had with others, but he found it very difficult to take favors he could not repay. It embarrassed him to be living with the Hales and forced to make a choice between the work he felt he had been called to do and the work he felt he ought to do to keep the Hales happy.

One night when he was with Emma in their room he said, "I think we should leave your father's house."

She had been lying on the bed. Now she sat up. "But we can't leave . . . we have no place to go. And our baby will be born in less than two months; then there will be three of us." She made the last remark gently, with a mother-light in her brown eyes.

He had been locking the records away in the trunk. He turned, his eyes caressing her. Then he came and dropped down beside her on the bed. "You are working much too hard, my girl, trying to keep up your end and mine. There are shadows under your eyes. And sometimes when you think none of us are watching you, your drooping body frightens me. You always say you are fine, but you are not fine, and I aim to get you to a doctor very soon."

She scoffed at the idea of a doctor. "Nobody goes to a doctor to have a baby. A midwife is all a woman ever needs." Her smile flashed suddenly. "If I get tired, Joseph, it is probably a sign that our baby will be a nine-pounder."

He smiled and kissed her, but his eyes were troubled. Emma was having many bad days. If Jerusha had had bad days Hyrum would have told him.

One evening after supper Joseph went for a walk alone to get away from tension in the Hale house, and this night he chanced to walk by the little cabin where he had first met Emma. Moonlight silvered the trees and gave the small house a mellow glow that seemed to shine from each window. Joseph walked around the house, impressed by the night beauty that bathed each tree in shadow. Could this be the answer to his soul's cry for privacy? He began to picture coming home to Emma here. He and Emma had never had a home of their own, as Hyrum and Sophronia had. Their happiness had always been in another's home, surrounded by people. Even when they were shut away alone in their room they could never feel entirely alone, yet here was an abandoned house in need of repair for lack of occupants to tend it. There was more room in this cabin than Hyrum and Jerusha had. Why, it could be as fine a home as the one Sophronia and Calvin claimed with such pride. With a little fixing up it could be a heaven on earth. But would the Hales let them live there? Given time, perhaps he could buy it. There must be some way for them to have it, his heart prayed. The cabin was all he could ask for—big enough to hold a father, mother, and baby, with woods awaiting small exploring feet. There was so much natural beauty here . . . trees, wild flowers, birds, small furry creatures. A child in these surroundings could learn wisdom simply by opening his eyes and looking. For a while Joseph stayed, drinking in the fragrance of the night, the stars, the sound of soft wind moving through the trees. An owl hooted and a squirrel swished past him. Joseph went to the well and let down the old wooden bucket. He drew himself a drink of the sweet, cool water. What would Emma say about his plan?

They talked for a long time that night. Next morning Joseph was ready to bargain, for Martin had offered to lend them enough money to buy the cabin and surrounding ground, provided the price should not exceed the land's value. At first Emma's parents were entirely negative. They wanted no daughter of theirs living in such meager surroundings.

Emma reminded them that an uncle had lived there in comfort and reared a family.

"Times have changed," Mrs. Hale told her with an annoyed frown. "You deserve much better than a rundown cabin no bigger than a pigsty." Then Emma heard again her mother's version of what made a woman a lady.

Mr. Hale glanced at Emma's body big with child and his face became suddenly gentle. "Our girl is right, Mother. She is in no condition to run a big house. I think we ought to let them have the cabin." Then he named a price considerably less than Joseph had expected to pay, and Mrs. Hale remained silent.

The day Joseph and Emma became homeowners no cabin had ever had a more thorough scrubbing. It had been the home of squirrels, small wildlife, bugs and spiders for years, and the accumulation of dirt was unbelievable, but with everything shining and clean it seemed a place transformed, and Joseph insisted upon carrying Emma across the polished threshold.

"It's our first home, Mrs. Smith. When you were a little girl you played at keeping house here. Now you will be the real homemaker. Emma, I do want you to be happy here."

She teased him about lifting two across the threshold, but he could tell that she was pleased.

The Hales, once they were reconciled to the move, donated many things to make the house more livable. Soon there were curtains at the windows, iron pots for cooking in the fireplace, linens for the table, and tidies for the chairs. Mrs. Hale gave Emma her bedroom furniture, although it seemed too elegant for the humble little house, but Emma was pleased. She loved the spicy-smelling down mattress, the commode and bureau, the washbowl and procelain pitcher, even the small china pot with the cover that went under the bed. Emma had a knack for creating beauty, and Joseph found it hard to get down to his work of translating, so interested was he in Emma's creations. Besides, he wanted to help her, for he knew she was overworking, and the only way to stop her was to pitch in and help. She was so full of plans. Joseph had never seen her happier, but she was pale, with dark circles under her eyes that worried him. He did all the heavy lifting and water carrying, and he worked with a part of his mind alerted so that he could be ready at all times to assist her, for he knew her independent nature and her determination to do whatever-she-was-a-mind-to, with or without his help. Their home had become her pride, as it had been his from the first moment of his awareness of the cabin's possibilities. Soon it was as fresh and sweet smelling as the lovely woods that surrounded it. And then things began to happen that both benefited and hindered.

It began with an outdoor oven. The Hale men with Joseph's help built Emma a good one where she could bake loaves of bread and pastry, roast meat, fish, and fowl, and cook vegetables. They donated a few chickens, a cow, and Emma's own horse. But now there was a need for outbuildings. Mr. Hale and his sons brought lumber, and gave their spare time to the building. There were two reasons for all this activity. The first was to help Emma. The second was to goad Joseph into giving up his translating. They were trying to force him into their pattern of living, for material success to them seemed the natural and most satisfying way of life. The result was that Joseph worked hard at translating when Martin was available for a scribe, and he worked as a carpenter early mornings and evenings until it was too dark to see, when he was not helping Emma. Soon there was a fair-sized barn, a chicken house, a latrine, a corral, a cold house, and a pigsty, as well as the outdoor oven. Then one day David and Jesse uncovered a cellar. It was overgrown with underbrush which they cleared away. This was the place where their aunt had stored vegetables and fruit, and perhaps milk, cream, and cheeses, for the dugout was very cool.

David, Jesse, Alva, and Isaac Ward spent part of a week helping make a garden. All this help was unexpected and welcome, but now Emma began to worry about Joseph's health, marveling that he could keep up with such a schedule.

Soon vegetables were springing out of the ground, and Joseph was overwhelmed at their prosperity.

One day Emma's sister Phoebe came to Harmony and stopped at the cabin for a visit. Emma had just finished putting wild flowers in a bright bowl on the table when she looked up and saw Bea standing inside the door. Then the

285

sisters were locked in each others arms. Bea's coming was a complete surprise. If the Hales knew, they had kept the secret.

She handed Emma a package. "It's the dress I promised. I hope it will do for the baby's christening." Emma opened the package and drew in her breath at the sight of such loveliness. She had never seen such a dress as this one, the drawn work dainty and perfect, the delicate embroidery, the lace of finest thread. "Oh, Bea!"

Phoebe's cheeks became warm with pleasure. "It is my very best work, Emma. You *will* have the baby baptized in it?"

Emma hesitated, feeling for her words. "I would, Bea . . . but . . . how can I ever make you understand? You see, we think baptism is not for babies."

"Whatever are you saying, Emma? Of course baptism is for babies! Why, every Hale baby that has ever been born has been baptized."

"I know. But we believe that baptism is a symbol of obedience to God, of faith and repentance, of cleansing from sin, a kind of door to the kingdom of God. We think none of this applies to a baby because a baby has never sinned. Some ministers preach little children into hell, but Joseph . . . we . . . think this is wrong. Jesus said, 'Of such is the kingdom of heaven' and blessed babies. We think a baby should be blessed when it is born and baptized when it is old enough to be accountable for its actions."

Emma could see Phoebe's disappointment. She had spent weeks making a christening dress, and now she was being told that the baby would never wear it as such. What could she say now that would lessen her sister's disappointment?

"We'll dedicate our baby to God in it, Bea."

"It won't be the same," Phoebe answered sadly. "I

wanted the ceremony in our church with a large congregation watching another Hale being christened. If I had known you felt this way about baptism I never would have . . ."

Emma's eyes filled, and Bea stopped talking and reached for her. Now both sisters were crying. Presently Phoebe smiled through tears. "I'm being silly, Emma. I suppose I wanted the whole world to see my first nephew or niece decked out in my beautiful handiwork and exclaiming over it. My vanity is showing, and I apologize. This dress was made for your child, and you have a right to do whatever you think best for your own baby. I just want to be on hand when he wears it for the first time."

Emma raised the dress and touched it to her cheek. "It's so soft and beautiful. It will be our pride—as much so as if a thousand eyes were admiring our baby in it."

"I'll be here when the baby is born, Em. That is why I came. I'll sleep at the big house, but most of the time I'll be right here keeping an eye on you. I'll help you work or loaf, because it's you I came to be with." She paused. "Isn't that Joseph's voice I hear reading?"

"He is translating from the plates while Martin writes for him. They are working in our bedroom. It is very strange, Bea, the way Joseph receives light and truth through the Urim and Thummim. They have translated over a hundred pages of foolscap already, and I have read it all."

"You really believe in these records, don't you?"

"Of course I do."

"Yet you have never seen them."

"Come close to the bedroom door and listen. If you are very quiet you can hear the metallic sound when Joseph turns a page."

The girls listened, and Phoebe heard. "But, Em, how can you be sure the plates exist when you have never seen them?"

"I've handled them many times when they have been covered only with a cloth, so I have seen them the way a blind person sees—by *feel.*"

"I . . . I suppose one could see that way." Phoebe's tone proved she was not entirely convinced.

"And Joseph has made facsimiles of the engravings on parts of some pages. These I have seen. I know what Joseph has told me, and I have read all that has been translated so far."

Bea didn't say anything, but her face showed that she wanted Emma to tell her more, so the girls took chairs side by side near the bedroom door, and Emma continued quietly: "God's great love has covered men through all the ages. It is a constant love, and when men become aware that God truly exists, and that he is interested in them personally, their lives become rich and meaningful. Most persons ask, 'Why was I born? What is life all about? And what happens when I die?' We go to our Bibles to find these answers, but now on these records, some of our questions will be answered more fully. They will give the world an added testimony that God has had a plan for man from his earliest beginning."

Emma paused, and Bea said: "Could I read it, Emma?"

"When the translations have been made and the book is published, we hope the whole world will read it, but now what has been translated must be carefully guarded; it must not leave this house. I worry because Martin seems to be taking the attitude that because he has worked as scribe the manuscript is partly his. He has always been so cooperative, so understanding and kind, but these past few days he seems to have become possessive. Although Joseph hasn't mentioned it, I am sure Martin's attitude is worrying him too."

"Em, I hope you and Joseph are not being deceived. I hope the records are of God as you say. Our pastor says it's of the devil, and it could be. Take the Bible story of Adam

288

and Eve. They were deceived by Satan and were driven from their garden to spend their days in drudgery. The scriptures say Satan can change himself into what appears to be an angel of light. All this is separating you from the family. It is keeping Joseph from becoming successful. With all due respect for the way you two have revived this little house, you are still living in poverty compared to the rest of us. And you deserve so much more."

"When the translations are complete, when you have read it all, then you will understand and believe it is of God," Emma said with a half-smile.

"That's what I want to do—to judge the truth or falseness for myself."

"I wish the rest of the family would be as fair. They won't let me speak about the records at all."

Bea touched Emma's hand gently. "I agree with the folks that you should be mistress of a fine house. When we were children you loved hair ribbons and frills, and you haven't changed. This whole house proves your love for beauty. Look, you have ironed the tablecloth, which means you must have sweltered with the fireplace going to heat the irons. You have lovely flowers on the table. It amazes me what you can do to a room. You could make a house like mine look like a palace, Em."

"But we don't need a palace. We are truly happy here. I love Joseph, and I believe in his work so much that I want to have a part in it."

"As long as Joseph persists in doing it, you'll have a part in it," Bea said dryly. "It may destroy you both, turn all your friends against you, and cause you to be persecuted, but you'll have a part in it."

"Will you turn against me?" Emma asked quietly.

"No." Bea's tone was positive. "I may think you addlebrained, but I'll always adore you. Anyway, who am I to say this thing is evil? Perhaps it is of God as you say. Perhaps some day I'll believe in it as you do. What a sad day that will be for the rest of the family!"

A bright smile appeared on Emma's face. "Let's walk out into the woods, Bea. The wild strawberries are ripe. It is almost lunchtime, and I'm sure we can agree on what is good to eat."

Bea arose from her chair, suddenly conscious of the dark circles under Emma's eyes. How frail her body looked! Even though she was big with child she didn't look well at all. "I'll be glad when the baby gets here," she said as they walked out into the sunshine.

"It could be any time within the next three weeks."

"I'll take as much work off you as I can," Bea said.

"That is what Joseph has been doing. Between the two of you I'll grow completely lazy."

Bea's hand tightened on Emma's. "Nothing would please me more."

Martin Harris planned to return to New York by the middle of June. By June 15 one hundred and sixteen pages of foolscap had been written, and Martin seemed determined to take it to New York with him. He wanted to show it to his brother, wife, father, mother, and his wife's sister, a Mrs. Cobb; he had never been so determined or so persistent. In Joseph's experience this was an entirely new role for Martin, and because he was so out of character, Joseph found himself puzzled as to how to cope with him. He and Emma were indebted to Martin for many favors. The very fact that he was here, giving his time to the work, was a great service. He had helped with money for their move to Harmony. Even the tiny house they both loved was theirs only because Martin had loaned them the money to buy it. Taking the manuscript for a short while seemed small pay for all Martin's favors, yet Joseph felt it should remain where his own eyes could watch

290

over it, for it was the result of many hours of work, and they had made only one copy.

Several times Joseph had gone to the solitude of the woods to pray about letting it go. Two times he had taken the Urim and Thummim, praying that the answer be revealed there. And it was! Both times he had been told that Martin must not take the manuscript. The denial had been sharp and plain, yet Martin persisted. Was he not capable of protecting it? What possible harm could come to something he was willing to protect with his life if need be? If he were to continue as Joseph's scribe, his wife must be advised of the work. She was growing restless and would be against his returning to Harmony unless he had something tangible to convince her that the writing was important enough to leave his own farm work to hired hands.

Without Martin for a scribe Joseph knew the work of translating must stop for a time, because Emma was doing far too much already, and when the baby came she would be too occupied with other duties, even if she should be well enough to write for him. So again Joseph took the Urim and Thummim to a quiet place of prayer, and this time he was told that Martin could take the manuscript if he would give his word to show it only to the five persons mentioned. This Martin promised to do, and although Joseph didn't require it of him, he made a solemn covenant in writing that he would do this. Then he took the manuscript. He packed it carefully with his other belongings, but Joseph's heart was filled with misgivings as he and Emma stood outside their house and watched Martin drive away. Joseph didn't mention his worry to Emma lest she too become unduly alarmed, but he prayed that Martin would keep his word. Why, then, this fear that lay like lead on his heart—a fear that seemed to cover him—a fear he couldn't shake?

Part 4

A few nights after Martin Harris left, Joseph was awakened from sound sleep to find Emma sitting up in bed. She was staring straight ahead with her hands clenched into tight little fists. Joseph bolted upright, reaching for her gently. "Are you all right, Emma?"

Her lips were clamped tightly, and she didn't answer at first. Then he heard her give a long drawn-out sigh as the pain ceased. "I think," she said, "we are going to have our baby soon."

"How long have you been having pains like this one?"

"This was the first hard one. Slight ones started late this afternoon, but Phoebe says most women have false pains with their first child, and that when they quit it could be as much as two weeks before the baby is born. I don't think these are false pains, Joseph. I think our baby is going to be born."

The room was bathed in moonlight, but Joseph reached to light the candle on the commode; then he was up and dressing. "I'll go for your mother and Bea, and we'll send one of your brothers for the midwife." Both worry and excitement were in his voice. "You would be better off at the big house the way your mother planned it."

"Then I'll dress and get ready to go there."

"Are you up to it? Do you think you can ride? We ought to time your pains. If they are far apart we may be able to make it. I hate to leave you, Emma, until I know."

"You have no choice, Joseph. I've packed clothes for me and the baby. They are in a box under the bed. You must ride to Father's and let them know. They will send someone in the buggy for me, and someone in the surrey for the midwife. I hope they will want you to bring the buggy back for me, because I want you with me all the time now."

He kissed her quickly and searched her face. "You are sure you will be all right alone here for a little while?"

"I'll be fine. Now go, hurry."

The horse was gentle and easy to put a halter on. This was Emma's horse. She had speed and fire, and Joseph rode her bareback, unaware of the beauty of the star-filled sky or the golden shadows that seemed to shimmer each tree. It was a beautiful night. The horse, as if she sensed Joseph's urgency, galloped without any urging and was soon racing down the familiar road that led to the Hale barn.

As Joseph rode in, the Hale dogs began to bark and lights began appearing in various rooms of the big house. Someone from the bunkhouse called out, "Who is there?" When Joseph answered, the bunkhouse remained dark and quiet.

Joseph's running feet rang out on the gravel path, and the dogs ceased barking and joined him. By the time he reached the house Mr. Hale appeared with a lighted lantern. He was fully dressed, and behind him the other members of the family were stirring, as if they had awaited his coming.

Alva joined them almost at once, and the buggy and surrey were made ready to travel, with Emma's horse hitched to the buggy and a fast team of mares to the surrey.

"I'll go for the midwife myself," Mr. Hale said. "Alva, you go with Joseph to fetch Emma."

"Would it not be better to have a doctor, Sir?" Concern was in Joseph's voice. "I want the best I can get for Emma. The cost doesn't matter. I'll find a way to pay the bill."

"You are getting the best." Mr. Hale was climbing into

the surrey. "This midwife knows more about women than most doctors. She's been bringing babies to the best families in Harmony for twenty years."

Joseph climbed into the buggy beside Alva. "Let's go." And both vehicles were on their way.

Mr. Hale's words had not reassured Joseph. Why, he asked himself, had he not insisted on a doctor?

Mrs. Hale was a most efficient woman. By the time Joseph and Alva returned with Emma the bedroom nearest the kitchen had been prepared. The bed had been moved to the middle of the room, the headboard had been removed to allow the midwife and those attending Emma to reach her from all sides. All nonessential furniture had been either removed from the room or pushed out of the way, and a table had been prepared with a flask of brandy and various other articles the midwife would need.

Young Isaac Ward had been put to work filling boilers with water, and two boilers were being heated in the cookout, in order to keep the heat out of the house.

A fortnight previously Mrs. Hale had made a pad for the bed to protect the down mattress by sewing large sheets of soft paper between clean old quilts. This was on the bed now.

Mr. Hale and the midwife arrived a little ahead of Emma. Emma came in walking. She had refused to be carried, insisting that she could manage fine by herself, but she looked haggard.

"When we got to Joseph's," Alva said, "Emma was having such pain that we had to wait before we could bring her."

The midwife ordered her at once to the bedroom. Phoebe and Mrs. Hale started to follow but they were refused admittance. Emma said: "I want my husband with me."

"Presently . . . presently. Right now we have things to do that require no audience." And with that remark they

294

were left staring at the door. Phoebe and Mrs. Hale remained with Joseph. Other members of the family went their separate ways. For all of them the night would be sleepless, for Emma was a beloved member of the Hale household in spite of misunderstandings and resentments.

Joseph had been so hurriedly introduced to the midwife that her name escaped him. She was tall, probably six feet, quick of movement, bony and thin, but she carried herself with a confidence which was transferred to others. Her straight white hair was pulled severely back from her temples and done in a neat bun at the nape of her neck. She could have been fifty, seventy, or any age between. Her complexion was so dark that Joseph thought she looked Indian, but Mrs. Hale was quick to deny this. "Her father is Irish and her mother Spanish," she said.

Suddenly the air was filled with the sounds of pain. The midwife opened the door and the three of them entered. The pain ceased, and Emma reached for Joseph's hand. He kissed her fingers. Her forehead was damp with perspiration, and her face was drained of color, but her smile was brave.

The midwife had her watch in her hand, timing. Then another pain came and Emma caught Joseph's hands, one in each of hers, pulling and bearing down, as she tried to stifle the groans that came involuntarily through her lips.

Time moved. An hour went by . . . two . . . three. The pains raced and receded, and when each one was gone Emma lay without moving, white and spent.

Mrs. Hale and Bea began crying soundlessly, and Joseph studied the face of the midwife. Was Emma going to be all right? He tried to read the answer in her expression. Was this the way babies came into the world—through a sea of pain? And oh, dear God, how soon would it end?

"Call me Sari." The midwife looked at him as if she read

his thoughts. "Your arms are better than pulling ropes," she said. "You give her confidence."

More time passed. More pains came, each one worse than the last. Joseph was so concerned for Emma that he did not know that his arms ached from her pulling, and that his body was tired and sore; he only knew he had never witnessed such pain before. He had not known that a body could spend itself into such complete exhaustion while the mind remained conscious. Again Joseph's eyes sought the face of the midwife.

"She is built small," Sari said. "I have seen such births as this one. They are always difficult."

"Would it help to have a doctor?"

"Who can tell? If you will feel better to have a doctor I will gladly give way to his judgment and assist him."

Now Joseph looked to Bea and Mrs. Hale for help, and Bea said, "I'll send one of my brothers. David or Jesse will go. You stay with Emma. The skill of two persons will be better than one." At the door she paused, "I'll be right back."

Time passed. Sari sent Bea and Mrs. Hale from the room, for she could not bear to look at their faces and see their constant pacing and soundless tears.

Mrs. Hale's voice as she left the room remained with Joseph to haunt him. "She will die. I know she will die."

Until tonight it had not entered Joseph's mind that Emma might die. Every person alive had been born of woman. He had supposed that giving birth to their child would be as it had been for Jerusha. Now icy fingers of fear gave his face an ashen color. He tried to pray, but the words fell without meaning, for his faith seemed dead. Emma's moaning filled the room like cold snow falling upon his heart. How long could she endure such pain and live?

Sari worked with hands like a doctor's, examining,

296

assisting, counting her pulse, watching her respiration, wiping her face with cold towels.

For no reason at all Joseph found himself thinking of Emma as she had been the first day he met her—eyes shining, hair falling to her waist. He had known with her first glance that she was the woman for him. Now he knew her sweetness, her love, her purity, her devotion. She was far dearer and more wonderful than his mind had been capable of imagining. Now he gazed upon her suffering face, drinking in each feature, as if by his very adoration he might impart some strength to her.

"Brave darling," he said tenderly. "Keep fighting."

The minutes ticked by. As each pain reached a climax her voice would ring out in anguish, then sink to a whisper.

Once, while he stood helplessly watching her strength ebb away, he remembered another night, a blizzard and a windy hill with Alvin holding a knife, bringing life to a newborn calf. One could cut flesh, but one could not cut bone. Oh, God, his heart cried. Don't let her stop fighting.

The doctor came, and the fight continued. Night gave way to morning, and morning to midday, then it was night again. Joseph seldom left her side. They urged him to eat. He refused. He tried in every way he knew to give her strength, wondering as he encouraged her with voice and love where in her precious body she found the strength to keep on trying.

"The baby should have been taken with surgery," the doctor said when he first made his examination. "but it is too late for that now if we would save both the mother and the child."

"A midwife can't operate," Sari reminded him.

"I know." The doctor's tone was weary. "Someday babies will be born in hospitals with equipment for emergencies like this one."

Sari nodded. Her tears fell silently.

The night was far spent when the doctor told Joseph sadly, "It is of no use, my boy. We can't save them both. Which will it be, the child or the mother?"

Joseph's voice was quick and intense. "Save the mother and end this suffering." But even as he said the words he knew how great Emma's disappointment would be. All her long hard fight, and then empty arms! How could he ever make it up to her for such a loss? They had planned so much for this child. His own disappointment was great, but now he was aching for her.

Emma lay quietly without moving. Her eyes were closed as if she were sleeping, but Joseph knew she was not asleep, and he watched over her, still fearful that she too would die. The doctor and Sari had tried to reassure him. Confident that Emma would be all right, they had packed up what they had brought with them and had gone their separate ways. David Hale had driven them home.

When Emma finally did sleep, Joseph helped Mr. Hale and Jesse build a little cedar box—as perfect a box as they could fashion—and his tears fell as he worked, for a man's dreams are not easily buried.

Phoebe lined the box, and Mrs. Hale made a dainty mattress of soft white satin. Now the baby lay wearing the beautiful dress that had been Phoebe's gift and her pride. He didn't look like a newborn infant—his face was soft and white, the cheeks delicately pink, like a fresh-blown rose. The struggle and the fight that had taken his life were not present now. Perhaps in a full lifetime few had done such an important thing as this one, for he had given his life to save another's—something persons were seldom called upon to do.

Joseph had watched Bea dress the baby, and his mind would forever remember the perfect little body, the pert little nose like Emma's, the long, curling, dark lashes like hers. His chest was strong and husky like the Smiths. The little hands and feet were more perfect than any artist could paint them.

Phoebe had looked up, her eyes swimming in tears, as she carefully drew the dress over the small, lifeless head. "This ... was to be ... his christening dress," she said. "But I have a feeling Emma would ... want him to wear it."

Joseph nodded, not trusting himself to speak.

"Joseph—my parents can't forgive you for not having the baby baptized. They say it should be done now, before the little casket is closed."

"And you, Phoebe—how do you feel about it? I am as sure of this baby's home with God as I am that the sun warms the earth with its rays."

"All I know is, no Hale has ever been buried without baptism. And Joseph, I stand with the folks—just in case you are wrong."

"If an angel told you baptism is not for babies, would you believe it?"

She gave him a searching look and remained silent.

A small group of family and friends buried the baby in the family cemetery in a most beautiful wooded spot not far from Joseph and Emma's home. They sang one of Emma's favorite hymns, but Emma was not there to hear it. She was too ill to know that her son was dead. The Hale minister spoke at the graveside, the little coffin was lowered into the grave and covered with warm earth. The minister said a prayer, then the group of mourners went their various ways, and Joseph found himself alone beside the grave that held his firstborn child. The baby had no name, nor would there be a name until Emma was well enough to have her say in the choosing. When he knew what the baby was to be called he would put a marker beside the small mound of earth.

The church bells in Harmony were tolling. Even at this distance Joseph could faintly hear them, and he knew every family living in the vicinity of Harmony would hear and know that Isaac Hale's grandson was dead.

Were bells in another world ringing to welcome a little boy who would grow and learn? It seemed to him that all persons who believed the scriptures had to accept and know that life continued after death.

Emma's recovery was slow. For three weeks she struggled to live, and Joseph stayed beside her, watching over her, hardly sleeping at all. By the end of the third week she was better, but Joseph and the Hales had not spoken to her of the baby. Then one day she began talking. No one had told her, but she knew—she had known from the time it happened that their baby was dead. "I would like to call him Alva, if that name suits you, Joseph. If he had lived your name would have been my preference, but I want a living baby to be called Joseph."

"Alva suits me fine," Joseph told her, and he was thinking, There must never be another child. Emma must never be put through such agony again.

Reading his thoughts Emma reached her hand to caress his forehead. "A woman soon forgets the pains of childbirth, Joseph. Someday I want to be the mother of a living baby."

Later that day Joseph started to carve a marker. The Hale relatives had fine marble memorials, but for the time being a wooden one would serve.

A week after Joseph finished the marker Emma surprised the Hales by getting out of bed and joining them for breakfast. Joseph had helped her dress, and he had teased her a little about her oversized clothes, for she was very thin.

"I'll gain my weight back," she told him with a toss of her head. "In time I may get to be the fattest woman in Harmony."

"Better start working on it," Joseph said, holding her tenderly.

This was the beginning of Emma's recovery. Soon she was walking out of doors a little each day, and one bright morning she told Joseph, "I want to go home."

Phoebe had packed up all the baby clothes. She would take them home with her, and if at some future date Emma should need them they would be waiting. Now Bea was restless to leave, for she had been away from home days longer than she had planned to be. The day Phoebe packed her bags and left by stage, Joseph took Emma home in the Hale buggy.

They did not go immediately home, for Emma wanted to see the little grave where a part of her lay buried. Joseph drove as near to the spot as he could, then he carried her, for the ground was uneven and there was a small hill to climb.

It was familiar ground to Emma. She could not even remember when first she had seen it, but the beauty of this place always moved her. It seemed set apart, quiet and holy. Here birch and pine trees were old, and they moved in the wind with graceful elegance. Ferns along their path grew damp and cool; wild flowers in full bloom were of many colors, and so thick that try as Joseph would to keep from stepping on them he could not. Brightly colored birds flew out of trees and bushes, sounding alarm at their intrusion.

Beside the mound of earth and the little marker bearing Alva's name, Joseph very gently deposited Emma on her feet. It was still here, and they did not speak at first. Emma knelt beside the mound and her tears fell silently. The only sound to be heard came from the woods.

Joseph's arm went around her, and he held her with his soul aching for her and for the small one who had come into the world without a cry. Some lilies were blooming not far from the grave, and Joseph looking at them thought of the face of their child. He wanted always to remember the face of that perfect little boy.

Emma caught his thought for she said: "I was so ill—I can't remember what he was like. It hurts that I can't recall how he looked—even though you and Phoebe say he was very beautiful."

"He was a handsome boy."

"And strong?"

"He would have been."

She took a handful of earth from the mound and let it sift through her fingers. "I overheard one of the neighbors talking with mother. She said, 'Isn't it a pity that the baby was never baptized. Without baptism he can never cross into the land of the redeemed. He will be one of those who will answer for Adam's sin.' Could she be right, Joseph? If she is, my heart will never be at peace again."

"The woman's words are foolish." Joseph plucked a lily and knelt beside her. "Our baby is as pure and sinless as this lily. Would to God we all had his perfection and his glory. Somewhere our baby is alive. I am very sure, Emma, that life is eternal, and that we—you and I and our baby— are living in a part of eternity right now. The little form that was Alva lies here in his satin-lined box, but our son, in a way known only to God, will never lose his identity. He will grow and learn in his heavenly kingdom, attaining heights that perhaps he never could here. It isn't easy to comprehend eternal life, Emma, but this I believe: The divine is in all men, and each will attain his own unending glory—glories as diverse as the sun and moon and stars of heaven."

"And what of Adam's sin? Who pays for that?"

"Adam—just Adam. But sin, every man's sin, affects all mankind on earth. It weakens in the same way that goodness builds and strengthens."

"You think our ministers are wrong to preach eternal damnation?"

"Their explanation doesn't fit the God I worship. There has to be a different interpretation—a different meaning to the words. We have to find it." He took her hand, lifting her to her feet. "Many of the mysteries that puzzle the minds of men are explained in the records, but it is even more wonderful to know that we can take our questions directly to God, and receive answers. It isn't easy to comprehend that the Creator of our vast universe, a mind so great that it is forever creating and forming worlds without number, is ready to reveal his secrets to those who come to him in faith; yet it is so. Those who have faith to receive will receive. Ministers blaspheme when they paint pictures of children screaming in lakes of fire. There will be no children in hell, Emma." He lifted her and carried her back to the buggy.

"Joseph," Emma said as they were driving home, "do you think God caused our baby's death?"

"I caused the baby's death. I gave the verdict because I could not bear the thought of losing you. And our baby, reared without you, would have been more than half an orphan."

"Yet one little miracle could have saved us both. How can you be so sure, Joseph, that God doesn't cause death?"

"Christ came to show us what God is like. He healed the sick and raised the dead. He comforted the mourners and showed us what love is, but never once did he cause death."

They were almost home when she said, "How does one adjust to a lost dream? My arms are . . . so empty."

"I wanted him too," he reminded her gently.

"Someday we must have a living baby."

He looked at her tenderly, a half smile touching his lips. "I'm not sure I could go through that again." But even as he lightly teased her, the thought of having another baby was one he dare not face. Next time he might lose Emma.

With Emma stronger, Joseph began worrying about Martin Harris and the manuscript, for they had not heard one word from Martin since he had taken the manuscript to New York with the understanding that he would return and resume writing for Joseph not later than the middle of July. It was now August, and Joseph knew he should be translating. Emma offered to write for him, saying she was quite sure she could manage an hour or two a day, but Joseph refused with a grateful grin.

She ruffled his hair and went for her bonnet. "I'll pick us some beans. I can't get over how many vegetables have matured in our neglected garden."

Joseph got his hat. If Emma were going to the garden, he would go along and make sure she didn't stay in the sun too long.

He began getting up early and going to bed late working his fields, but toil did not stop his worry. If Martin had lost the manuscript, what would he do? One hundred and sixteen pages of translating—all lost effort! If it should fall into the wrong hands before the rest of the plates were translated, the whole work could come to a sad end! An enemy could alter the words in Martin's translation in such a way as to make all Joseph's future translations appear a hoax. What should he

304

do? Did he dare leave Emma, who was but a shadow of her old self? Did he dare go to Martin's with so much of his harvesting still undone? Would she overwork in his absence? She was never one to be idle. He tried to pray, but remembering that he had been warned not to let Martin take the manuscript, he found his prayers were like dry leaves detached from the source that gave them life. He would tell himself that Martin was trustworthy, that he would guard the manuscript with his life if necessary ... then he would visualize Martin's wife, a shrewd and clever woman with many years of experience in furthering her own ends. If the manuscript had impressed her as being a work of unusual importance she would never be content to let it remain a secret.

Joseph's fears became so great that he slept and ate little. Although he did not mention his worry to Emma, one morning before they were out of bed she said quietly, "Joseph, you must find Martin. You have waited far too long already for the return of your manuscript."

"I can't leave you, Emma, not until all our harvest is in." His arms drew her close to him.

"You *must* go, Joseph. I'll stay at the big house if that will ease your mind. My brothers will take care of the livestock and chores." She kissed him. "I wouldn't put it past me to find a way to get them to finish gathering in our crops."

"You're a minx," he said, "and I love you, but I'll finish our crop gathering myself."

She took his face between her two hands. "You have lived with fear long enough. There are plenty of workers around here without me to do what needs to be done if you're afraid I'll overdo. You must go and learn Martin's reason for not coming back. Your clothes are already packed. The stage is due in an hour. You must be on it."

His eyes widened at her understanding. He didn't argue, but he was amazed at how well she could read his thoughts.

Joseph would remember the trip to Manchester as one long nightmare, for the weather was steaming hot, which meant the stage must travel slowly to protect the horses.

His only traveling companion was a middle-aged stranger—a most congenial fellow. Under other circumstances Joseph could have enjoyed being with him, for he was intelligent, with a philosophical outlook and a bright wit. But soon after the stage left Harmony Joseph felt completely exhausted. The long strain of Emma's illness, the sleepless nights, the worry and overwork had left him almost too worn to think. Several times the stranger told Joseph he looked sick, and Joseph, without mentioning the manuscript, gave the man an account of Emma's illness and little Alva's death.

The stranger was enthusiastic about the new building projects that were taking place in and around New York State. He had helped to build the Erie and Oswego canals, and he had attended the grand celebration in New York City when the Erie Canal had been dedicated. Now the Delaware and Hudson canals were soon to be finished, and he had a part in the Hudson project. Great things were in store for the country with all the development. If it were not for mountains and Indians, no telling how far the expansion might go.

Joseph listened with a part of his mind, as he tried to push away his lethargy. Dust blew from the dry ground, burning their throats and nostrils, smarting their eyes, and giving their bodies a dull brown color. Garments wet with perspiration clung to them. Even at night there was little comfort, for droves of mosquitoes left them with itching welts.

They were about twenty miles from Manchester when the stage lost a wheel. They had been traveling a little faster than usual, ploughing through dust. Because of the dust the driver and his assistant had been unable to see the hole in the road, and they struck it with such force that the spokes splintered. Luckily the driver was a good one, with his horses well in hand. He brought them to a quick stop, and the stage remained upright.

Joseph and the stranger got out to examine the damage, joining the men who were bent over the wheel.

"I'll be obliged to ride one of the horses back to the last town we came through and try to buy a new wheel," the driver said. "This one is gone, and we have no spare."

"How long will it take?" Joseph asked, noting that the wheel was beyond repair.

"We could lose a day."

It occurred to Joseph that he could be in Manchester by morning if he walked. He knew this country. Most of the way was through woods, but it was all familiar ground. Walking twenty miles seemed more logical than waiting. He told his plans to the others. "Let's settle my bill, and I'll be on my way."

"If you are bound to go, lad," the stranger said, "I'll go with you. You are a sick man. I have a feeling you'll never make it through the woods alone."

Just after dawn two weary travelers arrived at the Smith farm. There was a new fence around the house, but as Joseph pushed open the new gate he hardly noticed the improvements. He shifted his knapsack and canteen of water to knock on the front door. A moment later a surprised family welcomed them joyously. Lucy gave them breakfast and ordered them to bed.

Don Carlos showed Joseph's traveling friend to a bedroom, but Joseph lingered. Alone with his family he

307

explained why he had come. "I must go to Palmyra at once and find Martin."

"No." Father Joseph's voice was gentle as he pointed to the stairs. "Go to bed, son. I'll fetch Martin. I'll have him here in time for lunch."

Needing no urging Joseph climbed the stairs gratefully. The last few miles of the trip he had had difficulty keeping awake and on his feet. Soon he was in his old room, sleeping soundly.

Around eleven he awakened. Father Joseph had returned with the promise that Martin would come for lunch. William, driving the carriage, had taken the stranger to Manchester to catch a different stage to New York City, and Joseph was disappointed to find him gone. It made him sad to think their paths might never cross again, for the stranger had proved to be a real friend.

Shortly before noon Hyrum, Jerusha, and the baby came. William, on his way back from Manchester, had carried the news of young Joseph's arrival. Now an excited household was vying for Joseph's attention, but it was baby Lovina who captivated him. Hyrum and Jerusha put her through all the antics a baby learns in its first year. Soon the child had all the family laughing, but Joseph felt a sudden ache for the son he would never know.

At one o'clock Lucy was still holding dinner for Martin, and Joseph was becoming tense with worry.

They were about to sit down to dinner without him when they saw him walking with slow and measured tread toward the house, his eyes fixed on the ground. Coming to the gate he stopped. Instead of passing through he got up on the fence and sat there with his hat drawn over his eyes. Lucy sent Don Carlos to fetch him.

There were greetings, and they all sat down at the table.

Father Joseph said grace, then talk and laughter filled the room, but young Joseph and Martin were not laughing. Joseph was looking intently at Martin who sat with downcast eyes. He accepted a portion of food, took up his knife and fork as if he were going to use them, but immediately laid them down again.

Hyrum, observing this strange behavior in Martin who usually enjoyed both conversation and food, said: "Martin, you are not eating. Are you sick?"

Martin lifted tormented eyes to Hyrum's. Pressing his hands to his temples, he replied in a tone of deep anguish, "I have lost my soul. I have lost my soul."

Now it was Joseph who laid his knife and fork down. He had intended to wait until the meal was over and he and Martin were alone to speak to him about his great fear, but now his words came out for all to hear. "You have lost the manuscript, Martin!"

Martin's shoulders sagged as if he wanted to hide from every eye. "It's gone! I have searched for days." His words began a little above a whisper, and ended shrilly. "For weeks I have searched everywhere. It has been stolen from me."

Joseph was on his feet now. "Then everything is lost—everything."

Asking to be excused, he left the table. It took all his effort to hold back the quick flood of condemning words that sprang to his tongue. Martin knew the manuscript's value. He had pledged his life to keep it safe. How could he have been so careless?

Swiftly he walked out into the hot August sun, and the fire in him seemed hotter than the sun. He was so angry that tears stung his eyes, and his hands became tight balls. What would he do now? What could he do?

It didn't occur to Joseph that he should blame himself—that the fault was his as it was Martin's, that three

309

times he had been warned to keep the writings in his possession. He did think of it but only to blame Martin the more. Had not Martin refused to heed God's warning and implored Joseph to ask just one more time? He had been determined to have his way. Well, he had lost the manuscript; he'd just have to find it. Mrs. Harris undoubtedly knew where it was. It would be like her to steal it to make trouble. If it was not found he had no answer as to how he would proceed with the translating or what he would do. How long Joseph walked he did not know, but dinner was over and the other members of the family were about their various tasks when he returned to the house. He had not forgiven Martin, but his anger had spent itself. He found Hyrum and Martin in the parlor and joined them there.

"We must go to your house and search some more," he said. "The manuscript has to be somewhere."

"Search?" Martin's eyes were stricken. "It is all in vain. I have ripped open pillows, combed the house from one end to the other, tramped the premises . . . all to no purpose. I know it is not there. It is stolen, and for no good . . . of that you may be sure."

Joseph sank down into a chair. His eyes were two points of pain. "Do you want to tell me about it?"

Hyrum got up to leave and Martin said sadly, "Stay. You may as well hear too."

Hyrum sat down, and the room became suddenly silent. The only sound was the ticking of the tall parlor clock, the treasured gift of Lucy's brother, Major Mack. Now the ticking seemed too loud, like an intrusion in the silence.

Martin cleared his throat and swallowed, then he began to speak in a weary voice that seemed to come from a long way off. "I took the manuscript intending to follow instructions to the letter. I arrived home with it safely, and showed it to my wife and the other four. She read it through

310

a couple of times and was so pleased with it that she gave me the privilege of locking it up in her own set of drawers." A fleeting smile touched his lips and was gone. "This was a special favor, for I had never been permitted to look into her bureau before—she is that particular."

Martin paused, and the clock was heard again. "After I had shown the manuscript to those who had a right to see it, according to the oath, I went with my wife to visit one of her relatives who lives some fifteen miles distant. We stayed there a day and a night; then I came home and she stayed on. Alone, I began to go over in my mind all the work that had gone into the writing of the manuscript." Again he paused, and his fingers drummed the chair arm nervously. "I began to think how unfair it was of you not to let me have a try at translating with the Urim and Thummim, and especially not to let me feel and handle the plates. I felt that I had as much right to see them as you did. It seemed to me you had set yourself up as an ambassador for God and above your fellows."

Joseph felt his anger blaze again. "That isn't true. I was only following instructions."

Martin went on speaking as though Joseph hadn't interrupted. "While I was in this jealous frame of mind a friend came to visit, and I told him all I knew about the records. As might be expected his curiosity was excited, and when I told him I had the manuscript of course he wanted to see it. I knew I was breaking my oath, but I thought, Why should I let an upstart young enough to be my son dictate to me? I have judgment. This friend is an honest fellow capable of being trusted. Why should he not see this marvelous work? And contrary to my promise, I went to the drawer to get the manuscript, but the key was gone. I hunted, but I couldn't find it. The more I searched, the more determined I was to carry through my purpose. At last I picked the lock. After

311

showing it to this friend I moved it to my own set of drawers where I could have it when I wanted it." His eyes became deep pools of suffering. "Since I had made a sacrifice of my conscience I went on exhibiting the writings to those I considered prudent enough to keep the secret—except your family, Joseph. None of the Smiths have set eyes on it."

Joseph's temper flared. It seemed unbelievable that a man of Martin's integrity could have done such a thing, but he had! "If the devil himself had planned my undoing the job couldn't have been more thorough." His tone was as cutting as acid.

"Someone has the manuscript," Hyrum reminded them gently. He touched Martin's bowed shoulders. "We must find it."

"Where? The wife . . . family . . . friends . . . everyone claims to know nothing about it. But somebody has it, and that somebody undoubtedly intends to harm Joseph's work with it."

"Of that I am certain." Joseph's tone was bitter.

The kindness in Hyrum's voice did not change. "We'll go home with you, and we'll search your premises one more time, Martin. The manuscript has to be somewhere."

Joseph spent several days searching with Martin—but they found no clues, no leads. The manuscript was hopelessly lost.

For a long time Joseph had had a feeling that once the plates had been translated and made into a book the book would make clear certain disputed teachings of theology. It would prove that God was indeed the God of the Bible, a God as much alive today as in the past, and that all persons could contact him personally for wisdom, for knowledge, for enlarging their spiritual visions, for every needful thing. The

312

new records did not minimize the worth of the Bible or man's need for it, but he had long had a feeling that a spiritual awakening was about to sweep the earth, an awakening that would cause churches to change their creeds and thinking minds to open to new truths, bringing changes for good in almost every field of endeavor. Within the records were hidden truths with great new meanings. Joseph didn't mind retranslating the manuscript—he would gladly do it—but suppose he did. Whoever had the original could alter each page to his own liking and make any second translation seem like a farce.

His family tried to reassure him. Of course he would go on with the work. Of course he would begin it anew. Since this was God's work a stolen manuscript couldn't thwart it.

He had parked himself on a stool in the kitchen with Lucy one morning—a dejected, downcast figure watching her knead bread. "Joseph," she said, "what has happened to your faith? You are doing exactly what the devil wants you to do by sitting here wasting time to no purpose. I have even thought of a new scribe for you—a young schoolteacher by the name of Oliver Cowdery. I'm sure we wrote you about him."

"Yes. The fellow you took to board and gave Alvin's room."

Lucy stopped her kneading for a moment. Her liking for Oliver showed in her face. "We've told him about the angel's visits and the plates. He has shown a special interest, asking questions and bringing up the subject again and again, as if he can't get enough of the story. Right now he is visiting the Whitmers in Waterloo. He thinks he's in love with the Whitmer girl." Her eyes softened. "But I wish he were interested in Catherine."

"Matchmaker." Joseph smiled, then sobered. "You think he'd write for me?"

"I'm sure of it. He is a fine teacher, but since children can't be kept in school during harvest and crop time, or when the weather is bad, there will be weekly and monthly intervals when Oliver can't teach. He would relish going to Harmony to write for you."

Joseph wanted to go home to be with Emma, yet how could he tell her the manuscript was lost? Emma's heart was in the records. Her belief in their divinity was as strong as his. She was fighting with such courage to regain her health. How would she stand up against another of Joseph's failures? It seemed to him that he had failed in everything—at the translating, as a farmer, even as a husband, for Emma deserved more than the small cabin that had once been a home for insects and squirrels.

The day after his conversation with Lucy about Oliver, Joseph boarded the stage for a hot, uncomfortable return to Harmony.

At first, after Joseph left for Palmyra to obtain the manuscript from Martin, Emma stayed at the big house, but she was not happy there. Her family was still of one mind about Joseph—he was without purpose or ambition. They were devoted to Emma, but their jibes at Joseph kept her continually defending him. Her brothers teased her about his weed garden, then went out and gathered in the produce. They teased her about the livestock, then went to care for the two horses, the chickens, and the cow. They pretended not to notice that the animals were all in fine shape, that the cow was from their own herd and gave the same rich milk. Their comments kept Emma in turmoil most of the time, and she longed for the peace and quiet of her own cabin.

The second sabbath she bathed and dressed, expecting to accompany the family to church. It had been a long time since she had gone to the church of her childhood, and she really wanted to go. But when she came down in her old hat and dress, all the members of the family looked at her, and Emma knew they would be uncomfortable if she went along.

It was her father who broke the silence her entrance had caused. "Remind me to take you to town tomorrow, Emma, and fit you with some proper clothing. You are a Hale, but you look like a scarecrow in that dress."

"I can't allow you to buy clothes for me, Father. Joseph and I will manage." She took off her hat and laid it on the sofa. "I don't really feel up to going to church anyway. All of you go without me."

They hesitated.

"Please. I would find it tiring to sit through the long service."

She discerned a look of relief on their faces as they hurriedly kissed her and went out the door to get into the surrey. Emma hadn't noticed until now how elegantly each one walked. Had she once been so proud, so concerned with the cut of garments? Of course she had . . . for she was a Hale.

She touched the little bonnet. The flowers were fresh looking, the straw was brushed and clean. Its flaw was in being out of style. She was clean from head to toe, but the lines of her dress were dated. All at once, instead of being heartsick she was amused. She pictured the flutter and the turning of heads when her family entered church. Her mother's skirts would make a rustling sound as she made her way to their special pew. Father, beside her, would beam with pride; brothers would follow, heads held in the certain proud way that marked the Hales. Eyes in the congregation would note every detail and line of her mother's dress and hat, and the flawless attire of the men from their black polished boots to the perfection of their celluloid collars.

Some would envy; some would make notes of what to copy; a few would remark about Hale extravagance; but all would notice what seemed to be her father's unlimited prosperity.

Emma had no quarrel with riches. Money was important in a growing country or community. What she objected to was her family's thinking that a man with money was a success, and one without it a failure. It simply was not true. Many of the world's greatest contributors had died penniless, and many more would do so. Most men with thoughts bold enough to change the course of history were not welcomed by their contemporaries; many were dubbed odd and looked upon with scorn. Many died without seeing the flowering of their efforts. It took a truly great person to stay on course when the tide of human opinion was against him. Many with the courage to stand firm in their convictions preferred seclusion that they might bring forth new revelations and knowledge or push the frontiers of mankind a little further, or add more insight to what had gone before.

There was no staid pattern or form for living. Each person had to choose his own. There were persons of simple taste who preferred simple foods, clothes enough to cover them, a roof to keep out cold and heat, and friends of kindred spirits. Perhaps these were the successful ones—at least they were often the contented ones. This was the kind of contentment Joseph's family knew, and she had learned to appreciate the commonplace through their eyes. This was something her people were unable to understand—the joys to be found in simple things that money could not buy.

She put away her bonnet. The day was a fine one, warm but not hot. She found herself walking in the direction of her cabin, and a nostalgic feeling of homesickness came over her. Suddenly she found herself wanting her own things, her own moments to live and think, her freedom. But was she strong enough to walk all that way? Time was abundant. I'll walk

316

short distances and take rests, she told herself. There are birds to study, cloud pictures to see, wild flowers to pick, and thoughts to think. There are logs to sit on, the shade of trees, the good earth, and the morning breeze. Suddenly she knew home was where she belonged.

The walk had been long, and Emma was spent when she reached her cabin. Even by resting, the last part of the walk had been fatiguing. At home she sat on the stoop, aware of the breeze and the beauty around her. How fresh the air smelled. Green tree fronds danced and touched other trees in the slight breeze. After a little she went to a hiding place, a spot known only to Joseph and her. There she found the key to the cabin. Unlocking the door she went inside. The rooms smelled close and unlived in. They were hot compared to the high ceiled rooms of her parents' home, but to Emma it felt good to be in her own place with her own belongings. She made her way to the bed and stretched out on it, missing Joseph. She touched his half of the pillow sham, then she removed the sham and moved to his side of the bed, burying her face in his pillow. Turning over, she rested her head where his had been, wondering how things were with him. Had he been able to get the manuscript from Martin? She hoped it was safe in his possession, but the uneasy feeling that had been with her for days still persisted. If the manuscript were lost, what would Joseph do? Would he be able to finish his work? Lying there alone she tried to pray for the safety of the manuscript, but her mind was so filled with misgivings that the words had no meaning. It was as if a sixth sense were telling her to pray that Joseph would have strength to meet his trials and disappointments.

After a time she stopped thinking of Joseph and

thought of herself. Had she been foolish to leave her parents' home? Would she be able to do her work and prepare her meals? Joseph had been doing all the heavy work and most of the cooking for ever so long. She must have slept then, for she was not aware of her parents' presence until she looked up and saw them standing beside her bed. Concern was written on their faces, and her father spoke sternly. "Emma, why in heaven's name did you undertake this long walk home?"

Emma, wide awake now, gave him an impish smile. "You think I'm a brat."

His face softened. "I know you're a brat."

Her mother said, "We were wrong not to take you to church with us. But you were wrong to walk so far."

Isaac Hale spoke again. "We're taking you home with us to a good dinner and a decent house. . . ."

The slur against the house was for Joseph, and it triggered Emma. "Father, I'm old enough to know what is best for me."

Now it was her father's turn to be angry. "You have never known what is best for you." When he was angry his voice boomed. "Everything you choose is bad for you. And the worst mistake you ever made was marrying Joseph. . . ."

Emma stopped him with a look, and her mother cut in sharply. "Stop it, both of you." Then her face took on tenderness as her eyes covered Emma. "If you insist upon staying here, child, I'll stay with you. Drive me home, Isaac. I'll get together what things we'll need and bring back Emma's dinner."

There was a grateful softness in Emma's voice. "Are you sure you want to do this, Mother?"

"I'm sure," her mother said.

There were those who sometimes found fault with Elizabeth Hale's stubbornness, for it was a fact that once she

318

had set her mind to something not even Isaac Hale's temper and quick tongue could move her off course. Now that she had chosen to stay with Emma in the cabin, it was her determination to nurse her back to health. She stood with the family in her disapproval of Joseph, but Emma was her child and she was loyal to her brood. Since Emma's marriage, she termed her the willful child, for Emma often angered her, especially when she upheld Joseph in his supernatural imaginings. She was certain Emma could make Joseph into a man like the Hale men if she would take a firm stand against his wild schemes. She wanted Joseph molded into the pattern of the Hales. Hale men were strong and determined to turn every clod to see that the town of Harmony was run the Hale way, which was the best way. It made her sick the way Joseph was bringing ridicule upon himself and Emma. Ministers from their pulpits were beginning to refer to Joseph's golden bible with sarcasm, and this reflected on all the Hales. Elizabeth felt the humiliation. How could Emma believe in the divinity of plates she had never set eyes on? How could she accept their existence on faith? The thought occurred to her that the plates were in the cabin, and that it was within her power to destroy them, but she couldn't bring herself to go near the chest where they were hidden. In truth she was afraid to touch them. She might declare to Emma and all who would listen that the records were a hoax, and that Joseph's claims pure imaginings, but deep within her was a doubt. Suppose Joseph *had* received divine records from the hand of an angel? If this were true and she touched them, might not some awful consequence result? So she stayed well away from them and turned her mind to helping Emma regain her health. She insisted on good food, light exercise, and plenty of rest. She was rewarded by seeing Emma's pale cheeks take on color and her listless feet move with new life. It was a triumph for Elizabeth that by the time Joseph

319

returned Emma was well on her way to her usual buoyancy.

Joseph's back rested against the faded horsehair cushions of the stage as it neared Harmony. His traveling companions were two young ladies and a middle-aged gentleman. When they first boarded the stage the young ladies had given Joseph a quick, approving appraisal, but his lack of interest had turned them to conversations with the older man.

They had discussed the steamboat monopoly, New York's new constitution, the forging of new frontiers in the west, the laying of a railroad for trains that would run by steam, perhaps at the fantastic speed of twenty miles an hour. Now they were saying there was probably a way to tie down the safety valve of the steam engine to stop the hissing sound made by escaping steam. Joseph came out of his own gray thoughts long enough to remark, "Do that, and it will blow up."

They discussed Fulton's steamboat, wondering if trains would make shipping obsolete?

"Ridiculous," Joseph said, and turned his mind again to the worry inside himself.

Emma sat on the cabin steps idly watching two squirrels cavorting up and down the trunk of a nearby tree. The day was hot, and she welcomed the shade made by many trees surrounding the cabin.

She was thinking of Joseph, for he was seldom out of her mind. She began enjoying the squirrels through his eyes. He loved the little creatures, and they sensed it, for they would perch on his shoulders or his hand while he fed them.

Suddenly Emma's thoughts were arrested by the sight of a man walking in the direction of the little house. Joseph! The next instant she was racing down the road to meet him, then panting she was in his arms, her kiss telling him how very much she had missed him.

His embrace was warm as he held her, yet she sensed something was wrong. "What is it, Joseph?" Although her lips formed the words, she knew before he answered that the manuscript was lost. It was exactly as she had feared all along.

He told her as best he could what had happened as they walked with arms entwined, and she sensed his disappointment and frustration.

"What will you do, Joseph?"

His face was stricken. "What can I do?"

"We must start over. I'll help you. We must do it all again."

He told her what he feared if they did that. "The person who took the manuscript means to use it against any retranslation, to make it appear a fraud. I'm sure of it."

"There must be a way. There has to be a way. We must pray and wait for God's answer."

"Emma, my prayers don't reach the treetops. I blame Martin. I'm bitter with him. After all our work—and his part was as important as mine—he was jealous, he said, because I wouldn't let him translate with the Urim and Thummim, and I wouldn't let him see the plates. The lost manuscript is his fault. Three times he was warned not to take it, but he took it in spite of the warnings."

She knew it would be useless to reason with him until his hurt had lessened, so she said, "Look at me, Joseph. See how healthy I have grown?"

His face took on a kind of shine. "Do you think I

haven't noticed how well you look? I do believe you are the prettiest girl in Pennsylvania."

He reached for her, and she impishly slipped from his grasp. "Catch me," she dared him, and the race was on. They were breathless and laughing when they reached the house, and for a little while Joseph's worries left his mind.

Shortly after Joseph's return Isaac Hale stopped by the cabin and Emma's mother rode back to the big house with him. Emma was almost relieved to see her go, for the minute she saw Joseph her manner turned cool and unpleasant. Emma had been grateful for her mother's help and tender care during Joseph's absence, but why couldn't they see that by shutting Joseph out of their affections they were shutting her out too? He wanted them to like him, and if they really knew him, he would be good for them. But they were opinionated and stubborn. It was doubtful if they would ever change.

After thinking the matter through, Joseph decided to try retranslating the manuscript, for of what use was it that power had been given him, if he didn't try to rectify what had been lost. He knew that what he had translated bore out the angel's promise, for he could see that the records supported the Bible, bringing added light to truths written there. In ancient times men had been called to do special work, and it would be so until the end of time. And there was no use denying his own curiosity. He wanted to learn the secrets of the records. Here were histories of persons who had lived, fought, and died in the Americas long ago, unfolding like recorded histories in the Bible, and just as old. Why, some of it could have happened upon the very soil where he stood. He had no choice but to retranslate, for he dare not fail to bring forth this second witness. The words of the angel seemed to pound through his mind: "By these things men will know that there is a God in heaven who is infinite and eternal, from everlasting to everlasting, the same unchangeable God, the framer of heaven and earth and all things which are in them, and that he created man male and female, after his own spirit, and in his own likeness created he them, and gave unto them commandments that they should love and serve him, the only living and true God, and that He should be the only being whom they should worship."

Had he not been told at each meeting with the angel how sacred these records were, and with what infinite care he must protect them? Had they not been called a marvelous work and a wonder? Joseph recalled the hours of instruction he had received before he had been permitted to take the plates, and the hours he had spent in studying the Bible to prepare himself. Was it to come to nothing now? It seemed that retranslating was the only answer. Once he had made up his mind, Joseph sought Emma to tell her of his decision. He would accept her offer to act as his scribe.

Emma was overjoyed at the prospect of being a scribe. She knew the importance of the work, and with what painstaking care she must write in order that not one word would be lost or omitted. She understood and sympathized with Joseph in his disappointment at having to start again with all the weeks of labor lost. Could the work be finished *in time* now? By *in time* she meant could they complete the work before religious sects in town began persecuting Joseph the way he had been persecuted in Palmyra and Manchester? Already there were rumblings, and Emma was certain that Joseph was aware of them, and that he knew the time was not far distant when there would be trouble again. If he had not spoken of it, it was because he wanted to spare her undue

323

worry. It was Joseph's way. Well, she would not speak of it either, for why should she add to his burdens?

She washed her hands and made herself tidy while Joseph put up the quilt that would hide the records from her view. When he was ready she went and sat in the chair where Martin had sat so many times before.

Her parchment, quill pen, and ink were on the same little table Martin had used to do his writing. She sat now, pen in hand, waiting. She heard the metallic sound of a leaf turning which meant that Joseph was studying the engravings. It was very quiet in the room, for Joseph had made no other sound. She waited. A full minute ticked by in complete silence, then another and another. At last she said, "Joseph, are you all right?"

She heard the sound of a muffled sob. "Joseph!" her voice held real concern now. "What is it? What is happening?"

His voice came to her with such anguish that she was startled. "The Urim and Thummim refuse to work. I have lost the power to translate."

"You must try again."

"To what end? It is as if the gift had never been mine."

She started toward him and stopped. She was not permitted to look at the records and must wait for him to come to her. She could hear him putting everything away. She knew when he removed the breastplate from his body, although she could not see him. She knew when he opened the lid of the morocco trunk and deposited the records. She heard the lid close. But instead of coming to her, she caught a glimpse of his ashen face as he walked past her out of the house. Should she follow and try to console him? No, he would come to her when he felt that she could help. If he had wanted her he would have come to her. This was something he felt he must face alone. Then she wept for him as only a woman who loves can weep.

Joseph walked to a secluded spot in the woods and sat down on a fallen log. He hadn't come to pray. He was too bitter. Martin had brought this trouble upon him—all of it. In his mind he saw Martin showing the manuscript to everyone who wanted to see it.

He sat there entirely unaware of a songbird singing in the tree above him. He didn't see a rabbit that came close to eye him before bounding away to be lost in the brush. A snake crossed not two feet from where he sat, but he didn't see it. It was not like Joseph to nurse a grievance, for he had always been one to forgive freely and to hold no grudge. It was his way to analyze both sides of a problem, and he had the rare gift of putting himself in another person's place, figuring out why acts were performed as they were. But this ability was missing now; blame and anger toward Martin were like fires burning in his brain.

Suddenly the woods around the log where he sat became surrounded by light. At first Joseph was unaware of this too, so lost was he in thought. Then he looked up to confront the sorrowful eyes of the angel Moroni.

"My son," the angel's voice was sad, "I have come to reprove you for your thoughts, which are sinful, and certainly you know by now that God looks upon sin with no degree of allowance."

Joseph opened his mouth to say something in his own defense, but the angel, understanding his thoughts, rebuked him further.

"Martin Harris did a wicked thing by deliberately breaking his oath. Now his repentance is great, and his soul yearns to make amends. But you, Joseph, have been instructed to know the sacredness of the work that was put into your hands. You have been told not to put your trust in

325

man but to rely on God for instruction and guidance, yet you repeatedly entreated the Lord for his consent after he denied you. You knew that Martin was not a strong-minded man. The blame is yours, not his. Because you have sinned and have treated lightly that which was sacred, and have not measured up to the work for which you have been called, I have been instructed to take the records from you."

Joseph's face became almost as white as the angel's robe. Moroni, seeing his anguish, spoke less harshly. "It may be that after a season the records will be returned, but the matter rests entirely with you, Joseph. My instructions were to obtain the records and hide them from the eyes of men. I have not been told that they will be returned to you again."

The light receded then, and Joseph felt as if the punishment were more than he could bear, for he was sure, even before he went home and looked, that the records were no longer in the morocco trunk.

At first Joseph thought the angel must surely be mistaken, for why should he shoulder all blame for another man's sin? Yet as he pondered he knew in his heart that it was indeed so. He had known all along that Martin was a man easily dominated by his wife, and that he seldom crossed his friends. This made him a lovable person. Certainly he was usually easy to get along with, but this tendency toward amiability did not make him a man of firm decision. Joseph had been aware of Martin's nature when he let him take the manuscript; therefore the error in judgment was Joseph's. Deeply troubled, Joseph returned home to find Emma. She was one of the few persons who would believe his strange story and the grave punishment he was to bear.

The punishment was indeed severe, and Emma suffered with Joseph, for they had risked their very lives to preserve the records. How could they endure it if it all were to end in failure?

326

Joseph's grief was intense. He felt the anguish not only of losing the records, but of being rejected of God. His repentance was genuine, as he thought deeply on all the instructions he had received from the angel. And he learned through mental pain how sacred the work was that he had been called to do. He had lost not only the records but his chance to bring back the promised gospel with the divine truths that had been in the church since the time of Enoch, for this had been his promise. How could he have taken lightly such a calling? And how could he be forgiven for failing to see the importance of his sacred work?

The more he pondered, the more he was made to see that he had been lifted up in selfish pride over his power to translate so that Martin had coveted his gift. If he had been more humble—a servant through whom the power was made manifest by the intelligence of God—Martin would have had no cause to envy. He did not ask for a second chance, but his whole being longed for it. If only he could be forgiven and permitted to try again, surely he would abide by the commandments and instructions a second time.

At last, feeling a great need to be alone, he took his hoe and walked out to cut down weeds that would destroy his next year's planting. As he worked his tears fell. Joseph was not one to cry easily. He had never felt more repentant, more humble, or more alone. "Oh, God," his soul cried, "how can I gain forgiveness and be accepted again?"

What happened while he prayed is not easily explained. He had an unusual experience similar to those related by the apostles of old, for as his whole being cried out to be forgiven he felt the warm, quiet comfort of the Holy Spirit enveloping him with its enlightening power, and words that were both divine and prophetic moved soundlessly through his brain.

The works and designs, and the purposes of God cannot be frustrated, neither can they come to naught, for God doth

327

not walk in crooked paths, neither doth he turn to the right hand nor to the left, neither doth he vary from that which he hath said; therefore his paths are straight, and his course is one eternal round.

Remember, remember that it is not the work of God that is frustrated, but the work of men; for although a man may have many revelations, and have power to do many mighty works, yet if he boast in his own strength, and sets at naught the counsels of God, and follows after the dictates of his own will and carnal desires, he must incur the vengeance of a just God upon him.

Behold, you have been intrusted with these things, but how strict were your commandments; and remember also the promises that were made to you, if you did not transgress them. And behold, how oft you have transgressed the commandments and the laws of God, and have gone on in the persuasions of men—for behold you should not have feared men more than God, although men set at naught the counsels of God, and despise his words, yet you should have been faithful and he would have extended his arm, and supported you against all the fiery darts of the adversary; and he would have been with you in every time of trouble.

Behold, thou art Joseph, and thou wast chosen to do the work of the Lord, but because of transgression, if thou art not aware, thou wilt fall. But remember, God is merciful; therefore repent of that which thou hast done, which is contrary to the commandment which I gave you, and thou art still chosen, and art again called to the work; except thou do this, thou shalt be delivered up and become as other men, and have no more gift.

And when thou deliveredst up that which God had given thee sight and power to translate, thou deliveredst up that which was sacred into the hands of a weak man who has set at naught the counsels of God, and has broken his most

328

sacred promises which were made before God, and has depended upon his own judgment and boasted in his own wisdom; and this is the reason that thou hast lost thy privileges for a season, for thou hast suffered the counsel of thy director to be trampled upon from the beginning.

Nevertheless, my work shall go forth, for inasmuch as the knowledge of a Savior has come unto the world, through the testimony of the Jews, even so shall the knowledge of a Savior come unto my people, and to the Nephites, and the Jacobites, and the Josephites, and the Zoramites through the testimony of their fathers; and this testimony shall come to the knowledge of the Lamanites, and the Lemuelites, and the Ishmaelites who dwindled in unbelief because of the iniquity of their fathers, whom the Lord has suffered to destroy their brethren the Nephites, because of their iniquities and their abominations; and for this very purpose are these plates preserved which contain these records, that the promises of the Lord might be fulfilled which he made to his people; and that the Lamanites might come to the knowledge of their fathers, and that they might know the promises of the Lord, and that they may believe the gospel and rely upon the merits of Jesus Christ, and be glorified through faith in his name, and that through their repentance they might be saved. Amen.

Even after the power of the Holy Spirit which had enveloped him was gone Joseph felt as if he were standing on holy ground. He was about to seek Emma to tell her of his strange experience when his mind was again lighted by the same Spirit, and words again flowed through his mind as substance without sound.

Now behold, I say unto you that because you delivered up those writings which you had power given unto you to translate, by the means of the Urim and Thummim, into the

329

hands of a wicked man, you have lost them; and you also lost your gift at the same time, and your mind became darkened; nevertheless, it is now restored unto you again, therefore see that you are faithful and continue unto the finishing of the remainder of the work of translation as you have begun. Do not run faster or labor more than you have strength and means provided to enable you to translate; but be diligent unto the end; pray always, that you may come off conquerer; yea, that you may conquer Satan, and that you may escape the hands of the servants of Satan that do uphold his work. . . .

Verily, I say unto you, that I will not suffer that Satan shall accomplish his evil design in this thing, for behold, he has put it into their hearts to get thee to tempt the Lord thy God, in asking to translate it over again; and then, behold, they think in their hearts, We will see if God has given him power to translate, if so, he will also give him power again; and if God giveth him power again, or if he translate again, or in other words, if he bringeth forth the same words, behold, we have the same with us, and we have altered them; therefore they will not agree, and we will say he has lied in his words, and that he has no gift, and that he has no power; therefore we will destroy him and also the work, and we will do this that we may not be ashamed in the end, and that we may get glory of the world. . . .

Behold, I say unto you that you shall not translate again those words which have gone forth out of your hands; for behold they shall not accomplish their evil designs in lying against those words. For, behold, if you should bring forth the same words they will say that you have lied; that you have pretended to translate, but that you have contradicted yourself; and behold, they will publish this, and Satan will harden the hearts of the people to stir them up to anger against you, that they will not believe my words. Thus Satan *thinketh to overpower your testimony in this generation, that the work may not come forth in this generation; but, behold, here is wisdom, and because I show unto you wisdom, and give you commandments concerning these things, what you shall do, show it not unto the world until you have accomplished the work of translation. . . .*

And now verily I say unto you that an account of those things that you have written, which have gone out of your hands, are engraved upon the plates of Nephi. . . . You shall translate the engravings which are on these plates until you come to the reign of King Benjamin, or until you come to that which you have translated, which you have retained; and behold you shall publish it as the record of Nephi; thus I will confound those who have altered my words. I will not suffer that they shall destroy my work. . . . There are many things engraved on the plates of Nephi which do throw greater views upon my gospel. . . . The remainder of this work contains all those parts of my gospel which my holy prophets and also my disciples desired in their prayers should come forth unto the people. And I said unto them that it should be granted unto them according to their faith in their prayers; yea, and this was their faith, that my gospel which I gave unto them, that they might preach it in their days, might come unto their brethren, the Lamanites, and also all that had become Lamanites because of their dissensions.

Now this is not all, their faith in their prayers was that this gospel should be made known also, if it were possible that other nations should possess this land; and thus they did leave a blessing upon this land in their prayers, that whosoever should believe in this gospel in this land might have eternal life; yea, that it might be free unto all of whatsoever nation, kindred, tongue, or people they may be. . . .

And for this cause I have said, If this generation harden not their hearts, I will establish my church among them. . . . Behold, I am Jesus Christ the Son of God. I came unto my own, and my own received me not. I am the light which shineth in darkness, and the darkness comprehendeth it not. I am he who said, unto my disciples, Other sheep have I which are not of this fold, and many there were who understood me not.

And I will show unto this people that I had other sheep, and that they were a branch of the house of Jacob; and I will bring to light their marvelous works, which they did in my name; yea, and I will also bring to light my gospel, which was ministered unto them, and behold, they shall not deny that which you have received, but they shall build it up. . . . This I do that I may establish my gospel, that there may not be so much contention concerning the points of my doctrine. . . .

Behold, this is my doctrine: Whosoever repenteth and cometh unto me, the same is my church; whosoever declareth more or less than this, the same is not of me but is against me. . . . Whosoever is of my church and endureth of my church to the end, him will I establish upon my Rock, and the gates of hell shall not prevail against him.

And now remember the words of him who is the life and the light of the world, your Redeemer, your Lord and your God. Amen.

Again the Spirit left him. He was surprised to find out how tired his body felt, but his mind was exhilarated. He wanted Emma to share the revelations, for now he knew that the plates would be restored to him and the work of translation would be resumed in God's own time.

Not finding her in the little house he went at once to their bedroom, thinking he might lie down for a short while, but upon entering the room he felt an urge to write down what he could remember of the words that had been given to

332

him. No sooner had he picked up the pen and dipped it into the ink than he was again enveloped in the Spirit, and he found himself writing the revelations as they had been given to him in the garden.

Weeks passed without the plates being restored. This caused Joseph and Emma no concern, for they believed that in God's own time the work would proceed as promised. In the meanwhile Joseph cut and winnowed the wheat, gathered in the last of the late crops, and prepared some of the land for future seeding. Both he and Emma knew their scanty crops would not carry them through to another harvest, and Joseph blamed himself for letting his seeds mature without care in order to translate a lost manuscript. But Emma was quick to defend him saying that it was more important to be diligent in doing God's work, and that the lost manuscript was a misfortune that didn't minimize his efforts. "God will open a way for our needs to be supplied, if we trust him." Emma's voice had a quality of confidence that Joseph had come to rely on.

With Joseph working his land the Hales became friendly, almost cordial, and Emma went about singing at her work. But when cold settled over the land the plates were restored, and the day the translating was resumed with Emma acting as scribe, the Hales became cold and distant again with both of them, and Emma dreaded the approaching holidays.

There was nothing she enjoyed more than writing as Joseph dictated, but the translating proceeded slowly, for she was not one to neglect her house, and since they were too poor to buy ready-made clothes, she had to sew the things they needed. There were candles to make, churning to do, bread to bake, and routine duties that seemed never to end. Joseph helped her; if he had not, there would have been no time for the writing at all, but they both knew Joseph needed a full-time scribe.

The holidays were as bad as Emma had imagined they would be. Because she loved her family deeply, she was hurt. An invisible wall that had been long in the making seemed insurmountable by Christmas, shutting her and Joseph out. Eric and Phoebe remained unchanged, but their stay was short, and after their departure Emma felt like a stranger among relatives and old friends in her father's house.

One cold winter day in early January, when Joseph and Emma were discouraged because the work of translating was progressing slowly, a horseman brought a letter from Mother Lucy that lifted their spirits, for it bore promise of being an answer to Joseph's need for a full-time scribe.

My dear children:

I am writing concerning Oliver Cowdery, the young schoolteacher I suggested would make a good scribe for you, Joseph.

Emma, we met him through his brother Lyman and our Hyrum. Hyrum is trustee for the district school, and Lyman was hired to teach there. But the day after he was employed he came saying he couldn't serve, and suggested his brother Oliver as teacher.

Oliver is a fine teacher, and I can't begin to tell you how much we have enjoyed him in our home. Joseph, it astonishes us, the interest he has taken in your work.

Yesterday he told us, "I have been in a deep study upon the subject every spare minute, and it is impressed upon my mind that one day I shall write for Joseph."

Today he said, "The subject under discussion yesterday seems to be working in my bones, and I think about it constantly. I must tell you my decision. Samuel, I understand, is going down to Pennsylvania to spend the spring with Joseph. I shall make arrangements to be ready to accompany him, for I have made it a subject of prayer, and I firmly believe it is the will of the Lord that I should go. If there is work for me to do in this thing, I am determined to attend to it."

Oliver is so completely absorbed in the subject of the records that when he is with us we can hardly get him to talk upon anything else.

There was more to the letter, a heartbreaking part:

The time is at hand when we agreed to give up our house and land, and we are making preparations to move our family and effects in with Hyrum and his family. We feel so keenly the injustice which has placed a landlord over us in our own premises, one who is about to eject us from our home. I thought this was a good time to warn Oliver of misfortunes which may be his if he turns his back upon the world and sets out in the service of the Lord. When you were here, Joseph, I told you I thought he was in love with Miss Whitmer. This is true. He told us that one day he hopes she will be his wife.

"Oliver," I said, "see what a comfortable home we have here, what pains our children have taken to provide everything necessary to make old age comfortable and life desirable." I told him of Alvin, and how everything had been built as Alvin wanted it. These tender recollections make our present trial doubly severe. Upon what righteous principle has all this been brought about? Our house and land will go into hands that have never lifted a finger to build any part of it. But I shall try to leave here without a murmur or a tear. I shall try not to cast one longing look upon anything we must leave behind. We will be crowding Hyrum and Jerusha to the very walls. Perhaps it is that as much as anything which makes the breaking up of our home such a bitter trial. A part of all this we have discussed with Oliver. I told him he would be obliged to find lodging somewhere else and his reply was, "Mother, let me stay with you, for I can live in any hut where you and Father are, but I cannot leave you, so do not mention it." The compliment warmed my heart, for he has become like a son to us. He knows Hyrum would welcome him if only the walls of the house were made of rubber.

Joseph and Emma read and reread the letter, thoughtfully commenting upon its contents. It was plain that Mother Lucy blamed circumstances, not Father Joseph, for the loss of the farm. But the news hurt. Every bit of ground, every nail and log seemed a part of Alvin. It should not be a place for strangers.

They were both surprised and pleased that Samuel was coming. The end of school would be sometime in April. They were not wondering how they would feed four when their larder barely supported two. Their concern was for the work, and the thought of a full-time scribe made their eyes shine.

Perhaps there was no man in Harmony busier than Joseph, for he was shiftless and lazy only in the imagination of the Hales. Along with translating whenever Emma was available to write for him, and helping her in the house, he had built a snug shelter to winter his pigs and a shed to store firewood. He had sawed and chopped enough wood to carry them through the winter and had added a granary to one side of the barn. The supply of wheat and corn was not sufficient to last until spring, but what he had was safe and dry. The hayloft was filled with bales of hay, and his animals were well cared for. The meat in the cold house was getting low, however, and this worried him, for he had no calf to butcher.

On the first day of February snow began to fall. An icy wind rocked the trees until the roar was the sound of a tempest. Inside the little house the fireplace blazed, and Joseph had stacked wood from the floor halfway up one wall—enough to last several days. The fire gave them a feeling of well-being. With the quilt between them, Emma sat at the table writing with Joseph nearby dictating. They had worked a little more than an hour in this way when their attention was attracted by the sound of horses and a wagon.

Emma left the table. As she opened the front door a gust of wind nearly took her off her feet, but her cry was a happy one. "Mother Lucy—Father Joseph." Then she called over her shoulder as she ran out to greet them, "Joseph, it's your folks!"

Joseph snatched up a towel to cover the plates, and a moment later he was assisting his parents out of snow-covered wraps. Everyone seemed to be talking at once while he hung coats near the fire to dry. The Smiths were half frozen, but soon they were sitting on chairs close to the fire sipping hot cider.

"We brought you the spinning wheel and other things we hope you can use," Mother Lucy said. "There isn't room at Jerusha's for some of our treasures that we can't bear to let go of, so we're sharing them between you and Sophronia."

Joseph was putting on his coat and boots. "I'll unload."

"I'll help you, if you'll wait until I've warmed a bit," Father Joseph said.

Young Joseph gave his shoulder a caressing pat as he went out the door. "If I can't manage, I'll call on you."

"You can manage. I loaded it, so I guess you can unload it," Father Joseph called after him.

Emma bundled up and went out to help him. Together they carried in the spinning wheel and found a place for it in one corner of the room. Then they brought in quilts, homespun sheets, and a feather mattress soft as down.

"These were Alvin's," Mother Lucy said. "We thought you would want them, Joseph."

Joseph's eyes told her how very much he wanted them.

"And we brought you Major Mack's clock," she added with a twinkle. The twinkle was because of Don Carlos. The clock had been named the Major Mack clock by Don Carlos and the name had stuck. It was a rare clock made of fine ebony wood. Roman numeral letters marked the face, and the pendulum of brass, delicately engraved, had been ticking out hours, minutes, and seconds with constant accuracy for a long time. Emma found a place for it on the mantle. With the wagon unloaded she wondered where they would put everything. There were the Smiths' few books, a rocking chair, antimacassars, a china washbowl, pitcher, and chamber, and Lucy's newest flatirons.

Yet even as Emma wondered, she knew what Joseph had meant when he said all things are spiritual in the eyes of God if they are good. Here, with quilts and a feather bed, were precious memories of Alvin. The Mack clock was a symbol of Lucy's years of plenty, and all things that had gone into making her a lady. The spinning wheel meant children clothed and warm, sheltered and loved. How many times had the chair rocked a sleepy child, heard laughter and song, held a form brave in adversity, or a heart lifted in joyful appreciation for some unexpected blessing. Here, in every separate gift, was a love for the beautiful, from persons whose delight was in simple living. She would take care of them and cherish them because they were the treasures of persons who had grown to be almost dearer than her own family. Gratefully her eyes rested first on Lucy, then on Father Joseph. "If the day ever comes that you want them back, they will be with Joseph and me, waiting for you."

With the wagon empty Joseph drove the team around to the barn and unhitched. He had to crack the ice in the watering trough before the horses could drink, then he led them to two empty stalls in the snug barn and tethered them. He gave them hay and grain and made sure his own animals had their needs supplied, then he went back to the house, whistling a merry tune as his face reddened in the wind and his coat turned white with snow.

Inside, Father Joseph and Lucy were talking to Emma about the records. Joseph took off his coat and hung it up to dry. He removed his boots and drew up a chair close to the fire without interrupting the flow of talk.

In a little while Father Joseph said, "Son, we didn't come here to stop your work. Emma tells us her folks have about disowned you both because of it."

Joseph's eyes were on the dancing fire. He spoke thoughtfully. "Their quarrel is with the translating. If I would end it and live as the Hales do I would be accepted. But I believe these records were mentioned in the Bible, in the Old Testament." He got up and brought his Bible, opening it to the thirty-seventh chapter of Ezekiel. Beginning at the fifteenth verse he commenced to read: " 'The word of the Lord came again unto me saying, Moreover, thou son of man, take one stick and write upon it, For Judah, and for the children of Israel his companions; then take another stick and write upon it, For Joseph, the stick of Ephraim, and for all the house of Israel his companions: And join them one to another into one stick; and they shall become one in mine hand.

" 'And when the children of thy people shall speak unto thee, saying, Wilt thou not shew us what thou meanest by these? Say unto them, Thus saith the Lord God; Behold, I will take the stick of Joseph which is in the hand of Ephraim, and the tribes of Israel his fellows, and will put them with him, even with the stick of Judah, and make them one stick, and they shall be one in mine hand. And the sticks whereon thou writest shall be in thine hand before their eyes.

" 'And say unto them, Thus saith the Lord God; Behold, I will take the children of Israel from among the heathen, whither they have gone, and will gather them on every side, and bring them into their own land:

" 'And I will make them one nation in the land upon the mountains of Israel; and one king shall be king to them all; and they shall be no more two nations, neither shall they be divided into two kingdoms any more at all.' "

Joseph stopped reading, and his eyes were bright. "I believe the Bible is the stick of Judah, and the records I am translating compose the stick of Joseph, and someday—it may take a long time—these two will become one in God's hand, to establish the truth of the Bible and to convince people that Jesus Christ is in very truth God's Son, who took upon him flesh and became man to show us what God is like, and to give us a reason for the life that is in us."

The room was very quiet. As the flames warmed the

bodies of the four people there, their minds were warmed by new thought. Then Joseph spoke again. "If I am right, the promise is that the Jews will be gathered as one nation, and Lebanon will become a fruitful field. Even now they are becoming restless to gather. They are scattered, but they have kept their lineage pure. And someday they will accept Christ as the Son of God, their long looked for Messiah."

Father Joseph's eyes were on the fire now. "What will you do, Joseph, when you finish translating the records?"

"I shall spend my life trying to establish truth. I believe in a living God who was in the beginning of time, and that time, as God knows it, has no end. I believe we are living in a part of eternity right now, that God is what he says he is—all love, all knowledge, all wisdom, all truth, all goodness, all purity—and that he is in the heavens above, and in the earth, and beneath the earth. There is not any place anywhere that he is not. We can comprehend with our finite minds only a portion of what he is, but he is a living God, one who reveals his will to man. Christ promised, 'Greater works than I do shall you do by the Holy Spirit that is in you.' He expects his church to have the gifts of prophecy, healings, tongues, the interpretation of tongues, and all the gifts and blessings that he exercised when he was on earth. I believe teaching truth as it is revealed to me will be my work, along with translating the records."

"Do you think people are ready to accept such a spiritual awakening?" Lucy asked gently.

"I think everyone wants a life that has meaning and purpose."

The room seemed filled with the ticking of Major Mack's clock until at last Father Joseph spoke.

"Oliver Cowdery and I talk about you and your work just about every day. Now this may surprise you, but of late I can't sleep wondering if there is something I can do to assist

340

you." He paused, his eyes earnest, his voice shy. "God talks to you through the Urim and Thummim. Would you ask how I can help? If there is something special I can do I would like to know what it is."

For a moment Joseph didn't answer. He had gone to God in Martin's behalf, and it had not been good. The Urim and Thummim was for translating and for receiving instruction. Father Joseph was a praying man, a man of faith who believed every prayer was answered, whether the answer was to his liking or not. If a special message was to be given, would it not come in God's own way and in his own time? What should he do? He had lost his gift of translating once. He dare not lose it again.

Suddenly it was as it had been in the garden. His whole mind seemed filled with light, and the light was centered around his father. He began to speak:

Now, behold, a marvelous work is about to come forth among the children of men; therefore, O ye that embark in the service of God, see that ye serve him with all your heart, might, mind, and strength, that ye may stand blameless before God at the last day; therefore, if ye have desires to serve God, ye are called to the work, for, behold, the field is white already to harvest, and lo, he that thrusteth in his sickle with his might, the same layeth up in store that he perish not, but bringeth salvation to his soul; and faith, hope, charity, and love, with an eye single to the glory of God, qualifies him for the work.

Remember, faith, virtue, knowledge, temperance, patience, brotherly kindness, godliness, charity, humility, diligence. Ask and ye shall receive, knock and it shall be opened unto you. Amen.

Father Joseph and Lucy stayed in Harmony until the weather cleared. They met Emma's people and liked them. They sat beside Emma and heard Joseph translate from the records. At night they slept in Joseph and Emma's bed. The young Smiths slept in front of the fireplace on Alvin's feather bed, covered with Alvin's bedding. The house seemed empty when the Smiths went home.

One cold March day Emma, pink-cheeked from hanging out clothes, came into the cabin to find Martin Harris with Joseph. She greeted him warmly. It was the first time she had seen him since the manuscript was lost, but that unfortunate circumstance had been resolved by divine enlightenment, and Martin had been absolved of blame by both Joseph and Emma.

Martin told her he had come to see how the work was progressing, and she informed him it was going all too slowly. The three of them talked in generalities then.

Martin and Joseph were sitting on chairs at the table, and Martin seemed under a strain. His fingers thumped nervously on the tabletop. Joseph and Emma both knew he had come for some special reason, and they waited for him to reveal it.

Emma brought glasses of cold milk and her special pandowdy which Martin seemed to enjoy. At last, after some time, Martin looked steadily into the eyes of Joseph and said with some embarrassment, "Joseph, people back home are saying, 'Martin, if Joe Smith really has got gold plates, why hasn't he shown them to you? You claim to have been his scribe; then why haven't you seen them?' "

Joseph returned his gaze and said nothing. The silence seemed to get under Martin's skin, for he put his spoon down with vehemence. "I have come to ask you to let me see and handle those plates so that I can witness to all who inquire that I have seen, touched, and know that the work you are engaged in is divine."

Joseph shook his head sadly. "My instructions are to show them to no one. Emma has never seen them, but her faith is strong. She doesn't doubt their divinity or importance. If it were left up to me, she would be the first to see them."

"Has your request been urgent that she might see them?"

"No, Martin, begging for a special favor is something I'll never do again."

Martin colored, for he knew Joseph was referring to the lost manuscript. "But you could ask, couldn't you? There are times when I find myself doubting that you have gold plates. I know you have something, but when I'm pressed by questions from every side I need a witness. You told me once that in God's own time he would show the plates to others. How do you know the time is not now? I have a burning desire to see them, so how do you know I am not one meant to see them? No one has a greater need to see them, for I want to help you financially, but unless I have something tangible to tell the wife, she is in a mood to give you trouble, Joseph, and to stop the work if she can."

Again the room was wrapped in silence. Then Martin said: "Ask—don't beg. Just ask, and I'll try to abide by whatever answer you receive."

Martin and Joseph went into the bedroom together and closed the door. Emma watched them go, and a small frown furrowed her brow. It was one thing for God to give Joseph revelations, but for Joseph to ask for a special one was an entirely different thing. It had brought them trouble before, and it could again. Suppose Martin were granted a look at the

343

plates—this would not satisfy Mrs. Harris. The only thing that would satisfy her would be a look at the plates herself—and even then she might cause trouble.

Emma went to the cold house where the meat was kept. She picked up a sharp knife and began cutting three steaks from the hind quarter of a beef hanging from the ceiling by wires. She noticed that their meat supply was getting low. She must ration Joseph and herself with great care as soon as they were alone again, for the day was not far off when they would be embarrassed at not having enough to properly feed company. They must stretch what they had in order to have enough to feed Joseph's brother and Oliver Cowdery, if their stay were long. But tonight she would not skimp. She was remembering the sumptuous table Mrs. Harris always set. Martin was used to an overabundance of everything.

When she had sawed and cut the meat to her satisfaction she went to make a fire in her outdoor oven. She would bake cornbread and a cake. There was enough pandowdy for another meal, but Martin might extend his stay to several days, and she could serve it tomorrow.

While she worked she thought of Mrs. Harris and her mother. How much alike they were! Each had a great house to run, and each ran it with efficiency and dispatch. Both measured success by material wealth. The poor, in their eyes, were either unfortunate or shiftless. If shiftless, they merited the disdain meted out to them. These were proud women, elegant in dress and manner whenever they left their own premises, but they were not afraid of soiling their hands at home. Mrs. Harris had a temper and a biting tongue. Emma's mother's temper seldom flared, but when it did her tongue could strike with force. Mrs. Harris liked to be in the middle of everything. She had an avid curiosity, and when she thought people had wronged her she always retaliated to "give them their just dues." Emma's mother was not one to

344

get even; she simply withdrew. Emma felt keenly the breach now existing between her and her mother.

Yes, she understood Martin's wanting to please his wife. At best, she was a difficult woman to live with, yet in spite of her temper Martin loved her.

Minutes ticked by. Emma was in and out of the cabin several times before the men came out of the bedroom, and when they came she knew the revelation had been given.

The men sat down at the table conversing in low tones. Emma was curious, but she didn't ask. It was not until after the supper things had been washed and put away and Martin had retired to the Hale bunkhouse to sleep that Joseph let her read the message. It was lengthy, and most of it concerned Joseph.

Behold . . . my servant Martin Harris has desired a witness at my hand, that you my servant Joseph Smith, Jr., have the plates of which you have testified and borne record that you have received of me; now this shall you say unto him: . . . I have caused that you should enter into a covenant with me, that you should not show them except to those persons to whom I commanded you; and you have no power over them except I grant it unto you. You have a gift to translate the plates; this is the first gift that I bestowed upon you, and I have commanded that you should pretend to no other gift until my purpose is fulfilled in this; for I will grant unto you no other gift until it is finished. . . .

Verily I say unto you I have reserved those things which I have intrusted unto you, my servant Joseph, for a wise purpose, and it shall be made known unto future generations; but this generation shall have my words through you; and in addition to your testimony . . . three of my servants, whom I shall call and ordain, unto whom I will show these things; and they shall go forth with my words which are given through you; yea, they shall know of a surety that these things are true; for from heaven will I declare it unto them; I will give them power that they may behold and view these things as they are; and to none else will I grant this power to receive the same testimony, among this generation, in this, the beginning of the rising up, and the coming forth of my church. . . . And the testimony of three witnesses of my word will I send forth; and behold, whosoever believeth on my words I will visit with the manifestations of my Spirit. . . .

And now I command you my servant Joseph to repent and walk more uprightly before me, and yield to the persuasions of men no more; that you may be firm in keeping the commandments wherewith I have commanded you. If you do this, I grant unto you eternal life.

And now I speak to you concerning the man that desires the witness. Behold . . . he exalts himself and does not humble himself sufficiently before me; but if he will bow down before me, and humble himself in mighty prayer and faith, in sincerity of his heart, then will I grant unto him a view of the things which he desires to see. And then he shall say unto the people of this generation, I have seen the things which the Lord has shown unto Joseph Smith, Jr., and I know of a surety that they are true, for I have seen them; for they have been shown unto me by the power of God and are not of man. And I command him to say no more concerning these things, except "I have seen them, and they have been shown unto me by the power of God." . . . But if he deny this he will break his covenant which he has before covenanted with me, and behold he will be condemned. . . .

I say unto thee, Joseph, When thou hast translated a few more pages thou shalt stop for a season until I command thee again; then thou mayest translate again. And except thou do this, thou shalt have no more gift, and I will take away the things which I have intrusted with thee. And now, because I foresee these lying in wait to destroy thee; yea, I foresee that *if my servant Martin Harris humbleth not himself and receive a witness from my hand, he will fall into transgression; and there are many that lie in wait to destroy thee and for this cause, that thy days may be prolonged, I have given unto thee these commandments; yea, for this cause I have said, Stop and stand still until I command thee, and I will provide means whereby thou mayest accomplish the thing which I have commanded thee; and if thou art faithful in keeping my commandments, that shalt be lifted up at the last day. Amen.*

Several days later Martin returned home. If he had come to serve as scribe he didn't stay.

Warned that the records were again in danger, Joseph hid them, and became alert, watching for signs of harm that might come to him or Emma. Now he turned his attention to his land. If there were to be food for another year the ground he had prepared must be planted, and the garden spaded and seeded. Emma was busier than usual, trying to catch up so that she could give more time to writing when the translating was resumed, if there should be no other scribe available. They were up at dawn and filled each day to the brim. They both carded wool, combed cotton, and dressed cloth. Emma cooked, churned, spun, and sewed. Butter and eggs she exchanged in town for necessary household items. Joseph went with her on these trips, for there was a growing coolness now among the townspeople. The setting hens hatched baby chicks, and how Emma loved them! They clamored over her hands at feeding time, and she enjoyed picking one up in her palm to feel the softness. A newborn calf and a colt became her special pets as she took over their care to give Joseph more time in the fields. There was a litter of pigs now too, nudging one another for a spot at the sow's teats. Earth had awakened from its frozen sleep. It was spring.

347

April began with rain. The weather was disagreeable, and roads were almost impassable. In spite of this, on the fifth day of April Joseph's brother Samuel and Oliver Cowdery came. Joseph and Emma welcomed them happily and provided dry clothes. Then Joseph livened up the fire with a birch log, while Emma warmed them with hot milk and corn cakes. Samuel had come to do whatever needed to be done in order to free Joseph for translating. Oliver was volunteering his services as scribe. A lean young man of medium height with blond hair and blue eyes, Oliver was frank and appealing. Joseph recognized his intelligence and his humility, a rare combination in one who even at this early age, was considered an outstanding teacher.

The cabin was warm, and the four talked easily as rain beat on the roof. Oliver, with eyes aglow and a voice alive with conviction, said, "When I was with your folks we talked about your work. From the moment I first heard of it, there was an urgency within me that would not be still. I want to write for you, but even more, I think I've been divinely called to be your scribe."

"I'm sure of it," Joseph said.

"Then shall we begin?"

"I hope we can begin very soon." The answer was vague. Oliver looked puzzled but made no comment.

That night Emma put the feather bed and warm quilts on the floor by the fire for herself and Joseph, but Oliver and Samuel refused to take their bedroom, asking instead to sleep on the floor bed. The first night, the beds were hardly used, for the four talked until almost dawn. Most of the talk concerned the book and its mission. But they talked too of the coming forth of the church which Joseph knew of a certainty was to be a part of his work, a work in which both Oliver and Samuel hoped to share.

In the early hours of morning Emma and Joseph went

to bed, but there was no sleep in Joseph. He lay wide awake and wistful. He had a scribe now, but of what use was a scribe when he had been commanded not to translate? Dawn flooded the woods with light. The rain had stopped, and Emma lay peacefully asleep beside him. Careful not to disturb her he got up and took the Urim and Thummim from where he had hid them. Since the day he had been commanded not to translate, he had looked each morning for instructions, but there had been none, and he expected today to be the same. Listlessly he lifted them and felt the burning in his breast that always accompanied his study of the engravings to confirm the truthfulness of the translations. There was a message. With three men to protect the records, the work could be resumed again.

Joseph spent most of Monday morning acquainting Samuel with the farm work. By afternoon talk concerning the plates began again, and Oliver and Joseph spent a part of the afternoon by themselves. Oliver had unanswered questions, and they sought divine guidance together for the work which Joseph believed could be completed now without delay.

Monday evening, when it was time to cook supper, Samuel went with Emma to the cold house to help her cut meat. It didn't please her that he was to see their depleted rations, but she felt it would be rude to forbid his coming. Now she watched his eyes move over the scanty remains of beef, venison, and pork hanging from the ceiling. He said nothing, but concern showed in his eyes. She took a knife from the shelf and began cutting the last of the meat off the beef thigh bone. She didn't try to explain their low supply, for she had no intention of putting Joseph in a bad light, and she knew if she seemed concerned about food Samuel would return to Manchester and persuade Oliver to go with him. How she would feed two extra men over a long period of time she did not know, but if God wanted the plates translated he would have to provide. Samuel held the plate. It was well filled when they closed the cold house door.

"If Joseph will lend me his gun I'll try for a wild turkey tomorrow," Samuel said as they walked back to the cabin.

"That will be fine," she answered.

Oliver made a good scribe. He was used to doing detailed work. He could write for hours without tiring, yet Joseph sensed an unrest in him. At the end of a strenuous day he would leave the house and walk by himself. At these times he didn't want anyone with him. Once when Joseph and Emma were returning from a walk to the little grave, they came upon him all alone praying. They quickly left the spot before he was aware of them. Then one day a revelation was given almost in whole to Oliver, and Joseph understood, if only in part, certain things that troubled Oliver.

A great and marvelous work is about to come forth unto the children of men: behold, I am God; give heed to my word. . . . The field is white already to harvest, therefore whoso desireth to reap, let him thrust in his sickle with his might, and reap while the day lasts, that he may treasure up for his soul everlasting salvation in the kingdom of God; yea, whosoever will thrust in his sickle and reap, the same is called of God; therefore, if you will ask of me you shall receive; if you will knock it shall be opened unto you.

Now as you have asked, I say unto you, Keep my commandments, and seek to bring forth and establish the cause of Zion: seek not for riches but for wisdom; and behold the mysteries of God shall be unfolded unto you, and then shall you be made rich. Behold, he that hath eternal life is rich.

350

Verily I say unto you, Even as you desire of me, so shall it be unto you; and if you desire, you shall be the means of doing much good. . . . Say nothing but repentance unto this generation; keep my commandments, and assist to bring forth my work according to my commandments, and you shall be blessed.

Behold, thou hast a gift, and blessed art thou because of thy gift. Remember it is sacred and cometh from above. . . . If thou wilt inquire, thou shalt know mysteries which are great and marvelous; therefore, thou shalt exercise thy gift, that thou mayest find out mysteries, that thou mayest bring many to the knowledge of the truth. . . . Make not thy gift known unto any, save it be those who are of thy faith. Trifle not with sacred things. If thou wilt do good, and hold out faithful to the end, thou shalt be saved in the kingdom of God, which is the greatest of all the gifts of God; for there is no gift greater than the gift of salvation.

Blessed art thou for what thou hast done, for thou hast inquired of me, and as often as thou hast inquired, thou hast received instruction of my Spirit. If it had not been so, thou wouldst not have come to the place where thou art at this time.

Thou knowest that thou hast inquired of me, and I did enlighten thy mind; and now I tell thee these things that thou mayest know that thou hast been enlightened by the spirit of truth; yea, I tell thee, that thou mayest know that there is none else save God, that knowest thy thoughts and the intents of thy heart. I tell thee these things as a witness unto thee, that the words or the work which thou hast been writing is true.

Therefore be diligent, stand by my servant Joseph faithfully in whatever difficult circumstances he may be, for the word's sake. Admonish him in his faults and also receive

351

admonition of him. Be patient; be sober; be temperate; have patience, faith, hope, and charity.

I have spoken unto thee because of thy desires; therefore, treasure up these words in thy heart. Be faithful in keeping the commandments of God, and I will encircle thee in the arms of my love.

Behold, I am Jesus Christ the Son of God. . . . If you desire a further witness, cast your mind upon the night that you cried unto me in your heart, that you might know concerning the truth of these things. Did I not speak peace to your mind concerning the matter? What greater witness can you have than from God? Now, you have received a witness, for I have told you things which no man knoweth. . . . And I grant unto you a gift, to translate even as my servant Joseph.

Verily I say unto you that there are records which contain much of my gospel, which have been kept back because of the wickedness of the people; and now I command you that, if you . . . desire to lay up treasures for yourself in heaven, shall you assist in bringing to light, with your gift, those parts of my scriptures which have been hidden because of iniquity.

I give unto you, and also unto my servant Joseph, the keys of this gift, which shall bring to light the ministry; and in the mouths of two or three witnesses shall every word be established. . . .

Fear not to do good, my sons, for whatsoever ye sow, that shall ye also reap; therefore, if ye sow good, ye shall also reap good for your reward. . . . Go your ways and sin no more; Perform with soberness the work which I have commanded you; look unto me in every thought; doubt not; fear not. . . . Be faithful; keep my commandments, and ye shall inherit the kingdom of heaven. Amen.

The weather continued windy and wet through the first half of April. Roads were muddy, making traveling disagreeable. It was fine weather for translating, however, and Joseph and Oliver made the most of it. For Samuel, it was a disappointing time, because he had been able to bring in only a couple of young rabbits. Emma seasoned them well and cooked them as she would young chickens. To her delight the men ate them with relish.

We will be eating our chickens next, she thought, when the meal was over and she was scraping the plates. She dreaded killing the chickens. Most of them were laying, and while eggs didn't bring much on the market they did help supply necessities which they could hardly do without. It would be some time before the young chicks would be big enough to eat; then they would kill the roosters and save the hens to add to their egg supply.

One afternoon she wondered what they would have for supper. The venison, pork, and beef were gone, and their supply of corn was low. They had exchanged most of their wheat for necessities they couldn't do without. There were the vegetables she and her mother had canned, but she had traded some of these for cotton and wool, and most of their dried food had been traded for needed items too. She had three or four cups of dried beans. Her parents' well-filled larder entered her mind, but she dismissed the thought as it came. She would not embarrass Joseph by begging food from them—not yet. Beans and corn bread . . . a late supper . . . but what about tomorrow?

It had been some time since Joseph Knight had visited the Smiths. Like Father Joseph he had a great love for books and a keen awareness of growing change in the United States that was pushing the country beyond its borders to new frontiers. The Smiths were always good for lively conversations concerning developments. Father Smith might lack business sense concerning the forwarding of his own wealth, but he was well informed on the world around him. He was one of the few men with whom Joseph Knight could whet his wits and come away with an enlarged vision. Because of this he frequently drove from Colesville to Manchester to spend a few days. This he had done over the years, and the two families had become very close. He had seen Alvin buried and Hyrum and Sophronia married. Young Joseph had used his wagon to bring the records from Cumorah's hill. This had always been a source of pride to Joseph Knight, for he believed young Joseph's claims and he had fought many a battle defending him and his "gold bible." He was interested in the progress of the work, and from Father Joseph he learned that Oliver Cowdery had gone to Harmony to be young Joseph's scribe. Now, he had heard the tale of an awkward young rail-splitter named Abe Lincoln riding a flatboat from his home in Indiana down the Ohio River to New Orleans. He seemed to be creating quite a stir, and Joseph Knight wondered if Father Joseph had heard of him. He couldn't go to Manchester right now, but he did have to go to Harmony on business for the mill. He would stop off for a visit with young Joseph and Emma. Young Joseph was pretty well informed; maybe they might be able to trade some news.

Emma looked over her beans, threw out the bad ones, and washed the good ones. The water in the cooking pot that hung on a rod over the fireplace was boiling, and as she put the beans in a knock came on the door.

She could hardly believe her eyes when she saw Joseph Knight standing there. She greeted him warmly, gave him a chair by the fire, and called the men out of the bedroom. Young Joseph's welcome was cordial the way a son might greet a father, then Oliver gave his hand in friendship. He had met Mr. Knight at the Smiths.

After an exchange of pleasantries Joseph Knight said, "Get busy, young men, and unload my wagon. There is half a beef out there, and a lot of provisions we had no use for. We're overstocked, so if you don't mind helping us eat the surplus I'll bring you some more from time to time."

Emma's eyes filled gratefully. Young Joseph reached for his old friend's hand and a husky, "Thank you," came through his lips. That night Mr. Knight slept on Alvin's feather bed, in front of the fire for he too refused to take Emma's bed. Oliver and Samuel slept on pallets not far from where the fire made shadow pictures on the wall. Next morning after a hearty breakfast Mr. Knight went home, leaving four thankful young people to watch until he was out of sight.

"God sent him," Emma said, and the men agreed it must be so. Joseph Knight's generosity lifted their spirits like rain after a drought, and work on the plates was resumed at an increased tempo.

It was Oliver's habit to pen a letter each evening after the supper dishes were done and the tallow candle had been placed on the table. This he did, even though it might be a week before a carrier would be available in Harmony to take the mail. At first they thought he was writing to his family, but the tender or gay expressions they read on his face as he wrote made them realize these letters were to a young lady. After friendly teasing from Joseph, Oliver admitted that her name was Elizabeth Ann Whitmer, and that she had bewitched him entirely.

"I've heard of the Whitmers," Emma told him. "A fine

family from Fayette, New York . . . large farm . . . several grown children."

"I've met David Whitmer." Joseph's arm went around Emma. "It's a wise man who picks a wife from good stock." He kissed Emma's ear ever so lightly.

Emma dimpled prettily and tossed her head a little. "I thought the Whitmer girls were too young to be interested in men."

Oliver grinned. "One is married. Elizabeth Ann is in her middle teens, but in many ways she seems as wise as you, Emma. In my eyes she is the loveliest and the finest of women. I'll count myself fortunate if I can win her. She is one of the few persons I can tell my innermost thoughts to." He picked up the letter he had been writing and handed it to Joseph. "Read this portion and you'll see what I mean."

Joseph read aloud: "These are never to be forgotten days—to sit under the sound of a voice dictated by the inspiration of heaven awakens the utmost gratitude in me. Day after day I continue to write uninterrupted as Joseph translates with the Urim and Thummim, or as the Nephites would have said, the Interpreters—the history or record called the Book of Mormon."

Joseph handed the letter back to Oliver, saying approvingly, "That is stated well enough for the world to read and believe. Someday, when we have established the church, you must write it again."

By mid-April the rains ceased, the weather cleared, and the air became balmy and warm. The muddy ruts in the road leading to town dried up, traffic smoothed them, and travel became pleasant.

Joseph and Oliver continued to translate hour after hour but they worked daytimes, leaving evenings free. Or if they took an afternoon off now and then, they would work at night by candlelight. When it was necessary to ride into town

Emma went with them. She liked looking at everything the stores had to offer—farm implements, wagons, buggies, household furnishings, hats bedecked with feathers, and imported yard goods. From these she turned away with a sigh, for Joseph must not see wishing eyes that would cause him to spend money they couldn't afford. There were spices of all kinds, perfumes, china, silver, crystal, almost anything one had money to pay for—but best of all were the shoppers. She noticed the ladies particularly—some as elegantly gowned as her sister Bea, but seldom as pretty. It seemed a long time ago that Emma had worn such clothes, walking with a proud tilt to her chin, carefully swinging full skirts properly fashioned, and showing just enough of a shiny buttoned shoe to draw masculine attention.

Almost everyone knew who Joseph Smith was, or had at least heard of him. Many looked upon him as an oddity because of what they had heard about his "gold bible."

Until lately the clergy had more or less let him alone out of respect for the Hales, but when Emma's people began complaining about him the ministers were quick to denounce him from their pulpits. Oliver was another reason for their displeasure. Martin Harris had been a quiet man, careful not to draw fire that could stop the work as it had been stopped in Manchester. Not so with Oliver, who was on fire with what he had come to see as divine truths. He clashed with the clergy as Joseph had done in Manchester before learning the wisdom of remaining silent. A lesser scholar might have been ignored or brushed aside, but Oliver was an apt student who sometimes left the wise floundering. Joseph aligned himself with Oliver. The result was like setting fire to dry brush. Within weeks stories of Joseph's angel visits, visions, and revelations became major topics of discussion everywhere in Harmony. There were those who believed and defended Joseph, but there were more who did not. Emma's marriage

357

and prestige no longer held rumor down. What had been suppressed suddenly burst forth, and those who believed in Joseph found themselves ever on the defensive. Joseph, more than anyone, was aware that persecutions were soon to come. The plates were in his charge, and it was up to him to guard them. Now that there was real danger, what surprised him most was the Hale men. Alarmed by what they knew might take place they went about grim faced, letting it be known that any harm to Emma would be met with bullets. Joseph and Emma were grateful for this unsought help. It was good to know that her people would fight to protect her.

Trips into town were held to a minimum, and Samuel bought himself a gun. One particularly dark night when there was no moon or stars Joseph was on his way back to the house after milking the cow. The air was unusually still. He heard no sound at all, but suddenly he was jumped from behind by several men who knocked him to the ground. He remembered spilling the milk, and being held prostrate by several pairs of hands, while he struggled and fought to get up. He tried to make out features in the blackness but could see nothing. He got the impression that his attackers were wearing dark hoods that covered their faces and dark clothes. He heard no voices, only whispers, and these he couldn't recognize. A strong hand was clamped over his mouth and nose.

"If you cry out we'll kill you." This whisper came low and determined.

They began dragging him over rough ground while he struggled and fought. They pushed him against a tree and he felt the roughness of a coil of rope. Were they going to hang him? He fought while they tied him. All this was done in complete silence while they held him with strong arms. Someone's hand was clasped over his mouth and nose, making it almost impossible to breathe. Then he was gagged

358

and bound with rope around hands and feet. What were they up to? Were they after the records? And Emma—would they harm her? He moved his face up and down against the tree trunk in an effort to work the gag loose. And then he felt the sting of the lash on his back. The bullwhip was held in the hand of some powerful man who knew how to wield it. Joseph's face was bleeding now in his effort to dislodge the gag. The sting of the whip came again and again, and he knew his back was bleeding. The lashes struck with constant rhythm as if they were trained for darkness, and there was no other sound. Joseph's face continued to work against the tree trunk. The gag had been put on in the dark; perhaps that was the only reason he was able to loosen it. When he was free he cried out with all his strength, "Samuel—Oliver—help me! Help me!" There was the sound of feet running away and feet running toward him. The ones racing toward him were those of Samuel, Oliver, and Emma. His captors were gone—lost in darkness.

Oliver and Samuel got him free of the rope and half carried him into the house. He was a sight to look at with his face scratched and bleeding and his back oozing blood. Emma heated water and washed and dressed his wounds. Oliver was stunned that such a thing could happen among civilized men. He had heard about the persecutions without comprehending; now he blamed himself for talking too much and creating agitation.

"Don't blame yourself," Joseph told him through swollen lips. "I have been expecting this for a long time. Sooner or later it was bound to come. My regret is we didn't get all the plates translated before trouble began. We must work at top speed now to finish them."

"I'm for finding the men who did it and putting the law on them," Oliver said bluntly.

"It would be useless to fight them." Joseph's voice had

359

an edge. "These are not town ruffians. The hand clamped over my mouth and nose was soft and smooth. These are stalwarts of the church out to destroy me."

"You are not going to let them get away with it?" Oliver's eyes were like two sparks.

"It's the best way," Samuel said. "In Manchester we learned we couldn't fight a whole town." A hint of humor flashed in his eyes and was gone. "They think they're doing Joseph a favor flogging the devil out of him." Then his voice became grim. "Tonight we weren't expecting them. Another time we will be. If they come they'll be trespassing, and we'll deal with them."

"Our job is to translate the plates," Joseph said, "and this we will do in spite of them."

Joseph had never found sleeping so difficult. He couldn't lie on his stomach because it hurt his sore face. By lying on one side or the other with the pillow just so, he managed to get through a restless night. Emma too slept under a strain, fearful that she might rub against him and start his back bleeding again or hurt him in some way.

The next morning Joseph was really feeling the effects of his flogging. His face was sore only to the touch; the scratches weren't deep and wouldn't scar, but his back pained him. In fact, he hurt all over.

Emma redressed his wounds. She made a cool lanoline poultice to cover his back, one that would keep his clothes from sticking to his cuts. She had just finished and he was putting on his clothes when they heard Samuel and Oliver getting up. Presently they were all together in the little kitchen.

"How do you feel, Joseph?" Oliver wanted to know.

Joseph's eyes were roguish. "Like the devil. They say I'm possessed, and I believe them this morning."

"We'll do the chores," Samuel said. "You should go back to bed."

"I may have to. My head aches and I'm dizzy, but it hurts more to lie down than it does to sit."

"We'll see after breakfast," Emma said. "He says he's going to translate then—but he isn't, not today."

"Of course I am," Joseph contradicted her gently. "Last night was only a sample of what we can expect. Every minute counts now."

Breakfast was over, the chores were done, and Samuel had taken the hoe to the garden. In spite of protests from Oliver and Emma the quilt was in place and everything in readiness to commence translating—everything except Joseph. He sat in his usual place by the table with the records in front of him, looking through the Urim and Thummim, but his head was aching so that he could hardly think. He knew Oliver was on the other side of the quilt waiting, paper on the stand in front of him, the quill pen in his hand. Joseph pressed his hands to his throbbing temples. If only the dizziness would leave him!

Oliver asked, "Are you all right, Joseph?"

"No, but I will be in a little while."

"Cover the records, Joseph. I want to talk to you where I can look at you."

Joseph never put the records away without wrapping them, so the cloth was there beside him, and he covered them.

Oliver pulled up a chair and sat down beside Joseph. "Please let me try translating. Remember the revelation that came in February. . . . The promise was that someday I could try."

"I . . . don't know . . . Oliver. I was told not to show the records. I have to follow instructions."

"But you wouldn't have to show any more than one

engraved sheet—the one you are working on. You could let me have that one and put the rest away."

"I couldn't, not without knowing it was all right to do so."

"Then ask. I'll see if Emma will write for me."

"All right," Joseph said. "We'll go in the bedroom and ask. If we get an answer we'll abide by it. If we don't, I'll make myself translate."

Emma saw them go into the bedroom and close the door. Previously she had gone to the cold house for some cream that was ready to churn and had not heard their conversation. Now she scalded the wooden churn and poured in the cream. The churn had a paddle that turned with a crank, and these too were made of wood. Soon there would be fresh buttermilk, a special treat for the men.

It was very quiet in the cabin. The only sounds were Major Mack's clock and the swish of the churn. Minutes passed, and flecks of butter stuck together until there was a bright ball coagulated around the paddle. As she was pouring buttermilk into a pewter pitcher, Oliver walked in and said, with a kind of awe in his voice, "I'm going to translate . . . that is, if you will write for me."

"Hand me two mugs," she said, "one for you and one for Joseph." She filled the mugs, and he began drinking. "If you'll carry Samuel a small pailful I'll be ready to write when you get back. Give me Joseph's drink. I'll take it to him. I have something to tell him."

True to his promise not to show anyone the records, Joseph had removed one gold sheet for Oliver. The rest he had hidden away in a safe place. The intricate engravings on that one sheet, when interpreted, would cover several pages of foolscap.

Emma sat on her side of the quilt with paper and pen waiting.

362

Oliver and Joseph were on the other side. There was an excitement in Oliver's eyes as he took the sheet into his hands, examining the delicate engravings. He knew a little about ancient records. These Joseph had were only a small portion of the numbers of records that had been written on plates of brass, silver, copper, mixed ores, and gold as well as papyrus and parchments made of reeds and skins. This one was gold, he was sure of it, and the engravings might have been done yesterday instead of many years ago, the metal looked so bright and new.

Joseph handed him the Urim and Thummim, and again he felt the tingle of excitement. Had these once been held in the hands of Enoch or Aaron, the brother of Moses? Had Samuel of the Old Testament touched them? Had they been in possession of the Israelites during the Exodus as part of their sacred vestments? He put them on, adjusting them carefully, and felt a burning in his bosom.

"Now begin," Joseph directed. "Put your full attention upon each character. Think, and the burning in your bosom will tell you when your interpretation is right."

Out of the quiet in the room came the sound of Oliver's voice. Emma picked up her pen and began to write. Joseph stood for a moment, nodded in satisfaction, pressed Oliver's shoulder in appreciation, and went back to bed.

Emma, writing as Oliver dictated, was commencing her third page of foolscap when Oliver's voice faltered. She waited. The Major Mack clock became too loud in the room. Still she waited. Presently she heard a muffled sob, then his anguished voice: "I have lost my gift. I had it, and now it is gone. Tell Joseph the plate is out of sight under your tablecloth."

He moved past her, out the front door, then he was lost among the trees in the woods.

Joseph slept and Emma went about her work with a

heavy heart. Oliver had been doing so well. What could have happened? Where would he go? Should she awaken Joseph? No, better let him sleep; his night had been a difficult one. But he didn't sleep long. He came to her and she told him all she knew. "What will he do, Joseph?"

"He'll be all right. If you'll write for me, we'll go on with the translating. I feel much better now."

Minutes passed into an hour, then two; the translating continued, but there was no sight of Oliver.

"Should you try to find him, Joseph?"

"No. There are times when one needs to be alone."

Another hour went by and then they saw him. He was walking along the road leading to the cabin, head down, shoulders drooping.

Emma said, "Let's go to meet him."

"No, he'll come to us if he feels he needs us."

He came inside the door, closed it, and stood against it. Joseph came from his side of the quilt, his eyes touching Oliver's with warm friendliness.

"I had the gift of translating," Oliver said. "I was exulting in it. At first I used all my mind to concentrate on each engraving. Then I began to think that translating was a gift from God, and all I needed to do was ask, and he would give me the interpretation. Those were my last thoughts. After that, I lost the gift." He paused, waiting for Joseph to say something, but Joseph remained silent.

"It wasn't my intention to take lightly things that are sacred. I've walked; I've thought; I've prayed; and I've asked forgiveness . . . still I feel rejected."

Emma said, "Come sit at the table. I'll fix something for you to eat."

"I'm not hungry." His eyes were on Joseph. "If you feel up to it, I'll write for you."

Joseph's voice was gentle. "Why don't you try translat-

364

ing once more? I lost the gift once, and it was restored to me."

Oliver hesitated, thought about it longingly, and then shook his head. "I'll write for you," he said.

They worked. After a time Oliver ate; then they worked some more. It was nearing supper when Oliver's voice came across the quilt to Joseph, stopping the translating. "Help me, Joseph. I sit here writing and thinking of the gift I lost. I know it is my fault that you have been working steadily all day, first with Emma and then with me . . . work that I should have been doing for you. Do you think the gift of translating will ever be mine again?"

"We could ask," Joseph said.

"You mean now?"

"If you want to." Joseph was covering the records.

"Where shall we go for privacy?"

"The bedroom. No one will disturb us there if the door is closed."

They sat down on the bed together and Joseph said, "Don't be hard on yourself because of me. I'm feeling better than I ever thought I could in one day. Keeping my mind off myself has been good for me."

"I'm glad if you're better. But I really must resolve this inner conflict."

"We will pray, but the answer may not come through revelation. It may come in some other way, or you may not think you have received an answer at all."

"I understand."

"We must believe that we are entirely covered by the Spirit of God, that he is within us and around us, and that his enlightening Spirit will give us an answer as he wills it. We must pray that if God answers by giving us a revelation it will come to both of us, so that you will know it is of God and not of me. If we get an answer with the Urim and Thummim

365

you must write it as I speak it, for unless we write it, by tomorrow it may be gone from our minds."

"I have what I need to write it."

They prayed silently and expectantly then, without fear.

Time passed and Oliver's eyes became bright with awareness. Joseph began speaking, and Oliver recorded his words. The things he wrote came from two sources, his own mind, and Joseph's lips.

Behold, I say unto you, my son, that because you did not translate according to that which you desire of me, and did commence again to write for my servant Joseph Smith, Jr., even so I would that you should continue until you have finished this record. . . . Be patient, my son, for it is wisdom in me, and it is not expedient that you should translate at this present time. The work which you are called to do is to write for my servant Joseph; and it is because you did not continue as you commenced, when you began to translate, that I have taken away this privilege from you. Do not murmur, my son, for it is wisdom in me that I have dealt with you after this manner.

Behold, you have not understood; you have supposed that I would give it unto you, when you took no thought save it was to ask me; but I say unto you that you must study it out in your mind; then you must ask me if it be right, and if it is right, I will cause that your bosom shall burn within you . . . but if it be not right, you shall have no such feelings; you shall have a stupor of thought that shall cause you to forget the thing which is wrong; therefore you cannot write that which is sacred, save it be given you from me.

Now if you had known this, you could have translated; nevertheless, it is not expedient that you should translate now. . . . I have given unto my servant Joseph sufficient strength. . . .

366

Do this thing which I have commanded you, and you shall prosper. Be faithful and yield to no temptation. Stand fast in the work wherewith I have called you . . . and you shall be lifted up in the last day. Amen.

May 15 started like any other day. Joseph, Emma, Oliver, and Samuel awakened at daybreak, finished the usual chores, and ate a quick breakfast of corn cakes and sorghum. Samuel took the hoe and went to the garden to plant beans and peas and to thin tender shoots of radishes, lettuce, carrots, and onions that had come up from the April planting. Emma began putting the little house in order, and Joseph and Oliver were busy in the bedroom translating.

The sun was warm—a welcome change from the crisp days of April. Emma opened the front door to let the sunshine in, and the cabin was soon filled with the fragrance of pine. It was a good day, and she began singing a favorite hymn, her clear voice blending with the song of a lark close by.

Then something happened in the bedroom. The translating ceased and a discussion began. Emma stopped singing to listen. Joseph and Oliver were disagreeing over baptism for the remission of sins. They were not quarreling, but they seemed to be concerned. In a few minutes they came out of the bedroom, hurrying past her on the way to the front door.

She looked up inquiringly and Joseph said, "We've come upon something in the records that seems of great importance to us. We need additional understanding, and we're going into the woods to pray about it."

She watched them go, and began singing again with a light heart. Half an hour went by and she began looking for their return. An hour passed. The breakfast dishes were washed now and the cabin was thoroughly clean, with scrubbed floors and dusted furnishings. A pucker of worry formed on her brow. Were the men all right? Two hours passed. Would they pray so long? Had they walked far? What part of the woods were they in? She went to the garden where Samuel said he would be working. The hoe was lying on the ground, but Samuel was nowhere in sight. Emma was alarmed now. Had Joseph's enemies returned and hurt them? Had Samuel heard their cries and rushed to aid them? Had harm come to all of them? Emma ran in one direction for a while, then she turned and ran in another, and another. She called their names, her ears straining for an answer. She halloed, but all she heard was the echo of her words and familiar sounds of the woods. She prayed for their safety, scrambling up one knoll and then another. At last, exhausted and out of breath, she started back to the cabin, telling herself that if they had not returned she would go to her father's house for help.

Arriving home, Emma found the house empty. She was about to go to the big house for help when footsteps sounded on the gravel road outside, then Joseph cleared his throat. It was a habit of Joseph's to clear his throat in just that way, and she recognized the sound. Hurrying to the door, she flung it open in sheer relief, then she stopped. All three men had been in the water with their clothes on, which in itself was strange, but it was what she saw written in their faces that led her to know this was no ordinary homecoming. Each man wore the same expression, an excited glow. Their eyes were alive, lighted by some strange and unusual experience. They had encountered no enemy; rather it was as if they had glimpsed a portion of heaven itself.

As they filed past her into the house Joseph said: "As soon as we have put on dry clothes we have something wonderful to tell you."

"Something that will amaze you," Oliver added.

And Samuel said, "I hope you will believe what they tell you, Emma. I believe, yet I have only their word that this strange experience took place."

The men went into the bedroom and closed the door. Emma listened, hoping they would say something to give her a clue, but the room was quiet.

Presently they came out in dry clothes. Joseph pulled up a chair for Emma and they all sat around the table. The room became so still that a squirrel's patter on the roof could be distinctly heard.

"We went into the woods to inquire of God respecting baptism for the remission of sins," Joseph began.

"I already know that," Emma said.

Joseph's voice became deep-toned and earnest. "We walked to a place near the Susquehanna River on your father's property, because the trees are dense enough there to completely hide us from view. We wanted to feel shut off from the world and completely alone. You know how quiet and still the woods can be in that particular place."

"Yes," Emma said.

"Now this is what you will find hard to believe." Joseph's eyes grew intense and Oliver leaned toward her, his face alert and alive, as if he could force her to believe what Joseph was about to say.

Joseph said, "While we were praying, seeking for guidance and understanding—we both saw at the same time a cloud of light descending toward us from the heavens. It was a bright light, yet it did not burn our eyes. In the midst of this light as it came toward us we saw a personage. He came to us and laid his hands first upon me and then upon Oliver saying, 'Upon you my fellow servants, in the name of the Messiah, I confer the priesthood of Aaron which holds the keys of the ministering of angels, and the gospel of repentance, and of baptism by immersion for the remission of sins; and this priesthood shall never be taken from the earth until the sons of Levi do offer again an offering unto the Lord in righteousness.' He said this priesthood of Aaron didn't have the power of laying on of hands for the gift of the Holy Ghost, but that this should be conferred on us at a later time, and he commanded us to go and be baptized, and gave us direction that I should baptize Oliver, and afterward that he should baptize me."

Joseph paused in his narrative, and the room became silent again. Oliver opened his mouth, intending to say something, then he closed it without speaking, his face alive, confirming all that Joseph had said, and Joseph continued: "And so we went and were baptized. I baptized Oliver, and he baptized me. Then I laid my hands upon Oliver's head and ordained him to the Aaronic priesthood, after which he laid his hands on me, and ordained me to the same priesthood as we had been commanded."

"There is more," Oliver said.

"Emma, the messenger said that his name was John, the same that is called John the Baptist in the New Testament, and that he acted under the direction of Peter, James, and John who held the keys to the priesthood of Melchisedec, which he said in due time would be conferred upon us. He said I should be called the first elder and Oliver the second."

The story was very strange, yet not more so than other experiences Joseph had had. He had never lied to her, and the truth of what he was saying was written upon his face.

"Immediately upon coming up out of the water after we had been baptized we experienced great and unusual blessings. As soon as I had baptized Oliver he prophesied many things that would shortly come to pass, and as soon as he baptized me I too had the spirit of prophecy concerning the rise of the church and many things connected with this generation."

"I can tell you this much, Emma, knowledge will sweep the earth like a flood. Men's minds will be awakened to mysteries the like of which the world, as we know it, has never dreamed of. There will be amazing inventions to ease men's burdens . . . new ways of travel. New light in every field of endeavor will make the minds of men seem tall like mountaintops. America will push her borders from sea to sea and above and beyond the seas until there will seem no end to her glorious works. All this should bring about a paradise, but it will not, for in that day many will set their hearts on riches rather than on God. They will say, 'See the mighty works of men. . . . We have no need of God, if there is a God, and who knows if there is one, for we have not seen him, but we have seen our works, and we know that they are good.'

"Then the eyes of the greedy shall be upon one another and sin will abound. Because of this there will be wars and bloodshed, famine, earthquakes and fear until it would seem that the earth would come to a terrible end. But this is not all, for God has a plan to gather the righteous. In that day there will be many who remember him, trust in him, and keep his commandments, and it will be the work of the church to gather the righteous into a place called Zion, a new Jerusalem—a place prepared where Christ can come to reign a thousand years. Zion is not a new thought. It is mentioned in the Bible and in the records. It is not for any one race or church or creed. It is for all the pure in heart."

Joseph stopped speaking and Oliver said earnestly, "Emma, we can't even attempt to paint for you the majestic beauty and glory of our experience. Believe us when we say men cannot begin to clothe language in as eloquent or sublime a manner as words spoken by that holy personage, nor have they the power to give the joy, bestow the peace, or

371

comprehend the wisdom which was contained in each sentence as his words were delivered by the Holy Spirit. I shall always remember how his voice, though mild, pierced to my very center, and the way he ascended as he came, enveloped in that cloud of light."

A warm breeze touched Emma's curtains, and a hint of a smile brushed Samuel's lips. "I knew they had gone off by themselves to ask for help, for they stopped by where I was working and told me so. When they didn't come back—with the threat of mobs—I got worried and went to find them."

Emma understood all too well what he meant.

"They were about ready to come home when I found them, and after I had heard of their strange experience they said I too should be baptized. I have always believed in the divinity of the plates and Joseph's other visions, but what they were telling me now concerned the gospel of Jesus Christ, which they said was about to be revealed in all its fullness. This was a new thought to me, and I went into another part of the woods hoping to obtain wisdom to enable me to judge for myself whether I should be baptized or not. I didn't see an angel or hear a voice, but I received sufficient evidence to convince me that everything Joseph and Oliver had said was true. Oliver baptized me."

"It is all so strange," Emma said, "so very, very strange."

Shortly after the baptisms Samuel went home to carry the unusual story to his family and to make it possible for William to visit Joseph. But he went reluctantly, for Joseph and Oliver were in grave danger from mobs, and this would heighten if word of their baptisms became broadcast. As he bid them farewell he warned them to keep secret the circumstances connected with their baptisms and their ordinations to the priesthood. "You must put a seal upon your lips, until the plates are translated and in the hands of the printers."

Samuel was right of course. Joseph and Oliver both knew it, but when they began translating, after their experience in the woods, they saw new meaning in many passages of scripture. It was as if they were penetrating a different level of understanding, and this made it difficult for them to remain silent. Without meaning to let it happen they began discussing the scriptures with close acquaintances. Then with a few they shared the experience of their ordinations, and the news spread.

Joseph had friends—those who believed in his work and were waiting for the book. There were others who had no time for his religion, but who liked him and stood by him. From time to time these brought him warnings of impending trouble. His enemies warned him in various ways too. He read trouble in their grim faces and heard it in their insulting remarks. Now and then, along with mail from Seneca, Manchester, or Colesville would come a threatening unsigned letter. Once there was a drawing of skull and crossbones and another time a picture of a man being shot through the heart. These were unnerving because the senders were anonymous.

Some of Oliver's fears were reflected in his letters to the Whitmers. One day a letter came from Peter Whitmer urging Oliver to bring Joseph and Emma to Seneca. They would be welcomed at the Whitmers rent free, Peter said. The whole Whitmer family was anxious to learn more of Joseph's strange work. The neighbors too were curious and wanted to hear about it.

They began to make plans for the move. Joseph's brother William would attend to the crops during their absence. Oliver, of course, was jubilant over the move for it would mean being with Elizabeth Ann, but Joseph and Emma were sad. Perhaps the day would come when those who dared to differ from established thinking would cease to cause hatred and violence. Maybe in another generation strange claims would cause no stir, but why expect the people in Fayette to be more liberal than those in Manchester and Harmony? Human nature being what it was, wouldn't the persecutions begin there the same as here? But if peaceful existence meant giving up, conforming, they wanted no part of it. They were not cowards, and their course was set. This was God's work. They would accomplish it or die trying. If mobs formed there they would move and move until the work was done. But why should life be this way when all they wanted was the serenity of a home, the satisfaction of work well done, and the respect of people around them?

"William was wishing for someone to stay here with him after we go," Joseph said to Emma a day or two after Hyrum left for Manchester. "I keep thinking of the Knights. Maybe one of them would come. To find out would mean a trip to Colesville."

"Why don't you go and see, Joseph? It would get you away from here. I worry about you with mobs plotting to hurt you and ugly things happening. I can stay at the big house while you're away. You'd better take Oliver with you; then you'll both be out of danger for a little while."

He didn't contradict her or remind her that with mobs forming danger could be anywhere. "We'll start in the morning before daylight," he said.

Joseph and Oliver had been riding since dawn, and now the sun was well up in the sky. They rode along the Susquehanna River, following the wooded road. It was a morning to lift the spirits. White clouds drifting in the sky wore the color of the sea on a clear day. A quietness pervaded the woods, and the air warmed them without being hot. They had conversed on many subjects, and now were discussing new truths they had discovered in the records.

The woods became more dense, and they found themselves awed by the beauty of their surroundings. The air here was as fragrant as earth after rain. The river widened, and in the water were reflections of birch and pine and hemlock. A soft breeze touched their faces and moved through the trees with gentle motion. Almost as if their minds worked as one, Joseph and Oliver reined in their horses. For a time neither spoke. They seemed set apart from all the earth, for no other human traveler was in sight.

Oliver spoke first. "Let's find a place by the river where we can eat the lunch Emma has packed for us. She is very generous—your Emma."

They dismounted, watered the horses, and fed them, then went in search of a place where they could eat. They found a spot so quiet and lovely that they talked almost in whispers. They tied the horses where they could nibble on grass near the riverbank, then they sank to the ground. The water of the river was like a melody, and wind moving through trees relaxed them.

Emma had packed their food in an empty lard bucket. There were hard-boiled eggs, homemade bread, and four juicy apples. She had sent cheese and a canvas of cool water from the well. They divided the food, holding back half for their evening meal.

Joseph's eyes were on the slowly moving river, whose placid waters gave hardly a hint of the swift current beneath its surface. "Oliver, no matter what it costs us the record must be finished and sent to the printers."

Oliver nodded, adding, "I know it is the sealed book

spoken of in the twenty-ninth chapter of Isaiah and other Bible texts. I'll fight to the death for our work, if the need arises."

They became wrapped in thought. Joseph prayed silently for the protection of the plates and the safety of Emma and William, only to learn that Oliver had been making the same prayer. So in tune were they that their thoughts seemed to intermingle. Without a word being spoken, both men were remembering the promise that someday the Melchisedec priesthood would be given to them, and both were wondering when this event would take place. They knew only in part what the promise would mean to them, yet each felt he was ready to assume the responsibilities for a higher calling. Their prayers ascended simultaneously. Each asked for wisdom and understanding, and each promised to give a life of love and loyalty in order to fulfill the sacred trust. Suddenly the air about them became charged, and they were surrounded by a power that seemed to hum. The trees and the river stood out like bright engravings, and beyond them—where earth and sky came together—was a ball of light. It appeared white, yet from it poured all the colors they had ever seen, and it was moving, traveling toward them at incredible speed. Although it seemed impossible that something with such speed and energy could appear to stand still, this did, and as it came near them it spread to cover them like a thousand sunbeams. Even as Moses saw a burning bush and Paul a blinding light, these two were enveloped in this heavenly brightness, and standing in the midst of it they saw three personages.

Oliver and Joseph knelt in the light, humbly confessing their sins. As they did so the voice of the Lord spoke in their hearts:

This is Peter, James, and John whom I have sent unto

you, bearing the keys of the Melchisedec priesthood. The time will come speedily when you, Joseph, will ordain Oliver to the office of elder in the Church of Jesus Christ, after which he will ordain you to the same office. Then from time to time I shall make known unto you others who shall be ordained. The time of your ordinations will be when it shall be practicable to have those who have been, and who should be, baptized assembled together, that they may decide by vote whether they are willing to accept you as spiritual teachers.

There are in my church two priesthoods, namely the Melchisedec and the Aaronic including the Levitical priesthood. The first is called Melchisedec because Melchisedec was such a great high priest. Before his day it was called the Holy Priesthood, after the order of the Son of God. The power and authority of the Melchisedec priesthood is to hold the keys of all spiritual blessings of the church; to have the privilege of receiving the mysteries of the kingdom of heaven; to have the heavens opened, to commune with the general assembly of the church of the Firstborn, and to enjoy the communion and presence of God the Father and Jesus the Mediator of the new covenant.

The light remained, and a part of the fourteenth chapter of Genesis was brought to their remembrance:

Now Melchisedec was a man of faith, who wrought righteousness; and when a child he feared God, and stopped the mouths of lions, and quenched the violence of fire.

And thus, having been approved of God, he was ordained as a high priest after the order of the covenant which God made with Enoch.

It being after the order of the Son of God, which order came, not by man, nor the will of man, neither by father nor

377

mother; neither by beginning of days nor end of years; but of God.

And it was delivered unto men by the calling of his own voice, according to his own will, unto as many as believed on his name.

For God having sworn unto Enoch and unto his seed with an oath by himself; that every one being ordained after this power and calling should have power by faith, to break mountains, to divide the seas, to dry up waters, to turn them out of their course; to put to defiance the armies of nations, to divide the earth, to break every band, to stand in the presence of God, to do all things according to his command, subdue principalities and powers; and this by the will of the Son of God which was from before the foundation of the world.

And men having this faith, coming up unto this order of God, were translated and taken up into heaven.

The vision faded. The light that had been bright around them became the natural light of day, but Joseph and Oliver still knelt, shaken and humbled by the experience. Together they had seen and shared a supernatural happening. Together they would be called upon to establish the Church of Jesus Christ. They had known that once the translating was finished this would be a part of their work. Soon they would be ready.

Joseph and Oliver spent one night with the Knights. Father Knight said he could spare all of his sons if they were needed, and he would go too if that would help. Joseph told him that one son would be sufficient.

378

In the morning Father Knight insisted upon loading the three horses with supplies from his larder. "If there is more than you can use for your trip to Fayette, trade it for merchandise, or for whatever you'll need."

Joseph tried to pay him, but he shrugged away the offer. "It's from our surplus," he said. "And remember, there is plenty more where this came from. What we're waiting for is a copy of that book."

When Joseph returned from Colesville he suggested that they begin planning what they would take with them to Fayette, and what they would leave behind, in case they decided not to return to Harmony. It was the first time Emma had actually faced the possibility that they might never return, and the little house and the grounds surrounding it suddenly became the dearest place on earth to her. She packed with a heavy heart. There were times when her eyes were so blinded with tears that she could scarcely see what went into the barrels. Joseph tried by his gentle helpfulness to make her understand his concern for her, but in spite of all his tenderness the hurt remained.

Emma was careful to keep only what personally belonged to her and Joseph. She would give back all the lovely things her mother had donated from the big house. If they didn't come back she would not have it said that she and Joseph had taken advantage of Hale generosity.

She packed the dresses that had been donated to her by Bea, for without these she would have few clothes to wear, and she was as certain of Bea's love and loyalty as she was of Joseph's. Emma knew she could count on her anytime.

By the end of May everything was ready for the move to the Whitmers, and one bright morning in early June an almost new wagon drawn by two high-stepping black horses was seen coming down the road that led to the cabin. Oliver knew those horses. It was the Whitmer team and wagon.

379

Watching it, the young people had mixed feelings. Oliver was jubilant. Joseph and Emma were misty-eyed. How did one say good-bye to hallowed ground, to memories, and to living that had been deep and meaningful?

Emma turned from the window without a word and walked out of the cabin. Later she would greet their benefactor, but for now she would let the menfolk welcome him. She must take this little time to be alone with herself and her thoughts, for in her heart's innermost secret place she was certain this move would be a final one. Oh, there would be this year's crops, and William would keep things going, but Joseph's work was not cut out for Harmony. Where it would take him when they left Fayette, she had no idea, but it would not be here with a whole town against him.

She walked, holding her skirts high enough to make her stride free and easy. After a time she stood beside the little mound of earth where her son lay. The roses and lilies around the grave were blooming, and their sweet fragrance filled the air. She bent and picked a rosebud. Roses were not commonplace; they were miracles. And babies were even greater miracles. She pressed the rosebud to her cheek. It was soft to the touch and delicately scented. She was aware of it, even as she thought of Alva. A bee lifted itself from a full-blown rose and flew away. Emma, watching, drank deeply of the quietness of her surroundings. Bending, she took a handful of sod, warmed by the sun, and let it flow through her fingers. How did one say good-bye to surroundings that had been a part of her since birth? Suppose someday she should forget the sounds and the smell of these woods, the scolding of the squirrels, the cry of the owl, the whirr of birds' wings, the motion of trees in the breeze, and the pulsing throb of life that made this land dear to her?

She touched the little mound of earth tenderly. The Hales would tend the small grave carefully, along with the

380

others, and for this she was grateful. Holding the rosebud carefully, she walked to higher ground where she could see the big house. The pride of the Hales was in the gleaming paint that glistened in the sun from every building. There was no bitterness or envy in Emma as she gazed upon her father's possessions. She had been reared with love in a family that had brought her up well, and she felt only gratitude for such shelter and tender care. She had been wrong to expect them to understand Joseph's heavenly calling when she understood it only in part herself. Joseph was very unlike the Hales. They worked hard for a high place among their fellows; Joseph worked to fulfill the will of God. And he too had definite ideas of how life should be lived. He believed all things belonged to God, and that men were only stewards over earthly possessions. Her people looked upon wealth as a mark of distinction and a way to judge a man's worth. Joseph believed riches should be shared with those who were less fortunate. He was not lazy or shiftless. On the contrary he was ambitious, with a yearning not only to lift himself up to a higher level of living but to draw other men upward with him. His idea was that wealth was not in earthly riches so much as it was in educating the mind. It was asking too much for her husband and her people to understand one another while each retained definite points of view.

Footsteps sounded behind her. She turned to find Joseph looking at her with tender concern. For a moment the two of them stood without speaking, their eyes upon the abundant wealth of the Hales; then Emma put her hand in Joseph's.

His eyes dropped to the flower she was holding. "I stopped at the little grave too," he said. They turned then and began walking back to the cabin. For a while they walked without talking, each lost in thought. It was Joseph who broke the silence. "David Whitmer has a strange story to tell. Perhaps when you hear it your leaving will be easier."

At the cabin Joseph had supplied buttermilk and apple strudel which the young men had enjoyed. They were still sitting at the table when Emma and Joseph came in. Almost as one, each young man arose and offered Emma his chair.

She laughed. "Sit down, all of you."

Joseph introduced her to David Whitmer. He was very like the other young men in the room, with an open countenance that made her trust him at once. He was not unusually tall, but he was well built, bronzed and muscular. She liked his eyes—the direct way he had of looking squarely at her. He seemed a man of quality. Emma's smile was warm as she said, "Joseph tells me you have a story that he would like for me to hear. I hope you won't mind telling it again."

"Of course I'll tell it." There was an earnestness in his voice that she liked.

Joseph sat down on one of the packed boxes with a nailed-down lid, and she sat beside him. The room became suddenly still, evidence that all the young men wanted to hear the story again.

David's eyes touched Emma's, and truth was in them. "When I read of the dangers you face here I wanted to come to you in all haste, but I was responsible for a field of wheat that would take two days to harrow. Besides, I had a quantity of plaster of paris to spread which had to be done immediately. Common sense told me I couldn't leave unless I could get a witness from God that it was absolutely necessary."

He paused, but nobody interrupted. Then he went on: "My family was concerned about you, too, but all hands seemed needed to insure the crops. We all felt that I should come for you as soon as the wheat was harrowed and the plaster of paris spread. Next morning I went to the field

382

certain that three or four heavy workdays awaited me before I could leave. As I fastened the horses to the harrow, the thought came that instead of dividing the field into what is usually termed lands, I would drive around the whole thing. This I did, continuing until noon. On stopping for dinner I looked around and discovered to my surprise that I had harrowed full half the wheat. After dinner I went on as before, and by evening I had finished the entire field."

Emma's eyes widened a little, but she made no comment. David continued: "Father went into the field that evening and saw what had been done. 'There must be an overruling hand in this,' he told me. 'I think you had better go to Pennsylvania as soon as the plaster of paris is spread.' " Awe was in David's tone now, and Joseph's hand clasped Emma's.

"Next morning I took a wooden measure under my arm and went to spread the plaster of paris which I had left two days previously in heaps near my married sister's house. Her house sits beside that particular field—but there was no plaster of paris. I hurried to ask my sister if she knew what had become of it.

" 'Wasn't it spread yesterday?' she asked in surprise.

" 'Not to my knowledge,' I told her.

" 'I'm certain it was all spread yesterday,' she insisted. 'The children came to me in the forenoon, begging me to come and watch some men sow plaster of paris, saying they had never seen anyone sow so fast. I saw three men at work in the field, as the children had said. The work was being done swiftly and thoroughly. I supposed they were men you had hired to help on account of your hurry to go to Pennsylvania. I went back into the house and gave the matter no further thought.' "

David paused, then went on in a tone of wonderment, as if he were still trying to analyze the whole thing. "My family

383

and I made considerable inquiry among relatives and friends. No one seems to know who sowed the field. All of us are asking if these workers were friends, or was a supernatural power connected with this strange occurrence?"

Every face was thoughtful, and Emma said in a tone of wonderment: "It could very well be. Certainly it is a strange happening."

Silence continued to fill the room, then Joseph said, "All I know is, I'm grateful David is here and that soon we will have a safe place where Oliver and I can finish the translating."

Emma was surprised to discover that her heartache was gone, and in its place she felt a strange exhilaration and an anxiety to be on her way. The Whitmers had opened their home . . . she was ready now to open her heart.

Joseph and Emma disliked imposing on anyone. Because of this they were taking with them all the rations left from the Knights' generous gift of supplies, plus their best milk cow, their riding horses, about a dozen laying hens, a few fryers, the spinning wheel, and the Major Mack clock. In order to do this William would go along with Joseph's loaded wagon and a borrowed team. This way he could bring the team and wagon back to Harmony. With two wagons they could carry clothes, bedding, and other items plus any passengers who might grow weary of riding horseback.

David seemed pleased that Joseph and Emma preferred to be as independent as possible. It was a trait possessed by all the Whitmers, and one which he admired. Space, he assured them, was something his family had plenty of. Joseph and Emma were to bring whatever seemed wise to them.

By the following morning the wagons were packed, and

with one last lingering look at their beloved cabin, they closed and locked it. The journey would begin with Joseph and Emma riding horseback, David and Oliver in the lead wagon, and William following. William would take charge of the cow and carry the chickens, baggage, and equipment they might need for wagon breakdowns, as well as grain, food, and supplies packed in barrels, feed for the animals, and buckets and water canteens, with extra cans of water for possible emergencies. David's wagon carried the plates and manuscript well hidden, food supplies, spinning wheel, and all the rest of the items Joseph and Emma had decided to bring.

Joseph helped Emma mount. As they rode side by side he reached for her hand, and after a backward glance at a past that had been filled to the brim with experiences of living, they were on their way to accept the hospitality of strangers in a strange town. Whatever the future held, they would face it together.

Oliver had tried to prepare Joseph and Emma, by enthusiastically describing from time to time what the Whitmers were like and the merits of their farm, but they were totally unprepared for what they saw—mile upon mile of fertile acres, so beautifully cared for that even the fenceposts looked new. There was not a sagging wire or a leaning post, and the worked soil bore promise of abundant crops.

Peter Whitmer, Sr., was a big man—big in body but even bigger in spirit. Unlike the Hales he cared nothing for prestige. He was from the old country, and like most Germans he worked hard. To him work was a God-given right, joy, and duty. "Six days thou shalt labor" was a rule for him and one which he taught his children. As his children grew they became a happy working unit. Peter Whitmer never drove his family. In spite of his size, he was a gentle man who loved his wife and children and took pains to understand them. When a child was old enough, he was taught the proper way to saw a board and drive a nail. All the children learned that any job worth doing was worth doing well. Peter awakened in them a desire to create, to move with confidence, to accomplish, and as they grew his wealth grew. He bought more land and built more buildings, but this he did without pride, teaching his family that all things belonged to God and that they were partners with Him in the creation of good. Peter sought no power, yet his influence in the community was felt probably more than any man's. There was hardly a family within miles that had not benefitted in some way from the bounty of the Whitmers. Most rich men were envied; the Whitmers were loved. Peter was considered a wise man. When he spoke, his neighbors listened.

Fayette was a beautiful place situated on high ground between Lake Seneca on the west and Lake Cayuga on the east. On the north the Seneca River connected the two lakes so that the land was three-fourths surrounded by water. Until early in the nineteenth century Fayette and the surrounding territory was an unbroken wilderness inhabited by the Cayuga Indians, one of the six tribes constituting the powerful federation known as the Iroquois. Some said the temperature and climate favorably modified by the proximity of the lakes and river tended to promote longevity. Fayette boasted a Mrs. Orman, one hundred and four years old; Mr. Jolly, one hundred and seven; and Mr. Widner, one hundred and six.

Joseph and Emma were saddle weary. The men in the wagons were feeling the fatigue of travel, too, for the trip from Harmony to Fayette had required several days, and part of it was over an old road which was little more than an Indian trail. Joseph had spent part of the time driving the wagon teams in order to relieve the men, but Emma preferred the saddle. Now, as they neared the river, she and Joseph were riding side by side. The sun was far above the hills, and the road was smooth. They were riding directly behind the lead wagon when Oliver said, "Look."

They followed his gaze through acres of planted land to where the Whitmer home stood like a jewel among pine and maple and tulip trees. Behind it were the carefully spread outbuildings. Emma looked anxiously at the Colonial house with its four alabaster columns supporting the porch. What would it hold for her and Joseph? Would they feel at home or would they be strangers?

"It is Peter's idea to build his barns low enough to be easily accessible for repairs and upkeep," Oliver told them. "In this he is ahead of his time. Some of the neighbors find it easier to let their buildings deteriorate than to climb to paint and repair them."

As they entered the lane, marking the end of their wearisome journey, the front door of the Whitmer house opened, and a young woman came racing down the road. She was lovely of face and form, and she ran with a certain grace that inhanced her shapely figure.

The moment Oliver saw her he was out of the wagon and running toward her. The sight reminded Emma of her first meeting with Joseph. She glanced at her husband and knew that the same thought was in his mind.

"The wagon is too slow for Oliver's heart," Joseph said, and Emma's eyes danced in appreciation.

Later, when Oliver introduced Elizabeth Anne, Emma knew that she had found a kindred spirit. In that first glance they liked one another. Each saw in the other solid stock

387

with roots that could hold through stress and strain the way a giant tree holds in a storm, yet they were gentle women. As their eyes met with warmth and understanding, each knew that she had found a friend. Elizabeth Anne gave one hand to Emma and one to Oliver, and they walked that way toward the house.

"Oliver looks so well, Emma. I think you have fattened him up a little." Elizabeth's voice had tone and color, a quality that was exactly right for her. She was alive with happiness, and the glow in her eyes lighted her whole being. "We're anxious to learn more about the manuscript. Oliver wrote that Joseph will call it the Book of Mormon." She turned to Oliver then with a tender look and said teasingly, "Papa said you'd find half a dozen attractive girls in Harmony to take up your time. Did you?"

"It was more like a hundred, wasn't it, Emma? But none were as saucy as you, Liz Anne."

She tossed her head and let go his hand, then she caught it again and moved closer to him. They were together, and their cup of happiness was full.

The Smiths found Whitmer hospitality to be everything Oliver had predicted. Mother Whitmer, like her husband, was big and generous. Even before their children were born they had made up their minds to surround them with love and guidance, but to let them grow into individuals capable of thinking their own thoughts and making their own decisions. There had been no indulgent permissiveness, for Peter Whitmer had always kept his hand on the pulse of his family with the Bible as his guide, but when opinions differed, children had been given a "hearing." They had grown up without fear in a house where they could count on justice and understanding.

As a young woman Mother Whitmer had been small and dainty like Elizabeth Anne, but as her fame as a cook grew, so did she. Her increase in weight, she said, was due to having so many "younguns," but her daughter Virginia was still slender after having three children.

"It's the times we live in," Mother Whitmer would say. "These days new mothers stay in bed where they belong for ten days, until all their bones are nicely back in place. With my first three I was up and doing my own work before the end of the first week. Such foolishness should have killed me."

By nightfall the wagons were unloaded and Emma and Joseph were comfortably lodged in two rooms with windows that looked out upon a carefully tended garden, beyond which lay fertile fields.

The rooms held the comforts of their little house in Harmony, even to a fireplace with wood stacked to burn if the air became chilly. They would eat with the Whitmers, pooling the food they had brought. They would try to find a way to replenish the larder, and they would work to pay for their lodging.

"We're in good hands, Joseph," Emma said as she poured water from a porcelain pitcher into a matching bowl on the commode and commenced to wash her hands before going to the kitchen to help Mother Whitmer and Elizabeth with supper. "Imagine two rooms to relax and be alone in when we want privacy. How thoughtful the Whitmers are! Tonight Mother Whitmer has promised to show me a quick way to use a fluting iron on the clothes I've had packed away. While I'm here I can do petticoats and frocks for her and Elizabeth Anne. It will be one more thing I can do to show appreciation for all they are doing for us." She reached for one of the towels Mother Whitmer had hung on the clothes bar at the left of the commode.

Joseph was unpacking and putting things away. Now he

389

looked up from a squatting position to grin at her. "We have our own towels, Emma."

"I know. I told her we did when I saw them hanging here, and she said, 'Then use mine just until you unpack.' Feel this, Joseph. It's of the finest linen." She touched its softness to his face.

"Nice," he said. "It smells good too." He caught her and kissed her, then his eyes became suddenly serious. "I hope the Whitmers will believe the translations—that they are God's work." There was an urgency in his voice. "I hope we can do the work now without interruptions, finish it soon, and put it into the hands of the printers."

"We will, Joseph. You must work daytimes and help the Whitmers at night."

That night at supper, Joseph and Oliver told the story of Joseph's experience in the grove when he was fourteen, of the angel's visits, obtaining the plates, and the persecutions that had followed as he had translated from the Urim and Thummim. The Whitmer men and Elizabeth Anne listened in rapt attention and believed, but Mother Whitmer was skeptical. "Angels . . ." she snapped, "I'd have to see one to believe they come to folks in our day. And if I do see one I'll probably faint."

Eyes around the table twinkled, but Mother Whitmer could see no mirth in the situation. "Oliver's letters have been full of this talk. He believes it, same as you do, Joseph. But I think you're being fooled somehow." Her attitude said plainly that she wanted them there, that she respected their right to believe as they chose, but that unless Providence intervened she wanted no part of it for herself.

Next morning Joseph and Oliver commenced translating and writing. They would finish the manuscript with as much speed as their strength would allow. Peter Whitmer and his sons were so interested in what Joseph and Oliver were doing that they were reluctant to go to the fields.

Christian and John had sat up most of the night reading the finished portion of the manuscript, and each came to Joseph privately, assuring him they believed the work to be divine and asking permission to write some in Oliver's stead. An agreement was made that one or the other of them could write from time to time to relieve Oliver when he was tired, or when he wanted to be with Elizabeth Anne. Later, Peter, Jr., and David came, stating their faith in the work and offering their assistance.

Joseph was humbly grateful, not only because the translating could move more rapidly but because here were friends he could trust, men with open minds, willing to search for new truths and to be led by a power greater than their own.

The work of translating was done in much the same manner as it had been in Harmony. In one of the rooms assigned to Joseph and Emma the men sat at a table with a divider between them.

Soon Virginia Whitmer Page, her husband Hiram, and the children were spending every minute they could spare at the Whitmers. They too had been caught up in Joseph's work. Within a few days, along with the other Whitmers, they had read the manuscript as far as it was finished. Now all of them eagerly awaited the new pages that were added at the end of each day. Mother Whitmer could not be made to admit that she believed what she read, yet her behavior was not that of a skeptic. She began doing outside chores ordinarily done by her sons so that they would have time to write for Joseph, and she approved their waste of free time just to sit under the sound of Joseph's voice and listen. Milking she enjoyed. And although her family remonstrated, she went to the barn each morning, brushing their protests aside with the same casualness she had used when they were children. Were not Emma and Elizabeth Anne getting breakfast each morning? Had not the girls taken over the household chores? Why, then, could she not help outside? It was not her nature to be idle.

One morning after straining the warm frothy milk into tin milk pans in the cold house, she came into the kitchen where the others were assembling for breakfast. She was strangely quiet as she washed her hands and took her place at the table. Father Whitmer said grace; Elizabeth Anne dished up porridge; and Emma passed hot, golden biscuits to everyone. Mother Whitmer sat toying with her spoon. David, sitting next to her, passed her a pitcher of thick cream. Absentmindedly she passed it on without pouring any on her porridge. He passed her butter for her biscuit. She passed that on without taking any. Her body was with them, but her thoughts obviously were elsewhere.

"What is wrong, Mother?" Elizabeth Anne asked the question that was forming on everyone's lips. "Don't you feel well?" Her tone was concerned.

Mother Whitmer seemed not to hear her, and now concern was voiced around the table. "What is it? Tell us . . . what is wrong?"

After what seemed forever her eyes moved around the table, seeming to cover each one, then they rested on Joseph. When she spoke her voice was filled with such awe and wonder that a breathlessness enveloped the room. Everyone was looking at her.

"You, Joseph—you, Emma—and Oliver must believe me. The rest know I don't lie, even though what I am about to tell sounds like a whopper. I saw your angel, Joseph. I really saw him."

Joseph made no sound. They were all looking at her so silently that if a pin had dropped it would have been heard.

392

"I had finished milking. When I got off the stool with my filled bucket he was standing between me and the door." The awe in her voice deepened. "You described the light, Joseph, and that too I saw. It was all around him like sun boiling, only there was no heat. His robe was white and bright. And then he looked at me. His eyes sort of smiled into mine. I felt as if he knew all about me . . . my prayers . . . my bullheadedness . . . everything, but still I felt that I was his friend. I don't know how he got hold of your gold plates, Joseph, but he had them. I can tell you everything about them. I saw the engravings and heard the leaves turn. Then he smiled at me again as if to say, 'Now, old girl, go and tell the world this is true. You said you would believe if you saw an angel.' Then the light faded and he was gone. I have never believed in visions outside the Bible, but this I know, I saw your angel, Joseph, as plain as I am seeing all of you."

Joseph's eyes held her's with tender understanding, then he smiled. "Now there are three of us who see angels."

"I'd been praying to see one," she said softly. "Now I know that what you are doing is God's work."

The translating had gone even better than Joseph had hoped it would. "At this rate," he told Emma one night after they had retired to their room, "the manuscript will be ready for the printers before the month ends."

Emma was standing at a window looking out at the twilight. Usually she was attentive to Joseph's words, but this time her eyes were rooted on the garden swing. It was a new two-seated wooden swing that had been finished recently by Hiram Page as an excuse for spending time at the Whitmers. Hiram knew one sure way to stand in good with his father-in-law was to keep his hands busy, and the swing would be a special treat for Virginia and the children, as well as the Whitmers.

Joseph went on talking. "I wish I could do something special for Oliver—for the Whitmers—to repay them for the help they have given us." He waited for Emma's reply, and when she remained silent he went on, "What could we possibly give them? We're poor. The Whitmers have luxuries in abundance. As for Oliver . . ."

A dimple appeared in Emma's cheek, and her attention was again focused on Joseph. "What Oliver wants more than anything is Elizabeth Anne. If you'll stand by the window with me you will see them in the garden swing disgracefully close together."

He grinned and said, "Disgracefully? You can't mean that."

"Of course not." She turned toward him, and some of the rapture of the romance she'd been witnessing was in her eyes. "How tragic it would be if one of them should stop loving the other."

Joseph came to the window and reached for her hand. "Come away from the window, minx. You're peeping."

She didn't budge. "Not really, Joseph. I'm looking at their happiness. I want them to have what we have, for in spite of all our hardships and difficulties ours is a good marriage."

His fingers tightened on hers. His lips brushed her cheek. Twilight was very beautiful. The heat of the day was gone now. A soft, cool breeze moved the window curtains and touched their faces like a caress. Off to the east a thrush was calling to its mate. The scent of roses from the garden drifted to them, and quietness and peace seemed everywhere.

In the garden swing Oliver reached for Elizabeth Anne, and his arms enfolded her gently. He cupped her chin with his hands after a moment, and their lips met. Joseph and Emma moved away from the window. They both knew this was a moment not meant for their intrusion.

It grew dark. Candles in the room glowed from walls and table. The whole Whitmer house was agleam with light as it always was when darkness fell. Joseph and Emma were about to go down and join the family when there was a knock on their door.

"Have you gone to bed, Joseph . . . Emma?" It was Oliver's voice.

Joseph opened the door. Oliver and Elizabeth Anne were standing hand in hand. There was no mistaking the glow on their faces.

Joseph flung the door wide in welcome, and the two entered still hand in hand.

"We couldn't wait until tomorrow to tell you," Oliver said. The rapture in his heart was on his face. "Meet the future Mrs. Cowdery."

Joseph reached for Oliver's hand, and Emma hugged Elizabeth Anne.

"Oliver asked Father for me yesterday so he'd have *his* consent before he asked me," Elizabeth Anne said. "I didn't know he was going to do it, but it's about time. I thought Oliver would never get around to asking me."

They all laughed. It seemed such an unlikely remark coming from Elizabeth Anne whose childhood was hardly behind her. How beautiful she looked standing there with her starlit eyes meeting Oliver's.

"I'm glad he found the courage to ask you," Joseph teased her. "Otherwise you probably would never have had another chance."

They all laughed from sheer happiness and went downstairs to join the family.

Part 5

Almost every evening after the work was done the Whitmers and their friends gathered to be taught by Joseph and Oliver. Sometimes they met in the garden where cool breezes fanned their faces and brought the scent of flowers to their nostrils. When the weather was damp the teaching was done in the company parlor where the air smelled a little stale, for the family seldom used this room.

Joseph and Oliver knew they were teaching truths that sounded strange to many of the listeners, but they had no qualms. They knew that the time would soon come when they would organize the church, and that the Book of Mormon would be read and believed by many. One weekend Joseph's parents came from Manchester to see how the work was progressing. Hyrum had made several trips on horseback to talk with Joseph and Oliver, so it came as no surprise, after an evening of outdoor instructions, when Hyrum and Peter and David Whitmer announced that they were ready for baptism. The light shed by the moon was bright enough for them to see Father and Mother Whitmer's nods of approval. Only Joseph's face was questioning. "If you are sure you understand what it means to be baptized, then we will be happy to perform the ordinance tomorrow. Do you agree, Oliver?"

"I'm in full agreement."

Next morning after breakfast Oliver and Joseph took the three candidates up to Joseph's rooms for final questioning. Some of the questions came from Joseph, some from Oliver.

Did they believe Jesus was the Son of God, born of the virgin Mary?

Did they have a sincere determination to do what they

believed was the will of God even if it meant persecution at the hands of enemies?

Were they aware of their imperfections and willing to study the scriptures to learn the commandments of God, and try to keep them?

Were they willing to seek new truths wherever they could be found—by study, by prayer, and by the quiet enlightenment of the Holy Spirit?

Did they understand that baptism by water was the symbol of burying a careless way of living and rising again to a life of purpose?

Were they striving to understand the baptism of the Holy Ghost even as Joseph and Oliver were striving to understand it?

Hyrum had been committing scriptures to memory for as long as he could remember. Now solemn-faced he began almost as if he were reading: "And it came to pass in those days that Jesus came from Nazareth of Galilee and was baptized of John in Jordan. And straightway coming out of the water, he saw the heavens opened, and the Spirit like a dove descending upon him. And there came a voice from heaven saying, 'Thou art my beloved Son, in whom I am well pleased.' And John bore record of it."

With Hyrum taking the initiative the two Whitmer candidates relaxed. Hyrum's eyes were on Joseph and Oliver. "We know baptism of water and the Holy Spirit is one baptism, that only those called of God as was Aaron have the right to baptize and perform the ordinance of the laying on of hands to bestow the gift of the Holy Spirit, which is a divine gift. The promise is that if the Holy Spirit lives in us we can speak with new tongues and take up serpents or drink a deadly drink without harm. This doesn't mean we should take foolish risks. It does mean that there is a power at our disposal greater than any we can comprehend. Perhaps we are on the threshold of a great discovery that the spiritual part of man is an undiscovered area of living with vastly more possibilities than the material. I'll admit we're in the dark. We can only dimly comprehend Christ and the spiritual realm, but we are ready to take the initial step; then we'll have to learn together as we go along."

The questions ceased and five minds began exploring.

Peter said: "We are to add to our faith virtue, and to virtue knowledge, and to knowledge temperance, and to temperance patience, and to patience godliness, and to godliness brotherly kindness, and to brotherly kindness charity. I'm not sure any man can reach such heights."

Downstairs Emma, the Whitmers, and some of their friends were waiting. As the men joined them, Emma scolded, "It's about time you came. We've had our bonnets on for more than an hour."

But the day was too bright for discord, and soon they were all walking to the lake where Hyrum and David were baptized by Joseph, and Peter was baptized by Oliver.

The day after the baptisms the earth seemed to wilt beneath the scorching sun. Inside the house rooms the air was stuffy. Opened windows brought little relief. Not a curtain moved.

In Joseph's room the men at work wiped perspiration from their brows. Even the scratching of pen on paper seemed a great effort, yet Joseph and Oliver kept on doggedly, working as they had done since early morning. It was a little before two when Oliver laid his quill pen down. "I'm out of paper, Joseph. We've used the last of it."

Joseph came from behind the quilt that stretched between them, and his eyes held their accustomed twinkle. "Now isn't this a sad state of affairs? My suggestion is that we ask Elizabeth Anne and Emma to accompany us into town to buy more."

398

Oliver grinned. "I'm all for it, but it may take a bribe to get them out in this heat."

"Want to bet?"

They found the girls in the grain house cording cotton, and looking hot and bored. Would they go? Their interest was that of two robins pouncing on night crawlers, for it was usually very little they saw of their men in the daytime. Soon they were fresh and clean in pretty, cool, starched dresses, and Joseph and Oliver's spirits lifted just looking at them.

Mother Whitmer suggested they take the best team and the surrey. Half an hour later they were riding along enjoying their unexpected holiday. Grasshoppers by the roadside arose from dry weeds along the fences as they passed; rabbits buried themselves in dry grass waiting for the coolness of evening. Bees moved slowly among wilting wild flowers, and dust came up from the road like haze, stirred by the surrey wheels and horses' hooves, but to the young people it was a day to enjoy.

The general store carried everything from Paris bonnets to harness. The girls looked over imported yard goods, and did some planning for Elizabeth Anne's wedding trousseau.

Oliver and Joseph bought paper and bonbons for their ladies, then they went to look at breeches and boots with Oliver's wedding in mind.

After a time the four of them met again, and the girls tried on bonnets to delight their men. They were about to leave the store when Elizabeth Anne saw the pastor of her church making a direct path to where they were standing. She smiled, but there was no answering smile on her minister's face, and Joseph and Oliver exchanged looks. Would there be trouble again?

The man was tall, fine looking, middle-aged, and he seemed to grow taller as he came up to them. Giving

Elizabeth Anne a curt nod, he began speaking to Joseph and Oliver before she had a chance to introduce them.

"By what authority do you baptize? You did baptize two Whitmer boys, and they have withdrawn from my church. Is it not so?"

"We baptized Peter and David Whitmer."

"By whose authority?"

"Authority through priesthood ordained of God, bestowed by divine revelation." Joseph's tone was kind and unruffled.

Anger deepened in the minister's face. "This is blasphemy."

"Why?" Oliver's query was low and calm.

The very calmness increased the minister's anger. "I had planned to visit you today at the Whitmers. Instead I will give you a warning. This morning the Fayette pastors held a meeting concerning you and your baptizings. Our warning is that if you continue to baptize and teach your false doctrines, we shall force you to leave Fayette, even if it means tarring, feathering, and riding you out on rails." He started to leave, then came back. "Every minister in Fayette is agreed—we won't tolerate losing any more members."

They watched him go, and for a moment silence followed his departure. The ultimatum had been given so quietly that two customers and a clerk standing nearby were unaware that the meeting and the parting had been more than a friendly greeting, but Joseph, Oliver, and Emma knew, and were gravely concerned. Experience told them that persecution lay ahead again, and perhaps trouble for the Whitmers if they were to continue the work there. Elizabeth Anne was unaware of the danger, for she hadn't experienced any harassments, but the other three knew that their very lives could be in danger.

400

The translating was almost completed, and it must be finished.

Oliver had kept from his letters to Elizabeth Anne everything that might cause her or her family to worry, so the insidious meaning of the pastor's words escaped her, and she was the first to break the silence. "I've always liked that man, but now I'm not sure I'll keep on attending his church. By whose authority does he threaten us, as if he were law to govern our thinking!"

A hint of a smile touched Oliver's lips and was gone. "No one can stop thoughts we keep to ourselves, dear girl. But let them be spoken, and there are those who will try with all the powers of Satan to govern our speech and our actions. Few persons want change. New truths upset old ways and patterns. If Joseph and I were to write our experiences, if they were printed in all the weeklies in the land, how many would believe them?"

"Truth is truth whether it is believed or not," Elizabeth Anne said, and four subdued and thoughtful people rode back to the Whitmers.

Joseph and Oliver unhitched, fed, and watered the team. This done, Joseph went in search of the Whitmers. He found Mother Whitmer in the herb garden, and together they went to the close forty where Father Whitmer was at work. Joseph had to make them understand that the minister's threats meant danger for all the Whitmers if he and Emma remained with them. The church would grow; the priesthood would grow; and Joseph's claims to divine revelation would bring wrath from an established clergy. Should the Whitmers risk persecutions by continuing to keep the Smiths and Oliver under their roof? These things Joseph explained with all earnestness, pointing out the dangers, and warning that events could shape into something even worse than his own past experiences had been. He went into detail, sparing

401

nothing of what he had gone through, then suggested that he and Emma leave at once.

When Joseph stopped speaking Father Whitmer pulled himself to his full height. "You are staying right here until that manuscript is finished and in the hands of the printers. We will not be dictated to by men who come to us for help to build their churches and care for their needy. You came to us because we wanted you here. My boy, nobody tells a Whitmer how his business shall be run."

"Amen," Mother Whitmer said.

It must have been somewhere near midnight when Emma awakened Joseph from sound sleep. He bolted up in bed, every muscle tense, his ears straining for the sound of an intruder, for it was not Emma's habit to awaken him. The stars were out and the moon made the room almost like day. "What is it, Emma? What do you hear?"

She pushed him back on the pillow and stifled a giggle. "There is no danger," she whispered. "I'm sorry to startle you, but morning seemed so long to wait to tell you my plan."

He was entirely awake now, and his mood to scold vanished. Instead, he was moved by her nighttime beauty. She was sitting up in bed, brown curls falling to her waist. Her cheeks looked like alabaster in the moonlight, and the ruffled collar of her blue nightdress enhanced the lovely curves of her throat. The seriousness of her eyes, that a moment ago had been teasing, made her face even more beautiful, and he pulled her gently to him. Then, with his face touching hers, he murmured, "What is this great plan that can't wait until morning to be told?"

"Well," she began, "I know how anxious you are to finish the manuscript."

402

"We must finish it with all haste now, and hope there is time."

They were speaking in low tones, careful not to disturb other sleepers in the Whitmer household.

"I know there is danger," she said. "But aren't we overlooking something very important? I think you should go to New York City and find a printer, Joseph. You ought to know exactly where you will be taking the manuscript to have it printed, for the real danger will be when you move it away from here to have it made into books. As soon as you know where you'll be taking it, it could be moved a few pages at a time without attracting the attention of those who will want to destroy it."

He thought she had finished speaking.

"I think you should start tomorrow and ride our fastest horse. If you leave by daybreak you'll be less apt to meet enemies."

She was right of course. He must find a printer—someone with a good reputation, someone trustworthy who wouldn't overcharge them. He wasn't even sure where the money to pay for printing would come from, although it had entered his head that Martin Harris might advance the money, which could be paid back as soon as copies of the Book of Mormon were sold. Seeing Martin meant he could ride into Manchester. He thought of his folks living in the cramped little house with Jerusha and the baby. How good it would be to see them. Jerusha would welcome news of Hyrum, for he had never been away from her for any length of time before, and the only reason he was away now was so that he could work with the Whitmers in the fields to help pay lodging for the Smiths until the Book of Mormon was ready to market. The title page had been prepared for some time. It was a part of the translated plates, and this he could show the printer. The weather was fine for outdoor sleeping

403

now, so there would be no need for accommodations at an inn or at Jerusha's. Traveling by horseback was his swiftest and safest way. He would go as speedily as he could and return as soon as practical—but would Emma be safe in his absence? Would the Whitmers and the rest be harmed? This was God's business. He must leave everything in His hands. "I'll leave by daybreak," he told her, holding her tenderly.

Shortly before dawn, after a good breakfast, Joseph brought the saddled horse to the back door. Emma helped him tie two knapsacks to the saddle. One contained two changes of clothing, the other held food enough to last a week or more. There was feed for the horse, and a canvas bag filled with ice from the sawdust house and fresh water. The ice would melt, but Emma hoped the water would remain cool.

The household was just beginning to stir when Joseph embraced Emma for a second time and swung himself to the saddle. Then he was away, carrying the title page carefully concealed on his body, along with a few other painstakingly written sheets. He turned once to wave. Beautiful Emma—she filled his heart completely. How empty life would be without her. His prayer was earnest and simple: "God keep her safe." Then he added a second petition, "And guard the Whitmer household." His prayer was short but it filled his whole being.

The trip to Manchester was so free of incident that even Joseph was surprised. He rode into Jerusha's lane in good time, with not even a hint of trouble along the way. The welcome he received made his eyes shine. His mother was heavier, his father thinner. Jerusha looked the same, except that she was big with child. Looking at her he knew that Hyrum must come home before the end of the month.

Baby Lovina would be two in September, a beautiful child with dimpled cheeks and dark hair that framed her small, oval face. In a way she reminded Joseph of Lucy at that age, for she spoke full sentences with a plainness of speech hard to believe in a child so young. Looking at Joseph solemn-eyed she said quite matter-of-factly, "Do you know what Momma has in her tummy? A baby!"

"Lovey," Jerusha said embarrassed, "that was our secret. It's something we don't talk about in public."

Quick as a flash she turned to Joseph and begged, "You won't tell, will you?"

Don Carlos at thirteen was as tall as his father. Lucy, eight, was still small and dainty. Samuel was away digging a well for someone.

A soft breeze touched the trees. It was pleasant and cool outside, so they sat on the grass. Lucy curled up beside him, and his arm encircled her. Don Carlos sat at his feet; Lovina climbed into his lap; and the rest sat as near to him as possible, plying him with questions, telling him the news. Joseph marveled how they were able to manage in Jerusha's small house, yet they seemed congenial and happy. He was even more amazed when Jerusha told him Catherine was in the house with six of her young friends. They were having a party at which each girl was making herself a bonnet. About that moment Catherine came rushing out of the house to embrace her brother, and he arose hastily to hold her, thinking how changed she was—from a gangling girl to a lovely young lady, all in one year's time. She resembled Sophronia now—tall and slender, but with a beauty all her own.

"I'm going to be married," she said, and her eyes took on a special glow. "You'll like Will, Joseph. His name is Wilkins J. Salisbury, and he is the finest man I know."

"He had better be," Joseph told her fervently.

She excused herself with a promise of a chat later and went back to join her friends. Joseph's eyes followed her—seventeen and engaged. Why, she was hardly more than a child!

Mother Lucy seemed to read his mind. "The wedding won't be soon, possibly not until January of '31. He wants to have a house and the furnishings. It will take awhile. Catherine has always known what she wanted. I suppose that is why we permitted the engagement."

Father Joseph said, "I've been meaning to ride to Fayette to see how things were with you and to see how you are coming with the manuscript."

Joseph told them how well the translating was progressing and his reason for visiting them. Later, after supper on the lawn and a walk with Catherine, he slept with Samuel and Don Carlos on a bed of fragrant hay in the haymow. Next morning the family feasted on strawberries from the garden, thick cream, and yeast buns baked in Jerusha's outdoor oven. Joseph pronounced it food for the gods. Soon afterward he left them to visit Martin Harris.

Joseph sat alone in the cool Harris parlor waiting for Martin. Mrs. Harris had let him in, then perhaps sensing that he had come for a loan she had motioned him into the most uncomfortable chair in the room, watched him seat himself in it, and left him. Joseph was quite certain she would return again when Martin did, and he dreaded having her listen in. It was so much easier to talk to Martin without her.

While he waited he looked around at the lavish room, comparing it with Jerusha's. Life seemed unfair. Ten persons were housed in Jerusha's three small rooms and Martin's house of elegance held two plus what hired help Mrs. Harris was able to keep. Help came and went like the change of the moon, for Mrs. Harris' acid tongue was no easy thing to take.

If material blessings brought happiness Mrs. Harris should be one of the most contented persons alive. The room had been tastefully decorated when he was here last, but now it had been redone with satin draperies, fine carpeting, furniture of the finest design, mirrors, pictures, a new organ, and even a sculptured bust of their daughter who had recently married.

Joseph wondered what Jerusha would do with such a house as this . . . and decided that perhaps it would bring her no greater joy than she already had, for she was one whose heart seemed to overflow with contentment at all times and in all places. She was in tune with earth and people; harmony was a part of her very being. Mrs. Harris, unfortunately, seemed forever out of tune with herself and everyone else; she was a most unhappy woman. If Jerusha had a house such as this one, it wouldn't be a showplace, for whatever Jerusha had was shared to make comfort and pleasure for someone else. He looked about, deciding in his mind's eye which things Jerusha would love to own and which she would grimace at. The chair he was sitting in would probably be the first to go.

His musing came to an abrupt end. Martin entered with outstretched hands. His greeting was genuine, and as Joseph stood up to grasp those hands he knew old misunderstandings were gone. There was only admiration which each man held for the other. Martin led Joseph to a comfortable chair and was seating himself in another when Mrs. Harris came in, embroidery work in hand, and sat where she could watch each man without turning her head. Joseph felt suddenly uncomfortable and wished he could leave and come back another time, but what would he gain? Now, or another time, she would still be around.

Martin asked about the translating and how it was progressing. "I've been intending to travel to Fayette to see for myself how the work is coming along, but Mrs. Harris was

407

remodeling and refurnishing the house. I felt I was needed here."

"You needed!" Mrs. Harris jabbed the needle into the material with such force that her thread broke. "I can't see where you were needed here at all. You didn't do anything."

His tone was patient. "Maybe I kept you from spending more than we could afford, Pet."

She was rethreading her needle. "I spent only what was necessary to do the job right."

Joseph had meant to compliment her on the fine parlor, but her outburst changed his mind. She was a spoiled woman who exalted herself by making Martin feel low. Martin chose to ignore her remarks, and Joseph went back to talking about the manuscript. He showed Martin the title page and explained that he was ready to look for a printer. Then he added, "We'll need to borrow money for the first printing, Martin. It was Oliver's thought and mine that you might be willing to advance it."

Mrs. Harris spoke before Martin had a chance to. "I think this is something you are foisting on the public to get gain. We'll have nothing whatsoever to do with it. Gold plates! Who has seen them? Have I? Has Martin?"

Again Martin chose to ignore her. "We have a good printer right here in town. Shop around if you like, go to New York City, or wherever you are a mind to, but I think you'll find E. B. Grandin as reasonable as any. I sinned and brought condemnation upon myself and family by losing an important part of the translations. The least I can do now is to see that the book is published."

Mrs. Harris bit her lip and said nothing, but her eyes held a fire that was bound to erupt. Joseph, feeling that anything he might say could bring an outburst, arose to go. Martin didn't try to stop him, but his handclasp at parting

408

was warm. Their eyes met in understanding. "Thank you, good friend," Joseph said.

Martin followed him as far as the entrance hall, and they clasped hands again.

Joseph untied his horse with a feeling of relief. How fortunate to find a printer close at hand. From inside the house he could hear Mrs. Harris giving Martin full steam. How he tolerates that woman I'll never understand, he thought. He mounted, looking at the house without envy.

Glad that a trip to New York City wouldn't be necessary, Joseph followed Martin's suggestion and went at once to see Egbert Grandin about getting the manuscript printed. He also saw a printer in Manchester and one in Lyons. After comparing prices he decided upon Mr. Grandin for the work. This would please Martin, and it would be his money paying for the books until enough copies could be sold to pay back the loan.

Joseph found Mr. Grandin to be a businesslike gentleman. After learning the approximate length of the manuscript he said he would print five thousand copies for $3,000.00. The printing would commence as soon as the manuscript was put into his hands. If Martin agreed to the price, Joseph felt the matter was settled.

Next he took the title page to B. R. Lansing, clerk of the U.S. District Court in Western New York. Here, in order to protect himself under the law, he signed his own name as "author and proprietor" as provided by act of Congress, but in order not to deceive anyone as to the divine nature of the book, he also left for the front page a description from the book itself. This was the title page he had secreted on his person with such great care:

THE BOOK OF MORMON

An account written by the hand of Mormon upon the plates taken from the plates of Nephi.

Wherefore, it is an abridgment of the record of the people of Nephi, and also of the Lamanites; written to the Lamanites, who are a remnant of the house of Israel; and also by the spirit of prophecy and of revelation. Written and sealed up, and hid unto the Lord, that they might not be destroyed; to come forth by the gift and power of God unto the interpretation thereof; sealed by the hand of Moroni, and hid up unto the Lord, to come forth in due time by the way of the Gentiles—the interpretation thereof by the gift of God.

An abridgment taken from the Book of Ether also, which is a record of the people of Jared, who were scattered at the time the Lord confounded the language of the people, when they were building the tower to get to heaven—which is to show unto the remnant of the House of Israel what great things the Lord hath done for their fathers; and that they may know the covenants of the Lord, that they are not cast off forever. And also to the convincing of the Jew and Gentile that Jesus is the Christ, the Eternal God, manifesting himself unto all nations. And now, if there are faults they are the mistakes of men; wherefore condemn not the things of God, that ye may be found spotless at the judgment-seat of Christ.

Translated by Joseph Smith Junior.

He had brought along a brief analysis of the book which he felt was the quickest way of explaining its contents. Now with a light heart he rode back to Jerusha's. He did not doubt that Martin would lend him the money for the books. Thinking about it exhilarated him, lifted him. After all these months of work and persecution the Book of Mormon would soon be ready to carry its heavenly message to the world. And it would sell. He was sure of it. Perhaps at some future date it would be printed in many languages.

To his family he related the happenings of the day. They were overjoyed. Jerusha said they ought to celebrate with another picnic on the lawn, and everyone agreed heartily, knowing full well how crowded the little house would be if they all tried to eat in it at once.

Later the family sat in the evening coolness enjoying the bounties of Jerusha's planning—golden loaves of bread, a

410

mound of fresh butter, vegetables from the garden, all the cold milk they could drink, and wild honey Father Smith had taken from a bee tree.

What was it that made this such a joyous occasion, Joseph thought as he compared it to the meeting in the Harris parlor. The answer, he knew, was love. Joy, peace, contentment—these were the things Joseph felt as he sat with his family. And looking at the children he saw their good fortune. Reared in love and understanding, they would have a foundation to bolster them if the time should come when they too might be called upon to face ugliness and unkindness in a prejudiced world.

The meal was half over when a man on horseback turned into the lane that led to the house, and Samuel said: "I do believe that is Lyman Cowdery, Oliver's brother, coming to pay us a visit." Surprise was in his tone, for while Oliver had always been an intimate friend of the Smith family and a most welcome guest, his brother took pains to let it be known that he had little use for the Smiths or their gold bible.

"I wonder what he wants?" Jerusha's tone was apprehensive.

"Probably coming to ask about Oliver's welfare," Father Smith said reassuringly.

They watched him tie his horse by the watering trough. Then he covered the distance from the barn to them. The wind blew stray strands of hair across his handsome face as he made his way toward them.

Samuel greeted him with "How are you, Lyman?" and Jerusha asked him to join them for supper. He declined the supper offer, nodded brusquely to the adults present, and addressed young Joseph. "I have a warrant for your arrest."

"Oh, no!" The startled outcry came simultaneously from several throats.

411

"On what grounds?" Joseph was trying to think of some way he might have broken the law.

One by one Joseph's family arose from the grass. Consternation, disbelief, and anger were the expressions written on their faces.

Young Joseph said, "Show me the warrant."

Lyman Cowdery handed it to him. "You're to appear before the magistrate in Lyons at ten o'clock Thursday morning. That is three days from now. If there is any doubt about your being there I will have to take you with me now."

Joseph looked at the faces of his worried family. His face too was grave, but his tone was light. "Lyons," he mused. "Now what could I have done that would bring me trouble in Lyons? Why not Fayette, Harmony, Manchester, or Palmyra?"

Samuel said, "This could be a trick of your enemies. I'll ride to Fayette for Hyrum."

Suddenly young Joseph's attention was drawn to Jerusha. Her face was whiter than usual and her hands had involuntarily gone to her stomach.

"Are you having pains?" Concern was in his voice.

She gave a wan smile. "Maybe I'm just scared for you. The baby isn't due for two weeks."

"Samuel," Joseph's voice was stern, "you get Hyrum here as quickly as possible. Never mind me. I can take care of myself." He cupped Jerusha's face in his two hands. "We must get you into the house. You must lie down and stop worrying about me." A twinkle flashed in his eyes. "They can't hang me for uncommitted murder."

She smiled through tear-wet eyes. "Why won't people let you alone? Why must they always be making trouble?"

He didn't answer. Instead he took her arm, walking her toward the house. Over his shoulder he said to Lyman, "I'll be in Lyons at the appointed time."

412

Some of the family followed Joseph and Jerusha. The rest waited to bring in the supper things, eyes following Lyman as he walked across the lawn and mounted his horse.

By morning Jerusha seemed her old self. "I guess he's waiting for the arrival of his daddy," she told Mother Lucy and Catherine. And then to Catherine. "They were false pains. Lots of expectant mothers have them."

"I know that." Catherine's voice had a worldly edge. "I know all about it."

Thursday morning Hyrum and Samuel came riding home. The Whitmer sons and Oliver had intended accompanying them to Manchester until Father Whitmer reminded them that it would leave the farm practically unguarded, and if Joseph were walking into a trap, trouble might be brewing in Fayette also. It took some persuading to keep Emma at the Whitmers, but finally she was convinced that it would be better for her to remain.

Hyrum wanted to ride into Lyons with his brothers but decided against it; since Jerusha's time of delivery was so near, he felt he dare not risk being away from her.

Joseph dressed with meticulous care, hoping that if he looked the part of a gentleman he might be judged one when he went before the magistrate. Don Carlos, proud to be of some use, polished his boots to a mirror shine. Samuel loaned him his best silk tie and a starched white shirt with a stand-up collar. After he was dressed, Joseph said he felt like a well curried horse. Little Lovina asked him to bend down for a farewell kiss and said, "You smell like a girl."

All members of the family were present for the departure, offering their prayers and good wishes. Joseph lifted Lovina high in the air and kissed her cheek. She stood on the ground then, watching them solemnly. Don Carlos and Lucy-Lu ran to untie the horses. The men mounted, and with a wave of their hands were off, riding toward Lyons.

The day seemed unending, but near nightfall the waiting family saw the two horsemen returning. As they rode up the lane toward the house they were singing. The blending of their voices in the night air was a welcome sound to those who had waited at home in great concern all day. As they dismounted the family, unable to wait longer to hear the news, trooped out in a body to meet them.

"Tell us . . . tell us. . . ."

Expectant faces looked toward Joseph and Samuel. "I'll begin it," Samuel said. "It seems Mrs. Harris, peeved at Martin for his interest in the Book of Mormon, undertook to prove that Joseph never had the gold plates, that he only pretended to have them for the purpose of getting money. After Joseph left their place the other day she rode from house to house, inquiring for those who would be against Joseph. You know how she can stir up feelings. She must have been impressed by the number and strength of her adherents; they were even greater than she had hoped for. Then she entered a complaint against Joseph before a certain magistrate in Lyons."

"A nice friend to have around," Hyrum said, half in jest, half bitterly.

"Why Lyons? Why not Palmyra or Manchester?" Jerusha asked.

"She had found some special witnesses in Lyons, men who didn't mind lying with their hands on the Bible. She made affidavit to many things herself, telling the officers whom to subpoena. Among the number was Martin."

Joseph said, "Let me take it from here." His blue eyes were twinkling. "I'll be the first witness," he said. "Samuel, you swear me in."

Samuel produced the Bible, and bidding Joseph place his hands upon it he said with mock gravity, "Mr. Poindexter,

414

do you swear to tell the truth, the whole truth, and nothing but the truth, so help you God?"

"I do, your honor."

"Poindexter?" Father Joseph mused. "That's the one I've always thought shot at Joseph when the cow was killed—way back when he was but a boy."

"Mr. Poindexter," Samuel went on, "did Joseph Smith ever show you the box he claimed held gold plates?"

Joseph ran his hand through his blond hair, walked over to an imaginary spittoon, and replied, "Yes he did. He showed it to me many times."

"How big was it?"

"Sir, I didn't measure it."

"Approximately."

Joseph pretended to eye an imaginary box on the floor. "Three feet long maybe—two high—two wide." Measuring with his hands.

"Did you ever see inside the box?"

"Certainly I did."

"What was in it?"

"Sand, nothing but sand. Joe only said it held gold to deceive the people." Joseph took a few shuffling steps to show that the witness had finished his testimony.

There were cheers from the family, then Jerusha said dubiously, "Did this really happen, Joseph?"

"It really happened," he assured her. "Mrs. Harris was counting big on three witnesses, but they should have gotten together on their testimonies. The second witness said the box was filled with lead. The third said I told him there was nothing in the box at all, that I had bragged of making fools of everyone, and that I was aiming for Martin's money. He said I planned to get as much of it as I could, and that it was a known fact that I had already got two or three hundred dollars from him."

415

They were in the house now and the room became strangely silent. Nobody thought this was funny.

"Mrs. Harris' affidavit was read, stating that my chief objective was to defraud her husband and that it was her belief that I had never possessed the gold plates. The magistrate then called Martin Harris and swore him in. Martin testified resolutely to a few simple facts. He raised his hand to heaven and said, 'I can swear that Joseph Smith, Jr., has never got a dollar from me by persuasion since God gave me life. I did once, of my own free will, put fifty dollars into his hands in the presence of witnesses, for the purpose of doing the work of the Lord. This I can prove, and I can tell you furthermore that I have never seen in Joseph Smith a disposition to take any man's money without giving him a reasonable compensation for the same in return. As to the plates which he professes to have, gentlemen, if you do not believe in them but continue to resist the truth, they will someday be the means of damning your souls.'

"After Martin's testimony the magistrate told them not to call any more witnesses. He ordered them to go about their business and trouble him no more with such folly."

For a few seconds no one spoke, then Mother Lucy said, "There is more."

"More?" Puzzled eyes covered her.

"I was so frightened for Joseph, and I know so little of law, I went to Hyrum for assurance. His answer seemed the sensible one: 'About all we can do is wait and pray.' So, I went to the woods, and there I was given to know that not one hair of Joseph's head would be harmed. We have a great deal to be thankful for this day."

Hyrum was looking at Joseph with earnest eyes, and his tone was intense when he spoke. "I have a feeling you will never be free of trouble, Joseph. You are offering new concepts in religion, and your enemies will fight you. For the

416

least cause they will bring you before the courts. Just wait until the church is organized and trouble will really begin. It may cost you your life, but I'm with you all the way."

"We are all with you." It was a family chorus.

That night Jerusha gave birth to another daughter. She was named Mary.

Once again in Fayette the work of translating continued, but now there were interruptions from callers. Some came seeking the truth as Joseph and Oliver taught it; others asked hard questions, hoping to confound the listeners. In spite of warnings from the indignant Fayette clergy, Joseph and Oliver continued to administer the ordinance of baptism.

The translation and publication of the Book of Mormon was a sacred responsibility, but another responsibility also weighed heavily upon them. They knew a part of their calling was to establish the church. They were aware of the confusion in the religious world, with reformers striking at the very heart of various church creeds. The angel had said that a marvelous work and a wonder was about to come forth, and certain religious thinkers had predicted for a generation or more a new order of things. All through the United States new concepts were being formulated, causing compromises and departures from established beliefs. Joseph felt that these changes were not sufficient. The church needed not reform but restoration—a gospel restored in completeness by God himself. And because Joseph believed he had been called to do this task, he was not afraid to speak out, saying that the authority to minister in the things of God must be restored from heaven itself by those who held the keys of divine authority, and that no one must take this honor unto himself unless he was called of God as was Aaron.

The translation of the Book of Mormon, he told his

believers, was a manifestation of the power of God to communicate his mind and will to men, and soon it would be accepted by many as scripture, even as the Bible was sacred scripture.

When they were alone, he and Oliver talked of their experience in the woods on the Susquehanna River where they had seen in vision a great organization with the same gifts and blessings that had been in Christ's original church. They looked forward to the fulfilling of the promise that soon the Melchisedec priesthood would function as an everlasting blessing, if they were faithful. Had they not seen in vision the multitudes of men who would hold this priesthood?

With the translation nearing an end, members of Joseph's family were constant visitors at the Whitmer home, helping Father Whitmer with his work but showing keen interest in the final chapters of the book.

Martin Harris was a familiar figure also, for life with Mrs. Harris was difficult, and the manuscript seemed all-important to him. Remembering his carelessness in losing a portion of the early part of the work, he elected himself to stand guard so that no harm should come again to what he called the angel's message.

The Whitmers also were drawn to the upper room. From time to time one of the sons or Emma would relieve Oliver with the writing, but for the most part Oliver did the work of transcribing.

Then came a special day. It began like any other day, with prayers preceding the translating. All had gathered for early worship, as was their custom, then each had gone to his special task, until only Oliver, Martin, David, and Joseph remained to continue work on the book. They were translating from Ether, a history of the Jaredites who had come to ancient America at the time of the confusion of languages about 1200 B.C. It was the story of the Brother of Jared, a man of such strong faith that he was shown all the important happenings from the beginning of the world to the end of it.

The translating was going well. Joseph's voice and the scratching of the quill pen Oliver held were the only sounds in the room, and then Joseph's face took on a strange expression.

A moment before he had been absorbed in deep thought, but now the words he was reading caused him to remember a promise the angel had made long ago, a promise he had awaited with patience even as he longed for its fulfillment. Now, here in the ancient plates written by the hand of Mormon, were words which the angel had spoken:

Behold, I have written upon these plates the very things which the Brother of Jared saw, and there never was greater things made manifest, than that which was made manifest unto the Brother of Jared; wherefore the Lord hath commanded me to write them, and I have written them. And he commanded me to seal them up, and he also commanded that I should seal up the interpreters, according to the commandment of the Lord.

Joseph continued to translate, and Oliver continued to write.

Behold, ye are privileged, in that ye may show the plates unto those who shall assist to bring forth this work; and unto three shall they be shown by the power of God; wherefore they shall know of a surety that these things are true. And in the mouth of three witnesses shall these things be established; and the testimony of the three, and this work, in the which shall be shown forth the power of God and also his word, of which the Father, and the Son, and the Holy Ghost bear record—and all this shall stand as a testimony against the world at the last day.

Here was the same promise the angel had made to Joseph, not once but many times. For had he not said that he himself would show the plates to three witnesses, that they would see the records, behold them with their eyes, handle them with their hands, and declare with knowledge that this was indeed a divine work?

The room seemed charged. Had words written so long ago moved through eons of time to this very moment in history, and were they in truth a part of it? The promise was that after three had viewed the plates and the angel, Joseph would show the records to a few whom the Lord would appoint. But only these three would see from the hands of the angel. Every man in the room knew of the promise, for Joseph had related his visions to them many times. He covered the plates and pushed back the divider. The three men looked at Joseph, and he knew it was not doubt but belief that held them silent.

Oliver was the first to speak, and his voice came humbly with great earnestness. "What do you make of it, Joseph—ancient records speaking of promises made to you? Some might say your translating is a hoax, that you made up the part about the witnesses to impress us. But I know you did not. Suppose this is the day when three will see your heavenly being? With all my heart I should like to be one of them."

Martin Harris and David were looking at Joseph with eyes expectant and wishful. "You have almost finished the translating, Joseph," David said. "The time must be near when this experience will happen." His voice took on a kind of longing. "I'd like to be a witness."

"And I." Martin's voice was hardly more than a whisper. "Do you suppose I would be worthy?"

420

Joseph looked at his friends. Who could be more worthy? If this were indeed the time for the fulfilling of the angel's promise, surely God would make it known to them. Joseph loved these men. If it were left to him he would choose them.

"Why don't we go to the woods?" Oliver said. "Perhaps in the silence of the forest we will find our answer."

The men walked to their accustomed places in the woods without talking, their minds firmly fixed on their inward meditations.

Joseph held the Urim and Thummim in his hand. "Our Father," he prayed, "if these three friends are worthy in thy sight, permit them to see what I have seen, that they may witness before thee and the world that the plates intrusted to my care are divine records. Let their words stand as a testimony to all men that they have seen the angel face to face and know that the work is true. They yearn for a testimony from thee. They do not ask that the vision be given today; their prayer is that they may know whether this blessing may be theirs, in thine own time, and in thine own way." He prayed forgiveness for his sins of omission and commission, for he saw himself as the man he was and the man he ought to be.

For a long time their prayers and meditations continued, then the men gathered around Joseph. Each one knew that an answer had come. No one told them. They simply knew that the revelation Joseph had was meant for all three of them.

Joseph looked into the Urim and Thummim and began speaking:

Behold, I say unto you that you must rely upon my word, which if you do, with full purpose of heart, you shall have a view of the plates, and also the breastplate, the sword

421

of Laban, the Urim and Thummim which was given to the Brother of Jared upon the mount, when he talked with the Lord face to face, and the miraculous directors which were given to Lehi while in the wilderness, on the borders of the Red Sea; and it is by your faith that you shall obtain a view of them, even by that faith which was had by the prophets of old.

And after you have obtained faith, and have seen them with your eyes, you shall testify of them, by the power of God; and this you shall do that my servant Joseph Smith, Jr., may not be destroyed, that I may bring about my righteous purposes unto the children of men, in this work. And you shall testify that you have seen them, even as my servant Joseph Smith, Jr., has seen them, for it is by my power that he has seen them, and it is because he had faith; and he has translated the book, even that part which I have commanded him, and as your Lord and your God liveth, it is true.

Wherefore you have received the same power, and the same faith, and the same gift like unto him; and if you do these last commandments of mine, which I have given you, the gates of hell shall not prevail against you; for my grace is sufficient for you; and you shall be lifted up at the last day. And I, Jesus Christ, your Lord and your God, have spoken it unto you, that I might bring about my righteous purposes unto the children of men. Amen.

The men looked at Joseph with quickened hearts. David was the first to speak. "How does one obtain the faith necessary to see and to know?"

"We must strengthen one another," Oliver said. "We must trust . . . and put out of our lives, if we can, everything that will make us unworthy."

Martin Harris said nothing, but the longing to be one of the witnesses was reflected in his eyes.

The finished manuscript lay on the table. Oliver put down his pen and wiped his brow. Joseph came from behind the curtain, the joy of accomplishment glowing in his eyes. The same friends were together in the room. David and Martin stood beside Oliver scanning the page so recently completed. The many days of work . . . were they really over at last?

Oliver handed the manuscript to Joseph, who touched the pages reverently. Was this not indeed God's holy word made manifest, a work which would bring to thousands a greater knowledge of God and man's reason for being?

Oliver said, "We must be very careful in delivering it to the printers. Our enemies will be looking for a chance to steal it and destroy it."

Remembering past experiences, Joseph said, "We must take a few pages at a time to the printer. Nothing must happen to the manuscript now."

"I'd suggest Oliver do it," David said. "If it becomes known that the manuscript is ready for printing, you'll be the one they'll watch. They'll expect you to deliver it."

Martin nodded. "Oliver could proofread what he takes each time, to make sure everything is correct, and we ought to have two copies."

Joseph weighed their suggestions carefully, and agreed. "A thousand copies of the book will be printed by March," he said with a kind of awe in his voice as if he could hardly believe the truth of his statement.

"One thing more," David said, with such earnestness that they looked at him curiously. "The witnesses. They will be needed more than ever now, to testify that the book is a holy record and not something Joseph made up. I wish . . ."

423

Joseph put the manuscript in its hiding place. "God's promise will be fulfilled in his own time and his own way."

"But we could ask," David persisted. "We could go to our accustomed place in the woods . . ."

Without another word, the four men descended the stairs.

It was a rare day—not hot like so many preceding ones had been. The woods were as silent as if each tree had paused for prayer. Only the crackling of underbrush as the men walked, or the whirring of birds' wings, or the movement of small animals broke the stillness. They entered the grove without conversation, hoping for a faith strong enough to receive the divine Spirit that they might behold this marvelous work and wonder. But were they worthy? This was the question each man asked himself. This time they did not separate but decided to take turns praying aloud. Joseph prayed first. As he had done so often before, he stated his need for witnesses who could testify that the plates were indeed ancient records, written by the hands of righteous men who depended upon God to lead them—men who needed direction and knowledge, light and truth, even as did they.

Oliver prayed next. At this moment he did not feel like the intellectual, purposeful, dedicated young man who bravely went out to meet the challenges of life. As he compared himself to the greatness of God—a greatness far beyond his comprehension—he became very humble, and he promised to be true all his life to the heavenly vision should it be granted.

David prayed, and then Martin. These were trusting men who believed and were willing to risk their lives to bring about God's purposes. When all four had prayed as earnestly as they knew how they waited, but nothing happened. Again they prayed in turn and waited. Their faith didn't falter, for had not God said if they came with clean hearts and willing minds the vision would be theirs?

At last Martin spoke brokenly. "I may be the reason we aren't getting what we ask for. Because of me part of the manuscript was lost. And there was a time when my sinful ambition was to do the work you were called to do, Joseph. I wanted this honor for myself."

Sorrowfully he withdrew, a lonely figure walking to where he could pray alone in the thickness of the grove. Voices called after him, bidding him to stay, but he would not.

And now again the men petitioned in faith. They had not been engaged in prayer many minutes when they felt a strange and wonderful power enveloping them. Each heart beat faster, being quickened by the Holy Spirit, and then they beheld a light above them in the air, a light as gloriously beautiful as sun shining on snow, only more brilliant.

In the midst of this heavenly brightness an angel appeared, dressed in a robe so white there were no words to describe it. And with the angel, surrounded by the light, there appeared a table on which were the gold plates, the breastplate, the Urim and Thummim, the sword of Laban, and the miraculous directors that had led Lehi through the wilderness.

The angel lifted the plates from the table, and each man knew that these were in truth the plates from which Joseph had translated. Coming first to David, and then to Oliver, he turned over the leaves one by one so that each could distinctly see the engravings. Then into their hands, in turn, he placed the records so that each could touch them and know that they were in truth the records Joseph had protected with such great care.

Addressing himself to David in a voice that penetrated to the very core of his heart, and to the hearts of Joseph and Oliver also, he said: "David, blessed is the Lord and he that keeps his commandments."

Immediately after the angel spoke they heard a voice that seemed to come from above the light which covered them: "These plates have been revealed by the power of God, and they have been translated by the power of God. The translation of them which you have seen is correct, and I command you to bear record of what you now see and hear." The same words were addressed to Oliver for all three men to hear, then the light faded, the vision ended, and the men were alone. No one spoke; there was only the sound of rustling leaves to break the stillness.

At last Joseph left them and went in search of Martin. He found him alone, pouring out his heart in penitence and prayer. Quietly Joseph knelt and prayed with him. Then, to Martin's great joy, the vision was repeated. He too saw the angel and the table, handled the plates, heard the angel speak, and the voice from above commanding him to bear record of what he had seen and heard.

In deep contemplation the men walked home. Never again would Joseph need to ask these friends to trust his word. They walked with knowledge now and could confirm that the work was as he claimed. Yet along with the happy thought that he would no longer walk alone, Joseph felt concern for these he loved. If they spoke out boldly, proclaiming what they had seen and heard, they would be in danger of persecution. And they would not keep silent, this he knew, for it was for this very cause that they had asked to be witnesses.

The thoughts of the three other men were similar to

426

Joseph's, for as they neared the house Oliver said, "Before we talk of what we have seen and heard we should go to the upper room and put it in writing, while every detail is vivid in our minds."

Quietly the men slipped into the house and climbed the stairs.

Joseph went immediately to see if the plates were where he had left them. The visions had been so vivid he expected to find them gone, but they were safely locked away.

The men seated themselves at the table and Oliver took up his pen. After writing for a while he stopped to read what he had written. David and Martin made certain suggestions. At last, when all three felt satisfied, Oliver read aloud the whole document, asking for Joseph's approval.

Be it known unto all nations, kindreds, tongues, and people, unto whom this work shall come, that we, through the grace of God the Father and our Lord Jesus Christ, have seen the plates which contain this record, which is a record of the people of Nephi, and also of the Lamanites, their brethren, and also of the people of Jared, who came from the tower of which hath been spoken; and we also know that they have been translated by the gift and power of God, for his voice hath declared it unto us; wherefore we know of a surety that the work is true. And we also testify that we have seen the engravings which are upon the plates; and they have been shown unto us by the power of God, and not of man. And we declare with words of soberness that an angel of God came down from heaven, and he brought and laid before our eyes, that we beheld and saw the plates and the engravings thereon; and we know that it is by the grace of God the Father and our Lord Jesus Christ that we beheld and bear record that these things are true; and it is marvelous in our eyes. Nevertheless, the voice of the Lord commanded us that we should bear record of it, wherefore, to be obedient unto the commandments of God, we bear testimony of these things. And we know that if we are faithful in Christ, we shall rid our garments of the blood of all men, and be found spotless before the judgment seat of Christ, and shall dwell with him eternally in the heavens. And the honor be to the Father, and to the Son, and to the Holy Ghost, which is one God. Amen.

427

Joseph nodded. "This is a valuable document. It should go with the manuscript and become a part of every copy of the Book of Mormon."

It was signed then, first by Oliver, then David, and then Martin.

The men decided to wait until everyone was at the supper table before telling of the day's momentous events.

Emma and Elizabeth sensed that something unusual had taken place when they brought the men fruit juice in midafternoon, but after being shown the finished manuscript they left, thinking that the completed script had caused what they termed a joyful and knee-bending dedication.

It was the usual thing at the Whitmer home to find from one to a dozen guests seated with the family at mealtime, and tonight was no exception. Around the long table were Father and Mother Whitmer, Christian, David, Jacob, John, and Peter Whitmer, Jr.; Virginia and Hiram Page with their children; Joseph Smith, Sr., Emma, Joseph Smith, Jr., Samuel and Hyrum Smith; Oliver and Elizabeth Ann. Hyrum and Samuel had returned to Fayette feeling that they might be needed to help protect the manuscript once it was finished, and Father Smith had come along to check on how the work was progressing.

Everyone at the table knew the manuscript had been finished that day. Father Whitmer said grace, then all eyes turned expectantly toward Joseph. He looked from one to another of them. These were his family and his friends. Love was in his eyes and his voice when he arose and said, "I have a feeling you know that we finished the manuscript today. All that remains now is to send it to the printers."

Cheers came from all sides of the table. But Joseph didn't stop speaking, and the faces of those who listened became sober. Then, with the help of those who had shared the great experience he told of the angel's visit and the viewing of the plates.

Food became cold while they listened. As the strange narrative concluded he had expected everyone to rejoice, but everyone except the witnesses and the children sat gravely silent. Then Hiram Page pressed the table hard with his strong work hands as if he were striving for self-control and spoke in a voice strained with emotion. "Why did you do this, Joseph, without telling the rest of us? You *knew* how much we all wanted this chance. It's been a dream of mine to see those plates and bear witness ever since the day you brought the records here."

"We've all had this dream," Father Smith said.

Christian and Father Whitmer nodded agreement, and Hyrum Smith added a fervent "Amen."

Emma's eyes filled with sudden tears. Her voice came low and muffled, so that only Joseph heard. "I too . . . have carried . . . this dream. I've wanted so much to see."

No one except the children felt like eating. Martin, Oliver, and David said nothing. Their eyes were on Joseph, waiting for him to answer.

Joseph sat down, picked up his fork and toyed with it. What could he say? Silently he prayed for a way to answer them. There were to be other witnesses . . . but how was he to know which of these would be chosen? It was not up to him to name anyone; if it were he would name them all, for all were worthy in his eyes. This was something he couldn't answer without a knowledge greater than his own. They must take the problem to God.

His eyes moved from one to the other of them, and under his expression of compassion the tension eased.

Joseph placed the fork beside his plate. "There are to be other witnesses, but who they will be I can't say. When the time comes, those who are called will know. Until then, we must pray for this knowledge."

"Eat, all of you." Mother Whitmer's voice seemed to gather them all in as if it were a relief just to speak in an atmosphere that had been so strained. "We've fixed a good meal, and it's gettin' cold. I reckon God knows his mind, and wishin' won't change it."

After the evening meal, Joseph excused himself from family and friends and went alone to the woods for meditation and prayer. He had grown to trust the Father even as a child would trust a parent. He had come to know that God revealed his will to trusting hearts, and that His love and interest encircled all mankind in both great and small things. And, he thought, choosing witnesses is no small thing.

Stopping at a secluded spot where his presence would hardly be noticed even by a passerby at close range, he sat down on a fallen log, his mind alive with his problem. Bending, he picked up a twig and began breaking it into small bits. How amazing that every adult at the table, except Mother Whitmer who had seen both the angel and the plates, wanted to be witnesses. The cause was unpopular and even violently opposed. All had reason to know that persecution would be their lot once they made it known that they had seen the plates. And dearest Emma—he could understand her longing to see them, for she had moved them from place to place in their wrappings, dusted around them, handled them, and sometimes hid them, but always making sure they were hidden from her view. Words were inadequate to describe her loyalty. She had given up family and friends, accepted handed-down clothes and poverty that the book might be. She had known dangers and heartache, facing whatever problems he faced without flinching. How blessed he was that she loved him.

Moved to his knees he began to pray: "Great God, open

my eyes that I may know which of these loved ones will be strong enough to take ridicule and oppression, to stand alone and declare that this work is true. Almighty and eternal God, maker of the earth and heavens, whose power is too great for man to comprehend, show me the way."

One by one faces moved through his mind as he prayed on.

Unknown to Joseph, at about the same time, Oliver, David, Martin, Samuel, and Hyrum Smith were in other wooded spots joining their prayers with his that light might be given.

In other sections of the forest Christian, Peter, Father Whitmer, Hiram Page and Father Smith also were praying.

Emma, Elizabeth Anne, and Mother Whitmer made up another prayer group, and Virginia, who had taken the children home, was praying with them. All of these, unknowingly, had joined Joseph in his supplications.

It was time for family worship. Singly and in groups they came to the rose garden. How cool and fragrant was the air about them—how much a part of God's world they seemed!

Tonight was a little different from other nights. They came without talking, as if their prayers and meditations were still a part of them, for God had been very near as they had prayed for light.

Young Joseph entered the group, and the hush became more pronounced. He knew without asking that all were waiting to know whether he had received an answer to their petitions. He had, and this should be a moment of happiness and joy. Those who were to be witnesses he was sure already knew it, however silent their lips were; but the others

431

yearned to see the plates and to witness—how disappointed they would be. Emma . . . would she think he had purposely left her out?

There were chairs in the rose garden, and they sat down. Their eyes covered him, waiting for him to speak. At last he addressed them—sadly, brokenly, because of Emma: "If this were my will, in at least one instance I would have chosen differently." His eyes met Emma's and held for a moment as his love enfolded her. He fought for composure, for tears were very near. "The names," he said, "are Christian Whitmer, Jacob Whitmer, Peter Whitmer, Jr., John Whitmer, Hiram Page, Joseph Smith, Sr., Hyrum Smith, and Samuel Smith. You are called to be witnesses. May God be with you now and always."

Later that night, in the upper room, Joseph showed the chosen eight the plates. They too, made a written testimony:

Be it known unto all nations, kindreds, tongues and people, unto whom this work shall come, that Joseph Smith, Jr., the translator of this work, has shown unto us the plates of which hath been spoken, which have the appearance of gold; and as many of the leaves as the said Smith has translated we did handle with our hands; and we also saw the engravings thereon, all of which has the appearance of ancient work, and of curious workmanship. And this we bear record with words of soberness, that the said Smith has shown unto us, for we have seen and hefted, and know of a surety that the said Smith has got the plates of which we have spoken. And we give our names unto the world, to witness unto the world that which we have seen. And we lie not, God bearing witness of it.

Christian Whitmer	Hiram Page
Jacob Whitmer	Joseph Smith, Sr.
Peter Whitmer, Jr.	Hyrum Smith
John Whitmer	Samuel H. Smith

"There is a part of the record you didn't translate," Father Joseph said, after each man had signed the document. "Why?"

432

"Because a part of it is sealed, and I was told by the angel that the sealed part is to come forth at a later date. Generations may pass, but the sealed part will come forth eventually."

"I wonder what the earth will be like then? I wonder who will be called to translate?" Hyrum's eyes seemed to be looking forward into time. "I wonder if he will face persecutions as you have, Joseph?" He looked from face to face. "I suppose persecutions will follow all of us now. Perhaps for us trouble is just beginning."

The hour was quite late when the eight witnesses left the upper room to go to their beds, and Joseph went in search of Emma. The big house was silent, for most of the family and guests had gone to bed some time ago.

In the parlor, seated on the uncomfortable, straight-backed, horsehair sofa he found Elizabeth Anne alone in the dark. It was not Oliver she waited for; this he knew, for Oliver had retired early that he might be on the way to the printers by daybreak with the first part of the manuscript so that the typesetting could begin.

"Isn't Emma with you?" Joseph asked.

"No, she wanted to be alone. I've been sitting here praying that no harm will come to Oliver tomorrow. Will the danger be great, Joseph?"

"Hardly any at all, I would say. The word can't have reached our enemies yet that the work is finished. But praying for those we love is always a wise thing."

She came to him, and the moonlight from the front window revealed the lines of worry on her face. "I love him so much, Joseph. If anything should happen to him I wouldn't want to live."

"Nothing will happen to him. I'm the one our enemies want, not Oliver. Besides, Hyrum and Samuel will be along. I'd go, and so would your brothers, if we thought he'd be in

433

trouble." He turned her toward the door. "Now go to bed, for you'll be up before the cock crows to wish him a safe journey."

She brightened then. "And to fix him a good breakfast . . ." At the door she paused. "You'll find Emma in the rose garden. We were together there until just a little while ago."

He had expected to find Emma crying. Instead she sat in the swing with moonlight falling on her hair and casting highlights on her face and throat. Her eyes were turned toward the stars, and she was singing softly to herself the words of a favorite hymn. He paused to listen. She began the second verse unaware that he was near her.

> Oh, may this bounteous God,
> Through all our life be near us!
> With ever joyful hearts
> And blessed peace to cheer us;
> And keep us in his grace,
> And guide us when perplexed,
> And free us from all ills,
> In this world and the next.

He came to her then, and she made room for him beside her in the swing. He sat down without saying anything and they began singing the song from the beginning. They sang in low voices so as not to disturb any of the sleepers in the house. His arm encircled her. No doubt they would be called upon to make great sacrifices in the days ahead. Probably there would be persecutions and trials as God, through personal revelation, reestablished his church—the Church of Jesus Christ. This was his work now, and his calling, of which the Book of Mormon would be a part.

Emma must have been sharing some of his thoughts for she said, "Whatever comes in the future, I want to be a part of it."

434

He took her hand in his big one and raised it to his lips. "You have helped me more than you know already. The Book of Mormon will be printed soon, and it will increase the faith of thousands. Perhaps millions will read and believe." He brushed her cheek with his lips. "Do you mind so much not seeing the plates?"

"Yes." He felt her sigh. "Oh, yes I do mind, Joseph. Perhaps someday I'll know why this blessing is for others but not for me. I've been sitting here alone trying to pray through to the reason I wasn't allowed to see them. I've tried hard to do everything right. So many times I could have sneaked a look. I never did. What will become of the plates now?"

"The angel will come and take them away, perhaps bury them again until the time is right for the sealed part to be translated—in some future generation when more light is needed."

"When it comes it will add more proof that the records you translated are what you claim them to be." She reached and drew Joseph's face down to hers. Their lips met. The scent of roses was all around them, and the stars seemed to enfold them. Then hand in hand they left the swing and walked toward the house.

Next morning most of the household arose early to bid the men a safe journey. Martin left with a heavy heart. He was going home to a wife he loved, but he dreaded their reunion. That she would make unhappiness for him he had no doubt, since she believed the Book of Mormon to be a hoax.

Days passed. Joseph took extreme precautions that no harm should come to the copied pages. The original manuscript was in his keeping, and only the copy made by Oliver, a few pages at a time, was entrusted to the printer. Oliver was never alone on these trips to Palmyra. Sometimes

Joseph went with him; when he could not go, then someone else guarded. Mr. Grandin seemed trustworthy, but there was always danger of theft once word got out that the printing had actually begun. Secretly Joseph, his family, or friends guarded the Grandin Printing House, watching day and night for troublemakers. Even so, a garbled account of the Book of Mormon story very nearly reached publication before the book did.

An individual by the name of Squire Cole was using the Grandin House to print a weekly periodical called *Dogberry Paper on Winter Hill.* The Smith brothers and Oliver knew this, but he seemed a likable fellow, and they trusted him.

Then, when almost the whole of the manuscript had been delivered, Hyrum and Oliver came upon Squire Cole about to publish in his *Dogberry Paper* mutilated extracts of the Book of Mormon.

"Where did you come by these?" Oliver's voice seemed to shake the very walls as his anger burst forth.

"They were obtained from the printer's copy. Now see what you can do about it." Squire Cole's eyes were pinpoints of determination, but Hyrum and Oliver seemed to tower above him, although he was no small man.

"Print this and you'll find yourself in the biggest lawsuit in the state of New York," Oliver told him, and they strode off to bring Joseph, who was spending some time near the printing office, taking his turn at guarding it.

It was not until Joseph confronted him with the threat of suit for the infringement of the copyright law that Squire Cole backed down and gave up his plans.

This was only the beginning. There was no way to keep the Book of Mormon from being spotlighted in the papers. Comments and criticisms found place in newspapers from as far away as Rochester. Joseph was handed a copy of the *Rochester Daily Advertiser and Telegraph* days before the

436

Book of Mormon printing was completed. In it he read: "The *Palmyra Freeman* says, 'The greatest piece of superstition that has ever come within our knowledge now occupies the attention of a few persons in this quarter. It is generally known and spoken of as the Palmyra Prophet's *Golden Bible*. Its proselytes give the following account of it.' " There followed such a garbled story of the discovery of the plates and their translation that it sickened Joseph, and he crumpled the paper in his hands.

As news spread and comments increased Emma and Elizabeth Anne became apprehensive, and Joseph, noting their unrest, took a different approach to all this adverse criticism. At first it was only to alleviate their fears, and then he came to realize the truth of his new approach: "Never mind all this free publicity," he told them with a twinkle. "Aroused curiosity will hasten the sale of the book."

"Now you're sounding mercenary," Emma told him.

"Not at all," Joseph countered. "The book has a unique message that men need to know about; being inquisitive, they will read and sift for themselves."

When the last pages of the manuscript were in Mr. Grandin's hands, Joseph and Oliver felt jubilant—their minds finally at ease. And then trouble came from an unexpected source.

Joseph's sister Sophronia and her husband Calvin Stoddard had moved back to Manchester, and their home had been placed at the disposal of Joseph, Emma, and Oliver until the Book of Mormon was off the press . . . and for as long afterward as they wished to remain. Oliver had spent a few nights there, but his heart was in Fayette. The Whitmers, reluctant to see Joseph and Emma move, insisted on keeping their personal belongings and quarters as they were, with the understanding that their home be used when Joseph was ready to organize the church. All this was a help to Joseph, who wanted to keep an eye on the Grandin Publishing House until the five thousand copies of the Book of Mormon were delivered into his hands. But he also felt a need to be in Fayette to organize the church.

Breakfast at Sophronia's was over and the dishes were washed. Joseph went into another room to study, and Cal was off somewhere when Emma saw a lonely figure coming up the walk. It was Martin Harris, walking slowly with head down and shoulders drooping. Emma went at once to call Joseph, and Sophronia flung the door open to welcome him into the parlor. Her greeting was cordial, for although it had been several months since they had met, his kindness to the Smiths over the years was vivid in her mind.

His smile was genuine and his handclasp friendly, but she sensed that something was wrong as she seated him in their most comfortable chair. By that time Joseph and Emma had entered the room.

They greeted him warmly and as the men shook hands Joseph noted the uneasy look in his eyes. Everyone sat down. The room became suddenly still, and Sophronia said to Emma, "Perhaps the men want to be alone."

"No." Martin waved them back into their chairs as they started to get up. "What I have to say you'll be hearing from others soon enough. My wife has left me. She is getting a divorce."

"Oh, no!" Emma and Sophronia spoke as one. The disgrace of it seemed to hang in the room. No woman divorced her husband without great cause; it was something women of breeding simply did not do. A woman might divorce a wife-beater or an alcoholic, but not a man of refinement and respectability such as Martin.

"I'm giving her the house and eighty acres of land. You can see what this means, Joseph. All I'll have left is land. I promised you three thousand dollars to pay for printing the
438

Book of Mormon, but this changes my plans ... it changes everything except my belief in the book and the work you have been called to do."

The grandfather clock in the corner of the room seemed too loud in its ticking. How the books would be paid for now Joseph had no idea. He felt completely dispirited, but Martin obviously felt even worse. "Can we do anything to help you, Martin?" Joseph asked.

"If I deny the vision, proclaim the book a fraud, ridicule you as an imposter ... " He clutched the chair with tense fingers. "But this I can't do. And if I did she would despise me for it, even as I would despise myself."

He got out of his chair now, standing uncertainly as if he had lost his way.

"I'll talk with Oliver and Hyrum," Joseph said. "Your own trouble is enough for you to bear right now without worrying about us or the books or the money. If we can help in any way, Martin, we'll be standing by."

They offered him refreshments which he refused, and the conversation seemed to stop. "I must be going," he said.

Joseph walked with him down the steps and across the lawn to his horse. He watched him mount. Where would home be now for this man whose house had been the pride of Palmyra?

Joseph returned to the house. He must let Oliver and Hyrum know immediately that money from Martin Harris for the books would not be forthcoming. Mrs. Harris from the beginning had been determined to thwart the work, but to divorce Martin in order to have her way seemed unthinkable since she would be bringing the disaster of a gossiping village down upon herself. Three thousand dollars! Where this side of heaven could they raise such a sum?

Joseph had found no solution to his dilemma when to his dismay the professionally righteous citizens of Palmyra

439

and Manchester formed a committee and organized a boycott of the Book of Mormon. They presented a long list of names to Mr. Grandin, and he stopped the printing, refusing to resume it until he had been paid in full for five thousand copies.

"If you were a man, Emma Smith," Joseph asked her when this second blow struck, "how would you handle this situation?"

"I'd fight while I prayed," she told him. "And I wouldn't give up until those books were in neat stacks at my feet. I'm sure Mrs. Harris is at the bottom of this boycott, and she's probably gloating over her success."

Now, as his father had done before him in trying to save the farm, Joseph went everywhere trying to borrow money, but he had no collateral, nothing to secure a loan, and there were too many who knew him and had no faith in his "gold bible." Hyrum offered his farm as security, but its worth was too small to be considered, and Mr. Grandin continued to insist on full payment.

"Work while you pray," Emma had said. But how long would it take to save such an amount? Should he take the manuscript somewhere else? Who would print it without money? Sell the copyright? To whom? What had happened to his prayers? Had he lost the ability to communicate?

Before he left Fayette the angel had come, and he had given back the treasures. There were now only thirteen persons—one woman and twelve men, counting himself—who could actually swear that he had ever had the plates, and these were all relatives or close friends. No wonder there were those who believed he was out to defraud.

Where should he go? What should he do? Without any destination in mind he rode, feeling the March wind on his face as he galloped, letting his mind wander. Did Martin know word was already circulating through Palmyra concern-

440

ing his marital difficulties? Not more than twenty minutes ago he had been asked questions concerning Martin, not Mrs. Harris, that he wouldn't have answered if he could. Should Martin be made aware of what the townsfolk were saying?

He turned his horse in the direction of Martin's daughter's place. That is where his informers had said Martin was staying until he could build a house for himself on the upper forty. Forty acres would be separating him from Mrs. Harris and the big house that had been his pride. In Palmyra news traveled faster than steamboats through the Erie Canal.

Martin answered Joseph's knock, and his greeting was cordial. Presently they were seated in the comfortable parlor. "The Book of Mormon . . . did you get it going with the publisher?" Martin asked.

"No." A frown flashed across Joseph's face and was gone. "But I didn't come about the book." He paused. In his mind's eye he was entering Palmyra's largest commercial store and making his way toward the circle of men gathered there to chew, spit, and swap news, rumors, and yarns. It was a familiar circle, with chairs around a potbelly stove. Joseph's eyes met Martin's. "I spent a little time in the men's sanctum. I was looking for a Mr. Lord from Lyons, hoping he might either loan me some money or buy the copyright. He did neither, but his refusal was friendly."

Joseph paused again, remembering questions about Martin and his wife that had brought snide remarks from the dozen or so men gathered there. These were earthy men with earthy minds. Joseph had no intention of repeating the questions as they had been put or the answers that had come from other mouths than his. If their intent had been malice Joseph would have struck in anger, but their aim was at divorce in general. They were against it, just as the whole state of New York was against it.

He spoke now embarrassedly, because he didn't quite

441

know how to proceed. "I came because . . ." he colored, and his words came out in a rush, "I think you should know what they're saying about you and Mrs. Harris."

"I can guess what they're saying." Martin's voice was crisp. "They're asking if I committed adultery, or if she did—while they add to the rumors floating through Palmyra."

"Tongues wag because in New York State adultery is the only grounds for divorce. Who started the talk, Martin?"

"She did. She's never been one to hold her tongue about anything. It was her idea to leave me, and she wouldn't do it without broadcasting her intentions. She gets satisfaction out of . . ." he paused searching for the right word, and finished lamely. "She enjoys shocking the townspeople." His fingers drummed restlessly on a nearby table.

"But there is more." Joseph's eyes flashed and then cooled. "They've linked your name with someone. They say you're cavorting with another man's wife."

"Do you believe that?"

"No."

"Good."

"This is the era when men and women are expected to get along under one roof, Martin." He studied his friend's face. "What will you do?"

"What can I do? Do you want me to make a public statement that the Book of Mormon is a hoax and the angel a myth? I can't deny truth to hold her."

"You could send her to New Hampshire. After a three-year waiting period she might not want a divorce."

"Mrs. Harris is not one to be *sent* anywhere."

Joseph stood up to go. He had come to help, but everything he had said seemed all wrong. And there was something unbending in Martin, an attitude he couldn't quite make out, as if a part of him cared that the marriage was failing and another part of him wanted it to fail.

442

Martin walked with him to his horse and watched him mount. Joseph turned in his saddle as he rode away and waved. Martin stood immobile as a statue, and Joseph shook his head as he rode away. Something was out of tune. He sensed it without understanding it. Martin was holding something back—but what? And why?

He crossed the river to the Manchester side, and his mind switched to his dilemma. Where could he get three thousand dollars? If it were not to be had, what would become of the Book of Mormon? When one was doing one's best, why must life be so difficult?

With no destination in mind he rode. Ahead of him loomed hill Cumorah with the lesser hills like Indian sentinals on either side. Suddenly he had an urge to climb the hill again and stand at the spot where he had conversed with the angel on other days.

He tied his horse to a maple in such manner that the animal could graze on the tender new grass growing on the foot of the hill. The ascent was exhilarating, and Joseph was caught up in the beauty of the day. Soft wind fanned his face and hair, and burdens dropped from him in the magic of awakening spring.

He reached the hill's crest feeling the excitement of viewing mile upon mile of river, land, and town. White clouds drifted in the bright sky above him, and nothing seemed out of tune. Life could be like this, he thought—all beauty, all joy, if there were no sin. For no reason at all he began to think of Enoch and his perfect city described in Genesis. Here was a city so righteous that those who dwelt in it were translated into heaven. Prophets predicted that at some future day a new Zion would appear—a dwelling place of the pure in heart. Suddenly things the angel had said began to take on new meaning. Perhaps he would not live to see such a Zion in its completeness, but he could put its image before

443

the people. When it was reality—perhaps soon, perhaps sometime in the far distant future—the wicked would say, "Let us not go up to fight against Zion for the hand of the Lord is over it, and the terror of the Lord surrounds it." In that day Christ would be its governor, to reign with the just in the earth for a thousand years.

In that moment his thoughts encompassed all the righteous of the whole earth. He walked down hill Cumorah lost in the magnitude of his dream, and mounting his horse he rode toward Sophronia's home, feeling a strange excitement as he contemplated what it would be like to dwell where men were self-governed by all that was good.

As he neared the house his contemplations and dreams came to an abrupt end. He was looking at a black and shining surrey and a team of matched horses tied to Cal's hitching post. He recognized the vehicle and team as the pride of the Harris ranch. Was Mrs. Harris calling on Sophronia? It was the team she drove. Had she come to visit with Emma perhaps? Sophie barely tolerated her, but Emma had the talent of finding something to like about almost everyone.

He removed the saddle and bridle from his horse and turned him into the corral where he could get feed and drink. Joseph was tired, and a visit with a woman who had little use for him was something he wished to avoid. He started for the carriage house, determined to stay there and mend harness until she left. He was on his way when Emma spied him and called to him from the back porch.

"Joseph, Mrs. Harris has been waiting for more than an hour to see you."

He stopped walking and put his hand to his chest in a gesture of disbelief. "To see me? Why?"

444

"I don't know. She didn't say. One suggestion though . . . you could come into the house and find out."

"I'd rather not."

She came racing down to where he stood with her skirts billowing behind her, and the obstinacy in him melted. How did Emma always manage to stay so neat? It was a talent few women had, and even after all this time of being married to her he was as moved as the first time he met her.

"You knew she was here," Emma scolded. "You were going to hide from her."

He grinned. "She makes trouble for me as easily as you make pleasure."

She tossed her head. "Blarney will get you nowhere today. She came to see you, and she'll stay until she does. Come on."

"I'd rather swallow bitters."

"She's not that bad." She caught his hand. "Come on."

When they were almost to the porch she lowered her voice. "I know you don't like her, but you can be polite anyway."

He made a face at her, opened the door, and followed her in.

Mrs. Harris was sitting primly and looking uncomfortable in Sophronia's favorite easy chair. She sat up straighter as Joseph and Emma entered, and the joy he had felt with Emma only a moment before turned to impatience. This woman was always trouble for him, and he felt it now.

Emma gave him a meaningful look, and he crossed to shake her hand.

"You'd better sit down," Mrs. Harris said, "because what I've come to tell you won't be what you want to hear."

"Is this private talk?" Emma asked her. "Shall Sophronia and I leave?"

"No. Stay."

Sophronia moved over on the sofa, and Emma and Joseph sat down beside her. The room became suddenly silent. Joseph had time to wonder what sort of unpleasantness she was conjuring up, when she said, "What would you say if I told you Martin has left me for another woman?" Her head lowered and her cheeks became crimson.

"I've heard the rumors," Joseph said with the coldness he felt. "I suspect you started the talk that is circulating in town."

"Won't you let me tell you who the woman is?"

"I already know the person they are linking with Martin. Why would he be interested in someone almost young enough to be his daughter? Let's end this conversation, and say no more about it."

"You won't hear me out at all."

"I'd rather not."

"Oh how I wish you would." Her words came wearily and her eyes filled suddenly, so that for a moment she seemed entirely out of character, a helpless woman imploring aid. "I didn't start the rumors, but I have investigated them. You think I'm breaking up my marriage because of you— because of your gold bible. But that wouldn't have been enough for me to disgrace myself. Do you think I like the public image of a divorced wife?" She straightened suddenly. "Would you be willing to prove the rumors true . . . find out the way I did by spying on him?"

"I've already asked him, and he denied it. I believe him."

"You believe him!" She stood up. "I came intending to give you all the proof you'd need, but what would be the use? You wouldn't believe me. You'd say I was trying to hurt him to salvage what little reputation I have left. All right, believe what you want to believe; it won't change the truth. But I challenge you to find out for yourself. Or are you

446

afraid he'll fall from the pedestal where you seem determined to keep him? Now if you'll excuse me ..." She gathered her skirts primly and swept toward the door, showing plainly that she believed all that she was saying.

Emma stepped in front of her. "I'll go with you to your surrey. Come on, Sophie; walk with us."

Joseph stood alone in the silent room. Could it be true about Martin? Such a thing would put him entirely out of character. Or would it? The girl was young, attractive, and not too happily married. And Martin hadn't really denied the rumors. His question had been, did Joseph believe them. Joseph shook himself. What was he thinking? Why was he letting Mrs. Harris' words sway him? But she seemed so sure, and she had challenged him to find out for himself. Well, that is exactly what he would do—find out for himself, not tomorrow, not at some future time—*now!*

In the saddle again Joseph headed toward Martin's daughter's place. He rode reluctantly, half doubting the wisdom of confronting Martin with what seemed to be none of his business.

After he and Martin were seated in the room where they had sat earlier in the day, Martin's daughter came in to light the candles, then left. Outside darkness had settled, and wind moved through the tree branches. Locusts sang in the grass. Martin sat near a table and drummed his fingers on the top of it.

Joseph moved in his chair, his mind on the conversation that had cleared up nothing, for Martin had neither denied nor confirmed his wife's accusations. The room seemed charged with words that had been spoken, and words that had been left unsaid.

Joseph was wrestling with his desire to go home and a force that seemed compelling him to stay. It was not that he wished to pry into Martin's life for the sake of knowing, it was that he was counting on Martin's help in organizing the church, not just his money but his example. It was for this reason that he wanted Martin's conduct to be above reproach. And there was another reason.

Joseph had translated by the power of the Holy Spirit, and he had received revelations by the same Spirit. Every man had access to this Spirit to a greater or lesser degree, for it permeated the universe. It was everywhere. There was neither height nor depth nor space where it was not, for it was in all things, and around, above, beneath, and within all things. He remembered other times when he had spoken by this power, and now, at this moment, words seemed to burn through his mind, and he felt compelled to speak them. A part of the message seemed strange to Joseph, as if it were in answer to questions Martin might have been pondering, and a part was what Martin would not want to hear. This was not fortune-telling, and it was not mind willing; it was supernatural only in that it was not something he could explain, and it had to be experienced to be understood. His eyes met Martin's.

Martin's hand became suddenly quiet. When he had worked with Joseph during the translating he had felt the quiet, penetrating power of the Holy Spirit. Now, without being told, he knew that Joseph had a message for him. Both men knew that receiving divine instruction was not something to cause one to lose control of his mental faculties; rather it was an enveloping Spirit that caused the mind to function with greater clearness.

Joseph's voice came quietly, filling the silence in the room:

I am Alpha and Omega, Christ the Lord . . . and at the end of the world, and the last great day of judgment, I shall pass upon the inhabitants thereof, judging every man according to his works, and the deeds which he has done. . . .

Wherefore, I command you to repent, and keep the commandments which you have received by the hand of my servant Joseph Smith, Jr., in my name. . . . Learn of me, and listen to my words; walk in meekness of my Spirit and you shall have peace with me. . . .

I command you that you shall not covet your neighbor's wife; nor seek your neighbor's life . . . nor covet your own property, but impart it freely to the printing of the Book of Mormon, which contains the truth and the word of God, which is my word to the Gentile, that soon it may go to the Jews, of whom the Lamanites are a remnant, that they may believe the gospel and look not for a Messiah to come who has already come. . . . Pray vocally as well as in your heart; yea, before the world as well as in secret; in public as well as in private. And declare glad tidings . . . among every people . . . with all humility, trusting in me, reviling not against revilers. . . . Declare repentance and faith in the Savior, and remission of sins by baptism and by fire, yea even the Holy Ghost.

Behold, this is . . . the last commandment which I shall give unto you concerning this matter; for this shall suffice for your daily walk even unto the end of your life. . . . Impart a portion of your property; yea, even part of your lands, and all save the support of your family. Pay the debt contracted with the printer. Release yourself from bondage. Leave your house and home, except when you shall desire to see your family. . . .

Pray always and I will pour out my Spirit upon you, and great shall be your blessing; yea, even more than if you should obtain treasures of earth. . . . Be humble and meek

449

and conduct yourself wisely before me . . . your Savior. Amen.

Again the room was soundless. For several seconds Martin sat with shoulders drooping and head bent.

Joseph had not premeditated the things he had said; the words were there and he had merely spoken them. Now, disturbed by the implications his words portended, he sat silently, waiting for Martin's reaction.

Presently Martin lifted his head, and his voice came like a sigh. "It's true about her—the girl. I've wanted her. I haven't harmed her in any way, but I've coveted her. Without really wanting him dead, I've daydreamed her husband into the grave so that she could be legally mine. And I've found ways to be with her. She likes me, Joseph. I'm old enough to be her father, but a man knows when a woman responds."

"And a woman knows when a man stops loving her," Joseph answered him gently.

Again Martin's eyes dropped to his lap, and his hands began their restless tapping on the tabletop. In the flickering candlelight his face looked older. Without lifting his head he spoke again. "I've shunned my obligation to you too, Joseph. I've withheld the three thousand dollars I promised—not because I couldn't get it but because I didn't want to get it. Even after giving the wife her portion, I have plenty of land. A mortgage for the amount you need would be easy to get and easily paid off with crops that are already in the ground."

He waited for Joseph to comment, and when no word was said he lifted his head and straightened his bent shoulders. "It's true. I have coveted my own property. I've liked hearing the townsfolk speak of me as the wealthy Martin Harris."

"I know." Joseph's eyes were full of understanding.

"Men have to be truly great not to think more than they ought to think of material possessions."

Martin squared his shoulders, and the self-condemnation left him. "Tomorrow I'll bring you the money to pay the printer."

Joseph put a hand on his shoulder. "Are you sure you want to?"

Martin's eyes met his unwaveringly. "I'm sure."

In that glance Joseph knew without a word being spoken that the affair—if it could be *called* that—was over now. It wouldn't be easy to bury the dream, but Martin would survive.

Joseph hardly realized he was guiding the horse as he rode home. He knew that the Book of Mormon would be printed now in spite of all the opposition from his enemies. But would it be read and believed, or would it be scorned? And the church . . . would it become a part of the hearts of men, or would it be misunderstood and laughed into oblivion? It was a divine work so great that he understood it only partially, and he could proceed only as he was led into truth by the Holy Spirit.

Regarding things spiritual he felt that men had not even begun to explore the mysteries of their divine nature because the material part of them consumed so much of their time and efforts. Yet they were spiritual beings whose very life and breath depended on things not seen. Joseph's eyes took on a kind of shine. Suppose at some future day men's minds should plumb the spiritual depths? In that day Christ's promises would be evident. The blind would see, the lame would walk, and the mysteries of heaven would be revealed. This was what he wanted for himself and all mankind. It was no small thing to be a Christian.

They were on the main road now and he slackened the rein. It would be a different world if all persons knew it was their right to go to the divine Mind with any problem small or great and expect an answer. Had he not conversed face-to-face with an angel and received a vision from the Father and the Son when he was a lad outside the fold of a church? Christ's church must teach this reality. Searching after truths of every nature, how absorbing the quest! The receiving of divine revelation, how humbling the experience! He remembered some words that had come in such a way: "Behold, this is my doctrine: Whosoever repenteth and cometh unto me, the same is my church. Whosoever declareth more or less than this, the same is not of me, but is against me; therefore he is not of my church."

Priesthood . . . the church . . . these were not means to exalt oneself, but rather they were ways to teach the cardinal principles. He pulled his horse to a walk that he might better concentrate as he strove to remember them . . . faith, virtue, knowledge, temperance. . . . His brow puckered in thought. . . . Patience, brotherly kindness, godliness, charity, humility, diligence. The word *love* would cover them all. If men could be made to see that the life they were living on earth was part of an eternity that would never end, they would want to live by these principles. And when they did, Zion, as spoken of in the Bible and Book of Mormon, would be a reality. And this was God's purpose—to bring to pass the immortality and eternal life of man. It was not enough that men should live forever—they must live to a noble purpose.

March 18, 1830, was a gray day. Since early morning the sky had been overcast, promising rain. Some of the dreariness had rubbed off on the Stoddard household. Cal and Sophronia had had words, tempers had flared, and Cal had marched off in a huff to clean out the barn. In the next

452

room Sophronia was crying. This was a good marriage, and a dispute with Cal was doubly hard on Sophie for these two seldom quarreled about anything. Emma stood at the window wondering if she should try to comfort her. No, it wouldn't be wise. Sophie would take a word of sympathy as an affront to Cal and would jump to his defense.

In the barn Cal was whistling. Was his heart free from malice? Had he absolved himself of blame? Was he using this lighthearted ruse to lure Sophie out to talk through their misunderstanding, or was he using this method to tantalize? A smile touched her lips in spite of herself. Whatever the trouble, it wouldn't last.

Then Emma's eyes clouded again. Two hours ago Joseph had taken Cal's wagon and team and driven off without telling his plans.

"Come along," he had said. "Share the wagon seat. But I haven't time for you to change your dress or comb your hair."

Men! They could coax a woman out in a wrapper and then stop in the heart of town. No, thanks! She would enjoy a trip into town as well as the next woman, but only if she were presentable. And Joseph liked it too when men's heads turned, and he knew whatever beauty their eyes were seeing was all for him. She wouldn't go dowdy, without knowing her destination, even on a sunny day . . . but he could have waited fifteen minutes. What was the rush anyway? She turned from the window and began straightening the room without any heart for the work. And now the rain began falling, a quiet spring rain.

Suddenly the door was opened and Cal and Joseph burst in carrying a box between them. They set it down, and Cal closed the door. Before there was time to say or do anything Joseph rushed forward, picked Emma up, and twirled her joyously. As he stood her on her feet again he held her

453

tenderly and kissed her lips, laughing at her puzzled expression.

Cal was opening the box, and Sophronia, hearing all the commotion, came in red-eyed from the bedroom. She saw what it was all about before Emma did. With a happy little cry she was beside Cal—their trouble forgotten in the joy of this long-awaited moment.

She turned to Joseph. "The Book of Mormon! It's really printed!"

Reverently each held a copy, turning the pages carefully, their faces tinged with awe.

"At last!" Cal said. The meaning in his voice was clear. "All you have waited for . . . striven for . . ."

"Are all five thousand copies off the press now?" Emma asked, feeling the wonderment of the moment, the joy and the fulfillment of it.

"No. This is only the first printing. The rest will be finished soon though."

"Whatever will you do with so many?" Sophronia's swollen eyes held a radiant shine. "Why, you have more books here than the combined libraries of Palmyra and Manchester."

"I'm hoping five thousand copies are only the beginning. It will be if people will read them and come to revere them as scripture along with the Bible."

"Will they?" Sophronia asked.

Joseph reached for Emma, and they walked to the window, arms entwined. It was raining, but there was sun shining through the rain.

"We'll send men out with them—two by two." Joseph said, answering Sophronia's question. "Perhaps they won't be accepted right away. But truth cannot be hidden no matter how many lips deny it."

"What do you mean, Joseph?" Emma's eyes were questioning.

"I am thinking of our baby and voices damning him to an eternity in hell. The answer is in this book. Eternal punishment is God's punishment because God is eternal. Everlasting punishment is God's punishment, because God is everlasting. Can you imagine a God of love damning anyone to a lake of fire and brimstone to burn forever, worlds without end? So many questions that puzzle men now will be made clear through this new scripture."

"Our troubles are over . . . at last!" Emma said.

"Perhaps, my darling," he said, "they are only beginning."

"But you have accomplished what you set out to do," she said softly. Their eyes met—eyes of love and understanding, speaking of all the experiences, the joys and sorrows they had shared that the book might be. "Out of the dust light shall shine, and truth shall speak out of the ground."

Cal was kissing Sophronia, and for no other reason than that they belonged together and loved one another, Joseph's lips met Emma's. God willing, the book would be read.

The End